# Legends of Erin

## Dawn of Boyhood's Fire

Meadow Griffin

Legends of Erin
Dawn of Boyhood's Fire

Olympia Publishers
*London*

www.olympiapublishers.com
OLYMPIA PAPERBACK EDITION

A CIP catalogue record for this title is
available from the British Library.

ISBN: 978-1-84897-757-0

This is a work of fiction.
Names, characters, places and incidents originate from the writer's imagination. Any
resemblance to actual persons, living or dead, is purely coincidental.

First Published in 2017

Olympia Publishers
60 Cannon Street
London
EC4N 6NP


Printed in Great Britain by CMP (uk) Limited

# Published works

Legends of Erin: Beyond the Castle Door (2011)
*978-1-84897-152-3*

Legends of Erin: Towards the Restless Winds (2013)
*978-1-84897-288-9*

## Dedication

To Tristian, my youngest brother, I love your strong spirit. Who you are drives me as I weave the webs that create the innermost workings of who Fadin is and will become.

Acknowledgments

To my God, who has given me my imagination, creativity, and the characters to fill these pages.

Mom, for more than I can possibly say. Without you there would be no third book. If it weren't for all your tireless hours of helping me sort through my storyline and plot holes, pushing me to keep writing, then this book would remain unfinished.

Dad, your constant reminder to me that no one will make my dreams come true except for me. Thank you for instilling in me the work ethic that makes it possible for me to write these stories.

Logan, you have created the very essence of who Ciaran is. Without your voice, I would never truly have found his. Thank you for all the laughs you give me and the children we get to teach. Thank you too for being my Tase.

Alexa, for loving my books since the beginning. Your desire to read more of my stories and your love of my characters has helped drive me to keep writing even when I have seemed to hit a wall. Thank you so much for loving my story.

Raegan and Mykaela, thank you for the constant inspiration of what it is to be children and for your wide imaginations.

Kellen Benton, for going through and catching the grammatical mistakes of my first draft.

Zoe and the rest of the Production Team at Olympia Publishers, for working so hard to edit my manuscript.

Chantelle, for taking the time to answer all my questions as we moved into the publishing procsess.

# Contents

"The road goes ever on and on,

Down from the door where it began.

Now far ahead the road has gone,

And I must follow, if I can,

Pursuing it with eager feet,

Until it joins some larger way


Where many paths and errands meet.

And whither then? I cannot say."


"The Lord of the Rings" The Fellowship of the Ring

J.R.R. Tolkien

# PRONUNCIATION GUIDE

Aednat: Ey-nit

Afanasii: Aef-ah-ney-siy

Aimirgin: Av-er-yin

Ainobhack: Ain-o-vakh

Alroy: All-roy

Ardan: Are-dawn

Argonne: Are-goon

Bogán: Boh-gawn

Bojin: Boe-jean

Caoimhe: Kee-va

Cavan: Cah-vih-n

Ciaran: Keer-awn

Ciotógach: Kyut-ogue-uch

Clearie: Clear-ee

Colmcille: Colm-cill Cormick:

Kor-mick

Corr: Kor

Dalbhach: Dul-vakh

Desmond: Dez-mond

Declan: Deck-lin

Dia: DI-ah

Dubhlainn: Dove-lin Etain:

E-tane

Enda: En-dah

Erin: Erynn

Fadin: Fay-din

Faolan: Fwail-awn Faróg:

Fahr-oog

Fintan: Fin-tan Fiedhelm:

Fail-im Geartú: Gear-too

Glendan: Glen-done

Hogan: rymes with Logan

Igraine: Ee-grain

Ilchruthach: ill-khroo-ukh

Kyna: Key-nah

Kavanagh: Kav-na

Lorcan: Lor-can Lynch:

Lin-ch Mealla: Myal-ah

Nóinín: No-neen

Nugent: Noo-jehnt

Pucelua: Puke-you-lah

Quinlan: Quin-lan

Raegan: Ray-gen

Saoirse: Sear-sha

Tase: Tay-Z

Teagan: Tee-gaen

Xoor: Zoor

# CHAPTER 1
## Chains in the Ashes

The house was enormous, cold and dark. It was always dark, and hauntingly still, that is, until Master came home. Maldorf sniffed, a terribly loud sound in the silence – almost like the ripping of paper in an empty cave – and picked up a pawful of ashes. He watched intently as the ash tumbled from his padded paw back to the floor.

He sat in a pile of cinders, in front of a massive stone fireplace. The hearth was made from green stone and was intermeshed with metal crafted into the forms of snakes. The fire was usually lit, unless it needed cleaning, which was why, at the current moment, it sat cold and still, full of ash and partly burned wood.

Maldorf shifted his large, bulging eyes from the silent fireplace, to his blackened hands and feet. Tears formed and tumbled down his blue fur-lined cheeks. He covered his small face in his paws and shook with the power of his sobs.

The shackles encasing his wrists and ankles glistened silver in the slight grey light, terrible and constant reminders that Maldorf was no longer free. He was now a slave.

He peered up, into the large mirror situated on the left side of the fireplace, and stared at his reflection. He examined his sapphire pelt, his great chocolate eyes, his tiny blue nose, the freckles that dotted his cheeks, and his wide mouth, now forever turned into a frown. He touched his thin silver horns and his horse-like tail, noting how dirty every part of him was. He looked like a prisoner, and that's exactly what he was.

He took a great gasping breath and, curling himself into a ball on the floor, wept bitterly. As he sobbed, his mind wandered to his master and how he was indebted to her – for life – because he owed her currency, which he could never pay off.

Senssirra Sesshiss was a truly horrible master – actually a truly horrible being if you wanted to look at it honestly – she was always angry and would beat Maldorf for the smallest mistakes. For example, the week before, he brought her tea – or her version of tea. It was a foul smelling liquid, and what it actually was Maldorf never wanted to know. He told her it was hot and to be careful, but she slapped him, so hard, in fact, that he hit the stone floor. He kept quiet at once. She took a sip of the tea nearly in the same moment and scalded her tongue. He was beaten severely for this and locked in the basement for three days with no food or water. Maldorf had wished incessantly for a drop of water or a crumb of bread, but he was given not a bit, not even when he wailed from the pain of it or when he passed out from exhaustion.

On other occasions Senssirra would throw *her* food at him, if it was slightly too hot, too cold, too salty, or not raw enough. She would make him re-clean entire floors of her mansion if she found one spot on the floor, or one wisp of dust. She would make ridiculous commands she knew Maldorf could not carry out, and punish him when he failed.

There were no rules Maldorf could live by, no guidelines to stay in to please her. He couldn't tell himself, 'If I do this, or if I do that, or if I obey her, I will be okay.' No, Senssirra *liked* to hurt her slave, she liked punishment. She took unnatural joy in bringing harm to him, and she would never, ever, let him go.

To make matters worse, he didn't even have memories of warmth and happiness to comfort him in his darkness. Some time ago, his memories had been wiped. He obviously couldn't remember when, or by whom, but it was clear a Memory Charm had been put on him, and no matter how hard he tried, he could not remember before a few years ago. During the time he did remember, Maldorf had been alone, living in one of the poorest parts of Cavan Corr, with other small creatures who were considered to have little value.

"At least now I have a constant roof over my head," he whispered to himself. But this sounded empty, a pitiful try at making his horrible situation not sound so bad. He let out a little whimper and screwed up his face at the blank wall he saw in his head any time he tried to remember his past.

There was a noise from down the hall.

Maldorf jerked up, and wiped his face of his tears. If Master came home and saw him crying, he would be beaten within an inch of his life. He cocked his head to one side and listened.

The noise came again, and Maldorf recognized the sound, a rat running overhead.

He let out a great sigh and looked down at the pile of ash he had been sitting in. There was a lot of residue from the long put-out fires. He had to get started before Senssirra came home.

He turned around and grabbed the small broom, dustpan, and rubbish bin. He began to clean and winced a little as the shackles dug into his skin.

*BANG!*

Maldorf jumped and dropped the dustpan to the stone floor. "Ahhhh!" someone screamed.

The sound of a glass object being thrown and crashing into pieces was unmistakable.

Maldorf whimpered and scrambled into a corner. Senssirra was home, and in a terrible mood. She would be looking for more than just breaking glass soon, and he was a wonderful target.

"Trat nolpim sssusssuw imjestel jairy lumn!" Senssirra screamed, and flung something to the ground.

Maldorf shrank further into the shadows of his corner. Senssirra, part human with scaly green skin and the lower part of her body a massive snake, was furious. She was speaking in Fherish, the tongue that used to be the most commonly spoken by magical creatures in Ireland – now it was a tie between Gaelic and English. Fherish was now generally used when someone was greatly overcome by emotion.

Maldorf knew small amounts of Fherish. He could speak a few words, and understood most of it, but he was terrible at writing and reading it. From what he understood, Senssirra had called someone a goblin sucking, something or other?

It was a rough translation, but close enough for him to understand she was angry with someone in particular.

"You sshould not sssay sssuch thingsss, Sssensssirra," the voice of Silass, Senssirra's husband, rang clearly through the stone mansion.

Maldorf was not so afraid of Silass – though he had hit him before – because Silass did not seem to enjoy inflicting pain as much as his wife, nor did he have the insane fire behind his eyes that Senssirra possessed.

"I will sssay whatever I want to sssay, umlorm lissssussst," she hissed. She had called Silass something quite nasty.

"You mussst control yoursssself," Silass snapped. "Cursssing isssn't going to help anything. What'sss done, isss done. We mussst now move on and find thossse missssing prisssonersss."

"What'sss done isss done?" Senssirra shrieked. It sounded as though she threw an entire table over.

There were several extremely loud crashes, telling Maldorf that many objects had been broken.

"Thisss," Senssirra yelled, "thisss isss acccceptable? Thisss isss all right with you? Did you sssee what wasss done to me? I'm sssupposssed to jussst be okay with *thisss*?" She screamed horribly loud and threw many things into the walls and on the floor.

Maldorf had become curious. What were they talking about? What was "*thisss*"? He carefully and quietly wiggled out of his crook and slipped to the wall that was near the door. He peered around and saw Silass – his top half looked like a human man, with long red hair, except for his green scaly skin, and his bottom half was that of a giant snake. His hand was on his forehead, covering his eyes, and he was shaking his red head.

Maldorf didn't see Senssirra.

Silass picked his head up and looked down the hall that was blocked from Maldorf's view. "No, you sshould not be okay with what wasss done to you. I'm not either, but we knew what we were getting into when we decided to join thisss ssside of thingsss. Sssensssirra, thessse people are evil, they are ruthlesssss, and they are going to be the ones to come out victoriousss if a war ssstartsss. That isss why we are on their ssside, becaussse they are powerful. But they are alssso terrible, and when they get disssappointed... well, sssomeone mussst pay." Silass slithered into the hall and out of Maldorf's sight.

Maldorf took a deep breath and scurried to the wall near the hall. His heart was pounding in his small ears. If he was caught eavesdropping, he may as well hang himself, because he wouldn't survive the punishment he would receive.

"I know all that," Senssirra yelled, "but what wasss done to me isss unacccceptable!"

Maldorf peeked his head around the corner and gaped into the hall. It was dark, too dark, in there; he could only see their outlines as they spoke to each other.

"How could I have ssstopped them from essscaping?" Senssirra continued. "The children, the boysss, they have sssome kind of power, sssome kind of ssstrength, none of usss undersssstood." She growled deep in her chest and flung herself out of the hall and into the room opposite Maldorf. Silass followed her. "And it ssshould be Lynch who wasss punissshed. He isss the one who caved under their power, twice! He isss the advisssor, the one in charge down here. *HE ISSS RESSSPONSSSIBLE*!"

Maldorf scurried into the dark rounded hall, covered in pictures. He could see their snakelike shadows as they moved further into the next room. He ran on all fours to the end of the hall, and listened.

"Sssensssirra," Silass tried, but she cut him off.

"How isss thisss my problem?" Senssirra roared. "How am I sssupposssed to get the prisssonersss back? *Everyone* essscaped and ssscattered to the four cornersss of thisss issland. We may catch sssome, but not all, and there have been no sssignsss of the Kavanaghsss."

In the shadows, Maldorf saw and heard her slam her fist down on the stone table, knocking the candleholders over. "I never asssked to be a prisson guard, nor did I asssk to be raisssed to the title of Prisson Massster. I had a feeling when

Lynch gave me the promotion. A sssick sssensssation in my gut. I was made ressssponsssible for all thossse prisssonersss. I was in charge of the Kavanaghsss, our most prized captivesss." Her shadowed figure put her hand on her bald head. "He did not want that burden on hisss ssshoulders. He did not want to be held ressssponsssible if anything ssshould go wrong. He made me the ssscapegoat, the one to carry the main weight of any problemsss that ssshould transsspire." She took a deep breath and turned to Silass. "He mussst have had a feeling, he mussst have known, sssomewhere insside him, that they would essscape, and he did not want to be punisshed for it."

Maldorf moved his head around the corner. This room too was dark, and still he could only see their outlines.

Silass put his hand under Senssirra's chin. "He wasss punisshed for the loss of the Kavanaghsss," he said. "He was burnt by them when they tried to essscape the firsst time. After the breakout he had to go tell the Bojinsss what had occurred in the penitentiary. Vladimir beat him. He keepsss holding hisss ribsss painfully, and have you ssseen hisss face?"

Senssirra let out a furious breath and slithered over to a massive torch on the wall. She slid her index fingernail against the stone and the stick of the torch. It lit instantly, and a line of gas that was in a small troth along the wall also caught fire and made the other torches around the room burst into flames.

She turned quickly to Silass and spat, "Have you ssseen mine?"

Maldorf recoiled.

Senssirra's face was a bloody and bruised mess. She had a large gash above her right eyebrow, her left eye was bruised and puffy, her lip was busted open, and she had bruise marks around her neck that looked like handprints.

"How about thisss?" Senssirra hissed, turning her back on him and taking off the coat she had been wearing.

Maldorf covered his mouth.

Her back was a chaotic labyrinth of gashes that could only be caused by a whip. The cuts marked every centimetre of her backside and also travelled to the rear of her arms and neck.

"Or thisss?" Senssirra said, and turned her right shoulder to her husband. There was a bloody brand there, made by a hot metal of some kind. The mark looked like an A and V combined, with intricate circles inside the letters.

Maldorf turned his cocoa eyes to his own right shoulder, where an old scab showed two S's, one above, one below, which looked like snakes. His mark, showing he belonged to Senssirra Sesshiss. He turned again to his master and stared at her nearly matching wound.

Senssirra had been branded like a slave.

Maldorf couldn't help but allow a smile to play on his wide mouth.

"You're branded," Silass gasped, gently touching her shoulder and staring at the mark. His yellow eyes were wide, and the horizontal slits that served as his pupils were open as far as they could stretch.

"I *belong* to them now," Senssirra spat, jerking her arm away from him. Her red eyes were furious and terrified, and her narrow form shook with either fear or anger, Maldorf was not sure which. "I am bound to them, whatever they wisssh I mussst obey. My will isss no longer my own."

Silass appeared frozen. "Ssso, if they sssay jump…"

"I jump. If they sssay go, I go. If they sssay throw yoursssself from a cliff, I do it. I cannot ssstop myssself from a direct order. If I fail a tasssk they ssset for me, I die. There is no perhapsss, there isss no way out of it. I am bound forever to them, my massstersss."

Maldorf quivered. The brand on his shoulder bound him to Senssirra, and made him obey certain things – like the fact that he could not leave the mansion without a direct order. If he tried he would hit an invisible barrier. He was a slave, but mostly he was ruled by fear from beatings, but his brand did not force him to obey or die. No, this magic that ruled Senssirra was far stronger than the spell cast upon him.

"Only the blackessst magic can produce sssuch a fate," Silass said, shaking his head. "No, thisss can't be."

"Oh yesss," Senssirra shivered. "Only my thoughtsss are my own now, but they can ssspeak to me through theirsss, if they whisssh." She slithered over to a chair and sat down.

"They've given you an imposssssible tasssk, haven't they?" Silass asked. Maldorf turned his eyes to Senssirra.

"I'm to find the Kavanaghsss," she said, "or die trying. I leave tomorrow." Maldorf swallowed hard.

Silass took a deep breath and moved over to his wife. "Then I'm coming with you. We *will* find them."

"No," Senssirra whispered, "we won't. They don't expect me to sssucceed. In fact, I sssenssssed that they themsssselvesss plan to sssearch for the Kavanaghsss sssoon. Thisss isss a punisssshment. They want me to fail."

Silass ran a hand through his long hair. "Then we will prove them wrong."

Senssirra let out a sarcastic laugh. "What are we doing?" she asked, looking out at nothing. "Why did we ever agree to ssserve thessse people?" She turned around in her chair so she was facing her husband. "They are mad, you know. Obsesssssed. They have planssss for thisss issssland, oh, horrifying planssss. I sssaw bitsss of hisss thoughtsss, Vladimir'sss, when he penetrated my mind to make the bond. He isss evil, Silasssss. I mean, pure evil, far more then we could ever comprehend or imagine. You don't know what he wantsss to do, and he isss getting ever clossser by the minute. He wantsss that book, and the Kavanaghsss have it. He will never ssstop until he hasss it in hisss handsss, and after he doesss," she took Silass' hand in hers. "I pray we are not here to sssee that day."

Maldorf gulped.

"We cannot ssstop what will happen in the future," Silass said, "nor can we change the passst, or the decisssionsss we have already made. What we can do isss pressss forward, and try to prove oursssselvesss to them. We will find the Kavanaghsss, and when we do, we will earn the Bojinsss' favor."

Senssirra shook her head. "You do not undersssstand, but it doesssn't matter. Thisss isss the beginning of the end, and we are on the wrong ssside. We will die, Silasssss, that I can promissse you." She licked her lips and peered upward. "Wouldn't it have been better to die with a clean conssscience?"

Silass gently took her face in his hands. "We won't die," he said. "You're ssstill ssshaken up from your beating. Come, we will ressst. Tomorrow, we leave, and thingsss will look a little better."

Senssirra got up and slowly slithered her way out of the room and up the ramp that served as their stairs, leaning against Silass.

Maldorf let out the breath he had been holding and slumped to the floor. What did all this mean? How bad were things going to get? Would it really come to war? He didn't know, but one thing he did realize was the peril the Kavanaghs were in.

The Kavanaghs. He knew the name, of course, the most famous of the Six Key Families, the kin that had gotten away the night of the Black Massacre when every member of the Six Families was killed. Declan, his wife Igraine, and their four children, Glendan, Dubhlainn, Teagan, and Etain, had managed to get away. They had run to England, and there they had stayed for many years. Later on they had returned to Ireland, and again their name went down into the magical history books, as they were some of the biggest supporters of Dia, and fought in the most terrible battles of The Great War of Ireland.

Sadly, during the war, all the members of the magical Kavanagh family had been murdered, except for Teagan. When Afanasii was overthrown, she took a page from her family's history and repeated it, by vanishing off the face of the magical map for fourteen years, along with her leprechaun friend, Alroy. At least, it had seemed at that time that Alroy was only her friend, but clearly their marriage had just been a well-kept secret. Perhaps they wanted things quiet because of what had happened with Teagan's daughter's father. He had become a werewolf, that much was clear, and then he ran away, leaving Teagan heartbroken and a single parent. Alroy had then moved in, helping Teagan with whatever she had needed, and fallen completely in love with the little Saoirse. It wasn't long after Saoirse had turned five that the three of them had disappeared. All this was a well known fact, spread from one gossip to another, until nearly everyone in the magical world knew of Teagan and Alroy's disappearance, and speculated at a kidnapping, or worse, murder.

Maldorf had heard the rumors spreading, however, and it soon became well known that Teagan Kavanagh had returned to Glas Cavan. Not long after the rumors started, she, and others helping her, had been captured and thrown into the Cavan-Corr Penitentiary. They were held there for several months, until, obviously, someone had broken into the prison and let everyone escape.

Who could it have been? Maldorf didn't know, but he was grateful to them. If anyone could help overthrow Lynch, and those terrible Bojins, it would be one of the Kavanaghs.

If he could only get a message to them, warn them of the dangers looking for them. But he didn't know where they were, and even if he did, how could he send a message? He was only a slave.

There was a flash of green in the corner of his eye.

Maldorf jumped and spun round, jerking back a little in surprise. The goblin wasn't much bigger than him, perhaps a centimetre or so taller, but that was all. Besides size, the fact that the creature was a goblin diminished Maldorf's fear. Goblins were lowly creatures, and generally looked down upon, not beings to worry about. However, it would be foolish to rule out that this creature didn't mean harm.

"I wants to talk, Bwca, that's all," the goblin said.

So, the goblin knew what he was. Not many did, Maldorf was a rare kind of brownie, and one not usually found in Ireland.

Maldorf eyed the intruder carefully, and saw no threat. The goblin was missing a leg, after all, and the only thing he was wearing was a torn loincloth. There weren't many places he could be concealing a weapon, and he didn't appear dangerous.

Maldorf lowered the poker, but kept it in his paw. "Speak, goblin."

The goblin put his hands down. "My names is Ciaran," he said, "and I haves heards what your master has been saying." He turned his hazel eyes up to the ceiling, as if he could see her through the walls. "She is goings to look for the Kavanaghs, and so is the Bojins." He turned his gaze back on Maldorf and stared at him. "They cannots be alloweds to find them."

Maldorf watched him warily. "Oh?" he said, wanting to know what this goblin's agenda was.

Ciaran took a step forward and his wooden leg again clacked on the stone floor. "Come nows, Bwca, you don'ts want the Bojins to gets their hands on the Kavanaghs any mores than I do. You know as wells as I that they are the only threats to their evil."

Maldorf thought for a moment. "Yes, but what is it you are wanting from me? I is a slave, you said so yourself, my master is going to look for them. Besides, I think they is safe, someone is watching out for them. They were, after all, set free from prison."

Ciaran let a small smile play on his face, but it vanished quickly. "They weres set free by childrens," he said, "Teagan's childrens. They brokes into the prison using a herd of stampeding manticores."

Maldorf blinked. "What?"

"I knows, I not sure how they does it myselfs, but they did. Now they have disappeared again, and the word among the small in Cavan-Corr is thats Leprechauns helped them."

Maldorf wondered at this. Children breaking into prison? Leprechauns helping the Kavanaghs? Well, at least they had some allies. He peered into Ciaran's hazel eyes and asked, "So, what is it you is wanting from me?"

Ciaran moved a hand to his pocket. Maldorf raised the poker.

"I is justs grabbing somethings," Ciaran said, pausing his motion. "Nothings bad, I swears."

Maldorf nodded for him to continue, but did not drop his poker.

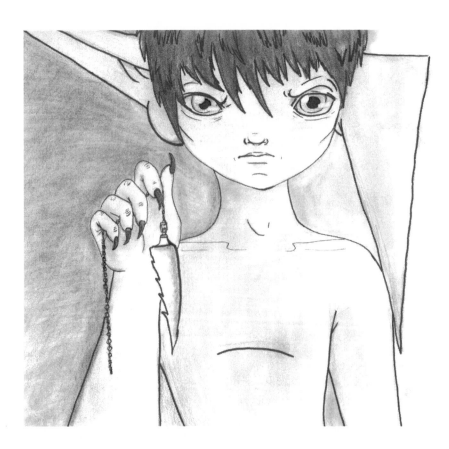

From his dirty loincloth, Ciaran pulled a necklace. From the thick brown cord there hung a tooth, about the size of a large shark's, and silver in colour. He let it dangle from his hand for a moment and then he flung it at Maldorf.

Maldorf caught it with his free paw, and gazed down at it. For some reason, this object stirred something in him, a burning in his mind, like something wanting to get out. His mouth popped open and he turned his eyes on Ciaran. "This is Alroy O'Callaghan's," he said, not sure how he knew this for certain, because it could be anyone's necklace, but he did, without a doubt. This was no small thing he held in his paw, it held great power. Why would this goblin give it to him?

"Yes," Ciaran nodded. "How dids you knows?"

"How did you get it?" Maldorf asked, ignoring the goblin's question and gazing back at the tooth.

"It is his son's now," Ciaran said, "I tooks it from him, lasts I saw him." Maldorf jerked his head up, distracted from the powerful thing he held.

"You know them?"

Ciaran got an odd sort of look on his face. "Knows them?" he asked indignantly. His hazel eyes suddenly flashed completely yellow in irritation. The tips of his ears and his fingers shifted from green to the brilliant yellow of his eyes. "Of course I knows those things! Uh, thems causes me so many troubles!" The goblin began to grow. "I tries to helps them, they makes stupids decisions. I goes to finds them, we almost crashes in a car, which, for your information, child things shoulds not be driving!" His entire body had become yellow and he was twice the size he had been. Maldorf lifted the poker high. The goblin no longer seemed unthreatening. He had heard of goblins having special abilities, most commonly when they got angry; however, he had never seen it happen before. He had always assumed it was a legend, like the story of the Grand Goblin, Sukert. No one really believed in magic like that goblin was supposed to have possessed.

"Now, you calm down," Maldorf growled, "or I will use this!" He clasped the poker in both hands, preparing to swing if necessary.

Ciaran looked at him and then down at himself. "Sorry," he said, closing his eyes. He began to shrink and once again turn the olive-green. "They brings up memories is all." He opened his now hazel eyes and sighed, still sounding a bit irritated. "They is braves though, they never gives up."

Maldorf suddenly noticed the shadows under the goblin's eyes, the lines on his face, and the sharp cheekbones protruding from his green skin. He was older than he first appeared, and there was something else too. "You is not what you seem," Maldorf said, his brown eyes widening. He couldn't tell exactly what it was the goblin was hiding, but it was something, something the magic of his bwca sight told him.

Ciaran turned his eyes back on him. "No, buts neither ares you."

Maldorf made a crease between his eyes.

"You don'ts even knows what it is yourselfs," Ciaran said, "but I cans see you have not always been as you ares now."

Maldorf felt rather confused, and his mind burned again. "What do you mean?"

Ciaran shook his head, and his ears flopped from side to side. "I don'ts exactly knows, but there is somethings hidden. You is not the onlys one with magical sight."

Maldorf let out a deep breath and swallowed hard. He clutched the tooth tightly and set the poker down. "Why would you give this to me, Goblin?" he asked, holding the necklace up.

"Because," Ciaran said, gazing at the brown cord, "its is important that the Bojins do nots find the Kavanaghs. And with this, you cans help stops them."

Maldorf looked down at the tooth. It was true, this tooth held the power to let him break the slave bond for a short period of time. He could defy an order with it, but then the power would be gone and it would need to recharge. With this he could actually be useful in helping the Kavanagh family, because if Senssirra and Silass were going on a search for them, then he was going too. He could disobey a direct order with this magic; he could hide things his bwca sight allowed him to see from his master. "Why do you want the Bojins stopped?" he said, eyeing Ciaran. "Besides the obvious reason of them coming to power, why do you want to help the Kavanaghs?"

Ciaran didn't answer right away. He seemed to be seeing something other than Maldorf standing in front of him. "I… I owes them a debt," he said. "I hads forgotten... forgotten who I was." He stared off into the empty room. Suddenly, his eyes snapped back to Maldorf and they held his gaze, firm and hard. "I *NEEDS* to helps them."

Maldorf stuffed the necklace into a pouch he had on his stomach, folding his blue fur carefully so that it couldn't be seen. "I will keep the Sesshiss's away from the Kavanagh's trail, the best I can," he said. "But just so you know, I see it in you."

Ciaran seemed taken aback by this, and his hazel eyes widened.

"I see that you have not always been so willing to help." He could sense darkness in Ciaran that lingered. It was faded, and the most of it was gone, but its shadow remained. He had done things in his past that left a dark mark, a mark only those with magic sight could see. "You once caused great harm, and great pain." Maldorf felt it, like a scent that wafted off the goblin's skin. "Is helping these children how you plan to right your wrongs?" he asked, watching him carefully.

Ciaran didn't move for a long time. "I cannots right my wrongs," he said slowly, "but I cans do what I cans to help." He paused, and then added,

"Especiallys those children."

Maldorf decided to let the matter drop. Let the goblin keep his secrets if he so wished. What did it matter, really? The past was the past, and Maldorf's was a mystery even to himself. None of that was important, though; what was important was here, and now. In this moment, he had an opportunity to help the only family it seemed the Bojins were afraid of. Not many knew the Bojins had returned, and those who did were of little standing, creatures like him, like this goblin, or fugitives like the Kavanaghs and those helping them. If the Bojins succeeded in capturing the Kavanaghs, then it was only a matter of time before the Xoor was found, and if Vladimir got his hands on it, he was sure to bring Afanasii back. Doom would fall upon Ireland, and the dark days would return, perhaps worse than before. If Maldorf could help stop all that, he would do whatever it took.

"I will do what you ask," he said. "I will keep from my master whatever I can."

Ciaran nodded. "Thanks you, and I asks one more things." Maldorf nodded his head.

"Ifs you finds them," – he flung a small scroll to Maldorf, who caught it – "contacts me, and tell me as soons as you know wheres they are."

Maldorf looked down at the silvery parchment and saw, by its ebony swirling seal, that it was an Inks, a scroll that allowed you to speak to someone else who had its twin.

Ciaran held a green hand up and showed he held the other piece of parchment. He turned to leave and then stopped. "How dids you knows the necklace was Alroy's?"

Maldorf looked down at the stone floor, then back at the goblin. "I don't know, I just did."

Ciaran cocked his head but said no more. He walked into the dark corner and vanished.

Maldorf was alone once more, by his pile of ash. The house was dark and still. His shackles gleamed in the small stream of light, but they no longer seemed so tight, so binding, because now Maldorf had a way of being free, even if only for a moment.

He smiled to himself and began sweeping the ash into the rubbish bin, and thought of the first way he could defy his master.

# CHAPTER 2
## From the Waves to the Shore

TASE'S EYES SHOT OPEN. He jerked upright and nearly tumbled to the floor, but he remembered he was in a hammock, so he clutched the netting tight and steadied himself.

Fadin was not so lucky. He plopped out of his hammock and hit the wood floor with a dull *thump*. He jumped to his feet, swung around, and stared at his twin.

Tase's blue eyes were wide. "Did you see him?" he asked. Fadin nodded, his green blue eyes as round as saucers.

*In his head, he saw the beach and the fisherman, with his wide smile, his strange, jewel-like eyes. His words rang in Tase's ears. "You boys have done a wonderful job following my directions so far, even when you weren't sure what to do."*

"It was a dream, right?" Fadin asked.

"A dream we shared?" Tase questioned.

*"Why do you think I've come to you in your dreams? I'm trying to help you. I've kept a close eye on you, making sure you're safe. You have so much ahead of you, such a powerful future."*

"He was the one, wasn't he? The fisherman we've been seeing in our dreams for months," Fadin said.

Tase agreed, it was the same man. It was strange, that they had both seen the same man in their sleep, and stranger still they had shared a dream just a few moments ago. Tase couldn't make sense of it, but there was something else too, gnawing at his mind.

"He showed us that storm," Tase said, remembering the horrible clouds and the rumbling thunder.

Fadin looked beyond Tase, at nothing, his blue green eyes fixed on empty space. "It's not really a storm."

Tase gazed at him and whispered, "It's what's coming in the future. It's all the bad things that are coming." A pit formed in his stomach.

The fisherman's voice echoed. *"You are moving towards it with every step you take. It's going to be terrible, and difficult, there is no denying that, but... you are not alone."*

Tase and Fadin looked at each other, and said, at the same moment, "Who was he?"

*"When you're ready, you'll know."*

"I don't know," Fadin said, his voice full of confusion. He put his head in his hands.

"We've been seeing that dove and dreaming about a fisherman since we left Kavanagh castle," Tase said.

It was true. Ever since they had left their Aunt Kyna's castle because the Cavan-Corr guards were after them, Tase and his brother had seen a white dove that seemed anything but normal. They had also been dreaming about a fisherman on a lake, and the fisherman always knew more about their situation than they did. After Ma and the other adults had been arrested in Cavan-Corr and the children had escaped with Ciaran – the goblin who lived in the castle's attic – they had seen the dove in the forest, and Tase had dreamed about the fisherman just before they had been attacked by Puceula Lynch and the other guards in the forest. The fisherman had told him to wake up. From their time with Travis – the kind shopkeeper – in Sligo, to trying to get the Xoor in Waterford, to Dublin, and back to Cavan-Corr to break Ma and the others out, they had dreamed about the same man.

"Who could he be?" Tase asked, the vividness of the dream whirling around him.

The cabin gave a little lurch, and the sound of waves crashing upon wood rang clearly.

Tase had almost forgotten they were on a boat. After he, Fadin, and his other companions had broken the adults out of jail, Puceula Lynch, the advisor to the king, tried to stop them – actually, he tried to strangle them – but somehow Tase and his twin had found some kind of strength and had forced him to let them go, and knocked out all the guards surrounding the prison. How, Tase didn't know, but they had done it.

Afterwards the group had met Irrah, an elder elf, Balinor and Russet, two leprechauns, and Shemus O'Sheelin, a human man, who all swore their allegiance to Ma and her family, promising to protect and help them in any way they could. When things had been discussed and it had been decided that the O'Callaghans and their companions had to go into hiding, Irrah had gone back to the Elven Kingdom to get supplies, while the rest had travelled with Shemus to the underground town called The City of O'Sheelin, where Shemus was the leader. There they had met James, a burly blacksmith, who had taken Tase, Fadin, and Clearie to pick out their weapons.

Tase smiled in remembrance.

In the magical world of Ireland, every child got a weapon when they turned thirteen. The weapon actually sort of chose you and it was yours for the rest of your life. It helped you use the magic that was inside of you, and Tase, Fadin, and Clearie were overdue for theirs.

Clearie had picked a handsome golden bow and quiver after only two tries. That had apparently been a big deal, for the shortest time James had ever seen a weapon chosen had been four tries.

Next it had been Tase and Fadin's turn. They made many failed attempts but after Tase had fallen over and Fadin grabbed his hand to help him up, a sword and a shield had come flying at them, both weapons splitting themselves in two and giving half to each twin. This had been an even bigger deal. The sword had belonged to the famous Brian Boru, the Legendary High King of Ireland, hundreds of years ago. The shield had been Saint Patrick's, a strange coincidence as 'Saint Patrick's Shield' was also the name of the famous prayer of the saint. It was no mistake, however, that the shield had the prayer inscribed upon it. The shield had been Saint Patrick's, and after his death the actual object had gone missing and turned into legend, which became a myth that the shield had only ever been a prayer, written by Patrick himself.

It was nearly a miracle that these weapons had been given to Tase and his twin, for no one had been able to touch them without a covering over their hands – unless they wanted to be struck dead – since their original owners had died. It seemed Tase and Fadin were destined for something great. At least that's what the adults seemed to think.

When the weapons had been put away, the group had gone out and met Irrah. He had horses and supplies for them. Then it was time to say goodbye to the elves and the humans and travel with Balinor and Russet to one of the seven Fairy Islands, where they would go into hiding. They had reached the beach and there a mermaid brought a boat up from the sea, which was what Tase and his brother were on now, rocking on the ocean, headed for the island that would become their new home.

"So, we are seeing the same man come to us in our dreams?" Fadin said, looking up at the wood ceiling of the cabin.

"Yes," Tase said, rubbing the back of his neck.

"What does that mean?" he asked, turning to Tase.

"That he is watching over us, I suppose."

Fadin nodded. "I wonder why?"

"Will you two shut up?"

Tase turned behind them.

Aednat was poking her head out of her hammock and glaring at them, her dark red hair a frizzy mess.

"Agreed," Ruepricked, the little talking dishtowel, shouted, popping up from a bag on the floor.

"Sorry," Tase grinned.

Ruepricked blew a raspberry and dove back into the sack. Aednat rolled her auburn brown eyes.

"Go back to sleep, Freckles," Fadin whispered.

She grimaced at him, her freckled cheeks becoming flushed. She stuck out her tongue at him and snuggled back into her hammock.

Fadin shook his head and sighed. "Oh my goodness!" someone yelped.

Tase stuck his head far out of his hammock and peered down the line of sleepers.

Enda suddenly bolted from his makeshift bed, a hand over his mouth, and ran up the wooden stairs to the deck. The sound of vomiting floated down the stairs, terrible gagging noises and coughing.

Tase crinkled his nose.

Fadin sniggered. "Poor Enda, can't hold his sea water."

"Oh faires," came a voice from one of the packs placed in the corner of the cabin. "I suppose I need to go up there now and see if anything needs cleaning up."

Tase looked toward the voice.

Ruepricked was poking out from his sack. He sighed and flew out of the sack, up the stairway.

"You're actually being helpful?" Fadin asked incredulously.

Ruepricked turned and showed them his small pink tongue before vanishing out of sight and up to the deck.

Tase chuckled, lay back down, and grinned. He involuntarily let out a big yawn.

"Should we get back to sleep?" Fadin asked. "I don't think we are going to make any more fantastic discoveries at the moment, and it's still the middle of the night."

Tase smiled, "I think sleeping is a great idea."

"So do I," Aednat growled grumpily.

Tase grinned and flopped deeper into his hammock. He unintentionally touched his neck, looking for the thin rope that usually hung there. He couldn't find it. His eyes opened in alarm. Where was Da's tooth necklace? He kept it around his neck always. He sat up and thought about looking for it, but hopelessness found its way into his stomach. It had probably been lost in the escape from prison, or at the O'Sheelin City. The last time he remembered having it was before he had touched the Xoor.

He felt a pang in his chest. He had lost it, he had lost Da's necklace. He slumped down and buried his head into the pillow and pulled his blanket up around him. How could he have lost it? It was the one thing of Da's he had gotten to keep with him. Another thought hit him and he frantically dug his hand into his pocket. Relief swept over him as he felt the small leather pouch that held the wooden K, the key that had opened the secret stairway up into Ciaran's attic all that time ago in Kavanagh Castle. He clutched it in his fist and let it slip back down into his pocket. At the thought of the attic and Ciaran, Tase suddenly remembered Pathos, their beloved dog, and his heart stung with the loss of him. Fadin and the others had seen him when Tase had touched the Xoor, but not since.

Tase remembered something about the dream and shot up.

"What?" Fadin asked, sitting up as well.

Tase stared at Fadin. "When the fisherman was walking away, you said Pathos' name."

Fadin seemed to be thinking back. He nodded. "Why?"

Fadin looked deep into Tase's eyes. "This may sound cracked, but... when Vladimir showed up and Pathos came to save us, he spoke."

Tase nodded. He had heard Fadin say this once before, but only once. Probably in fear that Tase *would* think he was mental.

Fadin swallowed. "The voice that came from Pathos... I could have sworn it was the fisherman's voice. I only noticed in the dream."

Tase's expression involuntarily became surprised, not only because of what Fadin had said, but because of what he had remembered. "I think," he said, "that you're right, because when the fisherman was walking away, and I heard you say Pathos' name, I could have sworn I saw a shape in the distance, behind the fisherman, that looked just like him."

"Just like Pathos?"

Tase bobbed his head. "What do you suppose that means?"

Fadin peered into the darkness that was around them. "I don't know, Tase. I really don't know."

~~~

"Land ho!" someone shouted.

Tase jerked too quickly and his hammock tipped and he plummeted to the ground like a dead fish. He rubbed his aching head and glared at the wooden floor.

"Get up, up," the voice of Balinor shouted. "We reach land today."

Tase stood up and yawned. It had been two days since they had gotten on this ship, and they had been two quite long boring days, and Tase was more than ready to get off the rocking sea vessel.

He gaped around the cabin and noticed that most of the hammocks were already empty, except for those belonging to Clearie, Aimirgin, Aednat, and Aldabella, and Annata – Aednat's sisters. Everyone, besides Aimirgin, staggered up and away from their swinging beds and moved over to the bookcase where their sacks full of clothes were kept.

Tase rubbed his eyes and shook his head, trying to wake up. Sleep still had its hold on him, and he probably could have slept deeply for two more hours.

"Get dressed, ya guppies," Balinor chuckled. His brown curly hair looked puffier than usual and his hazel eyes gleamed mischievously. His rotund body was dressed in fresh clothes of vivid blue and auburn and he appeared to be in bright spirits, his pointed ears looking particularly pointy. "When you are clean and clothed, come upside." He beamed at Tase, snapped his fingers, and vanished in a wink.

"I love that leprechauns can do that," Clearie said.

"Oh wow, amazin'," Aednat groaned.

"I'm so tired," Aldabella whined. She rubbed her auburn hazel eyes and pushed some of her long blue hair out of her face. She was the eldest of the Aislinn girls, and annoyed her youngest sister, Aednat, to the extreme.

"Oh, stop your complaining," Annata – the middle sister – said, pinning her shoulder length dark red hair into a pony tail. "We could have gotten no sleep at all." Her light green eyes, so similar to her mothers, were lined with slight bags against her tan skin. She seemed alert though, even if she did look sleep deprived.

Aldabella scowled at her. "I hardly got any," she grumbled, also pinning back her blue hair. She twisted it and bunched it into a coil. "I was up half of the night because the sea was calling to me."

Tase, who had grabbed his pack and was picking through it, paused. "What do you mean, the sea was calling to you?"

Aldabella turned her auburn eyes to him. "You know we have mermaid blood in our family," she said, as if this answered the question.

Tase did remember, but that hardly explained it. "I know that, but I still don't understand what you meant."

She bit her plump bottom lip. "I don't really know how to explain it. All I know is that while I'm in this ship, and the ocean is around me, I can sort of hear it calling to me. I can hardly sleep at night, I try but sleep doesn't come, all I want to do is run to the deck and throw myself into the water."

"Wow," Fadin said. "Why don't you do it? You can breathe underwater, can't you?"

"We have to be careful when we are in the sea," Annata answered.

"Be careful? Why?" Clearie asked.

"We could easily fall in love with the ocean," Aednat recited, like an old story she had heard many times. Her tone was mocking. "We could get carried away with our love for the sea and never return to the shore. Often once a mermaid's descendant enters her watery home, she will at once receive a tail and can never again touch land."

Tase's mouth gaped. "Is that true?"

Annata shrugged while Aednat shook her head and rolled her eyes. "Of course it's not true! It's just a story our ma told us because she doesn't want us goin' out into the open sea." Aednat gave a little snort. "Not that there was much danger of that when we lived in Cavan-Corr, bein' as there are no oceans down there."

"Does seem like more of a worry now though, doesn't it?" Annata said, her green eyes peering up toward where the deck was.

Aednat arched an eyebrow. "You don't really worry if we went into the water that we wouldn't want to come back?"

"No," Annata answered, "but the open water bit does concern me. Do you have any idea what kind of creatures are in the ocean? There are giant squid!"

Aednat looked at her, dumbfounded. "That's what you're worried about? A squid?"

Tase was taking far too much pleasure in their conversation and Aednat's reaction to her sisters, but he happened to see out of the corner of his eye that Aldabella looked worried. She stared out at nothing and twisted her fingers around her nightshirt.

"Are you worried about the ocean?" he asked her.

Aldabella swallowed hard. "I don't know if I believe Ma's warning was only a story."

"What?" Aednat blurted. "You can't be serious. It's so ridiculous it can't be true. When, except from Ma, have you ever heard of Geartu's turnin' into mermaids and swimmin' off?"

Aldabella looked at her. "I haven't, but I have a feeling that if I were to dive into the sea I wouldn't want to come back. You don't hear the waves crying like I do. You don't hear the voices of our people singing under this ship." She closed her eyes. "I can hear the calling of the sea even now, feel the people of the ocean wanting me to come to them, I know I would forever fall in love with the ocean if even my feet were to touch its salt waters." She opened her eyes and smiled wistfully, wearing an expression of dreamy pleasure.

Aednat stared at her. "The voices of our people? Fall in love if even your feet touched the salt water?" She grimaced. "Wow," she said, putting both hands on her small hips, "you are *such* a *girl*."

Tase, who had for a moment been in awe, had to suppress a laugh.

The longing look on Aldabella's face changed. She crinkled her nose and made her lips thin. "For your information," she seethed, "I am telling the truth. Just because you don't have any mermaid traits. Plus, you troll, I *am* a girl, and so are you. Although it is clear you forget that, you short little red-headed boy!" She threw the shirt at Aednat, which wacked her in the face.

The top fluttered to the floor, and Aednat giggled. "Is that all you got? Psh, you throw like a girl too." She arched a dark red eyebrow, grabbed her sack and walked to the cupboard that served as a toilet. She winked at her older sister and closed the door.

Aldabella clenched her teeth, stomped her foot, snatched up her bag, and trudged behind a curtain on the far side of the cabin, trying to slam the drapes like a door. The result was a humiliating look on her face, followed by a yanking of the curtain to hide her fury.

Tase and Fadin burst into laughter.

Annata rolled her eyes and kept looking through her pack. "Children, the both of them," she sighed.

Aimirgin came up behind them, still looking asleep. It had taken her that whole time just to get up and walk over to where the sacks were kept. She was rubbing her eyes and yawning. "Morning," she smiled, her black eyes slits and her lengthy ebony hair a tangled mess. Her legs, tan and black spotted, seemed wobbly, and her hoofed feet did not seem stable.

Aimirgin and her family were not human, they were creatures called Faróg's, a magical breed from India, looking like a cross between humans and giraffes.

"Still in dream land there, Aimirgin?" Fadin asked, grinning at her.

She rubbed her long spotted neck and tried to suppress a yawn. "I suppose so. I sure feel like it." She reached up and grabbed her bag. "Lovely clothes, aren't they?"

"Yeah, and so many of them," Tase said, still fingering through the pile of garments that never seemed to end.

"It's a month's worth," Annata said, picking out a blue top and tan bottoms with silvery blue boots and belt. "You have thirty different outfits in there, seven pyjamas, three cloaks, and two pairs of shoes. Pretty great huh?"

"Wow," Clearie said, pulling out a male silky silver shirt and cream coloured bulky trousers.

"Impressive," Tase agreed, yanking out his own outfit.

The ship unexpectedly gave a great lurch and Aimirgin – being gracefully challenged – flew forward. She nearly went face first into the wood floor but Tase caught her.

"Will you be careful," he scolded, steadying her and letting go of her arms.

She half smiled. "Sorry, I guess I really am still part asleep. I'll work on that."

Tase rolled his eyes playfully and grabbed up his clothes.

"Will you children hurry it up?" Balinor called from above deck. "My grandmutter could move quicker than you!"

"Aye, shut it, you old bean curd," Aednat grumbled under her breath as she came out of the bathroom, hair brushed and clothes on.

Fadin laughed quietly.

Everyone took turns getting dressed and once they were all finished they clambered up the steep steps of the cabin and came up on deck.

As Tase stepped out of the dark cabin, the light of the day nearly blinded him. It was cloudy out, but the sun still lit the sky up through the clouds and made his light blue eyes sting. He shut them for a moment and opened them in slits. It was incredibly windy and the breeze whipped through his red hair, making it go this way and that way.

He took a deep breath and the wonderful, cool, salty sea air filled his lungs and senses. It was a marvelous good morning, and the wild blue-green sea seemed to kiss his face with the small flecks of waves that slapped against the ship and flew on deck. He smiled and turned his head.

Everyone was there, and it gave him a sense of peace to see them all in one place.

Mr Hogan, his jet-black hair whipping around his tan and well lined face, turned to smile at them. "Good morning," he grinned, showing his brilliant teeth. He always made Tase miss his father but feel safe at the same time. He opened his arms and Aimirgin ran to him. She wrapped her arms around his middle and he snuggled her close, being a breaker for the wind. The exchange made Tase beam.

Tase saw all four of the Hogan boys. Desmond, the oldest, with his facial hair and hairy body, always scraggily looking, was standing close to Saoirse. Quinlan, the youngest, with permanent smiling eyes and a joke on hand, was talking to Cormick, who was securing a rope with his large muscled arms. Colmcille, who was the thinnest of the brothers, with a long dark ponytail, was leaning over the side of the ship, seeming to listen for something.

Mr and Mrs. Aislinn, Aednat's parents, were talking to Enda, who stood almost at tall as Mr Hogan. Enda's talons were out, and he seemed to be sharpening them with some sort of tool.

Daireann, in her dryad form, was talking to Ruepricked and sorting through several of the packs on deck. Her arms were turned into vines as she held several things at once. Ruepricked seemed to be frustrated, but he was bobbing up and down in understanding to whatever it is she was saying.

Caoimhe and Aunt Kyna – her golden blond hair cropped sadly short – were in a circle with the leprechauns Balinor and Russet. Russet was pointing out to the skyline.

Ma sat a bit away from everyone, looking down into her lap. In Ma's lap lay baby Glendan, his curly red hair bouncing in the wind, the small dimple high on his left cheek showing. She seemed obsessed with looking at him; that's all she had done really over the last few days, look at Glendan, feed him, hold him, put him to sleep, and fuss over her other children. She picked her head up and her lovely face lit up to see them all. Her cerulean eyes appeared even more brilliant with the sea behind her, and her dark curls seemed alive with the wind. Angry with her or not, she was still one of the most beautiful women Tase had ever seen. He wondered how his father felt the first time he saw her, and quickly made himself think of something else, because the thought made him feel the pain of his father's loss.

The ship gave a little jolt and Ma, who had stood up to greet her children, stumbled. Mr Hogan was at her side in a second. He grabbed her shoulders to steady her, and put his hand under where Glendan's head rested in Ma's arms.

"You all right?" he asked.

Ma seemed surprised at his concern. "Oh, I'm fine. I think there was just some water on the deck."

"I'll clean it!" Ruepricked shouted. He happily glided away from Daireann and dropped himself onto the floor. He swished around and absorbed the water that was indeed there.

"Well, thank you, Ruepricked," Ma chuckled, looking at Mr Hogan who looked as surprised as Ma sounded.

Tase arched his eyebrows.

"Since when has he been helpful?" Fadin asked.

Ruepricked flew up and leaned over the side of the ship. He rung himself out, and quite a bit of water fell from him into the ocean.

"Since I informed him he needs a new purpose," Daireann said, standing next to them. "I told him I am an expert cook now, and that if he wants to stay enchanted, he must have a reason."

"In order to stay enchanted he has to do something?" Clearie wondered aloud.

Daireann nodded. "There are many rules of magic, and that is one of them. If an inanimate object is given life, it must be useful. Even if its original purpose is no longer necessary, it must find a new reason to exist, otherwise…" She trailed off.

"He'll just turn into an ordinary dishtowel again?" Tase asked.

She nodded sadly. "I never thought I'd worry if that happened," she admitted. "He can be quite annoying at times. But now that I know it could happen… I really hope he finds something to live for." She smiled at them and walked towards the railing.

"So do I," Tase said. He shifted his gaze and saw that the horses were also up on deck, beautiful cream coloured mares and stallions, with long flowing manes and sparkling purple eyes. They were elven horses, gifts from the elf Irrah. They were extremely well behaved, and quiet. Caoimhe talked to them often – whispering to them in a different language – and they responded in little ways that made Tase think they understood her. They were truly magnificent animals, and never gave them any trouble.

Tase made his eyes turn and linger on his sister, Saoirse. She was gazing out into the ocean, saying something to Desmond, but her face was forlorn, and her khaki green eyes were pools of confusion. Her ebony curls looped around her in the wind, and gave her an even more miserable appearance. She had not been herself since the memories of her time with the Bojins had come back. She had seemed badly affected at the truth coming out about her real father.

Tase shuddered. It was almost as if he could hear the echo of her and Ma's conversation.

*"You lied,"* Saoirse had wailed. *"You didn't tell me the truth about my father."*

Tase shook his head. Saoirse was not Alroy O'Callaghan's child. Her father was a man named Faolan Henessy, a man who had been Ma's *first* husband. There had been a picture of him in Kavanagh Castle, the picture that hung in their closet.

Faolan had left Ma before Saoirse was born. He had been helping the resistance when he had been bitten by a werewolf. Ma said he was fine at first, and then she had gotten pregnant. When he had found out, he ran away, never to be seen or heard from again.

Sad and shocking as the truth had been, it was not the worst of it; not only was Saoirse not Tase and Fadin's full sister, she was a half werewolf, and that was a whole other problem in itself. When she had been missing for all that time after Da's death – even though Tase and his family hadn't known she had been missing – the Bojins had held her captive. They were trying to bring out her wolf traits, feeding her wolfsbane, injecting her with it, making her watch the full moon. Their efforts had an effect on her, and she had been struggling with her wolf side ever since she had come back. The reason for their actions was, at the moment, unknown.

Tase hoped, with everything in him, that Saoirse was going to be okay. "Hey," Ma said, coming to stand next to them. Baby Glendan was peaceful and happy in her arms.

"Hi, Ma," Tase said. Fadin kept quiet.

Ma's cerulean eyes were filled with concern as she looked on her children. "How are you two doing with everything?"

Tase considered this question. "I don't really know. Surviving it all, I suppose."

Ma nodded, seeming to understand, perhaps even more fully than Tase did himself. "How are you doing about Da?"

That was a harder question. Tase tried to think of a way to answer, but anything he thought of brought a lump to his throat, and he had absolutely no desire to cry. He shook his head.

Ma shifted baby Glendan so she held him with one arm, and put her free arm around Tase. "I miss him too," she said, her voice sounding choked. "Fadin?" she asked. "How are you doing, love?"

He shrugged, but Tase could see the emotions he was stopping from breaking to the surface. Fadin was completely different than Tase, he often saw crying as weakness, where Tase knew it was not. However, it took a lot out of you to grieve, and Tase was tired already and had no desire to get emotional.

Ma patted Tase on the shoulder and moved to Fadin. She put her hand on his back and Fadin let her. Tase came and stood close to them, placing his hand on his twins' shoulder.

They stood together for a few long moments, and Tase felt comforted even though nothing was said.

"I spoke to Clearie last night," Ma told them, breaking the silence. "He's struggling with Da, but he seems to feel much closer to the two of you."

Tase grinned. "Yeah, we have a whale of a time together now," Fadin chuckled. "Clearie isn't such a pain in our backside anymore."

Ma seemed as though she would have liked to reprimand Fadin, but she shook her head with a grin and let it go. Her expression suddenly changed and she took her hand off Fadin's back so she could face them both. "Where is Pathos?"

Tase felt the pang back in his chest. "Oh, Ma," he said, "we didn't tell you, did we?"

Ma's eyes became sad. "What happened?"

Fadin let out a sigh. "He's gone. We lost him. The truth is, we don't really know what happened. But he saved us from Vladimir. That was the last we saw of him."

Ma breathed in deeply and looked out to the ocean. "He was a grand dog."

Tase swallowed the new lump that had begun to form in his throat. "He was."

Tase and Fadin looked at each other with mixed sorrow and curiosity.

Suddenly many of those up on deck turned and were staring out in the same direction, towards the bow of the ship, as Russet cried, "Look!"

Tase moved towards them and shifted his vision to where they were gazing.

Out in the thrashing ocean, not far away at all, surrounded by cloud and fog, there was a giant landmass, deep green and hilly with birds surrounding it and waves crashing at its shore.

Tase's mouth hung open.

"Welcome to the Sixth of the Fairy Islands," Balinor said, coming up beside Tase, "Bäle Rappõs."

"Oh, thank heavens," Enda gasped. "I think I'm going to be sick." He leaned his head over the side, and vomited.

~~~

The ship dug into the white sandy shore and sent a great jolt through its wooden body.

Tase stumbled forward, as did several others.

"I guess we're here," Russet said, running a hand through his brown beard and mustache. He gave a cackling hoot. "Leprechauns are many things, but I can't say we are great sailors."

"No bloody kidding," Enda agreed, righting himself and wiping his mouth.

"Ew," Ruepricked grimaced, looking over the side of the ship. "Quite the load there, professor."

Enda took a swing at him, but missed.

Tase and Fadin ran to the bow of the ship and peered out at the shore and the tangle of woods that were not even a metre from the water.

The island was lovely. The green of the foliage was like emeralds and it shone in the clouded sun. The sand was so pale it could have been mistaken for snow, and here and there, the beach was freckled with black and grey stones, smooth and shiny.

Aunt Kyna let out a sort of awed sigh at the beauty of it. Tase looked at her.

It was sort of odd having Aunt Kyna back with them. It had been so long since she had been in the picture. When they had first moved into her castle after Da had died, she had been warm and inviting, even if Ma and her seemed to share some hostilities and disagreements with one another. Then Aunt Kyna had changed; her demeanor became cold, short, and at one point almost psychotic. Tase remembered all too well the time she had had to be restrained by Enda because she was pulling chunks of her golden hair out.

The fit had turned out to be a hex put on Aunt Kyna by Puceula Lynch, because she was the only person standing in the way of a peace treaty he wanted signed.

*What was the name of it?* Tase thought. *Oh yes, Act of Unison and Peace to the Half-Breeds and other Discriminated Creatures.*

Aunt Kyna had thought it a plot to give Puceula more control in the Ministry. She had probably been right, but even after Ma and Caoimhe had made her sign it, she had really not gotten much better. She fought with the other adults all the time, and was hardly even tolerable at all.

Then she had gotten herself thrown in jail. She had been in there for several months, and she was only out now because of what Tase, Fadin, Clearie, Aimirgin, and Aednat had done to Cavan-Corr Penitentiary.

Tase eyed Aunt Kyna closely. The toll of prison life was all over and around her. Her once straight and lush golden hair that had hung to her shoulders was now cut ridiculously short – if it had been much shorter her scalp would have been exposed. This new haircut made her green eyes pop out, almost bug-like on her small face, as her nose and mouth were both petite. Her frame was even thinner than it had been when Tase and his family had arrived at the castle – which was saying something, because she had been naturally slight before – and her features appeared gaunt from the loss of her healthy weight. She also had fading bruises along her cheeks, a split lip, and marks up and down her arms and legs, signs of beatings and interrogations.

It made Tase sad to see her this way, but perhaps, now that she was free, she would begin to heal.

"Beautiful, isn't she?" Balinor asked.

Tase looked at him, confused. "Who?" he asked. He saw at once that the leprechaun was gazing at the island and he relaxed. "Oh… yes, yes it is."

Balinor took a deep breath. "Such a shame that so much blood was spilled here. It was a lovely place to live." He moved over to the anchor, and he, Russet, and Uncle Lorcan shoved it over the side.

Balinor and Russet had suggested this island to hide on because it was abandoned. The reason being that long ago there had been the Fairy Wars, a ruthless fight between the Fairies and the Leprechauns, and this island had been where much of the fighting had taken place. It was left uninhabited to show respect for those who had fallen on its shores, and apparently served as a cautionary reminder.

"You saw it before it was abandoned?" Aimirgin asked, walking loudly over to them. Her cloven hoofed feet were even less graceful on the wood of the deck than on dry ground.

"No," Balinor said, "but I have heard many stories. This island was said to have been the most peaceful, even if it was not the most beautiful."

"Balinor," Fadin said, pushing off the silver railing, "what were the Fairy Wars caused over? I don't really understand why there was fighting."

Tase inclined his head to the leprechaun. He wanted to know the answer to that question too.

"Well," Russet said, rubbing his hands together, "if you ask a fairy, you will get a different answer, but we have decided to agree to disagree on that subject. However, the way the leprechauns remember it, the fairies decided they were better than we were, because they had wings and could fly. They said they had stronger magical powers than we possessed and were wise in the ways of the stars and in the foreseeing of the future."

"Wait," Tase said, grimacing, "fairies can see the future?"

"Not really," Balinor said, patting his round belly, "they read the stars and say they can see what will happen from what the heavens tell them, and use their own brand of magic. It's a load of rubbish if you ask me, but fairies' eyes *were*, at one time, used to make dark witches' crystal balls."

Aimirgin gasped.

"Ghastly, barbaric thing to do, and utterly foolish," Russet scowled. "Fairies can no more see the future than you or I, but they believe they can. They have big heads, fairies, very proud folk."

Aednat bobbed her head in agreement.

"They are exceptionally knowledgeable in the ways of nature," Lorcan said, straightening his glasses and rubbing his nose. "They seem to think – and this is generally speaking – they think they are smarter and better than those who do not know everything they know. They learned how to look at the stars and read things there, signs, messages. *Sometimes*, the stars do tell when something unusual is about to happen, but no more than when birds fly away in flocks before a natural disaster. Fairies are like someone who notices the birds flocking away and decides to leave."

"Anyhow," Russet said, helping open up the ship so everyone could begin to get out, "from our standpoint, the fairies picked the fight by trying to take over our land and become the rulers over us."

Tase widened his eyes.

"Though, like we said," Balinor boomed, "you ask a fairy and you will get a whole other story."

"Truth is," Lorcan added, working with Balinor to place a rope ladder over the side of the ship, "no one is around who really *remembers* what happened. The true cause of the Fairy Wars is lost to us."

"But tensions are still high," Russet nodded. "There are spit spats that occur all the time between the young Fairies and Leprechauns. Us older wee folk have to keep them in line. Why, Balinor and I have had many a run-in with our young friends starting rows. We've put young ones in their place many times."

"Really?" Fadin asked, his blue-green eyes lighting up with excitement.

Balinor rumbled with laughter, "Right-o! You remember the time, about two years ago, when those four leprechaun lads and three fairy boys were starting a spell fight outside of Old Everdance Pub? Why, the spells they were using, they were out to kill each other! One of the fairy boys pulled out a —"

"As interesting as this all is," Enda said, "I would very much like to touch dry land again. I am not a sailor, nor do I ever intend to become one. So, if you don't mind, *let me off!*"

"Oh, touchy," Ruepricked half whispered. "Here, let me help, Professor!" He flew towards Balinor, rolled himself tight and snapped, hitting Balinor in the backside.

"Ouch!" Balinor cried.

"Let him off, let him off!" Ruepricked cried.

"You bloody dirty old piece of rubbish!" Balinor yelled, jumping away from Ruepricked.

Tase covered his mouth to hide the laughter.

"Bossy big fella, you are," Russet huffed, stepping to the side and extending his hand to the beach. "By all means, get off."

Enda gave him a sneering look and rushed off the deck. He jumped down into the water, and splashed in the small waves that came up to his ankles. He waded through the wet and trudged up to the sandy beach. Once he was on the dry land, he fell to his knees and scooped up handfuls of sand and smelt it. "Thank goodness for solid ground," he said, and flopped onto his back, his feet back in the water line, taking a deep breath.

Tase looked at Fadin and they both burst into laughter.

Enda picked his head up and gaped at the twins. "It's honestly not funny, you little buggers," he said, smiling despite himself.

Tase and his brother kept laughing, and Aednat, Aimirgin, and Clearie joined in.

Enda grumbled, stood up and threw a handful of sand at the ship. The children dodged it.

"Good job, Professor, great aim, great aim!" Ruepricked called. Whether he was trying to suck up or was being sarcastic Tase didn't know, but Enda seemed to think it was the latter.

Enda threw another handful and smacked Ruepricked dead in the middle, and sent him tumbling over the railing and into the water.

Enda laughed heartily and the children couldn't help themselves.

The ship began to get unloaded, the children staying on board and helping pass down what needed to be put on shore.

"All right, let's get you all off," Mr Hogan said, nodding to the boys.

Clearie bounded from the deck into the water more gracefully than Tase had known he could do.

"Show off," Fadin grumbled. He jumped from the deck to the water too, but he ended up landing wrong and his head went underwater. He got up, sputtering and coughing.

"Well done," Clearie nodded, lifting his hand, which held his bow, to him and giving a mocking salute.

Fadin looked round to Ma but she was walking to the shore, huddling baby Glendan close to her. He flashed Clearie a rude hand gesture.

Clearie chuckled and shook his head, continuing to shore.

Tase, not needing to repeat his brother's folly, climbed down the rope ladder.

The water felt cool and refreshing in his boots. He looked down and saw several gleaming fish swimming not far from where he stood. They almost looked like they were made of glass, so it was hard to completely make out their shape.

He turned his attention to the island and waded over to it. As soon as his feet hit the pale, dry sand, he felt a buzzing static rush through him. It made him a little lightheaded and he swayed.

"You felt it too?" Fadin asked.

Tase looked at him and felt the intensity of the feeling subsiding.

"The magic here is strong," Caoimhe said, putting her hand on his shoulder. "The strength of your sensitivity to it will fade rather quickly, but keep in mind that this island has a power source of its own, so have respect for everything that resides here." She gave him a stern look and headed over to help the others still on the ship.

Tase took a deep breath and found he was no longer lightheaded. "Wow," he breathed.

"I know!" Fadin cried. "Wasn't that intense? What on earth lives here that has that kind of power?"

Tase ogled at him. "I don't know, maybe it could be the fairies that were here?" He made a sarcastic grimace. "Moron."

Fadin wacked him on the back of the head. "Ouch!" Tase hissed.

"Tey cayn't be allowed to touch da wayter!" Alassandra's voice rang across the water.

Tase looked over at her and saw that her face was deeply panicked. "Don't worry," Ardan was saying, "I will get down first and carry each of them over myself."

"We will help," Mr Hogan told her, coming over with Enda.

Alassandra nodded but bit her fingernails. "Not ayven a toe can touch da wayter!"

Aednat was gaping at her. "Ma, you can't honestly be afraid of the ocean!"

Alassandra turned angrily to her youngest daughter. "Don't you argue with your ma, you obey me and gayt into your father's arms! Now!"

Aednat's face contorted into one of fear and she obeyed.

Tase watched the girls get carried off the ship one by one, Alassandra as well. "Maybe it isn't just a story after all," Tase said to Fadin.

Fadin was watching the whole thing with a look of utter bewilderment on his face. "I don't know, but she sure is hyper about it."

Tase shook his head. It wasn't worth the waste of breath it would be to try and explain why Alassandra would be worried about her daughters never returning to land. He kept his thoughts and snide remarks to himself.

After a short while everything and everyone was off the ship and placed at the point where the emerald forest met the shore. Tase kept glancing at the forest, wanting to really study it.

"Well," Balinor said, taking a deep breath and looking at each individual. "As much as I enjoyed the time we spent together, I think it's time for us to go."

"Yes," Russet grunted, "we have to be on our way, but I am so glad we were able to help you all."

"We are ever grateful and in your debt," Ma said. "Without you two, I don't know what we would have done." She bent down and kissed Balinor and Russet on their foreheads.

Balinor's cheeks went red and he huffed and mumbled something incoherent, letting out an embarrassed laugh.

Russet sighed and smiled. He jumped onto Ma's shoulder and hugged her neck tight. "Stay safe," he said. He pulled back and looked around, "All of you."

"I promise to guard them with my life," Lorcan said, straightening his glasses.

Russet jumped to the floor and shook Lorcan's plump little hand. "You make sure you do."

Lorcan jerked his head in understanding.

"Well," Balinor said, rubbing his crimson neck, "goodbye then, to you all. Keep hidden, and if you need anything, don't hesitate to call to the mer-folk, they can get news to us in the tumble of a wave."

Ruepricked made a rude sound. "Mer-folk?"

"We'll keep that in mind," Caoimhe said, ignoring Ruepricked's comment.

Russet patted his brother on the back, and together they clambered back up on the ship. Russet pursed his lips once they were safely aboard, and whistled his musical tune.

Almost immediately, the waves became more powerful and fuller. The tide rushed up and pulled the ship backward and out into the sea. In a moment the ship was away from the shallows and in open water, and Balinor and Russet were waving from the deck.

Everyone stood and watched the ship sail away. It gradually became smaller, until it was no more than a dot on the sea, and then the fog ate it up, and Balinor and Russet were no more.

# CHAPTER 3

## THE FAIRY RUINS

The Old One felt when the tall man had fallen onto the shore, but her sleep had been deep, and it hadn't awakened her. It had been a long time since anything other than animals and the occasional sea creature had placed its feet upon the white sands. She also felt the life force of the others, felt that they were magical, sensed the presence of leprechauns and an elf. This had made her curious, but she was still too deep in her sleep. What did it matter anyway? Too much time had passed and she was exhausted as ever.

It nearly startled her awake when the red-haired boys put their feet upon the sand, but not quite. They had something she hadn't felt in many years, but to her it mattered not. She had gone into the depths, she was almost completely immersed in the unseen realm and she had no desire to return to the world of men.

It wasn't until the girl with the green eyes and black curls had touched a tree with the tips of her fingers that the Old One awoke. Her eyes ripped open as she gasped at the surge of magic the girl had sent into the forest. She pulled herself apart from the ancient tree where she had hidden herself and staggered in her first breath in many long years. The girl was not what she appeared, and none who were with her knew what she really was. How interesting.

The Old One stared into the woods, contemplating this information. She cocked her head in curiosity and shot herself towards the shoreline. She needed to get a better look at these strangers.

~~~

Tase stared in awe at sand scattered across his feet. It shimmered, unlike natural sand, having a gem-like quality. It held flecks of gold, silver, pearl, and even some purple here and there.

He turned his eyes to the forest. All the trees were twisted and gnarled in their trunks; some trees even grew together and spiraled around one another. The leaves of the great trees glistened jade in the sun, and appeared like jewels, not greenery. He wanted desperately to go inside and see what it was like.

"We should start finding a place that will be our camp," Caoimhe said, finally.

Tase tore his eyes away from the woods.

"Yes," Daireann said, pulling a piece of frizzy white-blond hair out of her face, "the sooner we find a place the sooner we can start making breakfast. I don't know about the rest of you, but I'm starving."

"Right then," Enda sniffed, "I imagine we want to go deep into the forest?"

"If we could get near the centre," Desmond said, running a hand through his dark facial hair, "that would be the best. Make it as hard as possible for anyone to spot us from the sea or air."

"But," Fadin said, folding his arms, "isn't this island protected? Besides, it just looks like a normal island from far away. No one would know what it is."

"You'd be surprised some of the ways that have been invented to locate people and places," Lorcan grimaced. "If we can be based somewhere deep, that would be the smartest thing."

"Right then," Caoimhe nodded. "Lorcan, you come with me." He turned to her, his face looking paler than usual.

"You should know the ground better than I do."

"I've never been here," Lorcan said.

"No," Caoimhe agreed, "but I know you have heard stories." Lorcan nodded his head half-heartedly.

"Don't elves have dealings with fairies?" Tase wondered aloud.

Caoimhe looked at him, her eyes twinkling in the light. "We have a common respect for one another, but no, as a rule we usually do not. Our ideas of what are priorities are usually not in line, and elves don't customarily argue, we are keener to fall back into the shadows and hold onto what once was. Besides, we had absolutely nothing to do with the Fairy Wars."

Tase wondered on her mention of the elves *holding onto what once was* but he said nothing of it. Now was not the time to make more inquires.

"Layt's get away from the water," Alassandra said, eyeing the ocean. She herded her girls near the forest.

"We'll be back soon," Caoimhe said. She nodded her copper head to them, and then vanished into the thick forest, Lorcan perched on her shoulder.

It was almost as if she didn't even touch the ground. Tase could hear nothing as she took off into the shadowy forest. He envied the ability to be so silent. He crept closer to the tree line and peered into the darkness.

"Be careful," Mr Hogan said. "We aren't sure if the woods are cleared yet."

Tase heard him but he did not back off. He also didn't get any closer either. He didn't want trouble if there was something in the forest.

The world around them had become still as they waited. Tase could hear noises emanating from the woods, birdlike sounds, and other squeaking sounds too, things he couldn't identify.

As he listened and noticed the shine of a particularly light green leaf, a thought crept its way into his head. What if this island were not abandoned? What if dark things had found this place and were just waiting for unsuspecting people to come and take refuge here? Tase shook his head; imagining such horrors did them no good. They would be fine. Yet, as he tried to convince himself that everything *was* fine, the image of those thunder clouds rolling in off the ocean in his dream kept coming at him and filled him with a sense of fear.

Fadin put his hand on his shoulder. Tase turned to him.

Fadin was seeing the same clouds in his mind, Tase could feel it. He hoped they were just being paranoid.

Saoirse stared off into the forest, and Clearie followed suit. They were both listening with an intensity Tase could not understand. It was as if they could equally hear things everyone else could not, and the two of them inclined their heads– just a smidge – together every so often, as if hearing the same slight sound, that to Tase was nothing more than muffled bird calls.

He let out a small sigh and stared again in awe at the trees. As he gazed at one particular tree, he noticed something strange about it. He focused his eyes and saw that there were swirling carvings in its bark, and that it looked like there were windows etched into it, and tiny elegant stairs. There was also what looked like what once had been a small bridge, a door with a purple knob built right into the bark. He followed a particularly twisted stairway upward, and saw it climbed up into the trees branches, and blended against the emerald leaves. What was up above the leaves he did not know, but it made him want to climb the tree and find out.

Saoirse and Clearie's heads jerked up and to the right. Tase started. He prayed silently it was Caoimhe. Clearie placed his ear to a stone.

Tase held his breath.

A smile split across Clearie's face and before his head was completely righted, Caoimhe was standing in the middle of them, her face lighter and happier than Tase could honestly ever remember seeing it.

He sighed with relief.

"Come," Caoimhe said with a warm grin, "we found a wonderful place to make camp." She turned away and back into the forest.

The adults moved quickly, ushering the children inside. Tase needed no telling. He stepped gladly into the dark woods. As his face passed the threshold of the tree line, suddenly the forest changed. He stopped dead in his tracks and sucked in his surprise. It wasn't dark in the forest at all; in fact it was the opposite. The trees were alight with flowers that grew along the tree trunks and hung down from the branches. The flowers were illuminated purple and silver, and they glowed, giving the entire forest a magical light. The floor of the forest was covered in green and bluish moss, where shining diamond-like toadstools grew. Brilliant jade ivy crept along the ground and in many places swirled up the trees, which were not only green leafed. The leaves inside the forest were a multitude of colours: amethyst, sapphire, bronze, silver, gold, and even burgundy.

The leaves not only were unique in colour but they also picked up and reflected the light from the glowing flowers.

Tase breathed out as he realised he had continued to suck his breath in and had no more room. He turned his face upward and saw that the branches were covered in purple ropes, ladders, and many round hanging things that almost looked like mossy beehives. As he took a closer look at one that was more at his eye level, he saw the mossy hives were houses. The one he gaped at had a mahogany door, with a golden knocker, its windows were made from a bubbly shimmering glass, and it had a crooked chimney made from small pebbles.

He spotted a long rope bridge connecting one tree to another and saw that it was lined with glowing flowers and small baubbles on twigs. The baubbles shone too, but they were different from the flowers – they were brighter and appeared almost like stars.

"Do you like it?"

Tase turned and saw that Caoimhe was smiling at him. He shook his head in astonishment. Words couldn't seem to find their way out of his mouth.

"Fairies have a flair for beauty," she said. "They are purely magical beings, so anywhere they dwell takes on the magic for its own. This island is old, and fairies dwelt here so long it holds its own magic, unique from all other places. The other islands aren't the same as this one, just as no two fairies or people are ever the same."

Tase just wondered at the beauty around him. Caoimhe beamed and bade them forward.

"It's incredible," Aimirgin breathed in Tase's ear.

Tase nodded and nearly tripped, for he was focusing so much on the trees that he had forgotten to pay attention to his feet.

Aimirgin giggled and grabbed his arm. "Now it's my turn to tell you to be careful."

He smirked at her and laughed. As his laughter floated into the forest the flowers near him shone brighter. He pointed to them. "Did you see that?" he asked.

Mr Hogan leaned against the tree, where many of the flowers had taken on a stronger light. He lightly touched one and grinned. "The laughter of a child," he said, "has always been a favorite of fair folk. They used to collect it, and it sometimes gives strength to their magic."

Tase widened his eyes.

"The younger the child, the more powerful the effect would be. If Glenden were to laugh, he may be able to brighten up the entire forest." Mr Hogan winked and followed Caoimhe.

Tase eyed Fadin who ogled back. "It's not far," Caoimhe called.

Tase, Fadin, and Aimirgin sprinted to catch up and Tase found his heart felt lighter than it had in a long while. Perhaps it was the beauty and magic of this place, or perhaps it was just that the weight of everything was not only on his and the other children's shoulders anymore.

Whatever the reason, he delighted in running wildly through the forest and couldn't keep himself from chuckling as he, Fadin, and Aimirgin made faces of astonishment to each other. The flowers around them lit brighter in response to their joy and Tase forgot to watch where he was running.

He slammed into Aunt Kyna, who toppled forward. There had been a small hill Tase hadn't seen and the two of them went rolling down it, colliding with each other the whole way. CRACK! Tase crashed into a large rock and immediately clutched his head. He had hit it quite hard.

"Tase!" Aunt Kyna growled. "I would expect that of Aimirgin, but not of you." She made a noise that sounded like a gasp. "Let me see your head."

He pulled his hand away and peered up at her. She had grass and mud stains on her face and in her hair.

"It looks all right," she said grumpily and gave him a playful stern look. "I'm glad you can be a child again, even if only for a little while," she remarked.

Tase stared at her. Did she know about the storm that was coming too? "You two all right?" Enda called down to them, sliding down the hill.

"Fine," Kyna chortled. She stood up and offered Tase her hand.

He took it and saw that the others were coming down a less vertical part of the hill. Caoimhe, however, bounded down the steepest part and passed Enda easily, coming to the bottom with incredible grace, almost as if she had danced down.

Enda hit mud where Tase and Aunt Kyna had rolled and his feet went out from under him. He hit the mossy floor and slid with impressive speed into the same rock Tase had crashed into.

"You okay?" Aunt Kyna asked through her snickering.

Enda glared up at her and made a mocking laugh. "Ha ha, I'm just fine." He picked himself up and tried to wipe the mud away, but there was too much of it for his attempts to do any good.

"Let me," Aunt Kyna smiled. She pulled out one of her blades and in a swirling motion cleaned the stains. "There," she grinned, reaching up and straightening Enda's collar. She stepped back and gave Enda a strangely thoughtful look, one Tase had seen Ma give Da at times.

Tase screwed up his face, and Enda seemed just as taken aback by her. Aunt Kyna bit her lip playfully and turned to Caoimhe.

"Right through here," Caoimhe nodded, eyeing Kyna with interest. She stepped forward and pulled back what almost looked like a curtain of leaves.

They stepped through the dense foliage and came into a beautiful round meadow.

Tase stopped dead, and stared, in awe.

"Holy harpies," Ruepricked gasped, fluttering above him.

If the forest was beautiful the meadow was astounding. The clearing was wide, wide enough to fit Tase's entire old street on, if you were to take it and curl it into a circle. The floor was carpeted with moss like the forest floor, but this moss was softer, and a deep azure blue. Tase let his fingers dance over it and felt that it was like carpet. The trees around the clearing were larger than many in the woods, their trunks were snow white, but they sparkled as if imbedded with pearls and jewels. These trees held different homes, ones that looked much larger than the others Tase had seen. Grand doors of burgundy and gold were set into the trunks, many windows round and arching wound up the trees, and stairways had been cut into the branches, along with huge round holes that had been turned into what once must have been beautiful rooms. The hole-like rooms had chairs carved out of the tree, making the rooms look like places where many fairies had once gathered. The trees also grew in a unique way here, they had sort of huddled near their tips and had connected their branches together and had morphed into a dome shape, giving the clearing a sort of tree roof. There were small areas where the sunlight shot through, but for the most part the clearing was completely covered, making it impossible to see from the sky.

The meadow's trees not only had the same glowing flowers, but in the centre of the tree dome there was a massive cluster of flowers and violet grapes, all of which shone in beautiful incandescent light. Directly below the grand cluster of lights there stood ruins, beautiful rock ruins of a once great building, a building that had taken up almost the entire clearing. From the swirling broken bits of rock and stone Tase gathered it must once have been a castle, for pieces of towers could be seen here and there. Around the ruins a ring of the beautiful diamond toadstools had grown, making the broken stones appear even lovelier.

"There must have been a great battle long ago," Fadin whispered.

Tase nodded. Indeed. Someplace this magnificent didn't simply become abandoned.

Near the ruins Tase saw Uncle Lorcan, looking through the rubble.

He turned his attention to his far left and spotted Daireann and Ardan, who had begun working under instruction from Caoimhe, seeming to be doing something to the trees around the meadow.

Daireann had her arms turned into vines, which she attached to trees and bushes, creating new plants to further block the clearing from the rest of the woods.

Ardan was mixing herbs, flowers, and some strange liquids from his backpack. Tase strained his eyes and read some of the labels. *Unicorn Tears, Troll Spit, Star Dust,* and something that looked like it said *Pixies in a Jar.* Tase was certain he was making some kind of protection to make them even safer, although, in his opinion, this place was safe enough already.

"What do you think?" Caoimhe asked.

"It's wonderful," Ma breathed.

Alassandra gazed at the old ruins. "Whaht did tis oosed to be?"

"It used to be the Cashel of Ishland Bäle," Uncle Lorcan said, walking up to them.

Tase turned to look at him.

His face was solemn. This was a sad memory, the broken heap that was once a great castle.

"Was it really?" Ruepricked asked, turning his head to the mess.

Lorcan nodded. "It was home to the Fairy King of this island," he continued. "Bäle Rappõs was his name. He ruled here for many years in peace. Of all the Fairy Islands, I believe this was the most beautiful, peaceful, and wealthy. But when the war started, this island was caught in the crossfire. Hundreds of leprechauns invaded and the king was taken prisoner, his castle destroyed, his people slaughtered." Lorcan picked up a small piece of broken rock and cradled it in his hands. "Many died here, horrible deaths. There was much evil done in this place, so much beauty ruined." He swallowed and let the stone fall from his hands. "And for what?" He looked back at the mess of stone. "I am not proud of the past here," he said sadly. "These are the memories that make me cringe to think I'm a leprechaun. War, just for the sake of war, to fairies who wanted nothing to do with conflict." He gazed up at Tase and the others. "I don't care what Balinor and Russet say, the war was the leprechaun's fault. No matter what was done to our people, we fired the first shot." He snorted and ran a hand through his curly orange-red hair. "Anyway, you can't change the past," he kicked at another broken bit of rock, "you can only prevent its repetition."

Ma handed Glendan to Alassandra and bent down so she was at eye level with Lorcan. She put a hand on his shoulder and squeezed. "You're right, and this isn't *your* fault." She nodded to the ruins of the castle.

"I know," he said and gave her weak smile.

Somehow Tase thought that wasn't true. Uncle Lorcan clearly felt guilty for what had happened on this island.

"You wahren't ayvayn born yet when da wars took place," Alassandra added.

"I know," Lorcan repeated, "but… it's part of me, since it was my people who did this."

Caoimhe gave a small sarcastic chuckle. "Oh, Lorcan, if I blamed myself for everything the Elven people have done, or my father has done… or if Teagan blamed herself for her family's past, we would never be out of the burden of guilt."

Tase let out a sigh. That was very true. Tase could even beat himself up over Ma's past, but it would do him no good. His family line was filled with deceitful evil people, his betraying Uncle Dubhlainn was one shining example, but there was nothing *he* could do about it.

Caoimhe bent down to Lorcan's level too and put a hand to his face. "All you can do is decide how *you* live, not how others live or have lived."

Lorcan took a deep breath and nodded. "You're right, you're right." Caoimhe patted his head and stood up.

Ma fallowed suit.

"All right," Caoimhe said, clapping her hands together. "Well, since we found our hiding place, I think what we need to do now is collect our supplies and set up camp."

"Camp?" Ruepricked asked. "We are going to be here an awfully long time, aren't we? I'll be happy to help pitch a tent, or help cook, but can't we have something more stable than just a camp?"

Caoimhe rolled her eyes at him.

"He is right, in a way," Ma said. "We can't just stay in tents."

"Uck, please no," Aldabella said, eyeing a flying beetle that narrowly missed her head. She made a girlish squeak and checked her long blue hair to make sure it was still pinned up.

Aednat laughed wickedly.

"I don't mind tents," Annata beamed, looking up at her mother.

"Yeah, well you didn't go on *our* little trip," Fadin said, pointing to himself, his brothers, Aimirgin, and Aednat.

*No kidding*, Tase thought. They all had to stay in tents while they had been trying to find the Xoor and get their parents out of jail. He wanted no more of that.

Caoimhe smiled. "I didn't intend to stay in tents anyway. We are going to be here for a while, so I thought we would build huts."

"Huts?" Aldabella stared. Her auburn hazel eyes widened.

Aednat shifted her own hazel eyes to her. "And what is wrong with huts?"

Aldabella turned her gaze to her sister. "It's a hut! Like from the time when Ireland was invaded by Vikings! Civilized people from a great city like Cavan-Corr, in this day and age, shouldn't have to live in huts."

Aednat's mouth was hanging open in a dumbfounded expression. Alassandra grabbed her eldest daughters face suddenly.

Tase jerked, startled.

"Don't you ayver tink you are too good for tings, little girl," Alassandra reprimanded her. "Unappreciative girls can be given a tent and can stay in it until tey are grateful for da home her family has been given." She released Aldabella's face, which had turned scarlet.

"Sorry, Ma," she whispered.

Alassandra said nothing but held her head high.

There was a moment of silence, and Tase bit his lip, feeling the awkwardness.

"If we are going to build homes today," Enda said, coming up to them from the ruins. "We need to gather what is useful in this rubble, and get what else is needed to build with."

Lorcan spluttered. "We should be careful what we mess with in that *rubble*, as you so eloquently put it. Fairies are known for not only their great magic, but for enjoying tricks. I guarantee you there are spells upon those broken stones."

"I agree with you, Lorcan," Caoimhe said. "You can be in charge of the searching through the ruins. If we are going to stay here though, we are going to have to be able to interfere with what once was. We won't be able to leave this island untouched."

Lorcan nodded.

"Why don't you use the children's help?" Aunt Kyna asked.

There seemed to be a brightening switch in Lorcan's eyes. "Of course!" He turned and stared at Tase, Fadin, and the others. "Some of you are not so small anymore, but none of you are adults. All right then, come with me."

Tase glanced questioningly at Aednat and Aimirgin, but they all followed him.

"Children are never as affected by fairy magic as adults are," Lorcan explained. "Fairies think children are wonderful, and they delight in them, therefore their magic doesn't usually work on children." He brought them right up to the broken stones. "I know that the old king who reigned here loved maps. There should be some useful ones about this island. Try and find any papers you can, tools too, anything you think could be useful."

Lorcan walked into the rubble and the children did the same. The broken stones came up over Tase's head, but if Mr Hogan or Enda were to come by the stones, they would be close to their height.

As Tase looked in the broken mess he heard Daireann walk over to Caoimhe.

"I don't think we can get much denser if we still want to be able to get out," Daireann said. "The trees are thick and strong, and they are on our side. They have agreed to let us know if there is danger."

"Good work, Daireann," Caoimhe said.

"Wait, what?" Tase asked, his mouth agape, peering around a corner of stone. "The *trees* will let us know?" He looked to Aimirgin, who shrugged.

Daireann gave a small laugh and peered down at him. "Come now, did you really think that only things *you* think have ears know how to listen?"

Tase blinked in surprise and exchanged shocked looks with Fadin. Daireann chuckled again and shook her head.

"How about you, Ardan?" Caoimhe asked.

He was dusting some blue residue from his hands, which were missing several fingers. "Well, it was bit messy, but the protective charms are up, and the O'Sheelins gave me several light pixies – they will let us know if there is danger. I don't think anyone will be coming in this meadow unannounced."

"Well, let's hope not," Ruepricked snorted.

"What's a light pixie?" Tase asked.

Ardan smiled at him. "Sort of like a human light system. They turn on and shine if anyone unknown comes near."

Tase nodded, curious and amazed.

"All right now, boy," Lorcan said from behind him, "will you please pay attention to the task at hand?"

Tase smirked and returned his attention to the ruins. There must once have been many great rooms in the castle, he saw remnants of what once must have been carpets and grand beds. He felt a pang in his chest as he realized how horrible the destruction of this place must have been. Fire was clearly used, because many things had been burnt. He saw something gleam in a pile of ash and pulled out a small green knife. He gazed at it in recognition. It was much smaller than the other one he had once seen, but it was no doubt the same kind of knife as the one Aimirgin had sent him and Fadin all that time ago in Kavanagh Castle. He remembered the knife appearing in the kitchen fireplace. It had helped him and Fadin open Aunt Kyna's locked room, back when they were trying to get some of her golden hair.

"Hey, Fadin, look at this."

He almost tripped over a small seared chest. He righted himself and gaped at it. It was only partially made of wood, the rest was made from some sort of pale material; it almost looked like it was bone. The chest had swirls and strange writing on it. There had once clearly been jewels interlaid with the designs, but they had been yanked out long ago. Tase put the knife away in his pocket and bent forward to try and open it.

"What did you say, Tase?" Fadin asked.

Tase saw a lock and was about to reach for the knife to try and pry it open. "Wait!" Lorcan cried. "Do not touch that!"

Tase jerked backward. "Why?"

"It has a heavy curse upon it." He eyed Tase. "I can see it. Fairies, leprechauns, goblins, and other small creatures, have a special sort of sight. We can see things others cannot. Take a step back."

Tase obeyed and backed up.

Lorcan bent down and placed his hands over the chest. His eyes took on a glossy hue as he seemed to study it.

"What's in it?" Aimirgin asked.

Lorcan shook his head. "I'm not sure, but it has strong enchantments on it, whatever it is." He looked around and found a crumbled and burnt piece of tapestry that once clearly was purple in colour. He covered the chest with it and nodded to Tase. "It's better not to mess with something fairies felt should be locked up. Pick it up but make sure you only touch the cloth, and set the chest on its own near the forest. We will have to find a better and safer home for it soon."

Tase did as he was told. He picked it up and found it was surprisingly heavier than he imagined possible. It was just a bit larger than his two palms put together, but it felt like it was made of some incredibly dense metal.

He walked towards the edge of the woods and placed it on the grass. He gazed at it and wondered what could be inside.

There was a whispering in the woods just ahead of him. He ripped his head upward and studied the forest. There was something sparkling in the trees, unlike the leaves and flowers that grew on them. It was a sharp gleaming light but it vanished before he could focus on what it was. He felt a shiver go up his spine as he remembered seeing the black wolves green eyes in the dark. He stared out into the timbers, trying to shift ever so slightly in case the sparkling thing was only behind a few leaves or a branch.

"Hey! Tase!"

Tase startled and looked round.

Fadin was standing outside the crumpled castle with his arms raised high. "Would you like to join us?"

Tase took one last glance into the trees and then decided it had only been a trick of the light. After all, this island was abandoned, as he had been told. He tried not to let the doubt seep into his mind. He shoved the incident from his thoughts and ran over to Fadin.

"Day dreaming?" Fadin asked.

Tase smacked him playfully and took one last glance into the woods before entering the remains.

~~~

The entire rubble had almost been completely searched. It didn't take as long as Fadin had expected, but they did find many things. Much of it was old fairy tools and weaponry. There were partial books, and a few maps and papers were intact. Other chests like the first were found, and all of them appeared to be cursed, according to Uncle Lorcan. He had the chests all moved carefully and placed in a row near the forest line. There were eight in all when they were finished.

Fadin gazed at them in curiosity. What could possibly be sealed inside them? What had the fairies felt needed to be locked away?

"Fadin," Lorcan said, wiping some sweat from his brow, "make one last sweep, will you? I don't feel anything else of great power there, and the stones appear safe enough."

Fadin nodded, happy to oblige his uncle. The ruins were fascinating to him. "Just a tick," he answered him. He stepped over the toadstools and scrutinized the stones around him. He noted a golden door, still set in its place in a stone wall that had fallen to the floor. There was a small silver blanket in some ashes, which he picked up, but there was nothing under it. He went from one end to the other and sighed in satisfaction. There was nothing left. He turned and his foot swept through a thicker pile of ash. Something peered out from the dust and Fadin bent down to see what it was. It was a small scroll, bound with a scarlet string and sealed with amber wax. He was about to call for Lorcan but something made him change his mind. It was almost like a whispering in his ear, telling him it was nothing to worry his uncle about, that he should take the scroll, and keep it. Fadin was smart enough to know this had to be a trick, but his curiosity was piqued.

"All clear, Fadin?" Lorcan asked.

Fadin considered for a moment. He snatched the scroll up and put it neatly in a pouch on his belt. He would think more about it later. "Clear," he answered, and came out.

"The ruins have been thoroughly searched?" Caoimhe asked Lorcan, coming to stand near them.

"Yes," he said, eyeing the chests apprehensively. "I still think it's a bad idea to use the stones from a once great fairy castle, however. These chests make me think perhaps other things were left with shee escaine."

"Left with what?" Fadin asked.

"It's an expression used when there has been a particularly powerful curse left on an object by fairies." Lorcan explained quickly.

"I understand your concern," Caoimhe said. "However, it's either use the stones or live in tents. I think it has been long enough that any damage the magic could have done has subsided significantly. However, I think the boys can be the ones to move the stones, just as a precaution, and have Quinlan instruct them."

Tase made a face and Fadin silently agreed with it. It rather felt like they were being used as test subjects by the adults.

"Good idea," Enda said, "that will take care of the walls, but what about the roofs and the doors?"

"Cormick, Kyna, and Saoirse should go to gather plants to make thatched roofs. The girls," she inclined her head to Ma, Aednat and her sisters, "can make bundles and tie them down."

"Sounds good," Ma said, moving an ebony curl from her eyes.

Kyna seemed to like the idea and began to discuss the sort of plants they would find.

Fadin stopped listening. Something had glinted in the forest, quite near them. He wasn't sure how he had seen it, for it had been so quick, and it wasn't really seeing as much as he *felt* the glimmer of a strong presence watching them. The scroll in his belt began to hum quietly and quiver. Fadin placed his palm over it and darted his eyes from face to face to see if anyone else heard the humming. No one seemed to; they were still discussing the huts.

He let his eyes scan the trees, trying to find the glimmer again. What had it been?

Something slammed onto his shoulder and caused Fadin to leap into the air. Quinlan smiled. "Jumpy are you?"

64

Fadin pulled his shoulder away. "You almost gave me a heart attack." He surveyed the area and saw that everyone had broken off into their own tasks.

Quinlan snickered. "Okay, follow me, we have a lot of stones to move."

Fadin followed him over to the ruined castle and bit his lip as he thought about the scroll.

"What do you have in your belt?"

Fadin turned and saw Aednat staring up at him, her auburn eyes sure. "I don't know what you're talking about." he huffed.

"Sure you don't," she said and, with impressive speed, snatched the scroll from his side. "Quinlan," she called, before Fadin could make a grab for it.

"Yes, short one?"

Her face became livid but she did not spit a name back at him. "I think I saw more stones in the tree line, I am going to take Fadin to look at them. All right?"

Quinlan eyed them both but waved them on. "Don't take too long, we have plenty of work here."

"Right," Aednat agreed and, with a mischievous look, she waved the scroll briefly in front of Fadin and dashed toward the woods.

Fadin seriously considered not following her, on the principle of not allowing her to manipulate him. However, he knew he had to get that scroll back. His interest made him dash after her, but as he did he thought of ways he could teach her a lesson.

She stood a little way in, next to a thick trunked tree with almost all sparkling silver leaves. She held the parchment out in front of her, almost like a peace offering.

"You little thief," he hissed.

"I wouldn't have to be a thief if you weren't a liar," she retorted. "Now what is this?"

"I haven't the faintest idea."

"You found it in the ruins." It wasn't a question, it was a statement, and she proclaimed it with such surety there was no denying it.

Fadin folded his arms. "Why do you care?"

She smiled. "You tried to hide it. Of course I'm goin' to care!"

Fadin let out an exasperated breath. "Look, I wasn't sure what it was myself."

"Then why didn't you give it to Lorcan?"

"Because he would have put it away somewhere."

She smirked. "Perhaps that's for the best."

Fadin stared at her and she glared right back.

Fadin sighed angrily. "I wanted to find out what it did, okay?"

"Okay," she nodded. "But now you're findin' out what it does *with* me." She began to untie the scarlet string.

"Wait," Fadin tried, suddenly wishing he *had* given it to Lorcan. There was a faint sound, like someone quite far away shouting something.

The string fell to the floor. "You unfurl it," Aednat said, holding it out to him.

Fadin felt torn. He wanted to open it, but something told him not to. He bit his lip but curiosity won out. He took it and slipped his fingers under the gap in the parchment and began to break the amber wax seal.

As it broke, Fadin knew it had been a mistake. Whispers flooded around them in surprising volume. Words he didn't understand rang in his ears and screams seemed to emanate from behind him and above him.

Aednat jerked forward and covered her pointed ears.

"You have set them free!" was the only discernable thing that came from those whispers, and Fadin felt a sinking pang in his gut. What had he set free?

The hissing murmuring ended, and the power that had come with them vanished too.

"What was that?" Aednat asked, pulling her hands away from her ears.

Fadin shook his head. "I don't know, but I think we just made a big mistake, Freckles." The air seemed to buzz with whatever they had just done.

"Hey, you lazy gits!" Quinlan called. "There are clearly no stones in here." He came through the trees and glared at them, his hands placed irritably on his hips. "Stop being thick and come help us."

Fadin swallowed and exchanged one frightened glance with Aednat. He allowed the scroll to tumble, unseen, onto the green mossy floor. "Right, sorry."

Quinlan arched a black eyebrow. "Move it, the both of you."

Fadin dashed toward the clearing, Aednat right behind him, and he felt his heart pound as he wondered what it was they had just done.

~~~

Night fell like a warm blanket on the island. The Old One quietly watched the visitors from a high tree and swiveled her eyes to the unbound scroll. Only one with leprechaun blood could have opened it. These visitors were becoming more and more interesting.

They had let them out, but the ones who had done it were only children, so they could not understand the consequences of their actions. She smiled to herself, they may be too young to understand now, but they soon would.

As the light of the moon tapered through the leaves in thin strings, a beam touched the pale body of one of the chests that had been pulled from the ruins. All eight trunks moaned quietly and each one popped open.

The Old One bit her silver finger and watched as those who had been trapped inside crawled out. How fascinating this was going to be. She turned her eyes on the cabin where the girl was staying and flashed her light teeth in a wicked smile. How very fascinating indeed.

# CHAPTER 4
## CAUSE AND EFFECT

Ciaran sat at a small table in the noisy pub, sipping on his fairy nectar, a sweet and delectable liquid that could give someone with too much imagination the absolute surety they could fly. Ciaran had never had such an impulse when drinking the candy-like liquid: however, he had seen many others fall into this fate, some ending in dire circumstances. He glanced about the small crowded place for the one he was looking for but saw no one he recognized right away. A fat and particularly ugly grogoch sat at the table next to him, sloshing some sort of drink all down his chest. The grogoch, looking like a cross between a man and some sort of red-haired beast with fur over his entire body, gave Ciaran a gruesome snarl and the goblin quickly looked away. Grogochs could have horrible tempers.

Many creatures were out this night. Several other goblins occupied stools and couches, a group of six leprechauns laughed by the fireplace with mugs in their hands, two ballybogs, with their balloon-like bodies and bulbous fingers, sipped on aged swamp water, and there was even a gnome sitting on one of the stools. The gnome seemed quite sad, and Ciaran couldn't help but make the note that he looked nothing like his cousins from other countries, nor the replicas of his kind that humans sold in stores for garden decoration. The only similarity he held to the garden statues was that he wore a cap that looked like a large toadstool and he was short. He wiped his massive blue eyes of a purple tear with his bone-thin hands and raised his small glass to signal to the leprechaun behind the counter that he would like another.

"That's enough sugar water for you, Bob," the leprechaun said. "You should go home, you know what too much sugar does to you."

The gnome just stared down sadly. "Bob Omeshroom used to be a name of some respect among the small," he blubbered.

"Oh, come on now," the leprechaun tried. "How about I get you some tea?"

The door opened and Ciaran jerked his head towards it. It was just a pair of leprechauns, both with curly brown hair. The group next to the fire beckoned them over. "Balinor! Russet! Come over here, lads!"

Ciaran made a face. He knew those names. Weren't those two of the escapees from Cavan-Corr penitentiary? He was fairly sure they were, and if so, it made sense why they were here. This place was safe from the ministry, the small kept its secret, and it was far from Cavan-Corr. This was a place for exchanging information and lying low.

A group of fairy boys sat at a small leaf shaped table. They were huddled around each other and were whispering. Ciaran wasn't much interested in the affairs of fairies, but these ones were acting strangely, so he tried to have a listen. He focused his large ears solely on the fairies.

"I don't believe it," one of them was saying.

"Believe it or not, it's true," hissed another. "She saw it, and perhaps we aren't strong enough to see everything she can, but can't you feel the shift? The disturbance behind the veil? Something strange is going on, and someone just dabbled with some ancient magic."

Ciaran shifted his features in interest. Ancient magic?

Another of the fairy lads piped in, "What you're talking about isn't possible. They were sealed long ago. Besides, those were only scary stories to keep us away from the places where the fighting was the worst. Our elders didn't want us young ones to go and disturb the abandoned places, out of respect."

"Yes, our elders didn't want us to disturb the abandoned islands, but those are more than stories. Couldn't you feel the disturbance earlier today? I certainly could, and I'm telling you she's right. It came from one of the islands."

Ciaran considered this. They were talking about the fairy islands, what could be happening there?

"Oi," a new voice said, clearly surprising the fairies.

Ciaran turned his head ever so slightly and saw that one of the leprechauns with curly brown hair had come over to the fairy lads.

"You may want to keep it down," the leprechaun told them. "If we can hear you all the way by the fire, who else do you suppose can?"

The fairy boy he was closest to jerked away from him, stood up, and ruffled his wings. "Our conversation is no concern of yours, leprechaun."

The leprechaun raised his eyebrows. "I disagree, boy. When you shout in a public place about the fairy islands, it concerns fairies and leprechauns alike." He took a step closer but the fairy did not back away. "Keep your mouth quiet, all right?"

Ciaran's attention was suddenly jerked forward as something slammed on his table. He jumped and ripped his head in the direction of the noise. Someone had sat down. They wore a grey cloak that was dripping wet. The night had clearly become rainy.

The cloak hood pulled back and Ciaran let out a small breath of relief. He wasn't sure what he had been expecting, but he had felt frightened for a moment. "It's you's," he breathed.

Rinnerwood, a she-goblin with blue skin, large purple eyes, and white hair, nodded to him. Before she spoke she took a sip of the drink that had been slammed

into the table. It was some sort of hot tea, and she closed her large eyes as she took a sip, enjoying the warmth it spread.

Ciaran had never been interested in "settling down" as some would call it. However, as far as goblin women went, Rinnerwood – Rin, she preferred to be called – was quite pretty. She was much younger than Ciaran, however, and from a higher class of goblin; in fact, she was of the highest class. Her earrings of gold and silver, her golden necklace with the emerald encased in rose-gold hanging over her heart, her many dangling bracelets, and her fine clothes set her apart in every way from any other goblin present in the pub. She was the last of the royal line of Snugert goblins, and it was because of this fact that Ciaran knew her at all. He had sought her out after hearing of the terrible fate that had found her parents.

They had been murdered, and though an attempt at killing Rin had followed not long after, she had escaped and had gone into hiding ever since.

Ciaran hadn't been wasting time since he had vanished from Fadin and Tase's sides. He had felt guilty for leaving once he had done it, but he had to make a choice and once he had made it there was no time to let slip away. He was gathering knowledge needed to help the Kavanaghs, and this goblin made a wonderful ally and tool. She had information from inside the ministry as well as personal material about the inner workings of the castle, for her and her family had lived in the home of the king since her great grandfather had been born. Royal secrets were her specialty.

Though all this was true, and Ciaran had many meetings with her, he had not been planning to see her this evening. "What's you doings here, Rin?" he asked. "Supposeds to be meetsing our contact, nots you."

Rin let out a sigh. "He will not meet you in person."

Ciaran felt his temper begin to boil. He could feel the yellow creeping into his eyes and the tips of his ears. It was a cold and now rainy night, he had only come out so he could meet this contact, and now there would be no meeting in person? "Why's not?" Ciaran hissed.

"He is afraid," Rin said matter-of-factly. "He keeps his identity hidden. No one, besides me and few of those closest to him, know who he really is." She became quiet and glanced around the room suspiciously.

"What's?" Ciaran asked, feeling his anger subside a little.

She leaned in. "He thinks someone is watching him, that's all I know." She slid something over to Ciaran.

Ciaran glanced down and saw a stack of parchment paper. He flipped through it. There were many pictures of faces and notes in handwriting, some he recognized, others he didn't. There was a report that looked like an interview with one of the council members and he saw one page that stood out to him more than the rest. It was blueprints of a massive warehouse, one he had heard of, yet never seen. His hazel eyes became wide. "He is certains of this?"

Rin nodded. "Yes, and so am I. There is too much proof to try and assume otherwise."

Ciaran rubbed his head contemplatively and stared down at the paper. He flipped through several more papers of the blueprints and came across one that was scribbled with handwritten notes. Ciaran bit his lip and looked down at the signature at the end of the parchment, *Argonne Nugent*. Ciaran rubbed his pointy green chin and nodded to himself. This was the name of one of the most read reporters in Cavan-Corr, also one of the most controversial. He had wondered if the contact was going to be Nugent, but he hadn't been sure. He looked up at Rin. "I haves to see him."

Rin shook her head. "He won't." She began to stand up. " I assume you have heard that Puceula Lynch is searching for Nugent?"

Ciaran shook his head and his ears flopped from side to side. "I hads not heard that." He thought for a moment. "Lynch doesn't likes the reporters writising the truth," he sighed. "I undersands, but I still needs to meets him."

Rin shook her cloak out and reattached it. "I will see if I can convince him to meet with you a different time." She picked up her mug and drained it. She set it lightly on the table and made eye contact with Ciaran. "Until the next we meet?" She held her hand out, claws up.

Ciaran touched her claws with his, in the traditional gesture of goblins departing one-another. As Ciaran watched her pull her cloak up and head toward the door, he realised she probably had never received that respect from any goblin except her parents before. Being a royal made her wildly unpopular with the common goblins, for she had much and had been spoiled while the rest of the goblin race had to find castles, houses, cottages, or the streets of Cavan-Corr to live in. Being a goblin wasn't easy, and it more often than not required a lot of moving around. If people found you living in their attic, there was a chance of getting killed, not just by those who found you, but if it was in a human home and anyone from the magical world found out about it, well… Ciaran had heard of more than one severe punishment ending in the death of a goblin who had accidently been seen.

Ciaran looked towards the door as Rin stepped out. He was about to turn back to his own drink when he saw another hooded figure, this one still small but human in stature, stand and begin to head towards the door as well. Ciaran got a strange feeling as he looked at the hooded man, then the figure turned and looked right at him. Ciaran froze as he got the briefest glimpse of a man's face, with dark curly hair and light eyes, before he turned swiftly, disappearing out of the pub.

Ciaran slammed down a bottle of troll spit and called, "Keeps the change!" He ran out of the pub into the narrow passageway. He was about to pursue the hooded man but he saw Rin beckon him over, and the two of them vanished around another corner. Ciaran was baffled until a thought struck him. The hooded man was Argonne Nugent. He had been inside the pub all along, listening to the conversation between himself and Rin. Ciaran looked down at the parchment in his hands. He would follow the clues given to him, but he would find a way to meet the reporter. Ciaran didn't have time to waste. He went back into the pub, grabbed his own cloak, and, in a wink and a puff of green, disappeared to find out how many of the keys Vladimir had stolen.

~~~

Fadin stood on the beach. He stared down the shoreline and saw Pathos staring at him, perhaps four metres away. He blinked, surprised, and tried to call out to him.

No words came from his mouth as he moved it.

Pathos lowered his head and stared out to the water. Fadin followed his gaze and saw a huge wave headed right for the island. He tried to scream and to run, but he was stuck and not a sound came from his scream. In fact, there was no sound at all except for a low drumming which seemed to emanate from the ground.

The wave was nearly upon him. Fadin struggled with all his might to move but his feet held fast. He opened his mouth in terror as the wave towered over him. As the massive tower of water began to curl, ready to swallow him up, a white bird flew in front of him.

Fadin awoke with a start. He breathed heavily and his wide blue-green eyes told him he was safe, that there was no wave. He let out a sigh of relief and sunk back to his pillow when the scroll popped into his head. He jumped up and nearly knocked over a small table. He clutched it and hooked his index finger in the handle of a teacup before it plummeted to the floor. Eyes wide with the fear of waking Ma and the baby, he glanced around. Each silk hammock was still. His eyes flicked to the fur rug in front of the fireplace where Saoirse curled with a blanket – she continued sleeping soundly. He slowly let the table go, balancing it as it was meant to stand, and disentangled his finger from the teacup.

He considered waking Tase up, but Tase didn't know about the scroll, and Fadin didn't feel like explaining it. He also knew a lecture would be coming from Tase, and he wasn't in the mood for that either. Besides, he didn't even know what the scroll had done. Perhaps it was nothing, and if that was the case there was no need to tell Tase anyway.

He tiptoed to a sack which hung from a branch protruding from the wall near his hammock. Daireann had come into each hut and had created a living clothes rack, by giving everyone a thin indoor tree, which would continue to grow, but slowly. He dug in the sack, which was filled with his clothes, and slipped on the first shirt and trousers he found. After quickly donning his boots he grabbed his cloak from the hook at the door. He noticed one of the lamps, crafted in the shape of a lily, was on. He slipped over to it and blew the never-ending flame of the candle out. As quietly as he could manage, he opened the door and snuck out.

The air outside was near freezing and he watched his breath appear in puffs of white. He shoved his cloak on and wrapped it tightly around himself.

"There you are!"

Fadin stifled his gasp. He turned towards the voice and saw Aednat, huddled on the floor near his door, wrapped in her own cloak. "Freckles!" he growled.

"What?" she whispered at him standing up. "I've been waitin' for nearly thirty minutes! I was about to come in and shake you awake."

"Why were you waiting for me?"

"Why?" They began to move away from the cottage. "Because we opened a scroll yesterday and there were voices and who knows what else. I think we are responsible to find out what it did."

Fadin glanced down at her. "There was only one key person in what you just said," Fadin pointed out. "Me, I'm the one who opened the scroll, not you."

"You broke the seal, but I took the string off. We opened it together, it's on both of us."

Fadin wanted to argue but he knew she was right. "Fine," he sighed. "Where did we drop it again?"

Aednat smiled and pulled her cloak tighter around herself. "Over here." They made their way to the other side of the clearing and Aednat pointed.

"It was right around there, just past the chest —" Her voice caught.

Fadin felt his mouth become dry. The eight chests stood at the edge of the forest as they had the night before, but each one was open.

"Um, Fadin?" Aednat said, taking a step back.

Fadin gawked at the open chests. How had this happened? He had a horrible feeling it was their fault. "Did we do this?" he asked, voice cracking.

There was a shimmering flash in the trees. Fadin and Aednat jerked their heads in the direction it had gone, but there was nothing there.

"You saw that?" Aednat breathed. Fadin bobbed his head.

There was another flash and this time Fadin felt a tingle in his spine. "What is it?" Aednat wondered aloud.

"I don't know," Fadin said, pulling Aednat close to him.

A third blaze spun towards them and stopped directly in front of them, landing on a small branch not far from their eye level. The flash had turned into a point of glowing light. As it was still it was easier to see that it was mostly silver in colour, though it did have flecks of green and bronze.

Fadin and Aednat stepped closer. The bright light moved and the glow disappeared. Fadin saw that the glimmer had actually been caused by a ray of sun that had hit the small thing standing before them. Fadin allowed himself to stare, for he had never seen anything like it.

The creature took a step forward and stared back. She was small, not much bigger than Uncle Lorcan, but she was most certainly taller and longer than

him. Where Uncle Lorcan was squat and round, this being appeared stretched and narrow. Her arms seemed more fitting to a spider than to a small woman, her torso made her appear much taller than she was, and her legs seemed far too elongated for her body. Yet in all her strange length, she was beautiful and appeared graceful. The colours of her skin were remarkable; all the colours of the leaves of the trees, silver, gold, bronze, rose-gold, emerald green, and even some flecks of purple and sparkling blue. She seemed to be made out of crystal for the way the light clung and caught on her skin, and behind her hung magnificent wings. Her wings looked like sugar dipped leaves, but their shape was nothing like them. Her wings had beautiful veins in them, which seemed to be made out of pure gold, and as she fixed them with her stare Fadin saw that her eyes gleamed gold as well. She cocked her head from side to side and her hair, which flowed around her like water, caught the light and showed its colours of silver and rose-gold.

"Hello," Fadin said, keeping his voice quiet afraid he would startle her.

The small woman said nothing.

"Do you suppose she's a fairy?" Aednat asked.

The woman inclined her head to Aednat and in a blink she was hovering in front of her face.

Fadin stumbled backward.

Aednat gasped but recovered herself and smiled. "You are incredibly pretty," she told the small woman.

"You are incredibly imprudent," she answered.

Aednat's made a face. "Whats imprudent?" she asked Fadin.

Fadin shrugged. "I don't know, but by the sound of it, it wasn't a compliment."

The small woman flew over to one of the chests and perched on top of it. Fadin and Aednat moved closer.

"Foolish," the woman hissed and glared up at them. "Opened the scroll, the children did. Let them out. That is the height of senselessness on an island of this size. Not many places to hide."

Fadin felt his heart do a backflip. "What was in them?"

"Darkness," the creature said. "I was charged to keep them locked away for all time. The king of this island gave me the task specifically, and I was honoured to obey." She stepped off the chest and stood in the grass. "Long ago this was a place of beauty and prosperity. My people, the Sídhee, thrived here, we were wealthy and powerful. When the war came it nearly ended us, so out of desperation our king awoke what should never have seen the light of day again." She pointed to the chests. "They helped defeat our enemies, but at a terrible price, for their hunger could not be satisfied and their thirst never could be quenched. They like the battle too much, and when there are no battles to fight they create their own mayhem."

She stared out at where the ruins of the castle had been. "Disrespectful, your adults are, to touch something so old." She eyed the children with her glowing stare. "They drove the leprechauns back, but when the deed was done, they destroyed us as well. Warriors were chosen to catch them, which they did, but at the loss of much life. Our king sealed them in their chests and made the scroll for me to take into the realm of the unseen so no one could ever open them, but the leprechauns returned before he had time to place it in my hands. In the battle that followed it was lost to me, and when my people were taken I was made to stay by the spell our king had cast to make me the watcher of them forever. I could not touch the scroll however, for other magic had been set by our enemies, who were wiser than we gave them credit for.

"This island was abandoned for the wars ended and many lives were lost on these shores." She looked out into the distance. "There was a curse put upon here too which kept others away." She eyed Fadin suspiciously. "Clearly that curse has been lifted." She fluttered back up to the branch and watched them.

"So," Aedant asked, "what were they? The things in the chests?"

"Spriggans, they are creatures of darkness, powerful, and with a thirst for war. You will have to be careful, they will start out as nothing more than a nuisance, but over time their actions will become more malevolent. Unfortunately for the two of you, they will also take a keen interest in your futures, and they may take such a liking to you that they will be more than unwilling to leave you alone."

"What can we do?" Fadin pleaded, feeling his panic grow with each passing moment.

"Pray they don't want to go to war with you." She gave them a flashing smile, which faded as soon as it came. "They aren't what I would be most concerned with, however."

Fadin arched an eyebrow. "What do you mean?"

"They will take time to become a real problem, but you have a great problem on your hands right now."

"What problem?" Fadin asked.

The fairy smiled again, but this smile stayed and it made Fadin's blood curdle. "Your sister is not what she seems."

Aednat took another step closer. "Saoirse? We know she's a half were- wolf, if that's what you mean."

A chilling laugh came from the fairy and she flung her head back in delight. "That's not what I mean. I cannot say for certain what she is, in part because I don't fully understand myself. Furthermore, to tell you would spoil the surprise."

She leaned forward. "What I can tell you is that she is a great curiosity and puzzlement. Before long, that which is trapped will find a way out, and when that happens," she chuckled wickedly, "you all are in a lot of trouble. Far more than the spriggans could bring upon you."

Fadin could feel his heart pounding in his ears. "You can't help us?"

The fairy shook her head. "Even if I could, I would not want to. Playing with fire will burn you, or have you not learned that yet?" She cocked her head, almost like a bird. "That matters not though, for I can do nothing but what is required of me by the magic that holds me here. I must be certain the spriggans never leave this island."

"Will you help us catch them, then?" Aednat asked.

The fairy shook her head. "I am not strong enough to catch them, and neither are either of you. Besides, when you woke them you took the power over them out of my hands." She did not seem concerned by this at all, which made Fadin's stomach churn. "You will have to clean up the mess they make until they become too vicious. Once there is too much violence, you will all have to leave, and if they try to follow you I will use the power given to me by the king and sink this island into the sea, ending myself along with them."

Neither Fadin nor Aedant spoke for a long moment.

"You have a really bleak outlook on life, don't you?" Aednat asked, face contorted into a look of disdain.

The fairy did not seem amused. "I am more ancient than you can fathom, *child.*" She spat out the last word as if it left a foul taste in her mouth.

There was a noise from the cottages. Others were stirring.

"I must go, the adults cannot know I'm here." She peered down at Fadin and Aednat and made a sudden sweeping movement with her hand.

Something cut across Fadin's body, from shoulder to shoulder. "Ouch!" Aednat cried out in her own pain.

"What did you just do?" Fadin snapped.

She put a finger to her lips. "You will be able to tell the parents nothing of this."

Fear and fury overwhelmed Fadin. "Will we see you again?"

She nodded. "You will see me often, now that my task has changed there is no need for me to move on."

Fadin wasn't certain what that meant, but he decided not to ask. "What do we call you?" Aednat asked her.

The fairy turned to them. "I forgot my name ages ago. I am known only as the Old One." She seemed as though she wanted to do something else, but couldn't. "All I care for is my task, though the laws of magic I must obey... I must do what I have been charged, even when there are children in my way." She gave them one last glance and fluttered into the trees.

They both let out their breath. "Fadin," Aednat said, turning to him.

"I know, Freckles," he sighed. "We just got ourselves into a lot of trouble."

~~~

Fadin sat, feeling the worry bubble in his stomach, though how much of that was hunger he wasn't sure. He glanced at Aednat, who stared back, her auburn-hazel eyes full of her thoughts.

"What's the matter with you?" Tase asked Fadin, elbowing him.

Fadin put on a fake smile. "Nothing, I'm just hungry."

Tase made a face that told Fadin he didn't buy it, however he did not press the issue.

Fadin hated being dishonest to Tase. It felt wrong, but he wasn't sure what the fairy would do to him if he told.

Everyone was seated round a large table that had clearly been created from a fallen tree. They were all chattering happily and sitting on small stumps or large boulders, eagerly watching as Daireann placed the slices of steaming fruit pie down on the makeshift table.

"Oh my," Enda mumbled as a piece was set before him. He watched as Daireann turned her back and then reached out to touch the sticky sweet drop that was oozing out the side of the pie crust. A wooden spoon came down on his hand before he could reach it. "Owe," he hissed, pulling his hand back and shaking it.

"Rude," Daireann reprimanded. "You wait until it is all out on the table." She shook her frizzy white blond head. "Honestly, like a big child."

Ma looked at him and then burst into good-natured laughter.

Enda grumbled something under his breath and got up, seeming to feel that sitting near the pie was too much of a temptation.

Fadin tried to think of something besides the open chests he and Aednat had hauled into the woods, but his mind refused to obey. He jerked a little as Mr Hogan sat down next to him.

"Good morning," Mr Hogan beamed. His eyes crinkled up and fanned lines out of the corners, really making his smile look more joyful. His wavy jet-black hair that hung to the nape of his neck actually looked clean. It had been an almost ashy colour since they had left Cavan-Corr. Baths on the ship had not been something of a priority.

"Ah, there is our early bird," Quinlan teased, noticing Fadin. He leaned over Cormick, who was seated on Fadin's other side, and rubbed his head. "Up at the crack of dawn, eh? Not enough work for you yesterday? I suppose we have to work you harder then." He winked at him.

"Hump off," Fadin retorted playfully.

"Yeah, and watch your grubby sleeves," Cormick grumbled smacking his younger brother with his broad arms.

Quinlan was unfazed. He had a large smile on his tan face and leaned forward on the table. "Did you wake him like I said last night?" He asked Tase.

Tase was sitting opposite Quinlan. He smirked. "No, he was up way before I was."

Fadin's heart pounded at the thought of the Old One.

"Awww," Quinlan groaned, leaning back in his chair. "You have to, he won't know what hit him."

Fadin glanced warningly at Tase. Tase smirked and darted his eyes.

"And what mischief were ya plotting?" Ardan asked, taking a seat next to Tase. His dark red hair also looked freshly clean and brushed, and his pale skin was flushed at his cheeks, where his freckles were splattered.

Fadin pulled himself out of his thoughts and turned to Quinlan. "Yeah, what did you want Tase to do to me?"

His wide smile returned and his black eyes sparkled mischievously. He shrugged and looked down at his spotted hands.

"Taaase?" Fadin asked, realising Quinlan wasn't going to cop up to whatever his plan had been.

Tase was smirking. "He wanted me to flip your hammock over."

"Ahh, why'd ya have to go and spoil it?" Quinlan whined.

Fadin turned his attention back to Quinlan. "You mouldy tosser!" Quinlan stuck his tongue out at him.

"You really are a bloody devil," Cormick said, eyeing his brother. "Don't worry, Fadin," he said, turning to him. "I'll get him for you."

"Psh," Quinlan huffed, "I'm so scared."

Arden let out a hearty laugh and his hazel-brown eyes gleamed. "Ya boys crack me up. I remember being yer age, pulling pranks on me friends."

Mr Hogan leaned forward. "Me too. Remember that time we got Enda with that bucket of slugs?"

Cormick whipped his head in his father's direction.

Ardan let his head fall back a bit with his laughter. "Oh, of course! That was a great one."

"What?" Fadin and Tase said simultaneously, turning their full attention to the two older men.

Quinlan's mouth dropped. "I've got to hear this story!" Cormick tilted his position so he could listen better.

"Well," Mr Hogan said, "I think we were about twenty at the time, Alroy and I, which means, you were about eleven, right, Arden?"

He was wiping tears from his grinning eyes. "Ah yep, that sounds about right."

"We were mad at Enda for keeping us from exploring that cave. I think it was," Mr Hogan continued. "And now that I think about it, we were really a handful, and that cave went miles down, and we didn't have any idea where it went."

Fadin felt his mouth pop open as he listened.

"That's right. I remember being so furious with him," Arden chimed in. "I was getting to hang out with the older fellas, and he had to come and spoil all our fun."

Cormick chuckled.

"He loved doing that," Mr Hogan said, peering at the boys and rolling his eyes.

Fadin and Tase exchanged excited looks.

"So that night," Mr Hogan grinned, "all three of us got together, went and gathered a bunch of slugs from under these rocks we had seen by the cave, and put them in this huge bucket."

"Ahhh ha ha," Quinlan made an eager grunting sound. The corners of Fadin's mouth turned up.

"It was so full, we could barely lift it," Arden added.

Mr Hogan nodded. "But somehow we managed it, and we hung it right over the door to his tent."

"Oh, no," Cormick beamed.

"Oh yes," Arden cackled, "so that when he came out he'd step on the wire and, kersplat!"

Fadin and Tase glanced at one another, faces beaming. "So? What happened?" Tase asked.

"Well, we waited all night," Mr Hogan chuckled, "and that morning as he came out of his tent, he missed the wire!"

"No!" Quinlan howled.

"Yep," Ardan said, his face looking forlorn. "It seemed our brilliant plan had failed. We were getting ready to take it down, because we weren't sure who would go inside next, when Enda suddenly appeared near the door."

"AND?" Fadin questioned.

"He was talking to a pretty girl," Mr Hogan sniggered, "walking backward, going to get something from his tent."

Cormick grimaced. "Did you really let that happen?"

"Oh, we did," Ardan smirked.

"He backed right into it, and the bucket fell directly over his head," Mr Hogan made a movement with his hands and then slammed them on the table.

Fadin and Tase roared with amusement.

Arden burst into thunderous laughter. "I wish you could have seen his face!" Quinlan was beside himself.

"It was horrible," Mr Hogan said, his black eyes almost slits from his laughter.

"Ah, but worth all the trouble we got in," Arden chimed.

"I bet it was!" Quinlan cried.

Cormick chuckled despite himself and folded his muscle-lined arms. "Wow, you three were awful."

"That we were," Arden nodded, his red hair bobbing. "That we were."

"And the pretty girl he was talking to?" Tase wondered.

"That happened to be yer lovely Aunt Kyna," Ardan answered. "That was before yer Uncle Dubhlainn had claimed her as his own."

"And that little incident clearly helped her make her choice, didn't it?" Everyone turned.

Enda was standing, hands on his hips, looming over Mr Hogan.

Mr Hogan looked up and grinned slightly, his white teeth shining against his olive toned skin. "Remember Enda, we were quite young."

Enda shook his head. "Psh, young, as if that's an excuse. If the three of you were together again, I wonder what you would do."

For a moment Mr Hogan smiled, and then sadness came over his face. Enda's too.

Arden swallowed, his face void of the joy that had just been there.

Fadin felt the emptiness of his father's death fill him up. How much he wished he could see him here, with his childhood friends, sharing stories, and laughing at memories made long ago.

"Well," Arden said, his smile returning, "I'm sure Alroy would give you a run for yer money, Enda."

The emptiness in Fadin's chest lifted a little.

Enda chuckled, his bushy graying brows rising. "I'm sure he would."

Mr Hogan chuckled. "Maybe he'd stick a slug or two in your lovely piece of pie?"

Fadin crinkled his face in disgust but grinned at the thought.

"Uck!" Enda grimaced, and smacked Mr Hogan in the shoulder. "Don't ruin my pie for me. I won't be able to get that image out of my head."

~~~

"What are we goin' to do, Fadin?" Aednat asked as they stared down at the empty chests, attempting to cover them completely with leaves and other things about the forest floor.

"I'm not sure," he answered, dropping a pile of glittering silver and purple leaves over the chest most visible. His mind wasn't working at a quick pace, not after all the pie he had eaten. He was surprised they had actually managed to slip away unnoticed.

"We are magically banned from telling the adults, obviously," Aednat grimaced. "But I don't think we should tell the others either."

Fadin nodded. "I agree. It's our problem, not theirs."

The sound of close voices made Fadin and Aednat duck down. They were in a patch of long flowing bluish grass that concealed them quite nicely when they got low.

They watched as Saoirse and Desmond walked into the woods together. "I understand about not being able to always control yourself," Desmond was saying. "You should have seen when I first started to change. I could hardly think when it would come over me."

"Yes, but it's different now, isn't it?" Saoirse asked, her voice sounding hopeful. "I mean, you can control it? It seems like you are completely you when you change, like you don't lose yourself."

Desmond smiled at her. "I do have control now. It never takes over like before. I'm sure the same will happen with you."

Saoirse's face looked doubtful. "I really hope so, Desmond." Desmond put a hand on her shoulder.

They continued talking as they walked further into the trees, but Fadin didn't care to listen to anything else they said. "That was close," Fadin breathed.

Aednat put her face in her hands. "I can't believe we opened that scroll." Fadin let out an exasperated breath. Neither could he.

"Caoimhe!"

Fadin jerked.

"Caoimhe! They're gone!" It was Uncle Lorcan's voice. "The chests! They're gone! Where could they have gone?"

Fadin's heart pounded against his ribs.

"Oh boy," Aednat gulped.

"Go!" A voice hissed at them.

They both looked up to see the Old One fluttering over their heads.

"Into the clearing. I will hide the chests. No one will find them."

Fadin did not need any more encouragement. He grabbed Aednat's hand and together they snuck back into the meadow.

~~~

Two weeks went by in what felt like a blink. Uncle Lorcan had been in an almost frantic state for the first ten days. He had insisted on a search of the woods, had demanded guards be put on duty at night, usually Mr Hogan, Ardan, Enda, or himself. He had not known what was inside the chests, that much was clear, but he seemed to feel that whatever the fairies had locked away must have been terrible, and if the chests were missing it meant they were all in danger.

He finally calmed down, partly due to the fact that nothing had happened, and because Caoimhe was as vigilant as he was. She had taken the matter extremely seriously. Even after Uncle Lorcan's nerves had been soothed, she continued to keep a watchful eye at night and scouted the woods.

Fadin sat near the fireplace in his family's hut on the fifteenth night, staring down at his hands, a feeling of guilt gnawing at him. He reprimanded himself for the mistake of opening the scroll. Nothing horrible had happened yet, but a large bag of fish, caught by Mr Hogan and Enda, had gone mysteriously missing. Fadin and Aednat knew immediately what had taken it. They were going to have to keep a better eye out.

There was a soft knock on their door.

Fadin's body tensed, for his mind had been on the chests.

Ma looked at her children, surprised as they were. Clearie got up and opened the door. He smiled wide as Mr Hogan's face appeared.

"Hi, Mr Hogan," Tase beamed.

"Lee?" Ma asked.

"I had something for you, before we all turn in," he said from the doorway.

Ma beckoned him inside. "Of course, what is it?"

Mr Hogan grinned and opened the door wider. He pulled in one of the most beautiful cribs Fadin had ever seen, though to be fair he hadn't seen many. It was made from redwood and had beautiful designs of horses and swords carved into it. There was a small mattress and a fur blanket inside.

"Oh, it's lovely," Ma breathed.

Saoirse stood and gawked at it. "Wow," she whispered, touching the wood.

Mr Hogan nodded, patting the crib. "Shemus gave me the instructions and material for it. We thought Glendan could use a proper crib." He surveyed the cabin. "Should we put it near the fire? That way Glendan can keep warm?"

"I think that would be perfect," Ma agreed, seemingly beyond knowing what to say.

Mr Hogan placed the crib in a corner quite near the fire. It would keep the baby plenty warm. "There," he said with a smile. "Do you mind if I do the honours?" He held his spotted hands out for baby Glendan.

Ma laughed. "Of course." She handed Glendan to him and the baby smiled up at Mr Hogan as he was placed in his arms.

Mr Hogan let out a rumbling chortle and gently stroked Glendan's cheek with his large hands. He laid him down carefully into the new crib.

Fadin noted that the fur blanket made it look like Glendan was lying on a cloud. It took only a moment for the baby's large brown eyes to droop and then close with sleep.

Mr Hogan and Ma laughed softly, and as Fadin looked up he felt a sort of pang. They stood together, side by side, both leaning over the crib and staring down delightedly at baby Glendan. Mr Hogan's strong hands gripped the railing of the crib, and Ma hugged herself, but they both were leaning towards one another. Fadin couldn't help but think this is how his mother and father should be; standing together, enjoying their youngest child with those looks on their faces. Instead it was Mr Hogan who stood with Ma, and that for some strange reason made Fadin feel horribly sad but also in a strange way happy. At least Ma wasn't standing there alone.

"I'll let you all get some rest." Mr Hogan said. He gave Ma a sort of strange look, and then hugged Saoirse and each of the boys. "Goodnight," he smiled, and walked out.

Ma said something or other, and everyone began to get ready for bed, but Fadin's mind was on the strange look Mr Hogan had given Ma. He usually never noticed things like that, but this time he had, and he wondered what it meant. He thought about bringing it up to Tase, but he was too tired. He would remember to tell him in the morning. His mind went back to the missing bag of fish and tried to find a way to keep a better lookout for the spriggans.

~~~

The disappearances continued as time went on. They were sporadic and long periods would go where nothing would be missing, but the worry grew in Fadin and Aednat's minds. They tried to talk to the Old One, who was of absolutely no help. She agreed it was the spriggans, but insisted there was nothing she could do about it. They were in Fadin and Aednat's hands now.

Besides the spriggans, life on the island was simple. They all began to fall into a routine. The adults all agreed that the children needed to continue their education, so classes were set up. Enda taught history, which had always been one of Fadin's least favorite subjects. However, he found when you were dealing with magic history, things became much more interesting. Daireann and Enda together taught about the different magical creatures found in Ireland. Ardan's specialty was invention, potions, and the consequences of magic: a class that was quite important. Whenever he taught them about an invention or potion he made, he would have to have the help of one of his daughters, usually Aednat, because of his missing fingers. If you didn't have steady hands, things could go horribly wrong, he instructed them. Apparently all through his career either Alassandra or one of the girls had always been his assistant.

"Ya have to understand," Ardan told them one particularly cold and rainy day. "Anything you do in this world has consequences, right?" He had just shown them a nasty liquid that took the breath away from those you made drink it, until you were ready to give it back. It, however, wasn't a stroll on the beach to use; using it made it hard to breathe for all the air stolen from the other person entered the users body.

"I suppose," Clearie said.

"You suppose?" Ardan chuckled. "Okay, how about this, when you jump in the air, what is the consequence?"

"You come back down?" Aimirgin asked.

"Correct," Ardan nodded. "Every action has an equal and opposite reaction. It's the same with magic. What ya do in magic has consequences, because it is not in nature, nature must keep the balance, but you also have your own price to pay."

"Price?" Fadin asked, leaning forward.

Ardan leaned against his chair. "Yer magic is like a muscle, it gets stronger the more ya work it out, just like yer body gets stronger the more ya exercise and train it. If ya were to try and lift a car, Tase, what do ya suppose would happen?"

Tase laughed. "I couldn't."

"Right, ya couldn't, but what if ya were to try? What if ya were to have a car dropped on ya and ya tried to get it off?"

"I would probably die."

Ardan nodded. "If ya try something beyond yer strength in magic before yer ready, it could kill ya."

There was silence at this. Fadin had not realised how serious using magic could be. His experience with magic had been to see adults just do it, and he and Tase had the incident at the prison, but that seemed beyond their control. If magic could kill you if you were not strong enough for it… he would need to remember to keep himself under control.

Mr Hogan and the Hogan boys worked with them on training with their weapons. Mr Hogan, though a gentleman, proved to be quite formidable with his whip. It was incredible, the things he could do with it.

Fadin's favorite was when Mr Hogan would steal the weapons out of his son's hands.

With a good-natured chuckle, Mr Hogan bowed to him and beckoned him over.

Fadin was given a wooden stick, because Caoimhe felt it was unwise to train with their swords yet. She handed it to him and arched a copper eyebrow. "Watch yourself," she warned.

Fadin, frustrated at her for not allowing him his sword, gave a mock smile and turned round. He held his stick before him and watched Mr Hogan carefully.

It happened so fast Fadin hardly saw it. One moment he was staring at Mr Hogan, the next Mr Hogan was laughing and he held the stick.

"Wow!" Fadin exclaimed, wrapping his mind around what had just happened. "That was brilliant!"

Mr Hogan beamed at him. "Takes years of practice." He let out a tired breath. "I'm out of shape," he grinned. He wiped his sweaty brow and began to remove his shirt.

Fadin was reliving the moment the stick left his hand when he looked up and saw Mr Hogan's bare back. His jaw fell.

He had never seen Mr Hogan without a shirt on before, so he had never seen the scars. Long, dark, raised up scars lined his olive skin. These were wounds from a whip and they seemed to be everywhere. Others that could only belong to swords were on his side, along his right shoulder blade, and there was one across the length of his back ribs. There were burn marks too, and a few scars that even looked like bullet wounds.

"Mr Hogan," he breathed.

Mr Hogan turned to him, face still bright with his smile. Fadin had to suppress a gasp as more scars were visible from the front. Mr Hogan's grin vanished. "What's wrong?" he asked, voice full of concern.

"What happened to you?" Tase asked, coming to stand besides Fadin.

"What do you mean?" His dark eyes were genuinely confused.

Quinlan came closer and seemed just as perplexed as his father. Clearly, the scars did not bother him.

Fadin pointed to one particularly dark scar just under Mr Hogan's left ribcage, one that looked like it was inflicted by a large sword. "Your scars, what happened?"

Mr Hogan looked down and realisation dawned on him. "You've never seen them?" He rubbed the back of his neck. "I sort of forget about them, they've been with me so long," he smiled.

Fadin did not smile back.

"Don't worry," Mr Hogan said, coming closer to them. "If I had thought about it I would have warned you. These scars are quite old. I got them during the Great War." He touched the one under his ribcage. "This one nearly killed me, but I'm still here." He bent down so he was closer to their eye level. "I've had them for such a long time I forget they may surprise people. They are just a part of me now."

Fadin felt a bit sick thinking about each scar being fresh, the pain Mr Hogan must have been in, how long it would have taken him to heal. "I'm sorry," he said. "I don't suppose I realised what fighting in the Great War meant."

"Neither did I," Tase said.

Mr Hogan touched Fadin's chin. "I don't think anyone who hasn't been in a war would." He grabbed both of their shoulders. "That's the way it should be though. If everyone knew what war was really going to be like…" He seemed to be remembering something as his voice fell away and he looked far off. "… No one would ever go to war." He returned his attention and winked at them. "All right, let's get back to it."

He stood and began to talk about watching when an enemy is looking for an opportunity to disarm you but Fadin couldn't help but stare at his scars. Each one was a story of some battle long ago, each one told of the sacrifices he had made. How had he not understood what that war had meant to the people in it?

Fadin saw something out of the corner of his eye and turned.

Ma was standing not far from them, her hand was over her heart, and a look of pain was spread across her face. She was looking at Mr Hogan and clearly taking in his scars for the first time as well. Her cerulean eyes looked as though they could spill over with tears, but her chin was firm and she did not cry. She bit her plump bottom lip and turned away, going back to baby Glendan who had begun to shriek.

Fadin focused his eyes forward and tried to pay attention, but all he could think about was how Mr Hogan had received each one of those scars.

# CHAPTER 5
## BREAK THE BONDS

Rain pounded against the windows, sounding like a thousand softly clapping hands. Outside the day was beautifully grey and chilled, while inside the stone castle the large fireplace boasted a beautifully enormous fire warming the room it burned in significantly. The silver fur rug was inviting as it danced with the firelight, and on a small wood table two mugs steamed with a hot drink to take the chill out of any body. The only one there to enjoy the comforts the room held was the servant who had prepared it, and he stood near the back door, trying to listen to what it was his masters were doing up the cold long stairs. The roll of thunder that erupted suddenly made Maldorf jump backward, and just in time. The door swung open, and had he not moved it would have knocked him unconscious. He scooted back even further as the door rocked open and closed on its swinging hinges, his eyes wide with surprise.

A tall man had come in, with lanky legs and slicked back white hair. He wore a fancy human suit, and for a moment Maldorf's heart flew into his throat, thinking that by some horrible chance an Ainodall had wandered into the master's home. However, when the man turned, Maldorf's stomach plummeted for an entirely different reason. He recognized the man, and he almost wished it had been an Ainondall who had made a wrong turn somewhere. The man was Puceula Lynch, the advisor to the king, a man you did not forget. Though on a side note Maldorf mentally commented that with his new scars from the burns he had received at the hands of the Kavanaghs, Lynch was almost unrecognizable. Maldorf knew he was simple, and did not understand the great things of the world, but even he wondered at how a man like this had become King Raegan's advisor.

Puceula had a long coat on, which was covered with rain. His boots, which were black and seemed to be made out of ogre skin, were caked in mud. Had they been in the underground city there would have been no rain or mud to avoid, something about living underground Maldorf missed, no rain. Though Maldorf did like seeing the sky, in some ways the above world seemed frightening to him. The masters had left Cavan-Corr weeks ago, in search of information concerning the Kavanaghs. So far there had been little luck, and they had to be quite careful to make sure no humans saw them. They were staying in an abandoned castle, however, far away from the view of humans. It was a castle no Irishman would ever come to for superstition's sake and no tourist could ever find without the help of locals.

Maldorf ran out to Puceula and held his arms out. "Take your coat for you, sir?"

Puceula glanced down at him and shrugged his coat off.

The coat fell on Maldorf and he staggered under its weight, spluttering as the wet cloth had forced some rain in his mouth and nose.

"Bring me your masters," Puceula commanded.

Maldorf would of course obey, but he knew Senssirra and Silass were in a meeting with someone they suspected of having information. They did not like being interrupted. "Yes, sir, right away I go."

He scurried to the twisting metal coatrack that had the appearance of six silver snakes slithering up the body of a dragon. The snakes were each sinking their fangs into the dragon's hide and the dragon in turn had its head leaned back in a silent roar. Maldorf shuttered as he looked at it, but he tapped the tail of the metal dragon four times. The head of the largest snake turned to him, and the silver eye glistened.

"The advisor's coat," Maldorf said, nodding to the wet cloth.

The snake flicked its metal tongue and slithered down to him. Maldorf held the coat out to it and the snake ripped the coat away with its long silver fangs. It curled itself up the dragon, hung its head forward and froze. The coat appeared as though it was resting on an elaborated piece of furniture, not on the head of a snake that could become mobile at any moment.

Maldorf stole one last glance at Puceula, who was observing the warm living room, with its unfriendly looking decor, and dashed up the stairs. These stairs were made of old cold rock, and the handrails had been carved so that at the top of the landing there were stone horse heads peering at you from either side. Maldorf did not like the stone horses, though he wasn't sure why. He heard a blood-curdling scream explode from a room down the massive stone hall and all his blue hair stood on end. What were they doing?

Sensirra opened the door angrily and hissed down at him.

"What are you doing up here, ssslave?" Silass spat.

"Please," Maldorf bowed to them, lowering himself as flat as he could, "the Advisor to the King is downstairs, and he wants to speak with the masters." He was not allowed to use any being above his status's name. He could not call the advisor Puceula, nor could he call the masters Senssirra or Silass, it was disrespectful and he would be punished severely if he disobeyed.

He snuck a glance at them and saw the concerned looks on their faces. He couldn't help but feel a bit glad at their obvious distress.

"You will clean up the messss in that room, and ssstay out of our way." Senssirra commanded him.

Maldorf felt the magic bind him to obey her, and the shackles on his wrists and ankles stung with the orders.

They hurried past him, slithering gracefully down the stairs.

Maldorf considered his next move for a moment. He could choose to disobey the order and listen to their conversation, but if he did that he could not disobey for another five days. He reached down to his furry stomach and unfolded the pouch no one else could know was there. He pulled from his pouch the dragon tooth that had belonged to one of the Kavanagh boys, and before them to their father, Alroy O'Callaghan. He had used the tooth on more than one occasion: first to keep information he had learned away from his masters, three weeks ago to hide a young brown goblin who had mistakenly come into the house, a handful of times to leave and meet others he had learned wanted to help the Kavanaghs, and once just the week before for his own satisfaction to deliberately disobey an order to rescrub the entire downstairs floor because there had been four crumbs left in the stone kitchen. The tooth had worked at breaking the magical bondage every time, but it did not work again for five days, and if he tried it before it was ready he learned it had consequences – like blabbing uncontrollably the information he had managed to hide from Senssirra, or nearly blurting out where the young goblin was hiding before stuffing a handful of dirt from the nearest dustpan in his mouth.

He stared at the large tooth and decided the conversation was worth using the power for. He had to know what Puceula came for. He held the tooth firmly in his paws and closed his large chocolate-brown eyes. "Break the bond," he whispered to it. "Allow me to disobey my mistress, remove my order, to hold my own interests. Loosen these shackles, give me the freedom to choose, away the slavery, give me the power to refuse." He felt the weight of Sensirra's order fall away, the crackle of her magic failed and he grinned. He quietly scampered down the stairs and got as close as he dared.

"It's got something to do with mermaids," Puceula said. His voice was frustrated.

"Mermaidsss?" Silass asked.

Maldorf leaned his head around the corner, and watched silently. "Yes," Puceula said as he paced and bit his left thumbnail. "I have it on good authority that a mermaid was seen helping them. How or what she did to help them, I don't know. There is some magic preventing me from getting more information."

"In what way doesss that information help any of usss?" Sensirra hissed angrily.

Puceula stopped pacing. "I know you're still upset about that punishment you received," he snapped at her, while she snorted in disgust, "but disregarding the only information we have isn't going to help you keep your snake-like head attached to your shoulders, is it?"

"Punissshment?" She laughed coldly. "I don't care what you know, you cowardiccce filth!" She spat at him. "You got away with only a ssslap acrossss your ssscarred face, a kick in your preccciousss ribsss, and a broken nossse. How horrific. You ssshould have tried an ounccce of the pain I reccceived." Her features were livid and her ruby eyes glowed with her fury.

"Sssenssssirra!" Silass barked at her. She waved a hand at him furiously.

"Call me what you'd like, you belly crawling serpent," Puceula growled venomously, "but we are in the same boat, whether you want to accept that or not. Vladimir wants the Kavanaghs back, and though he may have made more of an example out of you, his anger burns just as blistering against me." He let out a deep breath. "I know my value to him only lasts as long as I am useful, as does yours." He nodded to the both of them. "Once we lose our worth, he will end us."

Senssirra and Silass said nothing, but Senssirra nodded ever so slightly. "We have to fix the damages done from the prison escape," Puceula continued. "I am working on obtaining the girl from the asylum. It's not easy, someone is protecting her and blocking my efforts, but I'll find a way around the protections. The Kavanaghs are another matter. I can find no trace of them, which leads me to believe…" He let his voice fall away.

"They are no longer on the mainland," Silass said.

Puceula Lynch gave him a look that said he agreed. "I just don't know where they went, nor who is keeping their whereabouts hidden. Not even our most powerful fairies can see where they are." Puceula was quiet for a moment then ran a hand through his white hair. "Besides being a threat," he said, "Vladimir believes they have it with them."

"The Xoor?" Senssirra questioned, surprised.

"No." He shook his head. "Vladimir thinks one of the Kavanaghs has the key."

Both of the enchidians eyes widened but Maldorf was confused. What key?

"Is he sure?" Silass asked.

"Fairly certain, yes."

"Well," Senssirra said, going to the silver coat rack and grabbing her own long jacket, "if mermaidsss helped them, then I think it'sss high time we paid an old friend a visssit."

Silass smirked at her. "I think that'sss a fabulousss idea."

Puceula did not seem to know what exactly they were talking about, but it didn't seem to bother him. "Find out what you can," he said, grabbing his coat from the silver snake. It relinquished his coat as soon as his fingers clutched it. "I have plenty I have to do, but I want you on the right track. If I hear anything else, I will let you know. In the meantime, keep from Vladimir our meetings if you can."

Senssirra nodded. "Hisss knowledge of our collaborating wouldn't make thingsss more pleasssant when we all have to deal with him."

Lynch grunted his agreement. "Contact me if you learn anything of significance." He went to the door. "And make sure you wipe that Ainondall's memory." He inclined his head toward the upstairs.

Senssirra smiled coolly. "We were consssidering keeping him for a sssnack."

Lynch stopped at the open door and turned to her. "That would be foolish indeed. Remember, the children got help from him, they may return to check if he is all right. If he's dead, he can't lure them into a trap for you."

Senssirra's eyes lit up malevolently. "Not bad, Advisssor."

He took no pleasure in her compliment but gave a slight bow and was about to exit when Silass grabbed his arm. Puceula stared at him with immense abhorrence.

"Isss there a reassson you're wearing ogre ssskin bootsss and wrissst

92

guardsss?"

Maldorf looked and saw that Lynch was indeed wearing wrist guards, ones that went all the way to his elbows.

Silass eyed the advisor suspiciously. "They usssually are to keep you sssafe from large clawsss. You planning on needing that sssort of protection?"

Lynch appeared as though answering Silass was the last thing he would ever want to do, but he turned and relaxed his stance. "An old friend of our master has returned. I am to go and convince her to join us." He sounded extremely unhappy at the thought. "I'm not sure what sort of state of mind she is in, so I thought protection would be necessary." He paused, then added, "It's not claws I'm worried about. Where I'm headed there is more need to fear fangs."

Silass and Senssirra glanced at one another.

Puceula nodded to them and trudged out into the hammering rain.

Senssirra and Silass hissed among each other, too quietly for Maldorf to hear. They seemed to agree on something and readied themselves to leave.

"Maldorf!" Senssirra cried.

He felt the power overtake him, and the bond reinstate itself. The tooth could help him no longer. He fought as long as he could and then scurried out to her, making it appear that he had run from upstairs. "Yes, mistress?"

"When you are finisssshed tiding up in that room, I want you to take our guessst back to hisss home." She flung a piece of parchment at him and Maldorf snatched it up. "Make sssure to give him a proper memory removal of all of the eventsss sssince he was brought here, but do not erassse anything elssse. It is crucccial hisss memory isss otherwissse intact."

Maldorf bowed to her.

"We do not know when we will return," Silass told him. "Have food prepared and keep the firesss ssstoked." He glared outside. "I am sssick of this blasssted rain."

Maldorf bowed his understanding.

They said nothing more to him but gathered a few more things and left into the storm.

As soon as the latch clicked in place he raced upstairs. He rushed to the door he had seen his master's exit and dashed inside, not sure what he would find.

The room was dark, and the sounds of the rain magnified as part of the room was made from some sort of metal. There was a heavyset man inside of a steel cage, who cowered against one side. His complexion was white as a sheet and he cried out when he saw Maldorf and covered his eyes.

"This can't be real!" he yelped. "First giant snakes and now this?"

Wiping this man's memory seemed like a kindness, as his fear was so clearly overpowering. Maldorf reminded himself this man was going to be used as a trap to trick the Kavanagh children, and he refocused his mind.

Maldorf looked down at the address Senssirra had given him. He reached inside his pocket and pulled out the thicker piece of parchment and a small ink pen. He wrote as quickly as he could and hoped that Ciaran wasn't too far away so he could tell him everything before the slave bond made him obey his masters every command. "Hurry, Goblin," Maldorf said aloud as he finished scribbling. He looked up at the man and frowned. "The Kavanaghs are in trouble."

~~~

"The Kavanaghs are in trouble!" Quinlan cried above the rain. "They are being pinned down by the terrible Hogans and there's no where they can run. They tried their best to defeat their enemys, but it turns out they are the lesser of the two clans." His voice sounded like a television narrator and Tase could hear the smile in it.

"Besides that being absolute rubbish," Clearie called from a tree nearby, "Our last name isn't Kavanagh, it's O'Callaghan."

"No one knows the name O'Callaghan like they do Kavanagh in the magical world," Quinlan retorted, "and you *are* in the Kavanagh family, let's not split hairs here. But I thank you for trying to reprimand me and giving away your position in the process."

Tase raised his hands in exasperation. "Thanks a lot, Clearie!" he hissed.

Clearie turned behind his tree and rolled his eyes. "You don't think they knew where we were?" His voice was a whispering shout. "We lost this game long ago."

This was Caoimhe's course. She taught them all about defence and combat. She also made them use magic as they did it. She had them do caber tossing – which basically meant finding a really huge stick and throwing it as far as you could, Tase was terrible at this – hammer throws, sheaf tosses – though they used sticks instead of straw – and she had them do target practice. Target practice was what they were doing now, though instead of starting with arrows, she made them fight each other with mud.

Tase, holding a ball of mud firmly in his fist, was not ready to give up. "I can't believe you are on our team," he spat at Cleaire. "Fadins out there somewhere scooping them out, and he has good aim."

"He is the only one in our group who does," Clearie pointed out, whipping some rain out of his line of vison.

*WHACK!* Mud splattered against the side of Tase's head and sent him colliding towards the ground. He caught himself and spun round, trying to spot his assailant. He could see no one.

A huge ball of mud hit him from the other side and this time he went down hard, cracking the branch of a blue bush as he collided with the forest floor. He jerked upright and sent his mud ball flying. By sheer luck he hit Quinlan in the stomach, but the hit didn't seem to faze the tall boy. He stumbled for a moment, reached down and came up with an armful of mud.

Tase's eyes bulged as he struggled to get up. He spotted Clearie, hiding in a patch of purple leaves like a coward. "Defend me, you git!" Tase billowed and got to his feet just as he heard Quinlan throw the massive pile of mud.

Had it been a fair fight, where the laws of physics were involved, no one could have thrown that large pile of mud as far as Quinlan chucked it. They were not fighting fair, however, and Quinlan was much better with his magic than Tase was. Tase ran but the mud boulder was too quick and it nailed him square in the middle of the back, knocking the wind out of him and sending his face in direct contact with a huge brown puddle.

Tase pulled his head out of the water and sucked in a horrible tasting breath. He felt the magic of it just before another massive pile of mud pounded down on top of him. He wished his magic sensing abilities were more developed, he could have felt that attack coming a lot sooner.

"Great job, Aimirgin!" Tase heard Cormick shout, and he heard the high five he gave her.

Caoimhe laughed and Tase glared up at her from her vantage point in a high tree. Tase thought it wildly unfair to team Aimirgin up with Quinlan, Cormick, and Colmcille, while he was teamed with Fadin, Clearie, and Aednat. None of *them* had much control over their magic at all, and the Hogan boys were all grown, and had many years of practice behind them.

"Feel the magic, Tase," she called to him. "If there is no challenge, how will you push yourself?" she said to his unspoken protest.

Tase would have liked to hit Caoimhe with a mud ball, but he knew that was a waste of brainpower to even consider. Caoimhe was so powerful she could stop the mud in mid hair with a word and send it colliding directly into Tase, no matter how far he ran or what he hid behind. In fact, as she perched on a tree branch the rain, which was drenching him and the others, the rain was falling around her in an unnatural way. No rain touched her, it fell close to her body in a curving fashion so that she stayed dry – that was the sort of thing she could do, allowing her to focus on the mud battle they were all having. Throwing something at her would do him absolutely no good.

Tase grimaced and pulled up a handful of mud. He felt the magic Caoimhe had taught him to locate within himself, felt the prickling of his anger and magic mixed together and flung it. So far, each time he had tried to use magic without his weapon, absolutely nothing had happened. This time there was the faintest blue glow as the mud left his hands. It disappeared as soon as it had come but it must have given the mud the little extra boost it had needed because it hit Aimirgin square in the face.

Aimirgin hit the ground and slid down the small hill she had been on.

Suddenly, mud balls flew from two sides and Quinlan, Cormick, and Colmcille appeared from their hiding places and covered their heads. One hit Quinlan hard on the back of the head and Tase smirked with pleasure.

Fadin and Aednat were nowhere in sight, but no one else could be sending the stream of mud besides them.

Clearie had run from his hiding place and had begun pelting Quinlan.

Tase grabbed another handful of mud and ran at Aimirgin, who squeaked in fear and stumbled as she tried to get up and run from him.

Tase chased her as she ran, almost falling over her own feet. She flung a pile of mud back at him, but Tase dodged it. She ran faster, heading toward the beach. Tase picked up steam and toppled over a stone concealed by leaves. He corrected himself quickly and dove for Aimirgin, who turned to see him leap for her. She screamed and the two of them went down.

He plopped the mud directly on top of her head and Aimirgin made a disgusted noise. Tase laughed with delighted satisfaction and was slapped across the face with mud and moss. Aimirgin tried to stand but Tase grabbed a handful of a sticky substance he saw puddled near a tree and got her on the back of the neck before she could completely right herself. She squealed and he pulled her back down.

The two of them began to tumble over one another, each cramming as much mud, moss, and anything else they could grasp in each other's faces. Without realising it, they had rolled near the edge of a small cliff and as Aimirgin thrust a slimy mushroom in Tase's shirt-front, they rolled right over the edge.

It was a slight fall, but it was enough to knock the breath out of both of them. Tase rolled over, away from her, and they both caught their breaths.

Tase, feeling the anger and energy of the battle drain out of him, looked over at Aimirgin. His face broke into a wide grin. She was an absolute mess.

Aimirgin scowled at him, her black eyes alight with a fire he hadn't seen in them before. She sat up and spit, frowning. She looked down, seeming to try and find a clean spot where she could wipe her mouth. There wasn't one. She shot Tase another furious look and he couldn't help himself. He burst into laughter.

She didn't laugh right away but after a moment her soft sounding amusement joined his. "You're going to pay for this," she said after they had settled.

Tase let out a snort. "You deserved it, after that huge mud bomb you laid on me."

She made a sound of contempt. "You really think I did that? That was Colmiclle and Cormick! Cormick only shouted my name so you'd come for me."

Tase raised his eyebrows. "That was a rather effective strategy." Aimirgin fixed him with a playful but irritated look.

Tase smiled and stood. He held his hand out to Aimirgin and froze. "Hey," he whispered, and nodded toward the beach.

Aimirgin turned round and the two of them gaped at Desmond and Saoirse, sitting together by the crashing waves. They were cuddled together on a large boulder and were holding hands.

Tase was bewildered. He had known they were spending a lot of time together, but he had never considered the idea that they may fancy one another.

"Are they holding hands?" Aimirgin asked.

"Looks like it," Tase nodded.

Desmond stroked Saoirse's dark curls and put his hand under her chin. "What's he doing?" Tase asked.

Saoirse looked up at him and, in a movement that seemed too slow, they brought their faces close together and kissed.

Tase's mouth dropped.

"What this?" a voice said by his ear.

Tase jumped and saw Fadin and Aednat had joined them. They were both covered in mud and grinning from ear to ear.

"Be quiet!" Aimirgin shushed.

"Why?" Fadin asked, and then he spotted Desmond and Saoirse. "What are they doing?"

Tase jerked his head in their direction.

They were gazing at one another in a sickeningly sweet way. Saoirse's hand was on his face and she said something to him Tase couldn't hear. Desmond leaned his face into her pale hand and closed his eyes. He let his lips touch her fingers and then leaned down and kissed her again.

Aednat's grin vanished and she gasped.

"Did he just KISS —" Tase and Aimirgin cupped their hand over Fadin's mouth.

Saoirse pulled away from Desmond and shifted her eyes towards the woods.

Tase, Aimirgin, Aednat, and Fadin dove to the ground.

Saoirse's green eyes surveyed the forest for a long moment, and Desmond asked her something. She shook her head and turned back to him.

Tase shot Fadin a frustrated glance. Fadin looked horrified and repulsed.

Tase put a finger to his mouth and slowly got up. The others followed suit and they all snuck away.

"They KISSED!" Fadin cried once they were well out of earshot, even for Saoirse.

"We all saw, Fadin," Aimirgin said, looking down.

Fadin seemed beyond knowing how to react. "I can't believe it." He stared out at nothing and kept shaking his head.

Tase didn't know what to say. He wished he could take seeing them back; he did not want the image of his sister kissing Desmond in his head. Just the thought made him shudder.

Aednat grimaced. "What do we do now?"

"What do you mean?" Aimirgin asked.

"Do we act like we know? Or not?"

"Not!" All three of them answered.

"I don't know about the rest of you," Fadin said, "but I don't want either of them to know we saw them snogging."

"Eww, Fadin," Aimirgin scowled, "don't use that word."

"Well what else would you call it? Your brother was *snogging* my sister!"

"I didn't see your sister putting up any kind of a fight!" Aimirgin shot back.

Tase could see that Fadin was spoiling for a fight. "All right, enough!" he barked. "It's none of our business, it's between the two of them. I say we try to forget it and don't act like we know when we see them. Agreed?"

Neither of them answered but they both nodded.

They all began to shuffle off and Tase glanced back towards the beach. He blinked. There was something there, watching him, something dark with eyes that reflected the light like a mirror. He moved toward it but it was gone. He shook his head. The darker area of the woods where the thing had been was empty. That wasn't possible, it had been there, he'd seen it.

"Tase?" Fadin asked.

"Coming," he said. He glanced back, wondering what the dark thing could have been.

~~~

"All right," Mr Hogan said, standing. "I think we all need to have a little fun."

Tase looked up: the children had all gotten washed, then dinner had been served, and once the meal was over the adults had been talking. It had been on more solemn matters, focused much on the Xoor and the mark it had left across Tase's chest. There had also been talk about the six keys and Puceula Lynch, rather serious and distressing stuff.

Plus Tase had been trying, and failing, not to notice how close Saoirse and Desmond were sitting, how their eyes kept finding each other, and how they clearly held hands under the table.

"What do you have in mind?" Ma asked with a smile. "A little music, perhaps?"

Tase smiled. He had wanted to hear Mr Hogan play his fiddle again since Halloween.

"We have instruments?" Daireann asked, her frizzy white blond hair was down, and it was much longer than Tase had realized. She looked quite pretty in her gown from the O'Sheelin city.

Ardan chuckled. "Of course! We didn't just get clothes from the O'Sheelin's." He stood, kissed Alassandra on the forehead and walked to a large sack not far from the fire. He dug through it for a moment and then cried, "Ah ha!" He came back with a smaller silver sack and held it out to Mr Hogan. "You first, Lee," he grinned, shaking it slightly.

Mr Hogan beamed, his white teeth standing out against his skin, and put his hand inside the sack. He made his eyes thin and pushed his arm in deeper. The sack wasn't much bigger than Tase's head, but Mr Hogan's arm, all the way up to his shoulder, disappeared into it as he searched. He removed his hand from the sack and pulled out a beautiful mahogany violin, its string glimmered in the firelight.

Mr Hogan looked at it, and clicked his tongue to the roof of his mouth. He balanced it in his hands and then plucked the strings with his finger. "Lovely," he said, speaking more to the instrument then to anyone else.

Ardan smiled at him. He passed the sack around, to Enda who was given a bodhran drum, Desmond bagpipes, and Kyna was given a penny whistle.

Last, but not least, Ardan dug in the sack and grabbed out a didgeridoo for himself.

The players arranged themselves in a group near one end of the fire.

Everyone else sat back down, as close to the fire as they dared, and watched as Mr Hogan started the music.

He pulled the violin up to his chin and brought the gleaming bow to the strings. The sound was beautiful, and started slow, and then picked up pace. Desmond's bagpipes joined him. Their sound nearly drowned out Mr Hogan, but only nearly, you could still hear the violin under the bagpipes cries. Enda began to drum and then Ardan blew into his didgeridoo.

The sound was fantastic, filling the clearing with wonderful beat and laughter from the listeners.

Most of the instruments tapered off, and then Kyna was given a solo with Mr Hogan's violin. Her pennywhistle made a golden sound as she played it, quick and upbeat. As she played the other instruments joined in, this time the tempo faster.

"Someone come up and dance!" Mr Hogan called. Everyone laughed but no one got up.

"Okay then," he said. He looked at Alassandra. "Hold down the fort?"

"Of course," she smiled.

Mr Hogan gave her his violin – which she played incredibly well – and strode over to Ma. He held his hand out to her.

This surprised Tase, and he wasn't sure why. There was nothing odd about Mr Hogan asking Ma to dance, was there?

Ma smiled but shook her long dark curls. "Oh no," she said, hugging baby Glendan close to her.

"Why don't you hand the baby over to Daireann?" he asked, his grin wide. Ma gave him a mischievous look but didn't budge.

Tase saw something in Mr Hogan's eyes, a look he had never seen before. He didn't understand it and was unsure what it meant. Looking at Ma's face and at Mr Hogan with his dark hand outstretched, he couldn't help himself. He called out, "Dance with him, Ma!" He hadn't seen Ma dance in a very long time, and he thought it had been long enough.

Ma gave a delightful laugh and Daireann leaned over and snatched baby Glendan off her lap gingerly. "Go on," she urged.

"Come on, you right old coward!" Ruepricked billowed. Mr Hogan smiled down at her, his midnight eyes twinkling.

Ma looked up at him a wistful look on her face and took his hand.

Mr Hogan wasted no time once he had her on her feet. He grasped her by the shoulder, his other palm clasping her hand as he spun her around the fire.

Tase clapped his hands to the music and laughed as they danced and whirled. Ma's face radiated joy as she moved gracefully with Mr Hogan.

The song tempo changed and became slower. Mr Hogan began to lead Ma into a slower dance. They still moved perfectly together, but this dance required them to be closer.

Tase felt something stir as Mr Hogan stared down at Ma, that strange look there again. Ma, not noticing, laughed and suddenly looked up. Her face changed and she gave him an odd look of her own. There was a meaningful moment between them and Tase knew he was not the only one who noticed, though he may have been the only one who didn't really understand what it meant.

Ma suddenly pulled away with a smile. "I think you ought to get back to that fiddle of yours, Mr Hogan," she said.

Mr Hogan chuckled, not seeming affected in the slightest. He nodded to her and walked back over to Alassandra, who gave him his instrument. He smiled wide and began to play.

Ma turned to Caoimhe. "Come on."

Caoimhe shook her head playfully but took Ma's hand and stood up.

Ma recruited Kyna, Alassandra, Aednat, and even Aimirgin, who Tase was certain couldn't dance. Perhaps Ma had not noticed how clumsy she was.

All six of them stood in front of the fire.

The music stopped for a moment, and then burst into life, and Ma gave out a little cry and jumped. Her feet moved like Tase had never seen them move before, and she held her long skirt up so they could be seen.

All of them whirled around the fire, Ma in the lead. They looked magical, their dresses flowing and their feet hopping and pounding into the ground. Tase had to admit, even Aimirgin looked graceful, though there were a few times she staggered.

Caoimhe grabbed Cormick's hand, who grinned up at her and jumped into the dance. They whirled around together, keeping time with the music.

Kyna jerked Enda away from his drum, and Aimirgin snatched up Fadin's hand.

Tase thought he would be safe, Clearie being the eldest, but Ma turned on him and before he knew what was happening, she had him on his feet. His eyes grew wide with embarrassment and fear of falling, but he didn't have long to dwell on that because the music was so fast he had to pay attention to where he put his feet.

Soon everyone, except those playing an instrument, was dancing, and Tase forgot about looking daft. He forgot about the secrets, the storm clouds in the distance, the Xoor, his dark scar along his chest, and even Vladimir.

In the midst of it all, as they danced and laughed, Tase saw Da with them. It was in brief flashes, perhaps even only in his mind, but as he would jerk one way or another he would see Da grabbing someone's arm to whirl around with them, Da smiling, his brown eyes sparkling with delight – he even heard Da's laugh. Tase decided not to try and figure out if it were real or not. He just smiled to himself, enjoying it, and kept on dancing.

# CHAPTER 6
## YESTERDAY'S FIDDLE

After a long while, everyone became tired and sat down around the still blazing fire. Tase, fascinated with the way Mr Hogan played the violin, was delighted when Mr Hogan handed him a beautifully designed banjo.

"Wow!" Tase beamed, stroking the wood.

"I thought you might like to learn to play it," Mr Hogan smiled.

Tase looked up at him. "Do you know how to?"

"I know how to play several instruments, Tase, but the violin just happens to be my favorite. You can thank Lorcan for the banjo, he found it in the old ruins."

Uncle Lorcan winked. "I thought of you when I saw it, Tase, I'm not sure why."

Tase stroked the banjo again and felt what was almost like magic crawling through his fingertips. He suddenly realised he had to learn to play it, he just had to. "Thank you, Lorcan!"

"I used an enlarging potion on it," Ardan chuckled. "It was made for a fairy, much too small for your fingers."

Tase grinned brightly. "It's brilliant!"

Fadin, Aimirgin, and Aednat crowded around him.

Aednat touched the strings. "Looks complicated," she decided.

"It's absolutely beautiful, Tase," Aimirgin said. "Do you suppose it will be hard to learn how to play?"

"Of course it will," Fadin declared. "We're going to have to walk around covering our ears for a while. This twonk is sure to sound horrible."

"Do dry up, you sodding git. Of course I'll sound bad at first, I don't know how to bloody play it." He wacked Fadin on the back of the head.

Fadin took the smack in stride and delighted in his own clever wit.

"I think," Clearie said, walking up with Quinlan, "you were meant to play it, Tase."

"Aww," Quinlan fuzzed the top of Clearie's hair, "what a brown noser!"

"Shove off," Clearie playfully growled.

Tase just stared at the beautiful instrument. He plucked at the strings and found, though their noise wasn't perfect, he was in love with it all the same.

Ma smiled at Mr Hogan, Uncle Lorcan, and Ardan. "Thank you, all of you."

Ardan winked. "Ah, it was nothin', love."

~~~

Mr Hogan settled into a slow tune, never seeming tired of playing. He smiled to himself and leaned into a long stroke of his bow against the gleaming strings of his fiddle, causing Tase to stop plucking at his own strings. "Have you ever heard the story of *The Three Golden Princesses*?" he asked, directing the question to Fadin and his siblings.

Fadin shook his head and backed up from Tase. "No, I haven't."

"I have," Clearie smiled.

Fadin looked at him. "How?"

"It's in that book I got from the Winter Fair."

Fadin shook his head. A book, why was he not surprised? Clearie spent more time with his nose pressed up against pages than anything else. Or at least, he used to, before they had been forced to run away.

"That is one of my favorite stories," Aednat said, leaning forward.

Mr Hogan continued to play a low and slow song. "I think now is a good time for a story."

Fadin scooted forward in his seat too, eager to hear a good tale. He noticed, just catching himself so he didn't jerk upright, that the old sídhee was watching them. She was leaning over on a tree branch just inside the meadow. Fadin wasn't sure what to make of this, but Mr Hogan began to talk so he kept his eyes on her but listened.

"A long time ago, hidden deep within the mountains of old, there was a great

kingdom called Nóinín. It was so named for the way the kingdom shone in the moonlight, for the city was made of a stone that no other kingdom had ever seen. King Nuadu the Wise ruled with a kind and gentle hand and was married to Duana, whose people had provided Nuadu with the unique stones to build their beautiful city. It is known that Duana was not a human, for she would shine just as bright as the stones of the city, but she was caring, generous, and extremely clever. The people of Nóinín loved her, and none asked who her people were.

"Nuadu was known as the wisest king in all the land, for

Duana knew more than any man could dream, and if anyone was keeping a secret from her husband she could see it and would inform him. With this gift, Nuadu could never be defeated in battle, and peace reigned in Nóinín. Time passed and Duana became pregnant, the people rejoiced with their king and queen, and all eagerly awaited the arrival of the child. As the time of the baby's birth approached, Duana fell extremely ill. An old man who was known for his skills in medicine was called to look after the queen. However, when he saw her, he informed Nuadu that she was dying. There was nothing he could do for her, but he could save the child.

"In tremendous grief, Nuadu gave the old man his blessing to save the baby. Duana gave birth to not one, but three beautiful daughters, whose hair glowed like the stones the kingdom was made of. They had golden eyes and gold freckles that splashed upon their pale skin, and Nuadu loved them. Before she died, Duana promised to watch over her daughters and Nuadu. With her last breath she gave her husband a piece of mirror, which she said held the key to her people's power, and then she was no more.

"The old man, under the instruction of the king, took the mirror and followed its light. It led him to a cavern filled with pieces of mirror and what looked like it had once been the place where Duana's people had dwelt. In her memory Nuadu had a mosaic statue of her, made entirely from those pieces of mirror. He set her statue in the throne room, where the moonlight fell most powerfully. Together Nuadu and the old man watched as the first light of the full moon fell upon it. As the moonbeam hit the image of Duana reflective light danced upon the walls, and in the many squares of light Nuadu and the old man could see the secrets being kept from the king. In this way Duana kept her promise.

"The two of them agreed this power should be kept secret, so they allowed none in the throne room at night, and the old man, who was a great Dalbach as well as a healer, agreed to stay with the king as his advisor.

"Years passed and the three daughters of the king had grown just as beautiful as their mother before them. So lovely were they that they became known among their people as the golden princesses, for their shining eyes and sparkling freckles. They were gentle and beloved by all who knew them; they held their father's heart and the advisor loved them as if they were his own children.

"Though great joy was in the city, Nóinín became a place coveted for its wealth and splendor. Nuadu could never be defeated and none understood why. Jealousy spread in the heart of a neighboring king, Draighean. He desired Nóinín above all else and would never be satisfied without it. He called to him his most trusted servant and created for him a powder of dragons teeth made from over two hundred dragons. So powerful was the magic of the dragon's teeth that when the servant drank it with any liquid, even the power Nuadu possessed could not pierce it. Draighean sent his servant to Nuadu's kingdom as a spy to find the source of his power. He would have to drink the powder three times a day to keep the magic protecting his true motives, and he would need to get as close to Nuadu as he could.

"The servant obeyed his master but found the task of getting close to Nuadu impossible. The only one the king trusted was his old advisor, and the only treasure he ever spoke of was his children. The servant spent two years searching, and he hadn't gotten any closer to the king or his secrets. His master's patience was wearing thin and the dragon tooth powder was almost spent. In one last attempt, the servant used a strong poison and made himself ill in front of the king. The king, being a kind man, took him to his personal physician and insisted the man stay there for the night. Never before had the servant been allowed to be in the castle at night. He pounced upon the chance – as soon as the castle had quieted he crept down the halls. A pale light shone in the throne room, and through magic and cunning the servant entered and found the king learning of the secrets being kept from him by his statue. Nuadu was puzzling over a particularly big secret that was not clear, though the servant knew it was his treachery that puzzled the king.

"The servant fled back to his master and told all he knew. With Nuadu's secret revealed, Draighean created protection about himself and his army that would not allow Nuadu even the briefest glimpse of their secret to destroy him. So it was that when the powerful army fell upon Nóinin, the kingdom buckled in moments, for no preparations had been made, no weapons had been set aside, and all had been so confident in their king's ability to protect them that nearly all the people were killed before they even knew what was happening.

"Nuadu did all he could, he fought alongside his soldiers and ordered the advisor to take his daughters and flee. The advisor obeyed, but the evil servant of Draighean had been watching. The mighty kingdom of Nóinin fell, and it was in Nuadu's throne room that the great battle of the two kings was fought. Legends have sprung up about the battle alone, however for this tale only its end is important. Nuadu struck the final blow that ended the evil king, but Draighean wanted to make sure he still had his victory, so as he fell he made sure he swung his weapon hard at the statue of Queen Duana. As Draighean's life ended, Duana's statue shattered into a million pieces, and Nuadu was left in shock, terror, and grief.

"Nuadu felt his heart splinter as he ran through his broken kingdom in search of his advisor and his daughters. All the enemies had fled when their evil king was destroyed, and all of Nuadu's people who had survived had run for their lives, so that no one but he was left in all of Noinin. The king called for the advisor and his children, but it was not until he went to the surface, to the place where the waves met the sand, that he found them.

"The servant of Draighan was ended by Nuadu's advisor, but that victory was forgotten in grief, for the advisor cried over the three princesses who had not survived the servant's attack. Nuadu's heart could hardly hold together under the sorrow, but he could not leave his princesses there on the beach. Together, Nuadu and the advisor created stone likenesses of the princesses, where they were buried. They were set in the middle of the throne room, where their mother's statue used to stand. The advisor was so overcome by grief that he left Nóinín, and what became of him, no one knows.

"The city remained abandoned, never to return to any of its former glory. King Nuadu lingered, keeping unnatural long life and living only in his sorrow. After years had faded into decades, and he had still not gone into death's hand, Nuadu began to wonder why. He sat and touched the statue of his wife, which he had tried time and time again to put back together, to no avail. He picked up a handful of her mirror pieces and, just as a tear fell from his eyes, a single ray of moon shone down upon the king. As he looked into the bits of mirror, illuminated by the moon's light, he saw something glimmer. He stared, and again something gold flashed in the fragments of glass. He pulled his handful of mirror close to him and peered down at the image of his three daughters dancing. He could see them, and they were happy, peaceful, and smiling in the palm of his hand, not alone but with their mother whom they had never known in life. He understood then, the magic of the mirror had stayed with him, prolonging his life, but allowing him to see his family one more time.

"No longer consumed by grief, Nuadu left, taking his queen and princesses with him in a glass bottle he hung around his neck. None know where he went after that, but many think he found peace, whether it was in this life or the next.

"Nóinín, deserted by her people, remained broken and forgotten. Yet rumors have sprung about creatures of darkness who found the secret way into the streets of Nóinín. It is said they have taken it over, and live there still, searching for the pieces of mirror, and the wisdom they may still yet hold."

Mr Hogan gave a long cry with his fiddle. When the bow left the strings, all became silent.

The air erupted with applause.

Fadin had sat upright, and his hands clapped together. "Great story, Mr Hogan," he said, beaming. "But it was awfully sad."

"Most Irish legends don't end on a happy note," Enda sighed.

Mr Hogan gave a small chuckle. "No, they don't."

"It was wonderful though… wasn't it?" Aimirgin said with a girlish grin.

Fadin smirked and looked up at the tree near the edge of the meadow. The Old One was nowhere in sight. He glanced around but could see nothing of her.

Aednat caught his look and made her eyes wide.

He nodded to her. He truly wondered how long they could keep this secret up.

~~~

Fall turned to winter, blowing cool air into the forest from the bitter waters of the sea. Christmas came and went, presents – such as they were – were given, and the meadow was warm and bright by constant fires lit in its centre. Mr Hogan played his fiddle, Tase practiced his banjo, as horrible as ever, and many stories were told.

Things continued to disappear. Though they were not extremely noticeable, Fadin and Aednat began to worry. They went to the Old One and asked her for advice, but she seemed either unable or unwilling to give it. The spriggans were in their hands now. The only problem was, besides fleeting shadows, Fadin and Aednat never actually saw them. How were they supposed to stop something they never saw?

"We need to train extra hard," Aednat said one day as they walked along the beach. They had managed to get away in search of a missing bag of sugar. "We need to learn how to sense magic, because if we can learn to be good at that, perhaps we can track them." She turned her dark red head to look out into waves. Her short cropped hair had begun to grow longer, and it didn't stick out as straight as it had done, but had begun to get some curl on the ends. She held her hand out before her and made the freckles along her arms dance and then fly to the tips of her fingers, making them look much darker than the rest of her pale skin.

Fadin considered this. "That's not a bad idea, Freckles." He threw a white pebble into the ocean waves. "The only problem I can see with it is that whenever Caoimhe tells us to feel, I get too much. It's like this whole island is abuzz with magical energy."

"Of course it is," Aednat said, sounding much older than she was. Fadin looked down at her. Her auburn hazel eyes were wide and staring back at him. "This island has been filled with magic for centuries. Bein' the home to leprechauns it has changed and become somethin'…" she seemed to search for the right word, "alive. It's different from normal islands, almost like it has a personality of its own. You can feel it." She sighed and smiled at him, looking eleven years old again. "Somethin' like that."

Fadin made his eyes large and let his mouth hang open in befuddlement. "You went way over my head, Aedant."

She laughed softly. "Well, my da is really good at explainin' that sort of thing."

Fadin felt a pang in his chest but grinned at her. "Train hard then, that's the plan."

Aedant nodded. She stopped and abruptly walked closer to the water. "What are you doing?" Fadin asked. He remembered all too well Alassandra's warnings to her daughters about the sea. "You said that even just touching the water you could get carried away with your love for the sea and never again touch land, because you all have mermaid blood in your veins."

"I don't believe that superstitious tale for one tick of the clock," she spat, and took off one of her boots. "Besides, even if I did believe it, do I look like I have blue hair?"

"What has that got to do with it?" Fadin asked.

"The blue haired girls are the ones with the mermaid traits," Aednat answered. "They can breathe underwater, and if the stories are true, they are the ones in danger of turnin' into mermaids if they touch the sea." She wriggled her bare toes and looked adventurously out to the waves.

"Aednat," he said cautiously, "maybe that's not a good idea. You may be right, but so could your mother."

She stared at him, her face arranged in a look of evident irritation. "It may be true for Aldabella, and it may even be true for Annatta, but I for one hear no voices at sea. I'm tired of havin' to tip toe around the ocean when we are surrounded by it! Besides, I intend to swim this summer, and if I don't do somethin' now, my ma will never let me anywhere near the water when the weather warms up!"

Fadin did see her point, but he still felt uneasy. "She probably won't let you even if you jumped in the water in front of her and nothing happened."

Aendat made a face and ripped off her other boot. Without warning, she dashed into the water.

"Aednat!" he cried.

She screamed when her feet hit the waves and Fadin's heart leapt in his chest.

"What is it?" He ran into the water, boots still on. He stared in fear of what he may see. Were her feet turning into fins?

Aednat ran back onto the sand, leaned against a tree and clutched her feet.

Fadin chased after her, heart still pounding. "What happened? What?" he yelped.

"It's absolutely freezin'!" She shivered.

Fadin gaped. "That's what you screamed about?"

"You go put your bare foot in that water."

Fadin let out a relieved breath and charged her. He picked her up over his shoulder with the smallest effort.

"Hey, you daft 'apeth, put me down!"

He held her firmly despite her struggling. "You knew I was waiting for something dodgy to happen to you in that water," he told her, "and you go screaming because it's cold."

"Let me down, Fadin!"

"You wanted to test your mother's theory out, eh?"

"Obviously, you git! Now put me down!"

"That's what I thought. But you know, you can't find out if you only put your feet in." He strode toward the water.

"What are you doin'?"

"Putting you," he heaved her up and flopped her into the icy water, which splashed up on him and made him gasp, "down."

She screamed as the freezing water soaked through her clothes.

Fadin began to make for the shore but Adnat dove at his legs and he went crashing head first into the sea. He cried out as the shock of the water bit at him from every angle. He didn't know water could get *that* cold. Then something felt like it pinched him and his head stung, like hair had been pulled from his scalp. He yelped again and struggled to pull in air.

Aednat sped to the shore and huddled in a ball. "Yuh-you are a b-b-bloody idiot!" she hissed at him.

Fadin yanked himself up and ran to the sand. "Yeah, w-well," he said through shuttering teeth, "ah-at least n-now we know yuh-you aren't going to t- turn into a muh-mermaid or will nuh-never want to c-come back from the suh- sea."

She grimaced, grabbed a handful of sand and chucked it at him. He laughed through his chattering teeth.

~ ~ ~

The Old One scowled down at the naiad who quickly swam away from the island. She looked down at the children and considered telling them what the naiad had just done, but... what good would that do? The water creature had taken hair from the boy's head, and blood from his arm. Whatever it wanted with them, telling the children now would change nothing.

Besides, no good could come of the naiad, and whatever it had needed the boy's hair and blood for concerned the island. The Old One knew the end of the island was drawing near, and she did not care. Let the island crash into the sea; let the dark beings be drowned with it, and her as well. Good riddance to it all. She was too old and too tired, and an end to everything would be good. If the island fell, or was attacked, she would pull it down to the depths, and finally her task would be done and she could go to the final rest at last.

No, she would not warn the children. She would wait, and watch, and hope.

~ ~ ~

Snow fell in slow featherlike flakes, landing soundlessly on everything, continuing to cover the world in white. He tore through the mounds of snow, sending waves of it crashing on either side as his strong legs propelled him forward. The castle came into view and he made a hard turn and slid to a stop, showering the ground before the dark haired woman in front of him.

She arched a black eyebrow and her pale green eyes shimmered. She wore a great coat lined with fur and a fur hat, and in her black gloves he saw something clutched, something glass.

He shook the snow off his fleece and changed from the massive beast he had been back into a man. As he walked toward her, Vladimir smiled widely. "You have good news." It was not a question, he could tell by the gleam in her eyes that she did.

Trandafira grinned at him. "Indeed." She held up a glass vial.

Before taking it, Vladimir closed his eyes and breathed in the cold air. He then stared out at the majesty of the Carpathian Mountains. It was good to be home. Romania held a power that was hard to explain, and the mountains were so commanding. To behold the mountains beauty, what a thing it was. Vladimir felt he gained some of their strength just standing upon them.

He turned, pulling his own fur coat higher on his shoulders, and shifted his bare feet in the snow. He held his hand out. She handed him the vial and as he looked in it, he beamed. "They got it."

Trandafira nodded, tossing her long black and silver braid over her shoulder. "Ve now have vhat ve need to drive zem out of zeir hiding place."

Vladimir laughed. "To be perfectly and completely honest, I did not think the snakes could do it. I was rather hoping Senssirra would fail."

Trandafira grinned. "Zey knew you did. Vhy else have ve received such results?" She paused, then added, "You know Puceula es vorking vith zem, even zough e vas given strict orders to keep his distance."

Vladimir chuckled. Of course he knew. They were fools, all of them, to think they could keep it hidden from him. "If I had told them to ally themselves, they would never have done it. Oh, they would have met and done what I ordered, but there would really have been no true working together. They needed a common fear, so I gave them what they needed." He held the vial up to the cold sunlight and gazed in at what it held. There was auburn hair and a red liquid inside. "In turn," he continued with a grin, "they have given me what I needed." He placed the vial in a pouch that hung from his leather belt. "It won't be long till the Kavanaghs have to come out from where they hide and right into our waiting arms." He offered his arm to his sister and she took it, gladly.

They turned to the massive castle before them and began to walk towards it. "Don't you concern yourself about all za time za children have to be trained? Vherever zey are, you can count on zat elf to not be idle."

Vladimir thought about the elf Caoimhe, he knew she would train them, but they were still only children. No amount of training could change that, and then there was the new little Kavanagh. He couldn't wait to get his hands on the baby, but he was patient. If he had waited as many years as he had already, what would a little more time mean, really? "Patience is on our side, Sister." He stopped and

110

turned to her. "Let them train, let them think they have become powerful, for their defeat will be much sweeter if they actually suspect they have a chance to win." He took in another deep breath of the cold air, the smells washing through him. "They are a priority," he continued, his rumbling voice undaunted, "but they are not our main concern. They are isolated, and the longer they stay hidden, the longer they have no friends to gain. The power we must fear is in numbers. Right now, they are so few, if they didn't have a key and if Teagan Kavanagh wasn't with them, I would not even concern myself about them." He thought for a moment about the children and how they had escaped him when the Xoor had nearly been in his reach. There was indeed a power on their side that gave him some worry, but no matter. All power had to follow the ancient laws, and there was only so far those laws could bend. Let that *dog* try that again.

Trandafira let out a laugh at this. "So, ve continue to find za keys, zen?"

Vladimir nodded. "That is our main concern. The Xoor is needed too, of course, but we cannot do anything with it until we can open it, though its location is known, more or less. Plus, we have the seals to worry about, but those can be dealt with, once the keys are in our possession," he smirked. "Besides, I have Dominique working to recover the book. She is using her wiles on the Sea King." He let out a vicious laugh that rumbled deep in his chest. "Let's see him deny her anything, especially something he doesn't even want in his oceans."

Trandafira did not answer and Vladimir looked at her. "I know your thoughts about the faith I place in Dominique, but I am aware she must be put in her place. That is why Gabriel is with her." It was a fine balance keeping Trandafira and Dominique; both were wild in their own right, which was greatly beneficial, but he had to keep them from going at each other's throats at times. He was profoundly aware of the need to control Dominique, though that unpredictable nature was one of the things that made her most valuable.

Trandafira nodded and they continued up to the castle door. It was elegantly built, as was the entire castle. This place held beauty, where their castle in Ireland held only their darkness, a necessity for the work they had to do there.

When Vladimir opened the door, their servants flung themselves at them. For the next few moments they were fussed over, as coats were removed, new fancy clothes adorned, and hot towels pressed to their hands and Vladimir's feet. Trandafira barked orders in Romanian to the servants and Vladimir enjoyed her relishing in the commands. She kicked one servant who, too eager to warm his mistress, accidentally spilt some hot water on her leg. The kick was not terrible, but it sent the rest of the water crashing into the floor, and the servant, begging forgiveness flung himself upon the floor to clean it up.

They left the servants to their work after they were clean and warm. They spoke no more until they had climbed many flights of stairs and entered a richly furnished room with a high ceiling made partly of dark wood and cream walls.

There was a roaring fire in a gigantic fireplace, which was nearly the width of the entire wall it occupied, and half its height. A small, brown, fur-covered creature ran at them, warm drinks steaming on the tray he held. Vladimir waved his away but Trandafira took hers and ordered the creature out. It bowed repeatedly as it headed for the door, and shot out as quickly as it could.

Once the door closed, Vladimir raised his finger and, with a small movement, as if he swatted a fly, contained all the sound in their room. None could hear what was spoken except for the two of them. He moved to the desk and shuffled through the many papers on it.

"We are getting closer," he smiled, as he picked up a picture of the key they planned to acquire next. "The more keys we gain, the more powerful we become. The Key Families did a good job of hiding them, I'll give them that, but we are finding them out, one by one." He turned to Trandafira and pulled her long black and silver braid so it fell from behind her to over her shoulder. He grinned at the blades knotted to the end of her braid, perfect for slicing anyone with a flick of her hair. "Just imagine when we hold the Xoor," he purred, "how none will be able to deny us."

She leaned over the table as well, gazing down at the information there. "And imagine vhen our old *master* vill come back with us, and vhat fear vill be struck into za hearts of za Irish."

Vladimir laughed delightedly, a roaring sound bubbling with his smoky voice. "Only the beginning," he chuckled. "It is only the beginning."

There was a knock on the door. Trandafira went to it. A young servant stood there and bowed to her, his body doubling where his head came about as low as his knees.

"Lady," he said in English, righting himself, "your guests have arrived."

Vladimir set his papers down. Good, the broader aspects of their plans could begin. This meeting would be the start of the insidious strategies the Irish would never know of, until it was too late.

Trandafira nodded to the boy, but Vladimir could see the irritation in her body language and he leaned forward to see what she would do. She looked down at her nails – they were quite long, and had been painted a deep mahogany red, perfect for frightening anyone who did not wish to feel how sharp they were. She turned her light eyes upon the child and slapped the boy across the face.

The child's head snapped to one side. He grabbed his cheek with both hands and looked shocked, but he did not cower away from her, in fear of what she would do to him if he did.

Vladimir folded his arms and smirked. Her vicious nature could never be dormant for long. Her conduct with the servants downstairs had been practically angelic. He knew that behaviour wouldn't last.

"Za next time you bow, you make sure your face touches za floor, boy," she hissed.

The child nodded, wide eyed. "Now go, tell zem ve are coming."

The boy bowed again, this time his forehead touching the wood floor. As soon as he stood, he dashed down the hall and rounded a corner.

Trandafira fingered her ruby necklace with the inscribed B and sneered. She turned to Vladimir, who was smiling at her.

"Shall we go and meet our guests?" He walked up to her and held his hand out for her to take.

"Love to," she beamed, and took his hand.

Everything was going as intended. There may have been some interruptions on the way, but at the present moment no one could stop what had already been set into motion. Vladimir would love to see anyone try.

# CHAPTER 7

## TROUBLE

Time is a funny thing. When you are miserable, it stretches on forever, making hours feel like days. However when you're happy, it almost slips through your fingers like sand, or blows away like flower petals.

Fadin decided he must have been incredibly happy, for as he stepped out the wooden door of the cabin on a particularly crisp morning, the light wind blowing his red hair, and his blue-green eyes picking up the small flecks of light, he realised that he had been living on Bäle Rappõs for nearly two years.

He and Tase were fifteen and Da had been gone for close to three years. In some ways it seemed like Da had been dead forever, but in other ways, it felt like no time had passed at all, and that he could pop around the corner any minute.

Fadin let out a breath full of sorrow and memory. "Hey," Tase said, coming out of the cabin behind him.

Fadin turned to him. A lot had changed in them physically over the last year and a half, and Fadin had really begun to notice how much.

Firstly, their voices. Tase's voice had somehow suddenly plummeted into a deep low bass and he no longer sounded like a child but a growing man. Sometimes Ma would mistake his voice for Mr Hogan's.

Fadin's voice had also gotten deeper and lower, but nowhere near Tase's volume. His tone was more like Ardan's, manly but not rumbling.

They had also grown quite a bit; both of them were taller than Ma. Their legs, torsos, and arms were spindly, and the clothes they had been given by the O'Sheelin City had long since become too small. Ma and Alassandra had to combine some of their trousers and shirts so they could fit into them.

Tase had become a hairy beast. His arms and legs boasted with red hair, under his arms as well, and to Fadin the most unacceptable part of it was the facial hair that Tase had sprouted, under his lip, over his chin, all along his jaw line. At fifteen, if Tase wanted to he could grow a beard. Fadin too had hair on his arms, under them, and on his legs – though it was not as thick as Tase's – but he had absolutely no facial hair, none at all. Fadin found this most unacceptable; how long had he wanted a beard or moustache? Now Tase had the ability and he *hated* it. He would shave his facial hair off so quickly, you could barely see he had any. Fadin made a face at the thought.

As if that weren't unfair enough, there was also the muscle tone that Tase had suddenly acquired. His calves were huge! Okay, well, maybe not huge, but they were far bigger than Fadin's, and Tase's shoulder width had grown while Fadin's seemed to have hardly outstretched at all, and Tase's arms were already becoming defined with muscle. Fadin considered his own arms and realised they too had muscles, but he was more sinewy than Tase, where just by looking at Tase you could tell he was solidly built.

Fadin and Tase still certainly looked like twins, but it was becoming clear the change of identicalness was happening, as Ma always said it would. They were looking more unique from each other, and it was becoming far easier to tell them apart. Besides their looks, you could tell them apart because Tase always had his banjo on his lap. During their time on the island, Tase had spent almost all his free time practicing, and Fadin had to admit, he had gotten quite good.

"Morning," Fadin said, looking at Tase as he came to stand next to him.

Tase had a small bit of white cloth sticking to his face, where he had cut himself shaving. He stretched his arms over his head and yawned, the air from his mouth making a puff of white. "Moooorniiing."

Fadin smiled and then let the grin fade as he saw a dark figure dash in the tree line. Spriggans, the pests. He and Aednat had learned a lot about the dark creatures with all their time on the island. They knew now how to keep them away from the meadow, and how to fend them off, but they still would try and test the boundaries now and then.

He caught sight of Aednat, who came out of her hut and gave him a knowing look.

"I'll be back," Fadin said.

Tase sighed. "You'll be late, and Caoimhe won't be happy."

Fadin waved him off and he could hear Tase snort in disapproval, but he did nothing to stop him. Tase had become more lax since they had been on the island, perhaps because they knew every inch of it now, or because they were surrounded by adults who would let nothing horrible happen. Whatever the reason, Tase didn't complain much when Fadin would do something rash. Really though, how much trouble could Fadin get in on an island this small?

Fadin made a face as he recalled the time he and Aednat had accidentally fallen into a fairy trap. They had been stuck in the tunnel cell for hours before

Uncle Lorcan could finally figure how to get them out. Fadin had also accidentally turned baby Glendan into a mushroom once, because while he was supposed to be babysitting he had decided to explore just a little ways from where Ma was working. He had stumbled upon a cursed fairy ring and had set baby Glendan in it to see what would happen. In his defense, he had thought children were supposed to be safe from fairy magic, but apparently because they were half leprechaun that protection was counteracted by their leprechaun blood. Glendan had, of course, been turned back after a while, so no real harm done, but Ma had been quite upset about that one.

Fadin shook his head and decided not to think about the many other instances when he had gotten into trouble on the island. He met up with Aedant and they ran into the forest together.

Aedant hadn't grown much taller, and her face still looked pretty much the same, but her dark red hair had grown past her shoulders, and she now wore it down with small braids here and there. Though she didn't look much different she had become quite good with a sword and with Aunt Kyna's blades, for she was allowed to use them. She also perfectly mastered her freckles, being able to do more with them than Fadin could have imagined.

Ardan, Alassandra, and Caoimhe seemed concerned with her of late though, for she had developed a rash on her left arm about a week before. This was apparently a sign that the time for her first bogán was drawing near. The Ailsinn's, being Geartús, had skin that had a special power, anything additional a Geartú child was born with on their skin – like freckles or a birth mark – they could make move, even fly off their skin as Aednat's freckles had the day he met her.

This ability was not only true with normal skin markings, in their culture every child got their first bogán, or mark, at thirteen. It was what marked their becoming an adult, as Aednat had explained. Each Geartú always got at least three bogáns, one at thirteen, one at seventeen, and one at nineteen, each one representing who they were, and who they would become. The marks came on their own, starting first as a rash. When the rash began to turn colours it had to be bandaged up, or the bogán would not properly develop and could not be controlled by the Geartú who possessed it. Fadin found the whole thing fascinating.

"You saw the spriggan too?" Aednat asked, breaking Fadin's train of thought.

"Yeah," Fadin sighed, "I saw it. They are always trying to get in, no matter how many times we drive them back."

Aedant nodded. "Keepin' them away has become a full-time job." She raised her auburn hazel eyes to him. "Serves us right though, doesn't it?"

Fadin ran a hand through his hair. "I suppose so." Fadin heard the sound of other footsteps and heard Ma's voice as well as Mr Hogan's. He looked down at Aednat. "Wanna hear what they're talking about?"

Aedant put a hand on her hips. "That's called spyin'."

Fadin grinned. "I know."

She smiled wide, her dimples showing, and nodded. "Come on."

They hid quite well in some bushes. Ma and Mr Hogan came towards them, Ma's voice full of worry. "It has nothing to do with Desmond, I hope you know that, Lee."

Mr Hogan nodded. "Of course I know that. I know your concern is for Saoirse, and I agree with you. She's getting worse."

Fadin looked at Aednat, who nodded. There was no denying it. Saoirse had done well for a while, but then she begun to have nightmares again, and she would have little fits, where she would break things and become furious for no apparent reason.

"Desmond seems to calm her," Ma said. "In fact, he often seems to be the only thing that helps, but... I don't want her depending on one person so much, because I want her to be able to help herself."

"You don't need to explain it to me," Mr Hogan answered. "I came in on an argument you were having with your daughter. I heard you talking to her about my son, but it is none of my business what your advice to her is about him. It was an accident that I overheard you, I planned to leave right away, but you saw me. I don't want you to feel guilty. Like I said, I understand, and in truth, so does Desmond. Though, his feelings may get in the way."

Fadin felt uncomfortable. He had gotten used to the idea of Desmond and Saoirse together, but he didn't like hearing all this talk about them, and he really didn't care if they were together or not. However, he couldn't just get up and walk away now, Ma and Mr Hogan would spot him and Aednat, and he didn't want a lecture about eavesdropping.

"I'm sorry for him," Ma said. "Really what I think is that Desmond is perfect for Saoirse, but I don't think Saoirse is good for *him*. She isn't well, the reason we got into a fight is that she suddenly became furious with me because I asked her how she was feeling. As if I have no right to be concerned for her. I don't remember how the conversation got turned to Desmond, but she is viciously protective of him." Ma looked out into the trees. "I'm failing her," she whispered.

Mr Hogan looked at her firmly. "No, you're not. You love her. You have only tried to do what is best for her since Alroy has been gone." He took a deep breath. "I think being away from everything and coming to this secluded island was a good plan. It just isn't working anymore, but it's no fault of your own."

Ma nodded gently. "Thank you, but my choice in her father does make her condition my fault. If I hadn't been so blinded by love for Faolan, I would have seen the signs, and I would have made different choices." She became still. "But then," she sighed, "Saoirse wouldn't exist at all, and there is nothing worse than that." She suddenly looked quite sad. "I wish Alroy were here."

Mr Hogan carefully took her hand in his. "So do I. I wish often that I could get his advice, hear his voice."

Ma forced a smile and lightly pulled her hand away. "His advice would be very helpful right now."

"We'll figure out a way to help her," Mr Hogan assured her. "Going to Enda can do nothing but help. He loves that girl every bit as much as you do."

Ma nodded. "Yes, he does." She followed Mr Hogan and in a wink they vanished into the meadow.

"I didn't realise it was as bad as all that," Aednat said.

Fadin stood. "Saoirse doesn't like to talk about it, but all the adults know." He looked down at her. "Let's go get that pest, shall we?"

Aednat got up. "Do lets."

They ran through the woods in the direction they had seen the dark figure go. They were nearly silent with their footfalls, Caoimhe's lessons had done them all a lot of good. Fadin wasn't worried about not being able to find the creature; spriggans usually left dark magic in their wake, and learning how to sense magic, as Caoimhe was teaching them to do, he could almost smell the spriggans trail.

Fadin allowed himself to take in the feeling of the island and his vision burned silver. It had taken him a long while to be able to do this. The power of the island was quite overwhelming. Once the initial wave of power hit, it was like keeping your head above water. Fadin felt the tingling of magic all around him, he almost saw the glowing veins of it running through the ground and up the trees. He got used to the feeling and then began to "look" for the spriggans trail. Strangely enough, he couldn't find it.

"What is it?" Aednat asked. Both of them hardly ever searched with magic at the same time anymore. They took turns because it made them tired when they used the ability. They found it worked best to have one find the trail and the other have the full strength to follow it and scare the beasts off.

"I can't sense a trail," Fadin told her. He looked harder and then jerked back.

Aednat didn't ask. Her eyes glowed silver and after a moment of them darting this way and that, her mouth fell open. "What is *that*?" she asked, pointing to the place Fadin focused on.

He took a step forward and studied the strange magic closely. It was strong, but not dark as a spriggan's was, though it wasn't light either. There was much fairy magic on the island, which lit up silvery white. This magic was neither. "I don't know," he said.

"Should we tell someone?" she asked.

Fadin considered it, but he ached for a real chance for something exciting, and they had taken care of the spriggans on their own. He doubted, whatever this was, that it would be worse than the spriggans. "No, let's follow the trail," he said.

Aedant's eyes once again became auburn hazel and she extended her hand to him. "After you."

Fadin began to run, Aednat right at his heels. The trail was strange, it faded fast and he knew if they didn't hurry they would lose whatever had made it. It wove through the forest and Fadin suddenly saw that it made a sharp turn out to the shore. Fadin followed it and as they broke through the trees he saw it continued down the shoreline. He dashed as the trail began to fade even faster.

"I don't understand," he said. "It's like the magic is disappearing."

"How could it do that so quickly?" Aednat asked.

"That's something we should ask Caoimhe." He stopped. The trail ended right in the middle of a great pile of boulders on the beach. "What?" he cried, exasperated.

Aednat gaped at the stones. "Why did you stop here?"

"The trail ends right into the rocks." Fadin huffed.

Aednat made a face but walked up to them and put her hand on them. She raised her eyebrows. "The stone is warm."

Fadin touched it too. "It is warm," he said, astounded and thoroughly confused.

"My word isn't good enough, huh?" Aednat grumbled.

"Oh, do shut it," Fadin threw back, but he gave her a quick glance and saw that she wasn't upset – it was all in good fun. He tapped the rock with his fist and it made a sound more fitting for wood than for stone.

"You things alone?" a familiar voice asked.

Fadin didn't need anything else to know who that voice belonged to. "Ciaran!" he shouted.

The small green goblin jumped from inside the stone and landed in-between Fadin and Aednat. He stumbled as his peg leg hit the sand first but he righted himself quickly.

Aednat's face burst into a wide grin. "Ciaran!"

"Yes, yes," Ciaran said, holding up his thin long clawed hands. "It's me, but hushes up. Do you wants the wholes island to knows I's here?"

Fadin considered this. "What does it matter now?" he asked. "You've got the whole castle to yourself. Who cares who knows about you?"

Ciaran smiled up at him. "It's a little mores complicated than that's now, Fadin-thing."

Fadin was about to ask what could possibly be more complicated when another small creature jumped out of the stone.

It landed with a dull *THWUMP* on the sand. It was small, when you measured it against a grown man, but it was considerably bigger than Ciaran. At first, its skin looked to be made out of the stone, but as the creature shook, the stone appearance fell away like dust. Beneath was bright orange skin that looked tough and leathery, almost like an elephant's. It turned its head to them and Fadin saw this creature too was a goblin, though he was quite different from Ciaran. Two pale horns protruded from his forehead, just before a mop of brown hair. His eyes were a piercing pale blue, almost like ice, and his ears were much smaller than Ciaran's, though they both stuck straight up. A small golden hoop hung from his right ear. He wore more than a loincloth, Ciaran's usual clothing of choice; he had on brown trousers and a dark cloak.

"This is my's friend," Ciaran said, extending his hand to the other goblin.

The orange goblin nodded to them both and touched his left horn. "I am glad to meet you both." His voice was quite deep. "I am Xemplos."

Fadin and Aedant nodded back.

"Nice to meet you," Fadin said, holding his hand out for the goblin to shake it. Xemplos made a face and looked at Ciaran questioningly.

Ciaran shook his head. "A greeting amongs humans," he told the other goblin. "We don'ts shake hands," he told Fadin and Aednat.

Fadin pulled his hand away and noticed that Ciaran was dressed nicer than he had ever seen him. He had on trousers and a cloak on too, though his one green foot remained bare. "Ciaran," he said, "not that I'm not delighted to see you... and to meet you," he added, looking at Xemplos, "but where have you been? Why did you leave us? Why did you vanish when you saw what the Xoor did to Tase?"

Fadin felt himself becoming angry. He hadn't realised he had been cross at the little goblin, but in fact he was. He was furious that he just left them right before Vladimir had attacked. "Why are you here?" he demanded, his voice full of his irritation.

Ciaran's eyes flashed a bit more yellow than normal. "I had business to attends to. I couldn't stay."

"Business?" Fadin snorted incredulously. "Right when we were about to be attacked?"

"Bads timesing, I knows," Ciaran answered. "Can'ts be changed nows, may as well forgets it."

"Forget it?" Fadin blurted. "Are you off your rocker? I can never forget it. You just left us there!"

Cairan's eyes turned pure yellow. "It couldn'ts be helped, Fadin-thing!" he snapped.

"Couldn't be helped?" Fadin cried, exasperated.

"He is a coward," Xemplos said in his rumbling voice. "That is the fact of the matter."

Fadin stared at him.

Ciaran's ear tips and fingers shifted to yellow and he swiveled his bright eyes to his goblin companion with a look of viciousness.

Fadin thought about the comment and decided Xemplos was right. If it had been Tase standing there, he probably would have told Ciaran he forgave him and to forget it. After all, Tase was the one most damaged by the whole thing, but Fadin wasn't Tase. He didn't forgive so easily. "He's right, you are a coward. You abandoned us and we were almost killed!"

"Fadin," Aednat hissed.

Ciaran's ears turned completely yellow and his hands and feet were a lemon colour all the way to his elbows and knees. "Words to remember," Ciaran hissed furiously. "*Almost*."

Xemplos stood in front of Ciaran, blocking him from Fadin's view. "Enough," he growled. "Pointless is this talk. He is a coward," he held his arm out to Ciaran, "this we know, and this many of the small in Ireland know too."

Fadin made a face. "What do you mean, many of the small know?"

"Ciaran has made bad name for himself," Xemplos said.

Ciaran said nothing but he flushed more yellow. "Fines! A cowards I am. Happy?"

Fadin thought and decided that he actually was. He nodded. "Fine."

"This talk is not why we came," Xemplos said, turning to Ciaran.

"No's, its isn't." Ciaran closed his eyes and his ears, hands, and feet once again transformed green. He opened his eyes, which still held more yellow than usual. "We is here to warns you, Fadin-thing."

"Warn us?" Aednat asked.

"Warn us about what?" Fadin demanded.

Ciaran took a deep breath. "They knows where you's ares." Fadin creased his forehead.

"Who knows?"

"The Bojins," Xemplos answered.

Aednat's mouth fell open.

"When are they coming?" Fadin managed around his dry throat. "Tonight," Ciaran said, "ands they don'ts come alone. They has an army."

# CHAPTER 8
## A STRANGE VISITOR

Dr Jason Guilfoyle leaned back in his chocolate wooden chair, set the piece of paper down on the table, next to the thick file folder, and sighed. He put a hand to his forehead and rubbed it lightly.

It had been a long and trying day.

Stillwater Psychiatric was a stressful place to work on a good day, and this had *not* been a good day.

The hospital was an open care unit; primarily having the task of taking care of the mentally ill and trying to get them back out into the world so they could lead as normal a life as possible. Although this was Stillwater's main goal, the Psychiatric Hospital also had sections designed for long-term patients, called Long-Term Care Facilities, as well as a Juvenile Ward, specifically made for the care of children, or adolescents.

This is where Dr Guilfoyle had been all day, in the Juvenile Ward – his professional expertise was in the care for mentally ill children – taking care of a particularly troubled patient.

He sighed. When he had done his schooling at university, he was so certain that when he became a doctor he would save the lives of many mentally ill children and give them normal lives. Reality hadn't turned out so wonderful. Sometimes he dreadfully wanted a different profession, one in which he could actually help the children he worked with. He often felt he was useless to his patients, even the ones who did leave and had some sort of a future. Perhaps it was being surrounded by mental sickness all the time that made him feel this way, but whatever the reason he knew for certain he couldn't leave, because there was at least one patient he was important to, even if he wasn't really helping her to get *better*. At least he was one of the only people who kept the child safe from the outside world.

Jason let out a deep breath and leaned forward. He picked up the papers on the desk and began to read again. Here was the child that was concerning him the most, the one always stamped on his mind. He peered down at the midnight ink letters, punching the girl's name onto the pale parchment.

*Marie Whelan.*

Dr. Guilfoyle shook his dark brown head. Poor girl, she was so disturbed, but even more so as of late. She had always needed to be kept separate from the other patients and staff – except for a select few – not because she was dangerous or violent, but because she was unique.

The child had not aged a day in the six years Jason had worked at Stillwater. She hadn't grown an inch, hadn't changed at all. No one understood it, but apparently she had been delivered to the psychiatric hospital fifteen years ago by a doctor from a different facility. He had a friend here, one Guinevere O'Malley, a nurse who then had been in her forties. She still worked at Stillwater and was one of the only people Dr Guilfoyle felt he could trust with anything. The doctor friend of Ms O'Malley had brought Marie Whelan to Stillwater because her secret was no longer safe in the hospital where he worked. The doctor was afraid someone would discover her and put the child through all kinds of tests to discover why she didn't age. Jason agreed with this fear, and that was why he stayed at Stillwater, to make sure the girl remained safe.

He made a face. "Keep her safe?" he snorted to himself. He hadn't done the best job at that. About a year ago, Marie had somehow escaped from Stillwater. Not that the hospital was a prison, but Marie had been held in a secure wing. She had no ability to care for herself and no family to care *for* her, so Stillwater was, to all intents and purposes, her home, and she had never expressed a desire to leave. A year ago, however, she had simply vanished, leaving no trace of where she had gone, when she had gone, or how she had done it.

Jason didn't understand how she had gotten out. All the doors, windows, and air vents had been locked and sealed tight. There had been security guards everywhere; even if she had managed to get out of her room, there was just no way she couldn't have been seen... but by some means she *wasn't*.

Guinevere O'Malley had pulled Dr Guilfoyle into a corner when they had found out Marie was missing. "I think someone took her," Guinevere insisted. "There was a strange man and a woman who came in about a week ago. They asked questions about the Juvenile Ward and they seemed as if they were scoping the hospital out. One of the nurses on the office floor said she saw them come out of the locked fileroom. She made them leave the premises at once, and I hadn't thought another thing about it until now."

If it hadn't been for the bizarre case of Marie herself, Jason would have thought the nurse was just being paranoid. As it was, he was inclined to believe her. "Did you get their names? Do you have any idea where they may have gone?"

Guinevere shook her greying head. "No, and they looked foreign, perhaps Russian or Bulgarian." The nurse insisted it was them, and Jason took her word seriously.

He tried to find more about the strangers from the other employees of the hospital, but to no avail. Even if they had taken her, it made no sense how they had done it. How weren't the strangers *seen* taking Marie from her room? And how was her door still locked and had no sign of forced entry? There seemed to be no logical explanation.

The Garda had been notified, and even the papers had printed stories about

Marie's escape, but there had been no trace of the girl... until little over a year ago.

She was discovered in the evening, as Dr Guilfoyle was leaving to go home. He had nearly stumbled over Marie's curled up body as he walked in the parking lot. She had been sleeping on the floor in front of his car, and seemed to have no memory of what had happened to her, but when she had been brought back into her quarters, things had become nasty.

Dr Guilfoyle cleared his throat and read down her file. A lengthy list explained her many illnesses and disorders.

She was diagnosed with dissociative identity disorder and schizophrenia. She had always struggled with depersonalization disorder, where she often felt she lived in a dream or that she would see herself doing things and couldn't control her actions, feeling disconnected from the world. She also struggled with primary insomnia, the inability to sleep, and dream anxiety disorder, where she had the same nightmare almost every night which made her fearful to go back to sleep, contributing to the insomnia. She was also a chronic nail biter, often nibbling her fingernails to painful shortness, but Dr Guilfoyle had never seen her as violent and as fearful as she had become, until she had returned to the hospital.

Everything had become worse. Suddenly she was hostile, angry, paranoid, and had frequent panic attacks. She would flare up and get furious for no apparent reason, she suffered great memory loss and her blackouts lasted for significant periods of time. She began to suffer from terrible headaches and her words became random, unclear, slurred, and she made no reasonable sense. Before her disappearance from the hospital she could communicate, and her speech was not beyond deciphering and understanding, now it was almost impossible without incredible effort to understand one half of what she was saying. Besides all this, it was clear that Marie was extraordinarily terrified.

"What happened to you?" Jason whispered as he touched the faded picture that showed what the girl looked like.

He had and was continuing to try and find ways to help her, but she was unbelievably aggressive and had harmed the few workers trusted to care for her, even Ms O'Malley, to the point where she had to be given stitches. To Jason's disappointment and regret, he had to have her restrained in her room, with no interaction from anyone, and no special walks outside with Ms O'Malley or himself. It wasn't what he wanted, but it was for her best, to keep her from damaging herself and others.

He rubbed his hand over his face and bit his bottom lip, feeling hopeless. "Dr Guilfoyle," a young man in a white trench coat said, coming through the office door. Peter Ryan, his name was. He was another of the few people trusted with Marie, a good and loyal man. When he was thirteen his grandmother had claimed she was magical and was hospitalised in a different asylum. While there, Ryan had met a pretty and distressed girl who he had enjoyed playing with on his visits to see his grandmother. When his grandmother had died, he knew when he became a man that he wanted to help mentally sick people. His first position had been to Stillwater and while he was being given a tour of the grounds he had seen Marie going for a walk with Ms O'Malley. He recognised her instantly as the girl he used to play with at his grandmother's asylum. After a long discussion with Dr Guilfoyle, Ryan had sworn he was trustworthy. After two years he had proven to be nothing but dependable.

"Yes?" Jason asked.

"We have someone here who wants to speak to you."

"Tell them I'm busy, Ryan," he said, looking up, feeling more worn out than he knew a man could feel. He didn't have time to bother with anyone outside the hospital today.

"I'm afraid it's urgent, Doctor," Ryan said. "He is a retired adolescent psychiatrist and he said he has some important information concerning," he dropped his voice, "the Whelan girl."

Dr Guilfoyle perked up at this. "About the Whelan girl?"

"Yes, he said he used to work with her."

Dr Guilfoyle was astounded. He only knew of one other doctor who had worked with her, the man who had brought her to Stillwater himself. Ms O'Malley would know about him for certain. "Get Ms O'Malley and bring me a file on him, I know there's one with the other information on Marie. And you can send him here, to my office," he said.

Peter Ryan nodded and left with a swing of the door.

Dr Guilfoyle leaned back in his chair put both hands to his face and brought

them slowly down to his neck. He prayed this doctor would have some information to help him with Marie. This other doctor must know more about her than *he* did. This brought him to another thought. How old was Marie? How long had she not been aging for?

The sound of footsteps rung outside the door, and Dr Guilfoyle sat up and folded his hands on the desk.

The white door swung open and revealed Peter Ryan and the other doctor. The retired psychiatrist was an elderly man, with long white hair that was placed behind him in a neat ponytail, a white and grey beard and mustache that were cut close to his face. His eyes were pale blue, heavily lidded and set beneath thick eyebrows. The lines on his face were numerous, seemingly cut from many sorrows, yet the man still seemed youthful somehow, and Jason couldn't figure out what it was that made him appear so.

Dr Guilfoyle got up from his desk and took the folder Peter handed him. "Thank you, Ryan," he said to the younger man.

Peter nodded and went back out to the hall.

"Dr Jason Guilfoyle," he said, holding his hand out.

The older man took it and shook his hand. "Robert Martinson." He had a deep voice, one that resonated in his chest.

"There's no 'doctor' before your name?" Jason asked.

Robert smiled, a surprisingly pleasant one to behold on a face which appeared to have known much grief. "It's been quite a while since I've used it, but yes, I suppose there is."

Jason grinned and offered Robert a chair.

The older man sat down and Jason moved to the chair behind his desk. "So, Dr Martinson —"

"Just Robert, please," he said, holding his hand up.

Jason shifted uncomfortably in his chair but smiled anyway. "*Robert*, I hear you worked with one of my patients?" He wasn't sure if Robert was the man who had brought Marie to Stillwater, and he didn't know how much this doctor was aware of concerning the child. Jason looked down at the folder Peter had handed him and opened it.

"Yes, I worked with Marie Whelan, the child who does not age."

Jason pulled his eyes to Robert's face. The old man's pale eyes were serious and clear, in no way muddled with age. "So you know about our strange girl."

Robert nodded. "And I can save you some reading time." He inclined his head to the file. "I was an adolescent psychiatrist for many years in Erin Asylum. I helped numerous patients, but my main priority always was Marie. She had to be taken care of and only trusted with a scarce few who would care for her, but not take her peculiar gift elsewhere. It was because I trusted the wrong person that I had to remove Marie from Erin Asylum, it was after I brought her here that I stopped my profession."

Jason took his eyes from the old doctor and scanned the file quickly, confirming everything he had just been told. "That was fourteen years ago?" Jason asked.

"It was," Robert agreed.

He looked up into Robert's face and made a crease between his dark eyebrows. Fourteen years ago? He looked back at the year printed on the paper of when Robert had retired. He would have been seventy-eight. Robert looked extremely good for being ninety-two years old, and he seemed extraordinarily clear headed.

Jason cleared his throat and folded his hands on his desk. "You look quite well for your age, Doctor."

Robert smiled. "Well, thank you, Dr Guilfoyle. I'd say it's a gift, but really it's always been more of a curse." He chuckled as if what he had said was ironic, but Jason didn't see the humor in it.

He felt there was something to Robert's appearance, but he didn't press it. "I see you're the one who brought Marie to Erin Asylum in the first place. Your file says you found her wandering the streets of Antrim?"

"That's right," Robert said. "She looked like she had been in some kind of fire and she wasn't making any logical sense, so I took her to the asylum."

"I see," Jason grunted, "so you were her doctor for a long time, did you ever discover why she didn't age?"

Robert arched a white eyebrow. "I don't think you'd believe the reason if I told you."

Jason sat straighter in his chair. This was not the answer he had been expecting.

Robert let out a deep breath. "Strange things are happening, Dr Guilfoyle. Stranger than a child who is timeless, but I'm afraid she has an important role to play in the events currently unfolding."

Jason felt uneasy. "What do you mean?"

"I see you have a file on me," Robert said. "Well, I too have a file on you. I know all about your childhood in America. I know about your unkind father and your reasons for relocating to Ireland. I also know about your request to be placed here in Stillwater after hearing about a strange child, and your wife and daughter's tragic death."

Jason gasped, the memories of his family hitting him like a runaway train. Robert continued. "I know you're here because that girl reminds you of the daughter you lost, and that helping her and keeping her safe are the only things that help with that emptiness your young family left."

"Now just a minute," Jason said, making to get up from his chair, his heart and mind racing defensively because of his pain.

"Sit down," Robert snapped, his voice demanding obedience.

Dr Guilfoyle was so caught off guard by this, that he did sit down.

"I too have lost people I've loved, many people," he sighed. "I felt similar to the way you feel now, that is, until Marie came along. She gave me a reason to keep going, as it appears she has done for you."

Jason swallowed, knowing it was true, that the protection of the girl made him feel as though he had a purpose.

"She has always been different," Robert said, "and I could connect with her in a way no one else could. I helped her, at least I made her suffering less when I was with her." He shook his head. "I failed her in the end, you see, and I couldn't forgive myself, but here in Stillwater, I knew she would be safe. I decided to go away and leave her in the capable hands of Ms O'Malley, which I did for several years. But then there was all that news in the paper about Marie escaping from this hospital, and I knew I had to come see her."

"That was well over a year ago," Jason said, despite his confusion at how this man knew so much about him.

"I'm aware of that," Robert rumbled, "but it's been a long time since I have been involved in the world. Besides I had to make sure no one would come back and take her, and I am not the only outside force watching over her."

"Take her?" Jason asked, his mind racing to the strange couple whom Ms O'Malley insisted had stolen the child.

"You and I both know she didn't escape." Robert gave him a perceptive look. "You know those dreams she has, the ones about her running through a burning castle. Watching people she loves, people she can't remember, being killed. Those aren't just dreams, those are memories."

Jason didn't know what to say. Robert had just explained Marie's nightmares, perhaps even better than *he* could. Marie was usually so hysterical when she woke up, that her words were undecipherable, but with Roberts's explanation, her words made sense. "*Fire, castle*," she would cry, "*burning*." "Memories?" he asked. He stared at the old man suspiciously. "How do you know all this?"

Before Robert could answer, the door opened and Guinevere O'Malley burst in. She was a squat woman, with a kind face and greying-brown hair. "Robert!" she cried.

The old man stood and Ms O'Malley flung her arms around him. 'I'm so glad you came," she said, pulling away.

"I don't think I could have done anything else," Robert said.

Jason was feeling more and more out of his depth. The confusion lead to fear at not understanding where the whole thing was going, which sprung up in him a spark of anger. "What's really going on here?" he demanded.

Guinevere put a plump hand on Jason's arm. "He is a friend, he can help the child. He has…" she seemed to look for the right word, "… certain gifts that he can use to keep her safe."

"Gifts?" Jason asked, wondering if he really wanted to know the answer. Robert exchanged a look with Guinevere.

She shrugged and sighed. "You may as well show him so we can get on with it," she said.

Jason felt a fearful twinge shoot through him. He took a step back. "Show me what?" He suddenly felt not like a doctor in his office, but like a child, getting ready to learn a hard lesson.

Robert cleared his throat irritably. "Oh, all right."

As Jason stared at him, the old man's blue eyes began to swirl and change into a silver colour. *No, I must be imagining it*, he thought. But then, suddenly, the folder, sitting near Jason's arm, began to rise off the table.

He stared, in disbelief, as the folder floated in midair, as high as his head.

Then the lamp on the floor to the right of the desk began to hover, and a picture frame, and the chipped teacup Jason had used that morning. Rubbish on the floor put itself in the bin, and the hole in the wall, which had been created by a violent patient who had escaped the nurses, repaired itself.

Jason decided he was having a visual hallucianation. However, knowing that didn't make it seem any less real. He jerked his bulging eyes to Robert and Ms O'Malley, terrified of them.

"It's all right, Dr Guilfoyle," Ms O'Malley said. "He's magical. He's what the magic folk call a Dalbhach."

"Magic folk?" Jason said, in shock and utter disbelief.

"I'm going to need you to let go of logic, Doctor," Robert said. "If you can believe in a child who doesn't age, can you accept that there are other things in this world you cannot explain?"

Jason let out a hysterical sounding laugh. *Could* he believe it? Jason thought for a moment. There was no doubt in his mind that Marie was unique, a mystery with no logical explanation. He stared at the hovering objects. They were real, they weren't just in his head. He looked back at Robert. *Yes*, he decided, he could accept there were other things in the world he would not be able to explain or understand. He did not need to know any more of them though, this was quite enough.

"You aren't mental," Ms O'Malley said, "this is real. I've known Robert since I was a young woman. He helped my family, and I have seen some things that are beyond believing, but I promise you, it's all really happening."

Jason nodded his head, overwhelmed. He decided his main concern was Marie, not his sanity, and if this man could help her, he needed to cooperate, no matter how illogical it seemed. "All right," he said, raising his hands. "You're telling me magic is real?" He gazed at the floating teacup. "That you," he gestured to Robert, "aren't human, at least, not like us?"

Robert nodded.

"Okay, so someone stole Marie over a year ago, and you are here to what?" Jason gazed questioningly at Robert. "Protect her from them?" He stared again at the floating objects. "For goodness sake, can you please have these bloody things stop hovering round my office?"

"All you had to do was ask," Robert said, smiling wickedly. He held his hand out and grabbed the folder. The other hovering items slowly sank back down to their original places.

Jason felt saner with nothing flying impossibly around him.

"You're right, I'm here to protect that child from the ones who stole her," Robert said. "The only reason I showed you my power is to convince you and prove that what I'm about to tell you is true."

Jason stared at him.

"That girl is in trouble, and not just because she's sick. The same people who took her last time still want something from her, something from her mind, which is why she has gotten worse since she's been back. I'm not entirely sure what they did to her, but they meddled with her thoughts somehow, trying to unlock something trapped deep within her memories. She doesn't even know what they want, but it's there, nevertheless, like a treasure hidden in a labyrinth."

"From what we understand," Guinevere said, "they tried to force it from her when she was missing, but it didn't work."

"And I'm afraid that if they get a hold of her again, they will resort to more drastic measures. If they take her this time," Robert's face turned grave, "I do not think the child will survive."

"What on earth do they want from her?" Jason asked.

"It's safer for you not to know," Robert told him.

Jason rubbed his aching head. "All right, so I'm going to choose to believe you. Cracked as it all is, I believe you." He lifted his tired eyes to Robert's, which now were no longer silver, but their normal blue. "What is it you want from me?"

"I need you on my side," Robert said. "I can't stay here to look after the child, though I wish I could. I have other things to do, important things, but I can't leave her here unprotected either, and this task is too much for just Miss O'Malley." He put his hand on Jason's shoulder. "I need you to trust me and to help me protect her. You are Marie's doctor; her life is in *your hands*."

Jason nodded, wondering what he was actually agreeing to. "All right, I'll help you. I must be absolutely off my rocker, but Marie is my responsibility, and I will do whatever I can to keep her safe."

"Thank you," Robert said. "I've put protection around the hospital. You don't need to know what it is, just that it's there, but I need you to be aware. Watch for the ones who took her, though I doubt they themselves will come this time. You need to be aware of anyone asking strange questions, anyone who seems not normal."

"Like you?" Jason asked sarcastically.

Robert eyed him, not amused. "And be on the lookout for a large black dog."

"A black *dog*?"

Even Miss O'Malley seemed surprised at this request.

"If I told you, you wouldn't believe me, but trust me, if you see a black dog, you're in trouble."

Jason nodded, as did Miss O'Malley.

"If anyone, and I mean anyone, asks to see Marie, or you get a new staff member who requests to be put in the Juvenile Ward, or you get any strange visitors, or see that dog, you contact me."

Robert handed Jason a small blue candle with a silver wick. "What's this?"

"When you need me, you light that candle and I'll come." He handed one to Miss O'Malley as well, who pocketed it.

"How will you know if I light it?" Jason asked.

"Just believe it, and I'll be here. Also, you need to be careful who you trust, tell no one about this conversation, but if you need help with Marie, Peter Ryan will help. He believes even more then he lets on."

Jason shook his head but was grateful for another ally. He peered at Miss O'Malley, who gave him a half-hearted smile.

"As for anyone else, be on your guard," Robert continued. "*You* need to be careful too, because with you helping me you two could become targets."

"Targets?" Jason asked. "For the people trying to find Marie?"

"Exactly. I've put protection around your house, and your car, but when you leave or you are out in the open, you're a sitting duck, so be aware."

Miss O'Malley's hand fluttered to her heart. "Oh, my goodness."

"This is insane," Jason said, putting a hand to the bridge of his nose.

"This is how we keep Marie safe," Robert said. "Now I have to leave but first I need to see her."

"Okay," Jason said, pushing his hair away from his forehead. He fumbled in his desk and grabbed a key. "Miss O'Malley, to avoid any suspicion you should get back to your duties."

She nodded. "I will come talk to you later." She gave Robert another hug. "We will keep her safe." With a look of distress on her face she left the office and bustled out into the hall.

"Follow me," Jason told Robert. He placed the candle in his pocket and led the way out of his office.

Their shoes made loud clicking noises on the tile as they walked down the hall.

Jason turned to the elevators and got into one, Robert right behind him. He pressed the button marked *3* and buried his face in his hands as the elevator began to ascend.

There was a small *ding* as the elevator made its way to their desired floor, and Dr Guilfoyle straightened up and dusted himself down. No matter how he felt, he had to look professional so as to avoid suspicion.

The door slid open. "It's just down this way," he said, pointing down the hall.

They made their way slowly until they reached the door Dr Guilfoyle knew was Marie's. He could see her from the small square window on the white door. She was standing in the corner, looking out her small window, which showed the outside world below.

"I don't know how long I can give you, so make it quick," he said, unlocking the door.

"Thank you," Robert said, "for all of this."

"Don't thank me yet," Jason said. "I'm still not sure if I'm cracked or not." Robert chuckled and went inside Marie's room.

~~~

Robert took a deep breath as the heavy door closed behind him. It had been hard to come here, but ever since those pestering children had come to his lighthouse on that horrendously stormy night, he hadn't had any peace of mind. He kept seeing the redheaded boy's blackened hands and how close the curse had come to the child's heart. He bunched his grey eyebrows together, remembering. Tase, the lad's name was Tase. He smiled at the memory of the other redhead, Fadin, and his absolute stubborn iron will to save his brother's life at any cost.

Robert let out a sigh. It had been them, and the other three ragged-looking youngsters caring for a baby, that had made him stop hiding from the world. He had known he needed to care again, and the first place he had gone looking was to the elven people, who were wild and powerful, like the Celts of old. They had already been watching and protecting Marie, so Robert offered his services to them. As he had hoped, his reputation had preceded him, and the elves were only too pleased to welcome his power to theirs.

He turned around and contemplated the child, not sure how she would seem

Marie stood still, gazing out the window, her small frame looking even slighter in the large pasty room. Her long brown hair was tangled, and her skin was pale white, clearly because she did not get enough sun.

Robert moved towards her, and she didn't stir. He got right up next to her, and bent down. He looked at her, at her big green eyes, her small pink lips, and wee nose. She had dark shadows under her emerald eyes, from lack of sleep, and her face was forlorn, looking almost devoid of life.

Robert got so close he could see her hair moving from his breath, yet still she remained motionless, she didn't even blink. She kept staring, unseeing, out her barred window, out into the free world, away from the cold white room that served as her cell.

Robert rubbed his hand over his mouth, thinking how to approach her. She evidently wasn't disturbed by his presence, but she didn't seem to observe him either, and he needed her to *know* he was there.

He licked his lips and swallowed hard. "Marie?" he said, his voice soft, calm.

Immediately Marie turned her head, and blinked over at him. She looked, her chest heaved with panicky and excited breaths, and she lifted her small hand up to his face and touched his cheek. "Bobby?" she breathed.

It had been the name she had always called him.

He smiled down at her, at the unchanged child. "Yes, Marie," he said, placing his large rough hand over her soft one, "it's me."

Marie's mouth spread into a grin, which quickly faded. "I do not like this place," she whimpered.

"I know," Robert said, taking her hand from his face and holding it in his. "I know." He wished there was somewhere better he could keep her, but at the present moment this was in fact the safest place. Besides, he had too much to do and could not have a mentally sick child with him.

"Am I going?" she asked, hopeful. "With you?"

Robert's face fell, she had always trusted him and he had loved her from the start, wanting to protect her, like the daughter he had never had. He wished he could tell her yes, could take her away from this place. "You stay here," he told her, with a look of sorrow. "This is a safe place for you."

She made a face. "Something is wrong," she said, and tapped her head with her palm. "It is not right in here."

Robert took the hand she had tapped her head with and held it in his too. "I know. That's why you're here, the doctors want to help you."

She made a snorting sound and her face contorted into a mocking look that appeared too old for her face. "Doctors are no help." She pulled her hands away and looked out the window again.

That answer has sounded pretty clear-minded, coming from her. He was taken aback by it. "You don't like the doctors?" he asked.

"Doctors, doctors, one and two,
Doctors, doctors, in white and blue,
Doctors, doctors, here they come,
They give medicine for your brain to numb."

Robert raised his grey eyebrows. "Did you make that up, Marie?"

She turned her eyes to him. "No, the woman did."

"What woman?"

"Long hair, black hair. Eyes black too, she liked to sing to me, but I did not like her. No, I did not."

Here is what Robert wanted from her. "The woman with the long black hair; did she take you?"

Marie nodded. "Yes, took. Her and others. They asked many questions, I did not understand them." She suddenly began to cry. "Too many questions, too many questions!" She grabbed a handful of her hair. "I don't understand!"

Robert carefully grabbed her up and hugged her. "Shh, Marie, it's all right. I'm here, they aren't asking questions now."

She stilled and released her hair. He let go of her a bit, but kept his hands on her arms so he could stop her if she tried to pull her hair out again.

She stared at him. "They ask questions all the time," she said. "Where's the key, where key?" She shook her head. "What key? I don't understand. They give medicine, they dunk me in water! Where key? Where's the key?" She began to cry out and hit her head.

Robert gasped and got hold of her again. "Marie, hush it's all right." She was throwing more of a fit this time and did not calm instantly. *Where's the key?* There was the proof. He had suspected the Bojins had taken her for information that was locked in her confused mind, but he was surprised they thought she knew the location of the lost key. They were looking for the key the Whelan family had been in charge of hiding. The *Bojins* were looking for the six keys to open the Xoor. Vladimir clearly wasn't going to wait until he had the Xoor in hand; he was gathering everything he needed until he could actually get his hands on the book itself.

Marie calmed down again.

Robert grasped her arms, and looked at her. "It's okay, you're safe now. The lady with the long hair isn't here to ask questions anymore."

Marie looked confused. "She asks all the time. Day and night she asks."

Robert's face darkened. "She asks now?"

Marie nodded.

"Where does she ask you at?"

Marie pointed to the window. "She comes here and asks me. Sometimes I can see her, sometimes I can't. But I can always hear her voice."

There was a sound like something banging against the window and Marie covered her ears and screamed.

Robert dashed to the window and saw a handprint fading from the glass.

Marie still screamed and the sound of shouts and running footsteps could be heard beyond the door.

Robert turned his head and saw a glint of magic near a corner. "Dominique," he growled.

The footsteps were closer and they were joined with the sound of jingling keys.

"It's down here, Doctor," someone cried.

Robert used his magic and sent a small flurry of rocks colliding with the glimmer of magic he had seen. For the briefest moment, there was a flicker and Robert looked into the eyes of Dominique Bojn. She hissed at him and her black eyes were full of malice. *"The child knows much,"* she said to his mind.

Dominque had always been skilled at penetrating minds, either when her target was asleep or awake. If he wanted Robert could block her out, and she knew it, but he was interested in what she had to say.

*"Ve have time to search, ve have time to be patient."* Her black eyes shone like raven pools on a moonless night that drew travelers in to their deaths. *"Ve vill feend vhat ve are looking for,"* she smiled, making her face more beautiful and frightening. *"Ve vill get zat key."*

Robert's mouth turned up at the corners and he chuckled. "Not if I have anything to say about it."

"Open the door," someone ordered, and keys were fitted into the lock of the cell door.

She pointed up at him with two fingers and sneered.

"SHE IS PROTECTED!" Robert's voice boomed. The whole hospital shook with the force of his words and the magic behind them.

"Get help," a voice outside the door cried.

*"You and those sprites cannot keep her safe forever,"* Dominique giggled. *"Ve'll feend a vay back!"*

"Perhaps not for forever," Robert said, his long white ponytail falling over his shoulder. He leaned closer to the window. "But you forget my power, girl." He strode over to Marie and took her in his arms. He went back to the window and locked eyes with Dominique, who stared mockingly. "YOU ARE NOT WELCOME HERE!" he cried.

There was a rush of some great invisible force, which shot from him. It flung the bed against the wall and shattered the glass windows and the glass on the door. It flung Dominque against a wall and knocked her head fairly hard. The entire hospital shifted with the power so that it felt as though an earthquake had hit.

"Find a way to force that door open!" someone shouted.

Dominque spat up at him and, as quickly as she had come into view, she vanished, and Robert knew better than to follow her. There would be some sort of trap awaiting him if he tried that and he was not strong enough to face more than one enemy alone, yet.

Marie had stopped screaming but she was clinging to him and crying in his arms.

He rocked her gently and enforced the protection on her window. He heard the door being banged against and scraped with some tool. He would need to let them in soon before they hurt themselves trying to force open the door. He righted the bed with a wave of his hand and pulled out a small purple leaf from a pocket of his jacket. He brought the leaf to Marie's head and as soon as it touched her skin, she stopped crying and her red-rimmed green eyes closed.

He placed her on the bed and pulled the covers up to her chin. "Sleep deep little one," he said. He touched her head with his fingertips and felt the confusion in her mind. He wished he could remove it, but her illness was beyond his skill.

The sound of metal against metal from the door made Robert smile at the persistence of the human doctors. It was time to go. He had other business to attend to. If he was correct, the Bojins would be on the move soon, and he knew just who Vladimir would target.

He removed the block he had placed on the door and it suddenly burst open. Robert turned to see Jason Guilfoyle and several others pile in.

Jason froze, looked at Marie's sleeping form, the broken glass, and then to Robert. His face became white, and he was clearly speechless, shocked by what he had heard. "What have you done?" he yelped.

"Only helped her, my young friend."

"Arrest him," one of the other doctors commanded, to a Guarda standing near the door.

The policemen began to move forward.

"I don't think so," Robert said. He looked into Jason's eyes and pointed at him. "Remember what I told you. Keep her safe, and if you need me," he nodded to his pocket where he knew the small candle to be, "just light it." He smiled and held his palm out.

There was a flash of white light which shot from his palm, a spell meant to erase the memory of all except Dr Guilfoyle.

Dr Guilfoyle would keep Marie safe, he was sure of that.

In the resounding flash of white, Robert took one last look at the girl on the bed, worry filling his heart, and vanished into thin air.

# CHAPTER 9
## MISHAPS AND MISFORTUNES

"How can you do nothing?" Fadin spat. The Old One sat on her chair, made from leaves and mushrooms, in a pale gnarled tree, which put her at human eye level. It was beautiful, even Fadin couldn't miss that, and the small blue and silver pixie lights which came out in the forest at dusk floated around her. She looked almost royal and the lights made her strange skin sparkle its many colours of gold, silver, blue, emerald, bronze, and purple.

She waved her thin, spindly-fingered hand and said, "Everything ends. I have been waiting for the end for a long time, and if it is to come tonight, so be it."

Aednat gaped at her. "You're completely mad," she gasped.

Ciaran and Xemplos murmured to each other. They had kept their distance and stood about three metres away. They seemed to have no interest in getting close to the fairy.

Fadin clenched his fists in frustration. "You have the power to stop them, I know you do. You said yourself you were made the protector of this place. Why not fight back?"

She looked at him, her golden eyes that held no pupil, appearing eerie. Her silver and rose-gold hair floated about her as if she were submerged in water and her marvelous wings, appearing sugar dipped with golden veins, twitched. "Because, *I do not care.*"

Fadin stared, not knowing what to say.

The Old One stood, her long body giving her the appearance of being taller than she was. "I fought my battles long ago. I was ordered to remain until the spriggans were destroyed."

Ciaran and Xemplose made surprised sounds at the mention of the word spriggans. Fadin winced – even goblins knew what those foul creatures were.

"If this island is overrun," the Old One continued, "the spriggans will be killed, and my task is complete." She fluttered into the air and came close to Fadin's face. She touched it lightly. "It is a pity that ones so young will perish," she pulled her hand away, "but such is the way of the world." She flew back to her chair and sat. "I will not help you. If you plan to survive you had better find another way." She stared off into the forest, dismissing them.

Fadin would have liked to yell at her, but what was the point? He grabbed Aednat's hand and they stomped back to the goblins.

"Wells?" Ciaran asked.

Fadin cursed under his breath and shook his head.

Ciaran's face became downcast. "I knew this islands woulds be protected by's a fairy, but I thoughts that fairy would wants to keep its islands safe!"

"Humph," Fadin growled. "Fairies have to be the worst creatures in the world."

"Oh no, boy," Xemplose said. "If you think that creature back there is so terrible, then you haven't experienced much of the world. Besides, fairies are usually reasonable and quite wise, depending which sort you're dealing with."

"Well, no matter what other fairies are like, this one won't help us," Fadin said, "so we are going to have to help ourselves." He looked at Ciaran. "I need you not to be afraid of everyone else. You have to come with us and tell everyone what you know. We don't have time for them to doubt what we're saying."

Ciaran turned his large hazel eyes to the floor.

Xemplos watched him, but didn't seem afraid at all himself. Ciaran shuttered. "I don'ts thinks I can, Fadin-thing."

Xemplos huffed.

"Come on, Ciaran," Fadin grumbled, feeling his irritation build.

Ciaran shook his head. "You don'ts understands."

"It can't possibly be as bad as your makin' it out to be," Aendat said. "Perhaps other Dalbhach treat goblins poorly, but you haven't met *our* parents. My father pretty much loves every creature he meets."

Ciaran didn't answer.

"Coward," Xemplos growled in his rumbling tone.

Ciaran shot an angry glance his way. "We have alreadys established the cowards thing, Xemplos," he spat at him, his eyes turning yellow.

Xemplos folded his arms. "Then you must be trying to prove us right."

Ciaran made his huge eyes slits. He gave Xemplos a growling hiss and bared his sharp yellow teeth. "All right, *Things.*" He addressed Fadin. "I wills go, I will tells adults."

Xemplos nodded, seeming pleased with himself. Fadin smiled and gave Ciaran a rough pat. Ciaran seemed vexed at the gesture.

"Come on," Fadin said, "we don't have time to…"

A horrible shriek rose up from the woods. In a flash they all dashed toward the sound. It clearly had come from the meadow and Fadin lead them through the tree line and they crashed into the clearing.

Tase was standing with Aimirgin and Annata. He rushed at them. "Where have you been? I've been looking all over for you!"

"What happened?" Fadin asked, ignoring all of Tase's questions.

"Saoirse. I'm not sure what happened but it was her…" His voice fell away as Fadin heard Ciaran and Xemplos burst from the forest behind him.

"Ciaran!" Tase cried and ran at him.

Fadin watched as Tase hugged the green goblin. He had no trouble forgiving him apparently.

"Can'ts breath, Tase-thing!" Ciaran chuckled.

"I'm sorry," Tase said, smiling and pulling away.

Annata leaned in to Aimirgin and whispered to her, staring at Ciaran. Aimirgin whispered back, and Annata seemed satisfied.

"What are you doing here?" Tase asked.

"And who are you?" Aimirgin nodded to the orange goblin.

Fadin was frustrated. He quickly recapped, skipping over the meeting with the Old One.

"What?" Aimirgin yelped. "An army is coming?"

"Of bads sea creatures," Ciaran confirmed.

"We have to find Ma and the others and warn them!" Fadin said.

"They all went looking for Saoirse and Desmond," Tase spluttered. "It's worse than that though, Fadin. Desmond was with her but Clearie and baby Glendan were outside, and they're nowhere to be found either."

Fadin's stomach churned sickly. The memory of what Saoirse had done to him when she had first arrived in Kavanagh Castle burned in his mind. He remembered her standing at the door; she had been a filthy, smelly, feather and grime-covered mess. Her clothes had been ripped and stained, her nails had looked frighteningly long, and her mouth had been caked with something red. Her eyes, usually so kind, had been deadly, and in a wink she had flung herself on top of him and had sliced at him with her nails. Fadin shivered in remembrance. "We have to find them," he said.

"I saw them," a choked voice yelled.

Fadin turned and saw something white flying towards them from the edge of the forest. "Ruepricked?"

"The flysing towel?" Ciaran asked.

Xemplos made a face. "A what?"

The white thing fluttered down and then staggered back up. It looked as though he was having a hard time staying in flight.

"What's the matter with him?" Aednat said.

Tase stepped forward and held his hand out. The tea towel barely made it to Tase's hand when he fell onto it. He had four long gashes that had torn all the way through his cloth.

"Ruepricked, what happened?" Tase asked him.

Ruepricked pointed a red-tipped corner toward the place he had flown from. "They're in there. You have to hurry, it's Saoirse." His voice was faint. "I was trying to protect Clearie and the baby by distracting her," he chuckled. "I suppose I did too good a job."

Fadin locked eyes with Tase.

"Leave me with Annata, and go," Ruepricked ordered. "Desmond is with them, and the last I saw Saoirse slashed at him."

Aimirgin gasped.

Tase passed Ruepricked to Annatta who took him in both hands. "We'll get you fixed up as soon as this is over," she told him.

"We musts hurry," Ciaran insisted. "We don'ts have much time."

Fadin nodded. "Follow me." He dashed into the trees.

~~~

Trandafira picked up the violet dust in her hands, and blew it into the burning seashells.

There was a great crack and purple sparks flew from the flames.

She rolled her head back and laughed delightedly, her beautifully shaped lips spreading into a pearly grin. Her lime green eyes opened and she stared at the sky and the countless stars. She ran a hand through her black and silver streaked hair and picked up another handful of purple dust, rubbed it in both hands, and began to dance around the burning opal seashells. She twirled, leaned in near the flames, pulled back, and blew the new handful into the roaring blaze.

"Za servants must obey zis call," she smiled wickedly. She flung her hand back. "Geeve it to me," she ordered.

Gabriel was at her side in a moment. He handed her the small glass bottle that contained the child's blood and hair.

"Mmmm," Trandafira hummed. She shook the bottle, mixing the contents, and then slammed it into the inferno. It was as if a dynamite stick had been flung into the fire – the sound was deafening, and the flames shot out in all directions. Trandafira laughed harder. It was a good thing they were in a bog, no humans would have heard the blast.

In the purple flames the form of the Kavanagh girl, Saoirse, could be clearly seen. She slashed at someone and then fell backward, seeming confused. "Zey can feend za island now," Trandafira grinned. "Our sea escorts vill bring za girl first, and once on za main land, Vladimir vill take her."

Gabriel sneered in delight but a sound from close by made them both turn their heads.

A pale and beautiful creature stood not too far off. A white bird was upon its shoulder. It was not clear if the creature was a male or female, but it carried its own source of light, and looked out of place in the darkened bog.

Trandafira grimaced and her heart fluttered in fear. She pointed her red painted nails toward the being. "You have no business here," she spat.

The creatures said nothing but suddenly disappeared in a flurry of pale sparkling dust. The bird flew away into the night sky, heading toward the ocean.

Trandafira snarled. "They have been warned." She picked up the red necklace that hung near her chest and rubbed it between her thumb and index finger. The red stone shimmered for an instant as she sent the news to Vladimir. Things had just become complicated.

~~~

Saoirse got up from the sand and looked down at her stained hands. The long nails shrank back into her fingers and she turned her eyes in horror to the two still bodies lying on the beach. Her mouth opened in a terrified grimace and her body shook. "What have I done?" she cried.

She hadn't been able to control herself. She had gotten so angry, over nothing! Desmond had been so wonderful to her, but with one word he had infuriated her and she hadn't been able to stop.

She didn't understand, she thought she had been getting better. Mr Aislinn, Enda, and Ma had been helping her, giving her potions, trying to suppress the monster inside of her. She shook her head, trying not to remember the vicious way she had attacked first Desmond, and then Clearie.

"Oh no," she wailed. She covered her mouth with her hands as she looked at Desmond and Cleaire. Perhaps the monster couldn't be tamed; maybe this was all she would ever be. The tears could not be stopped. She prayed she hadn't killed them, she couldn't live with herself if she had. Desmond was the one person she had met who understood what she struggled with, and she loved him, she couldn't lose him. She couldn't even think about Clearie, her brother – oh, what had she become that she could hurt him?

"Saoirse."

She flung her head around and saw a man standing by the shore. He had wonderfully kind eyes, eyes whose colour wasn't clear.

"I'm always near," he said. "No matter what may come."

Saoirse stared at him. She knew he was good, the precise essence of it, but she didn't understand how she knew. "Who are you?" she asked.

Another noise made her jump and she saw two forms diving at her from the waves. They were strange but magnificent creatures in their own right. As they got closer she saw they were pale grey skinned women, with white bellies and streaks of white blending with their grey. They had the lower bodies of dolphins, glimmering onyx eyes, and their hair was made up of silver strands, much thicker than human's hair. In their silver strands, seaweed and sea flowers seemed to grow.

Saoirse, feeling a pull towards the creatures, turned back to the man, frightened, but he was gone. She shook her head, wondering if he had been there at all, or if she was just going mad.

One of the women called to her, in a voice that sounded more like a flute, and the words were more like notes. Saoirse felt an overwhelming power pull her forward, and she could not resist. The beast inside her stirred but couldn't break free, and as she stepped into the water she fought the pull of the creatures and stared at Desmond and Clearie, who were still unmoving on the sand. The sight of their broken bodies hurled grief and self-hate at her, and the emotions swallowed her up, extinguishing any will she had to fight.

The dolphin maidens pulled her in and swam with her. Where they were going Saoirse didn't know, but she understood they were taking her, and in the pit of her stomach she knew she was in trouble. Her sorrow prevented her from caring what happened to herself, and she let the creatures take her wherever they wished.

~~~

Vladimir released his necklace and turned to Dominique, who stood at his side.

She was clothed in black bottoms and a black under shirt, with her small feet bare. Over her shoulders a wolf skin lay, silver and ashen, illuminating her milk-white skin. Her lovely face was streaked across her eyes with red, and the bridge of her hair was painted the lightest shade of silver.

She stared at him, the eagerness of the hunt clear on her face. She was wild, ferocious, a born huntress, and one of his greatest creations.

Vladimir held his hand up to her and took a few steps forward. His own bare feet moved silently in the wet grass. The bottom of his black trousers dampened, and his black shirt clung with the sweat of running.

He gazed up at the moon, the sharp wind rustling his shoulder length silver and black hair. He let the moon's light completely fill his eyes. He searched her brilliance for the connection he knew was there, if only he could see it.

Suddenly his mind's eye was overwhelmed with the vision of a young girl, with curly raven hair and green eyes, struggling to swim away from a small island. Her body bobbed up and down in the water, and as she paddled she tipped her head up, struggling to keep it above the waves.

Two sleek grey bodies swam near the girl. The two naiad women propped themselves beneath Saoirse's body to keep her afloat. The girl clung to the dolphin-like naiads and shook with the cold of the water, all her fight gone.

One of the naiads placed her webbed hand over Saoirse's heart. She would be able to sustain her body temperature until they could get her to shore.

Vladimir smiled and closed his eyes. The naiad women would bring the girl to him and his army would attack that island, getting rid of the Kavanaghs once and for all. Then he could take the girl and use her for his purposes. Never mind the intruder in the bog. Let one being *try* to overthrow an entire army.

"Vat deed you see?" Dominique questioned, her voice full of excitement.

"The girl is in the ocean," he said, his tone rumbling and smoky. "She will end up on a beach, east of here." He turned that way and gazed over the hills. "She will come across a village, and there we can overcome her."

Dominique yipped like a wild animal and peered to the east.

Vladimir smiled, his face lighting up. "Come, my dear," he said, taking her hand, "it's time to hunt."

Dominique's eyes filled with blackness and she grinned, her teeth sparkling in the moon's silver light. "Yaah, yaah!" she cried.

Vladimir released her hand and howled.

They sped off along the wet grass, their feet pounding into the earth, their lungs sucking in the scents around them.

The smell of the cool air and field filled Vladimir's nose, and he delighted himself in the pleasure of running. His heart beat faster each time his bare feet struck the grass, and his spirit soared as he let himself get swept up in the hunt.

Soon, they would have their prey. Soon, their waiting would be over.

~~~

Fadin ran through the woods, beginning to feel desperate. Where were they? This island wasn't that big, how had they not found Saoirse and the others yet? There was a sound like crunching leaves. Fadin turned and for an instant he could have sworn he saw Pathos standing in the shadow of a tree. The dog disappeared into the foliage. "Pathos?" Fadin cried.

Tase was right behind him. "What?"

"I could have sworn," Fadin said, and dove after the dog. Real or imagined, he was going to follow his instincts. There was a strange shimmer just ahead of him, between two winding trees.

"We will's go firsts," Ciaran called. He and Xemplose rushed into the shimmer and vanished.

Fadin, not trying to think about how the magic could be a fairy trap, burled through the shimmering piece of forest. He tumbled onto the beach, a cove in steep rocks he had never before explored. How had he never been here?

He darted his eyes, looking for Pathos, and froze.

Ciaran and Xemplos stood at the water's edge. Ciaran was completely yellow and he had grown significantly. At his normal height he had stood at Fadin's knees: in his current state he reached nearly to Fadin's shoulders! Xemplos flung a massive stone boulder – one far too large for him to possibly be able to carry – and roared. It crashed into the sea. A mournful shriek lashed out from the place where the boulder had collided and Fadin saw two grey women swimming away. They had something between them, a girl with black curly hair.

"Saoirse!" Fadin screamed.

She didn't turn, and the dolphin-like women were fast. There was no way to catch her.

Aednat suddenly gasped.

Fadin shifted his vison and choked. There, on the sand, not far from the water, lay Clearie. His eyes were closed, his clothing torn, and a large cut was streaked across his left cheek. He wasn't moving.

Next to him the wolf, Desmond, was sprawled. Deep gashes in his side could be clearly seen. His chest heaved slowly and Aimirgin held his head in her lap, tears flowing down her chin.

Aimirgin looked up at her friends, her face contorted in anguish.

Fadin couldn't seem to find his feet. He still stood there, shocked by what he was seeing. Saoirse had tried to kill them. *Oh, please,* he thought, *don't let Clearie be dead, don't let Desmond die.* As he stood, trying to let his mind catch up with his eyes, another thought struck him. Where's Glendan? That thought broke his paralysis. He ran toward his wounded brother and skidded to a stop near his cut face.

Tase and Aednat crashed into the sand next to him. "Is he breathin'?" Aednat asked, her voice panicked. Fadin shook his head, he didn't know.

Ciaran appeared beside him. He put his hand on Fadin's shoulder. Fadin moved so that Ciaran could get a better look.

The goblin, who had returned to green, lifted Clearie's head under his arm and felt his neck. "He lives," Ciaran said.

Fadin touched his neck and found there was a dull thud beneath his skin, but Clearie was cold and his breathing shallow. "I think he's hurt bad," Fadin said, fighting back the panic that had begun to creep into his mind and stomach. He glanced at his brother's shirt and saw deep gashes. He turned his head away, unable to come to terms with what wounds were distorted by his brother's clothes.

Tase leaned forward and moved back the ripped shirt, carefully. He stared, his blue eyes wide with horror, and he let the cloth go. "We need to get him to Caoimhe," he said, his voice quivering.

That's what he wanted too, but Fadin knew, in their present state, Clearie and Desmond could not be moved. Unless the adults found the shimmering magic that had led them to this cove, the chances of Ma and the others finding them were almost nonexistent. "Can't you help them, Ciaran?" he asked, voice threatening to tremble.

"Nos," Cairan said. "I is nots a healer, nor is Xemplos."

Aimirgin stroked Desmond's forehead, and as she did the fur began to fall slowly away. It looked like grey sand, tumbling from what was now a human face. As Fadin watched, all the fur vanished. The wolf was gone and only Desmond was left, looking lifeless, his wounds openly exposed.

Aimirgin, sobbing, pulled a jacket from a pouch on her belt and laid it over her brother's waist, so that he was not completely naked. She clutched him tight and buried her face in his hair.

"This is bad," Xemplos said quietly to Cairan. "These children will not survive if help doesn't come soon."

"We can'ts moves them," Ciaran said.

"No, we can't," Xemplos agreed.

Fadin turned away from Desmond, his head spinning, and peered out into the black ocean. He felt the hopelessness nearly drowning him. He was going to lose them both. "Oh, no," he half-sobbed half-moaned. His voice carried out to the sea, and he felt anger burn against the Old One, who surely must be powerful enough to help, but no help or sympathy would come from her.

His mind raced to the tonics Ma, Mr Aislinn, and Enda had given to Saoirse. She had seemed to be doing well, at least well enough that she hadn't attacked anyone in a long while. Why had this happened? He felt desperation begin to swallow him up.

"Someone help us!" Tase cried out.

A high sound unexpectedly carried through the air. Tase picked his head up, his vision distorted by tears, and stared out to the ocean.

Aednat noticed him sit up. "What?" she asked.

The noise faded and returned, carrying on the wind and hitting Tase's ears like a small bell. "Do you hear that?" he asked.

Aednat gaped into the sea, clearly hearing the sound. "It can't be," Xemplos breathed.

Ciaran stood and leaned towards the waves.

The noise came again, only this time it was closer, and sounded more like a whistle than a bell.

Aimirgin stopped her sobbing and listened. "What *is* that?"

A different whistle joined the first, and they cried together. The sound became more like a song, and it was beautiful, but heartbreaking.

"I know that sound," Aednat said softly.

Suddenly the waves began to roll in, come up higher, and splashed upon the children's laps and feet.

Ciaran and Xemplos backed up, more in a show of reverence than of fear.

Fadin thought of moving, but something kept him where he was, transfixed on the sea, and now soaking from the waist down. It was as if he had been rooted to the spot by some force beyond himself.

Something silvery blond began to break out of the water. As Tase watched, it was followed by an auburn brown something. He realised they were heads. The silvery blond and auburn brown hair was followed by eyes, noses, and mouths. The skin on these faces was pale and glimmered, and near the hair line shimmering scales could be clearly seen.

The eyes of the face with the silvery blond hair were brilliantly light blue, and the eyes on the face with the auburn hair were a deep golden green. Both women had thick lips that gleamed in the moonlight, and as they continued to break from the waves, their necks twinkled with the scales lining them, as did their shoulders. When their chests broke the water, Fadin saw that they were covered by shell necklaces, made from seashells that sparkled lavender, sapphire, and the deepest emerald.

The women continued to come further in the shallows, until the one with silvery blond hair had to pull herself along with her radiant arms. She kicked to propel herself forward and as she did a silvery blue tail broke from the water. It was long and magnificent. The billowy tips were coloured dark royal blue against the paleness of the other scales. The other woman kicked her tail as well, and hers shone golden red, with the tips the warmest shade of crimson.

~~~

"Mermaids," Tase breathed, as the two lovely creatures came up next to the children. He stared at them in awe and then shuddered. Ice began to penetrate his chest, originating just above his heart. It travelled quickly, sending the numbing cold cascading through his arms and legs, all the way to his toes and fingertips. He felt as though he would vomit and his head began to swim with dizziness. His face scrunched up in discomfort, what was happening?

He glanced up and saw the mermaids were upon them, so close that if he had the strength he could reach out and touch them. He felt his heartbeat galloping inside his chest much quicker than usual and his body shivered uncontrollably. He could feel the colour draining from his face. In confusion, he looked around to see if the others were having this same reaction, but they all looked fine. *What's the matter with me?* he wondered.

The mermaid who had the silvery blue fin lifted a long webbed hand that glittered with scales, and pointed to Clearie and Desmond. Her light blue eyes locked with Fadin's and her silvery eyebrows pulled together, making her look like she was in pain.

Fadin didn't move.

A tear escaped his eye and rolled down his cheek. Before it could tumble from his chin, the mermaid with the auburn brown hair lifted her own webbed hand and caught it with her finger. She held it up to her eyes and turned to her companion.

The other mermaid stared at the tear and opened her lovely lips. Tase thought she was going to speak, but instead she let out the most beautiful whistle, yet her mouth moved as if forming words. She stopped her whistling and pulled a small flask from around her waist.

As Tase looked, he saw that a string of seaweed was wrapped around her middle, much like a belt, and attached to the belt were many bottles, pouches, and even dead fish.

Tase felt himself becoming weaker by the moment, but he tried to keep himself focused.

The light haired mermaid held the flask up to her companion's finger and let Fadin's tear fall in. She shook the container for a moment and then handed it to the other mermaid.

The auburn-brown haired creature clutched the flask in her webbed hands, closed her eyes, and drank from it. She coughed and let the thermos fall into the water. Her chest heaved with the force of her coughs, as if she were choking. She took a deep breath, steadied herself, and lifted her head to Fadin. "If you permit me, child, I can save them," she said, nodding to Clearie and Desmond. Her voice was like a song, calming and more beautiful than any sound Tase had ever heard. "They *are* dying."

Fadin nodded.

The auburn-haired mermaid took a bottle filled with brilliant indigo liquid from her belt. She held the bottle over Clearie's mouth and let a few drops trickle in.

As soon as the liquid hit Clearie's lips, the mermaid let two tears fall from her own eyes. The two that fell were purple and jade. Once the second tear hit the wound and mixed with the indigo liquid, the wounds began to mend.

Tase felt a wave of relief come over him despite the fact that he was freezing from the inside out. Clearie was going to be okay.

"He's healin'," Aednat squeaked.

The mermaid placed her hand over Desmond's mouth and repeated the process she had done to Clearie. His gashes, too, began to close and his breathing steadied to a more normal rate.

A stabbing cold pierced Tase's chest and he clutched at it. The feeling of nausea worsened. He wasn't sure how much longer he could stand it.

Clearie began to stir. "Clearie?" Fadin gasped.

"Desmond!" Aimirgin shouted.

His eyelids fluttered. He let out a sigh and gazed up into Aimirgin's face. "Aimirgin?" he asked.

Aimirgin smiled and put a hand to her mouth to contain her sobs.

Desmond looked puzzled for a moment, then his face contorted into one of shock and he bolted upright. The jacket fell away and he stumbled in the sand staring into the woods. "Saoirse," he cried. "Oh no! Where is she?" But as he looked around, the fact that she was not there seemed to sink in. "She attacked us," he said, running a hand through his black hair and beard. "She, she attacked us." His black eyes were sad and frightened. "She didn't know what she was doing, she lost control." He took a shuttering breath. "She isn't a werewolf."

"What?" Tase managed, his voice sounding a bit slurred.

Clearie jerked upright. "Desmond!"

Tase jumped slightly at the abruptness of Clearie's awakening.

Clearie spotted Desmond and relief showed on his face. "You're all right? I thought she'd killed you."

Desmond nodded solemnly. "So did I, especially that last —" his voice fell away and he stared, his eyes wide. "Oh, my," he breathed.

Fadin looked up and saw him staring at the two mermaids, who peered back at him, their lovely forms barely covered by the tide.

Clearie turned, but before he could see the mermaid, he spotted Ciaran and Xemplos.

"Ciaran!" he cried. "What are you doing here?"

Ciaran gave him a small smile, "Hello, thing." He nodded his head toward the water.

Clearie shifted his gaze and became a living statue as he took in the sea women.

"You? You saved us?" Desmond asked. He arched his head to his sister – who had been prodding him in the leg – and spotted a pair of trousers in her hand. He looked down at himself and his olive toned skin turned scarlet. He quickly jerked the trousers away and pulled them on.

"Yes," the auburn haired mermaid said. "I am afraid there is not much time for explanations, but know we are friends." She placed a shining scaled hand to her chest and said, "You can call me Avalon, and my mother," – she placed her hand on the others shoulder – "Oona." She paused for a moment. "I have come to warn you, an army is coming, of some of the most powerful warriors of the sea."

Ciaran stepped forward. "Sorrys to bursts your bubbles, muirín, but we's has already warns them."

Avalon looked Ciaran up and down. "Goblins can only know what has reached the ears of the surface," she said. "We come to tell that Cashlin Muirghein was betrayed, and has fallen."

Aimirgin gave a gasp.

"Our people were driven out by Neres, a powerful nymph who has many sea creatures on his side. From what our spies have learned, we know his daughter was captured by land people, and unless Neres does the bidding of her captors, they have threatened to turn her into sea foam."

"To sea foam?" Clearie asked.

Avalon nodded. "It is what happens when we cease to exist." She turned to the sea. "Neres convinced those loyal to him to attack Cashlin Muirghein." She began to pull something from a pouch on her belt and Tase's heart began to slow. "Their purpose was to try to steal this." She placed something wrapped in seaweed upon the white sand.

Tase twisted his face as his body became numb. "What *is* that?" he asked, but in his heart he already knew.

Avalon pushed the parcel forward and some of the seaweed slipped away revealing black leather.

Tase's body felt like it was shutting down from the cold. "The Xoor?" Fadin cried.

Ciaran hissed and Xemplos made a surprised sound.

"Why is it here?" Desmond barked, panic boldly painted on his features. He glanced at Tase, but seemed to decide there was nothing he could do for him.

"We cannot hide it any longer," Avalon said. "Land creatures gave it to us, now you must take it back. We lost our home because of it, it is no longer our responsibility."

Desmond seemed hesitant to take it, and Fadin made no move forward.

Tase knew it was the book that made him feel the way he did, but if the mermaids didn't want it they couldn't just leave it on the sand. He moved forward and, with numb hands, grabbed it by its seaweed wrapping.

Everyone watched him hesitantly.

Tase didn't know how long he would be able to hold it, but a solution had to be found. "The army is coming here?" he managed to ask around the chattering of his teeth.

Avalon bowed her head in acknowledgement.

"W... we will keep the book," Tase said, "but w... we need a w... way off th... this island."

"We have already arranged for that," Avalon said. "A boat is on its way, but you must bring the others to the beach on the north end of the island. It will be here in less than an hour. The army is regrouping, I cannot confirm how long it will take them to reach this place, so move quickly."

Desmond nodded. "All right, we will get the others. But before we do, do you know what happened to Saoirse?"

Avalon seemed to know who he meant. "The dark haired girl was taken by two naiads loyal to Neres. I do not know where they have taken her to."

Desmond took a deep breath. "Thank you."

"Glendan!" Fadin suddenly cried. "Where is he? What happened to him?" Clearie and Desmond locked eyes.

Desmond's mouth fell open, his face a clear sign he didn't know. "You d...

don't know?" Tase yelped.

"The baby?" Avalon questioned. Everyone turned to her.

"You've seen him?" Fadin asked.

She turned and whistled to the water.

Everyone shifted their vision to the waves, and waited, breathlessly.

From around some rocks, where the beach pushed out in an arch, several seals' heads suddenly bobbed. They dove down and popped back up, struggling to swim with something tethered to their necks. Soon a little basket, woven with reeds and flowers, could be seen from around the corner as well, being pulled by the swimming seals. A small red head peeked up from the inside, followed by two big brown eyes. Glendan spotted his brothers and, smiling wide, he opened his tiny hands and grabbed at them.

"Glendan!" Fadin, Tase, and Clearie shouted as one.

Fadin and Clearie got up – Tase tried but he was too cold to even move – and ran into the water to meet him and his basket chariot.

The seals wiggled out of the harnesses and vanished into the black water, but something else reappeared behind the basket, a brown face with dark curly hair surrounding it.

Clearie and Fadin slowed.

The woman stood, her large, rich, tan eyes searching theirs. Her skin was a beautiful brown, and her face was lined with dark freckles. She wore a dress that looked like it was made from seaweed, and her neck was adorned with large pearls. She scooped Glendan up, who goggled at her, and took a few steps forward, holding him out to show she wished to deliver him to his brothers.

Tase glanced at Clearie, who looked spellbound. Clearie took a few steps forward and the woman handed Glendan to him. Clearie held him tight and kissed his plump cheeks.

Tase sighed in relief. No matter what came, at least Glendan was safe. "Thank you," Clearie said to the woman.

She smiled wide and her teeth sparkled like the pearls about her neck.

"We spotted him on his own, on shoreline," Avalon said. "The Selkies are fond of human children. They only took him to keep safe."

"Selkies?" Fadin asked, turning to her.

She nodded to the woman standing near Clearie. "Water creatures, from the depths of the sea, clothed in seal coat, hiding the beauty within, until they decide to show their second form."

"Don't you remember the stories about them?" Clearie asked, propping Glendan higher on his chest.

Fadin chuckled. "No, Clearie, I don't."

Clearie smiled at the selkie woman before him.

She gave him a quick kiss on his cheek and then dove into the water. Clearie, visibly smitten, put a hand to his cheek and stared into the water.

Tase smiled but began to feel his heart slowing to an alarming rate. He would need to find somewhere to put the Xoor soon; he wasn't sure what would happen to him if he didn't.

"Selkies are magical creatures who can become human by takin' off their seal coats. They can return to their seal form whenever they put their seal skin back on," Aednat said. "There are loads of tales about them, most about human men stealin' the women Selkie's seal coats when they are in their human form. If a man steals a Selkie's coat, she must marry him, but her true home is the sea and if she ever finds her skin, she will put it on and return to the ocean."

Fadin chuckled. "I think Clearie may want to take a Selkie seal coat and hide it."

Clearie gave him a glaring look. "Oh, do shut up, Fadin."

Avalon turned her head to the sea. "Something is stirring," she said. "You must go get the others, I will be waiting on the north beach. Be quick." Without another word, her and Oona flung themselves into the water, and with a powerful kick of their tails, vanished into the sea.

Clearie and Fadin came out of the water and Tase pushed the Xoor as far away from himself as he could.

Desmond bent down and picked it up.

"D... don't t... touch the l... l... leather," Tase stammered.

"I won't," Desmond said, placing a hand on Tase's forehead. "Tase!" he gasped. "You're freezing!" He turned to the others. "We have to get him warmed up."

"J... just keep the b... b... book a little away f... from me," Tase said. "I don't know how, but it's m... making me c... cold."

Desmond nodded. "Aimirgin, you take this." He handed her the Xoor and she was careful to only touch the seaweed. "Go ahead of us, to the meadow."

Aimirgin nodded and ran into the forest.

Tase almost immediately felt warmth returning to his body. Desmond bent down and lifted Tase into his arms.

"What are y... you doing?" Tase asked.

"Until you get your strength back, I'm carrying you."

Tase wanted to argue but he knew he couldn't move yet and they had no time to waste.

Desmond regarded the goblins but didn't ask who they were, seeming to know they were friends. "Lead the way?" Desmond asked Fadin.

Fadin nodded, giving Tase a knowing look. They looked at the black mark on Tase's chest, created when Tase had touched the Xoor's leather binding. It seemed the danger of the book's poison was not over. Tase would need to be careful how close he got to it in the future.

Fadin ran ahead of them into the trees and Desmond pounded in after him. Tase's body was feeling warmer every second, but his heart drummed in fear.

154

# CHAPTER 10
## FIGHT OR FLIGHT

Fadin, Desmond and Tase burst through the trees first. It was like coming up out of the water after a long swim, first it was a mess of green leaves, and then there was the meadow, open and lit up by the soft glow of the tree lights. Desmond stopped after he got a few feet from the woods and let Tase down.

Tase stood, feeling strong again, and saw Aimirgin come away from the horses. She must have placed the book somewhere on her stallion's saddle.

"You all right?" Fadin asked.

Tase smiled. "Better now, yeah."

Annata, Aldabella, and Quinlan came up to them, the only people in the clearing.

The others crashed into the clearing behind Tase.

"Where is everyone else?" Desmond asked, looking directly at Quinlan.

Quinlan's features were shocked. His mouth was open and his black eyes gleamed with happy surprise. He picked his spotted and olive tanned hand up to his forehead. "You're okay?" he asked his brother. "We thought the worst had happened." He looked around at them all. "Where's Saoirse?"

"Gone," Desmond said, pain in his voice. "We can't explain everything now. Where is everyone else?"

"Out looking for you," Quinlan answered. His face contorted as the two goblins clambered through the tree line. "Who are they?"

Ruepricked picked up his small white head. "Oh, greenie, nice to see you again. Didn't you abandon us all last time?"

Ciaran folded his arms and his ears, hands, and eyes scorched yellow. "We friends, all you's needs to know, you long necks," he snapped at Quinlan. His piercing yellow eyes shifted and he glared at Ruepricked. "And you's can go burns in a fire pit, for all I cares."

Xemplos did his best to cover the deep snicker that escaped his mouth. "They are here to help," Desmond said. "Listen, if we don't get out of here soon, we're going to have company."

"Company?" Aldabella quivered. She grabbed a strand of her blue hair and twisted her finger in it. "What do you mean?"

"Sea creatures attacked Cashlin Muirghein," Aimirgin replied. "They tried to steal the Xoor from the mer-people."

Tase turned to her. "I meant to ask, what exactly is Cashlin Muirghein?" Aimirgin appeared a bit frustrated that he asked at the present moment, but answered anyway. "It's the home of the coast of Ireland's Mer-folk, a large underwater city, housing many sea creatures. It was destroyed once during the Great War."

"Yes, and now it's destroyed again," Aednat added, "and the ones who did it are comin' here."

Annata gasped. "What?"

Aldabella began taking frantic breaths.

Quinlan stumbled backward. "Ogre spit." He looked up at Desmond. "If they make it here…"

"I know," Desmond hissed, "that's why we need the others. Do you have any idea which way they went?"

"Every way," Quinlan trembled. "They're all over the island."

"How are we going to get them to come here in time?" Clearie questioned. He pulled baby Glendan closer to him.

Desmond rubbed his forehead. "We have to call them all, we can't waste time going to get them." As soon as the words left his lips, Desmond lifted his head to the trees, closed his eyes and yelled. As he cried his body contorted and grey hair sprouted from his bare olive skin. His knees buckled and he fell on all fours, but he kept his head up. His scream transformed into a deep bellowing howl, and after a moment, all that was standing in their midst was the grey wolf, singing his song to the moon.

"They'll come," Quinlan shouted over his brother's call.

"Let's get some of our belongings while we wait," Tase cried. "We don't have time to waste."

Quinlan nodded. He and Aimirgin ran into their hut.

Aednat suddenly made a wincing sound and stared down at her arm. "What is it?" Tase asked.

"My rash," she hissed. "It's really burning."

Tase looked down at the rash she had developed about a week ago. It was a sign her first bogán was coming. He had no idea what you were supposed to do with a Geartú's bogán rash. "It that normal?" he asked Aldabella and Annata.

"It means it's getting close to developing," Aldabella said, pushing some of her blue hair away from her face. "We need to cover it. Before, it was too soon, but once it starts to burn it can't be exposed to the open air."

"What are we supposed to cover it with?" Annata asked.

"Allow me." Rueprickeds strained voice came from Annata's pocket. He poked one of his corners out. "I'm too ripped up to fly, but if you place me on her arm, I can secure myself to her."

Tase didn't like how weak his voice sounded.

"Are you sure, Ruepricked?" Aednat asked, wincing at her burining arm. "I'm supposed to find a purpose, aren't I?" he chuckled.

Aednat held out her arm and Annata carefully placed Ruepricked on the bright red bumpy skin of her sisters's left arm. He curled himself around her and tied a small knot with his corners.

"It's safe now," he sighed, sounding quite worn out.

"Thanks, Rue," Aednat said. "It already feels better."

"Make sure he stays firmly tied," Aldabella instructed. "We'd better go pack. Come on."

The Aislinn girls raced to their cabin.

Tase looked worriedly at Aednat and Ruepricked tied to her, but shook his head and focused on the task at hand. He, Fadin, and Clearie, along with Glendan, ran to their small cottage and began grabbing sacks and filling the contents of their home with them.

"We helps, things." Carian said. He nodded to Xemplos and they both began to grab handfuls of items.

They grabbed everything. The crib, books, blankets, pillows, pots, pans, backpacks filled with clothes, the rugs, food, the whole lot. The sacks they used had enlargement charms on them, which made the packing process quick and easy. Xemplos was rather good at lifting anything heavy and hurling it in the direction of a sack. Fadin was nearly crushed by the wooden chair he chucked at him, but Fadin caught it in the charmed bag, and it shrunk while flying toward the opening.

As Tase flung things into the sack in his right hand, his fingers moving swiftly trying to get everything packed as quickly as possible, he felt a pang in his chest. At first he didn't know what the feeling was connected to, but as he bent down and removed the loose stone in the wall where his hammock hung and pulled out the wooden K, shoving it into a small leather pouch which he hung around his neck, he felt and understood the sorrow. He was losing the one home he had felt safe and happy in since his father had died. He really hadn't realized how important this thatched hut had become to him, or the whole island for that matter. This *was* home, and it was time to leave it. He tucked the pouch into his shirt, replaced the stone, and ripped his hammock off the wall.

Ciaran noticed his sadness. "Okay, Tase-thing?"

Tase paused for a moment before nodding and putting his hammock away. "Fine." He swallowed and continued packing up his family's belongings. Now was no time to feel sad about moving on.

When their cabin was empty, everything collected in their backpacks, the three boys, and even little Glendan, became silent and still.

Tase memorized every crack in the stones, every line in the wood, every stitch in the thatched roof, and every imperfection in the bubbly glass. This was goodbye. He took a deep breath and then followed his brothers out. He took one last look at the hut, shook his head, and then closed the moss-covered door tight.

They moved swiftly over to the corral, where the horses were whinnying and pawing the earth. They clearly knew something bad was coming.

"You have horses?" Xemplos asked in his resounding voice.

"Yes, elves gave them to us," Tase answered as he hopped the wooden fence and strode up to his stallion, Morganius, who made an irritated grunt. "I know, boy," he said, placing his hand on the stallion's nose. "We're leaving."

"Horses are great for eating," Xemplos continued. "You have a lot, how many did the elves give you? Have you cooked them often?"

Tase stared back at the orange goblin, cerulean eyes wide.

Ciaran was staring, surprised at Xemplos too. He gave Tase a sudden uneasy smile and a forced chuckle. "Goblin's cans eats pretty much everythings."

Clearie cleared his throat. "We don't *eat* our horses, Xemplos. We ride them."

The goblin looked confused, but after a confirming glance at Ciaran, nodded.

Fadin covered a smile.

Tase grabbed a saddle from one of the hooks on the fence and dressed Morganius in it, trying not to be concerned about Xemplos and whether he was hungry or not. Once the saddle was on and firmly in place, he tethered his bundle to it.

Tase looked to Desmond, who was continuing to howl. The adults would be here soon, and the quicker they could all get back to Avalon and the boat she would provide for them, the better. He nodded to Quinlan. "Let's get to Aunt Kyna's cabin," he said to Fadin. "Clearie, you should stay here with the horses." He nodded to Xemplos. "They're... ah... anxious, we don't want them getting frightened and start running."

Clearie bobbed his head, "Okay."

"I will help him," Xemplos declared, folding his orange arms.

"Great," Clearie said.

Tase and Fadin, followed closely by Ciaran, dashed to Aunt Kyna, Daireann, and Ruepricked's hut. Once they reached it, they peered at the door, which was not only covered in moss, but purple and blue flowers as well, a detail clearly added by Daireann.

Fadin jiggled the handle and pushed the door open. It swung in easily, and as they stepped inside the fireplace lit up, casting the smallish home in a golden light.

Tase arched his eyebrows as he took in the cabin. He had thought – from looking at the outside – that the tree that grew so near was almost growing into the hut. Well, he had been wrong; the tree was growing right inside the house. In fact, the twisted branches were used as hooks for pots, pans, clothing, and food. The stone walls were sprouting with moss and flowers, and the thatched roof had grapes, ivy, and roses hanging down.

"I likes it!" Ciaran said with a wide toothy grin.

"You have to admire Daireann's taste," Fadin remarked.

Tase smiled a little. He moved to the fireplace and grabbed a sack that was lying there. "We better start packing."

Fadin also grabbed a backpack and the two of them began to empty the cozy hut.

Ciaran found a chest and began pulling things out of it.

Tase moved over to Aunt Kyna's side of the room as Fadin stood on the table and removed the items hanging from the tree branches.

Tase started with her hammock and then moved over to the piece of tree trunk that had been turned into a crude dresser. He opened the first drawer and packed away all the clothes stored inside. He had to suppress a shudder as he came upon Aunt Kyna's more intimate clothing, which he grabbed handfuls of and shoved inside the sack without opening his eyes.

When the first drawer was empty, he moved to the second. As he tried to pull it open, he found that it was locked. He thought nothing of it; instead, he grabbed the handle and thought with all his might that he would like to get inside.

There was a low rumble, not quite audible, but Tase could feel it, and there was a tingling in the air, almost like static. The familiar prickling pressure formed in his toes, then moved to his legs, splintering off all throughout his body. His vision burned silver for a moment and the drawer unlocked. He stood still, as the stinging in his body dimmed and then ended, suddenly realising what he had done. "Fadin," he gasped.

"What?" Fadin asked, standing on his tiptoes, trying to reach a metal spoon. He grimaced at the utensil placed so high up. "How the bloody hell does she reach this?"

Ciaran turned and laughed openly at him.

"I just unlocked this drawer with magic, and I don't even have my weapon on me!"

Fadin turned to him. "You unlocked it with your thoughts?"

Tase grinned at him. "Yeah, I guess I did."

"Tase-thing," Ciaran said, a handful of some sort of mushroom in his hands, "that's powersful stuffs."

Tase tried not to let it get to his head, but he couldn't help but feel proud.

Fadin looked down and made his hand into a fist. "What a load of tripe! I have been working on doing that for how long? I'll have to practice more." He peered over at Tase. "I'll do it with this spoon." He stared up at the spoon and screwed up his face. "Come on, come on," he whispered.

Tase chuckled, rolled his eyes, and went back to the dresser. He pulled the drawer open, and to his surprise, found it full of letters. He shrugged his shoulders and began shoveling them inside.

"Oh!" Ciaran said to himself from across the hut. "This is mys favourites mold!"

"Eww, Cairan." Fadin answered.

Tase placed an exceptionally large handful of letters into the sack, and one fell out and fluttered to the floor. He swung his head around and made to pick it up. He froze as he read the lettering on the envelope.

Cavan-Corr

Penitentiary

Fergus O'Mally

To Kyna Kavanagh

*From Cavan-Corr Penitentiary?* Tase thought. He looked at the date, scribbled in thin green ink in the right hand corner. It was marked for a date just a little before she had been arrested.

He grabbed the small grey envelope and turned it over. The seal was broken. It had been a mahogany wax seal, with a bear on the front, along with a crown, and six diamonds.

Tase pushed the flap up and pulled out the yellowed piece of parchment.

It has been a long time.

It read.

I can honestly say I didn't think I would ever hear from you again, not with how you were able to... how to put it... disappear, if you will? You were clever, though, I'll give you that, vanishing in plain sight, using your sister's identity. What an idea.

Tase crinkled his nose at this, but read on.

I do often wonder, however, can you sleep at night? Not just
because you stole her life, after her untimely demise,

Tase read that part over. Yes, this letter claimed Aunt Kyna had a sister who died.

but you stole that pretty castle you're living in too, didn't you? And all that lovely money. I imagine Teagan must hate you for that. Taking her family home, her fortune, right from under her. Oh, I know she ran away, but still. She has been living the life of a common woman, and you are soaking up the Kavanagh's wealth. Didn't I hear a rumour you two hadn't spoken for over fourteen years? And she doesn't even know your darkest secret.

Hum, I wonder how she'd feel about you
then.

Enough walking down memory lane. Time to get to business.
You want to know if you get thrown into this rat hole with me if I'll talk to you?

Let you in on what I know about Alroy's
death?

Tase's breath caught.

And about that pretty little girl who was smuggled in a few months ago? I'll tell you what, Ms Kavanagh, you get that proud, arrogant, holier than thou behind tossed onto this prison with me and I will tell you anything you want to know. We'll have all the time in the world to talk. Though, I don't know what good it will do you, because getting in is one thing, but how are you going to get out?

Think about it.

Be seeing you, I'm sure,

Fergus

Tase let his hand and the letter fall to his side. What did this mean? "Fadin," he said, his voice even. He picked the parchment back up and gazed at it.

"I've almost got it," Fadin said, making the table creak from the way he was leaning on it.

"Will you stop it about that bloody spoon," Tase shouted, spinning around to face him.

Fadin rocked a little and turned to his twin. "What's your problem?"

"Look what I've found," he said, holding the letter in the air and waving it around a little. The gesture was sarcastic.

Fadin stepped down from the table and moved over to him. Ciaran saw he had a letter but continued with what he was doing. Tase handed him the parchment.

Fadin's blue green eyes scanned from one side of the page to the other several times. His face froze, and he stared forward for a long moment before pulling the letter away from him. "She got thrown into jail on purpose?"

"It would seem that way, yes."

Fadin shook his head. "Who is this, Fergus O'Mally? I haven't heard Mr Hogan, Enda, or Caoimhe ever talk about him, and they talk about an awful lot of people."

"I knows him," Ciaran declared.

Tase and Fadin gaped at him. "Who is he?" Fadin asked.

"He was throwns into prison, six years ago. Durings the wars he was a spys, for the ministry."

"A spy?" Tase said, rather awestruck. "I wonder how Aunt Kyna knows him?"

Ciaran shrugged at that.

"You don't suppose the girl he could be talking about was that crazy looking girl from the prison? The one who was locked in with Saoirse, do you?" Fadin asked.

Tase gave him an affirmative look.

"I want to know what he means about 'using your sister's identity… after her untimely demise," Fadin said. "What is he referring to? Because after that he goes on to talk about how Aunt Kyna took Ma's home and fortune, but obviously he couldn't be talking about Ma earlier. Right?"

Tase ran a hand through his red hair. "Ah, I don't know. But I understand better now why Ma was so hostile about Aunt Kyna."

"Yeah," Fadin said, looking back at the parchment, "she stole her family's wealth, or at least she didn't hesitate to take it. It was rightly hers by marriage though, since there were no other Kavanagh's there to claim it."

Tase locked eyes with him. "What about Enda?"

Fadin bit his lip. "I don't know. He was adopted, but it sounds like, from everything I've heard, our grandparents treated him like he was one of their children… Maybe he didn't want it?"

Tase let out a deep breath. "I don't know, this doesn't add up. Clearly we are missing a big chunk of what happened."

Fadin snorted. "When aren't we?" Ciaran gave a small laugh at that remark. The howling outside suddenly stopped. Tase and Fadin stood silent and still.

Fadin slipped Tase the letter, ran back to the tree, and finished shoving things inside his sack.

Tase closed up the parchment inside the envelope and emptied the rest of the letter drawer.

They finished after a few moments, Ciaran taking great armfuls of the stuff from inside the chest and heaving it inside Tase's sack. They dashed out the door and into the meadow.

"They here?" Fadin asked as they both gaped around the clearing.

Tase screwed up his face. There seemed to be no one at all there, except Desmond, the wolf, who was staring blankly out into the trees.

"What is it, Desmond?" Tase questioned. Then he saw it. Water was creeping toward them from the thick black woods. It was moving like it had a mind of its own, slithering across the short emerald grass. It was seawater, with white foam bursting from its edges, and it stretched from one end of the meadow to the other, and continued steadily forward.

Tase had it in his mind to run, but something kept him rooted to the spot. Something about the white foam, and the way it sparkled in the moonlight.

There was a soft voice calling to him, like far away yelling, but Tase couldn't turn and see who was calling to him.

The water moved nearly to his feet, and then stopped. The foam began to bubble. It sprang slowly upward, like a geyser, and grew long. There were several pale foam mounds before him. Suddenly the mounds parted and rose higher, and Tase saw that the foam had been hair, pale sparkling hair, and beneath the hair there were women, and they were rising from the position they had been crouched in. As they stood to their full height Tase could clearly see them. Their skin was as white as their hair, and their bodies were clothed in flowing white gowns of sea foam. Their eyes were such a pale blue they almost glowed, and their lips were the lightest shade of pink.

The one closest to Tase opened her beautiful lips and began to sing. Her voice was unlike any he had ever heard before. It was like the song of a whale beneath the sea mixed with that of a woman, one who sang in an opera. Every thought he had went completely out of his mind, and the only thing left was the woman before him, and her song.

The faraway voice sounded more desperate now, but Tase could not listen to it. The pale woman in front of him beckoned him forward with open arms and with a smile he walked willingly forward. His feet hit the water and in an instant she was upon him. She took him in her arms and stroked his face.

Her touch was the sweetest thing he had ever felt before. She brought her pale pink lips to his and kissed him.

He felt the water enter his mouth before he really understood what was happening. Then it forced itself down his throat and hit his lungs. He tried to pull away, but it was no use, the woman had him in her firm grip, and her long white fingers had turned to barbs, which stuck into his clothes and pierced his skin as he tried to break free. The water continued to burst into his mouth; he spluttered and struggled to find some air, but the water was overwhelming and the woman didn't give him a centimetre.

He was drowning, he could feel his lungs spasm against the water, but it was no good. He was being consumed by it.

He was suddenly ripped away and flung backward. He hit the ground with great force and began coughing and throwing up water.

Tase could hear the sounds of weapons and horrid screams behind him. He turned round and saw the pale woman shrieking and Caoimhe, Ma, Mr Hogan, and Aunt Kyna slashing at them.

The woman no longer looked beautiful, but terrible. Their white faces were screwed up and their light eyes burned with fury. They hissed and screamed and retreated back into the water, though the water did not recede.

"You all right, Tase?" Enda asked, appearing next to him.

Tase gave another string of coughs, but nodded. He could breathe again, and the water was leaving his throat.

Ardan held up a small vile with swirling gold liquid inside. "Take a small sip

164

of this," he said.

Tase took it and did as he was told. The golden substance was warm, and as soon as it trickled down his throat he felt the water being pulled out of his lungs, and he could breathe normally again.

"You've got to be careful," Enda said, helping Tase to his feet. "Sirens are nasty creatures, beautiful, but deadly. They drown their victims and consume them."

Tase saw that Desmond was being helped to his feet, and the other children looked on in horror.

Ciaran stood wide-eyed next to Aednat and Fadin. Aednat was panting while clutching onto Fadin's wrist and Tase knew it had been her voice trying to call to him away from the sirens.

Ciaran didn't say anything to the adults, who it appeared hadn't noticed him or Xemplos yet. He did, however, say something to Aednat, which made her shiver, and cast a furtive glance to Fadin.

"Tase," Ma said, grabbing him up. She took his face in her hands. "You all right?"

~~~

Fadin watched as Tase nodded his head at their mother. He stole a quick glance toward the water and saw the menacing black shapes receding into the shadows. Silver teeth gleamed as the creatures gave vicious, sneering grins.

"How's did you's two morons gets mixed up with spriggans?" Ciaran hissed at them.

"By being stupid, Ciaran," Fadin answered. He stared at where the sirens had been called up by the horrible spriggans and shuddered. He was relieved they would be leaving soon, getting away from these horrible creatures before they could cause any real damage. "By being complete idiots."

~~~

"The others told us what is going on," Caoimhe informed Tase. "We need to leave, quickly. The water the Sirens brought is not going back into the sea, which means reinforcements are not far away. This whole island will be swimming if we don't get out of here." She turned and spotted the goblins. "Who's this?" she questioned, straightening to her full height.

Ciaran appeared afraid and his hazel eyes flicked to Ma, who had turned to them.

"They're friends," Tase said, surprised by Fadin's silence. "They came to help us."

"How do you know goblins?" Ma asked.

Aednat jumped in. "We've known them for a while. Well, Ciaran at least. He helped us in Cavan-Corr, when you were all in prison. He helped us as often as he could when we were on our own."

Ciaran gave a sheepish grin.

Tase liked how Aednat didn't mention Ciaran lived in the castle attic, but she didn't lie either. He glanced at Ma, who was still for a moment. Her face blossomed into a smile. "Anyone who helps my children is a friend to me." She bent down and before they could move she embraced both Ciaran and Xemplos. Ciaran's eyes were wide when she let go.

"Happy to help," Xemplos said, his orange face turning redder around the edges. He tried to look unaffected by Ma's hug, but it couldn't be clearer both goblin's had been flabbergasted.

For the next fifteen minutes or so, the meadow was pure chaos. People were running here and there, arms full of whatever they could carry, horses being loaded down with supplies, and voices shouting at one another.

"No, we can't take that," Caoimhe barked, "it's too heavy, leave it."

The things they couldn't bring were left scattered, making the clearing look like it had been ransacked.

"I don't think the horses can take anymore," Mr Hogan billowed.

"Agreed," Caoimhe said, jumping from the floor onto her stallion. "Let's ride."

Tase held his arm out to Ciaran, who took it and clambered to his back, where the goblin clung onto his shoulders. Tase ran up to Morganius, he jumped, grabbed a fistful of his mane, and flung himself onto his back. The stallion whined and dug his hoof into the earth. Tase patted his shoulder and peered over at his brother while helping Ciaran have a seat on Morganius in front, almost in Tase's lap.

Fadin shot onto his mare Nimueway in one smooth motion. He whispered in her ear and stroked her cheek. He helped Xemplos up and the mare let out a frustrated snort as the orange goblin plopped himself down. Fadin turned to Tase, and they stared at each other for a moment.

*Leaving home,* Tase thought at him, the sorrow thick in his mind. Fadin swallowed. *Nothing new though, is it?*

Tase turned forward. "No, I guess not," he said. He felt cold creeping through him as Aimirgin and her stallion moved towards him. Tase didn't want to mess around with feeling weak and frozen, so he jerked his heels down.

Morganius neighed loudly and blazed forward into the dense foliage. "Wow!" Ciaran cried, being shoved back against Tase.

The night was suddenly alive with running white horses. The sounds their hooves made as they pounded into the earth were minimal, however they all cried loudly, whinnying and snorting. As they flew through the forest birds shrieked, and other animals dove out of the way. The horses were evidently aware that something was happening.

Tase looked over his shoulder as they approached the beach, and the scene behind him was truly glorious.

The woods were alive with their own pale lights, and all their fantastic colours bounced off the stallions and mares and appeared to make them glow as they charged forward. The horses' violet eyes stood out, even against all the other colours and seemed to burn with a fire deep inside them. It was a lovely last look at the magnificent forest that had been his home for what now felt like such a short time.

Tase pushed down the sadness and turned forward once more. He ducked to narrowly miss a branch aimed at his head, his heart leaping in fear. He sat upright with a breath of relief and pulled on Morganius' mane as they burst out onto the sand.

Ciaran shrieked and nearly flew forward over the stallion's head, but Tase steadied him with his arm around him like a seatbelt. He sniggered and turned his attention forward.

Tase's mouth fell open.

There was a boat waiting for them all right, but he wasn't sure if he would call it a boat. It looked like a ship from the time when pirates ruled the seven seas, but that didn't even do it justice. It was magnificent.

The body of the ship was made from deep mahogany wood with golden and ebony trim. The masts were swirled in elegant designs, the bowsprit and rest of the deck were laden with carved figures and artwork, and the sails! Why, the sails gleamed with their breathtaking golden colour, shimmering in the bright moonlight.

"Wow…" Ciaran breathed.

Tase nodded. He was so overwhelmed with the ship's appearance that he didn't even notice the figure that was walking up to them.

"It is good to see you all."

Tase jerked his head in the direction of the familiar voice and his face broke into an abundant smile.

# CHAPTER 11
## BATTLE AT SEA

"Irrah," Tase cried.

The elf smiled back at him. He looked quite strikingly different than the last time Tase had seen him. His golden hair, which hung past his waist, was put in a labyrinth of braids and twists, and there were many blue beads adorning the braids, as well as silver jewelry. His skin was dyed with a blue-green colour on the tips of his fingers, and in small patterns near the edges of his face and around his neck. He wore splendid war-like clothing of the deepest blue, which brought out his intense silvery blue eyes, though the style was something Tase had never seen before. The clothes in some places appeared to be made of cloth, but in others the blue looked like metal. It was all adorned with green and silver designs, which made him appear as though he was wearing a piece of art.

On his shoulder sat the prettiest little bird Tase had ever seen. The bird was silver coloured in nature, but its belly and the top of its head were a brilliant shade of forest green.

The bird twittered and fluttered into the air as Irrah stepped forward. "Elves," Ciaran whispered. "I don'ts much likes elves."

Irrah, an Elven Lord, had pledged his allegiance to the twins and their family when they had escaped from prison. It was he who had provided them with their Elven Horses, and some of their most valuable supplies.

"Good to see you," Caoimhe said, swinging down from her horse, her pointed ears visible as her copper hair had been pinned back. "I wish it were under better circumstances."

"Indeed," Irrah said. He walked up to Caoimhe and gave her a large hug. The embrace was exceptionally warm, almost as if they were family who had been separated by time.

As Tase thought about it, perhaps they were. He really knew nothing of Caoimhe's past. Nothing could be more proof of that then finding out her father was a king. Tase didn't know the details, however when they had met Irrah at the prison, he had suggested they all hide on one of the Elven Islands – wherever those were – but Caoimhe had refused, saying her and her father did not see eye to eye, and she was not welcome.

Tase had tried to ask Caoimhe about her past but she was tight lipped and would always change the subject. There didn't seem any point in pushing her, and though Fadin had tried he had gotten nowhere. Tase was superbly curious, but he was resolved to believe that when the time was right Caoimhe would tell them what they needed to know.

Caoimhe backed out of the hug, but Irrah gave her a kiss on the cheek before she could move away. Caoimhe paused and stared at him, her face looking surprised yet sad. "Irrah," she whispered.

He patted her on the arm. "For good fortune, my dear, nothing more." He smiled at her and pulled back.

Tase traded a glance with Fadin. That had been an awkward exchange. "I'm afraid we have no time for proper greetings, the enemy is quickly approaching."

"Agreed," Caoimhe nodded.

Irrah turned to the vessel and shouted.

Several elves disembarked the sea craft, one Tase recognised. It was a particularly beautiful elf with long, thick, auburn hair. Lineth, her name was, if Tase wasn't mistaken. She was tall and thin, and her array of braids added to her already fierce look.

"Load them quickly," Irrah called to the elves.

The ground quaked and Tase nearly lost his footing. Irrah and Caoimhe snapped their heads to the woods.

Tase turned too and saw that the forest was shaking. The leaves of the trees began to vibrate and the ground groaned as if in pain. The natural light of the trees and plants flickered as if it were going out and sharp spiteful laughter rose from the shadows.

Tase took a step back as cold eyes shone from the darkness. Lorcan yelped. "Spriggans!"

Tase saw Ciaran jerk his head to Fadin. "You foolish thing!" the goblin growled.

Tase felt a stab and *knew* Fadin was involved with those creatures. He turned his cerulean eyes on his brother and glared at him.

Fadin acted as if he didn't notice.

"This island is losing its power," Irrah grimaced. "It's going to succumb to those dark creatures. We need to get out of here." He turned to his elves. "Let's go!" he ordered.

The elves moved swiftly, many of them having stained skin of green, purple, or blue, in the shapes of swirls, or intricate designs. They took the horses, leading them onto the ship in a matter of moments.

There was another tremor, this one Tase felt tingle through him. It was more than an earthquake, there was something magical about it.

"We're about to have company," Irrah said, drawing his sword.

There was a sound, like the tearing of a thousand papers at once, and a incredibly powerful jolt from the ground.

Tase jumped and turned himself around.

Fluttering before them, near the woods, were no less than two hundred flying beings in purple armour. Their wings shimmered, their small feet were bare, and in their hands they carried weapons of all sorts.

There was no doubt in Tase's mind, these were fairies.

One of them flew close enough that Tase could see him properly. His face looked young, his eyes were glimmering gold – no pupil in sight – and his cropped hair shone silver. His skin was like that of the Old One, glittering many different colours, and his wings appeared as if they had been dipped in diamonds rather than sugar. His face though, did not hold the look of indifference that the Old One always wore; he appeared sharp and courageous.

"I am Eferthun," he said. "This is my army." He held his hand back to gesture
to the hundreds of other fairies, male and female.

"I am Irrah, Elven Lord of Irial Ath Dara." Irrah bowed to him.

"We are the rightful people of this island," Eferthun said. "We have been gone
a long time, but word has reached us of the attack from the sea and what has been
awoken here. We are here to destroy the enemies of this island and to defend you,
if necessary." He lowered his head to Irrah, but his eyes were on the children.

Tase smiled.

"We are glad for the help," Irrah said.

Mr Hogan seemed rather stiff as he watched the fairy army, and Eferthun
turned his attention to him. "We don't know how you all found your way here,
but as long as you leave now, there is no harm done." His eyes lingered on Uncle

Lorcan, who shifted uncomfortably under his spiteful gaze.

"Greatly appreciated," Mr Hogan said.

A growl erupted from the forest and something black jumped out of the shadows and snatched three fairies from the air.

The flying army shouted and attempted to fight the creature, but the monster was too strong, it dragged them into the woods, their shouts fading.

Eferthun shouted, "Spriggans! They *have* been released, as we feared!" Irrah's face contorted into a look of shock.

Shouts of war resonated from the fairy ranks.

Another dark spriggan dove from the trees, taking five fairy warriors with him. Blasts of magic, swords, and other weapons rained down upon him, but the monster was lightening quick, and he vanished into the trees.

"Go!" Eferthun ordered his troops to prepare for battle. He turned to Irrah.

Irrah gave Eferthun an understanding bow. "Good luck to you."

Eferthun raised his glowing weapon. "To you as well."

"Move out!" Irrah bellowed.

In a matter of moments, everyone and everything had been loaded. Enda, the last one on the sand, was climbing up the ramp when the spriggans fully attacked.

Shouts rose up all along the beach. Fairies chucked glimmering explosives at the monsters, which erupted in clouds of different coloured smoke. The forest trembled and the whole island quaked, jerking the ship.

Enda jumped the last metre of ramp and immediately two elves stomped their booted feet and the ramp pulled itself in.

"Get this ship moving," Irrah boomed. "NOW!"

Tase's heart pounded as the ship jerked backward. He watched the raging battle and wondered how the fairies could win. The spriggans took out at least six of them with every swipe of their black talons.

Elves ran around the ship as Irrah barked orders, moving this, turning that.

The ship began to turn away from the island and Tase ran to the back of the ship, Ciaran at his heels. He watched as the fight carried on.

There was a splash and Tase looked down and saw the mermaid, Avalon, swimming next to the ship. She jumped above the water and crashed back down and dove deep, disappearing.

Tase adjusted his vision outward, to the open waves. It was fairly easy to see the water with the light of the moon, but he saw nothing unusual. The wind whipped through his red hair, making it shine a little in the moonlight and causing him to get a tighter grip on his shirt.

There was a cracking sound. Tase moved his eyes to the island; they were far enough away that he could see the whole thing. It gave a great shudder, the trees swayed, the light of the trees went out.

"What's happening?" Tase asked.

Bäle Rappõs moaned and in a great jolt was yanked down, into the sea. Gasps went up all around the ship.

"It sank!" Aimirgin cried.

A large wave came towards the ship from the place where the island had gone under.

"Brace yourselves," Irrah orderd.

Tase obeyed. The wave hit and everyone held tight as it rocked the ship with great force, sending water surging onto the deck. Tase got a face full of the water and shivered as it penetrated through his clothes.

Tase stood as things became still again, and looked in disbelief at the place where the island that had been their home used to be.

One of the elves suddenly screamed and pointed to the right side of the ship. "There is something in the water!"

Tase looked but saw nothing.

He was hurled forward, and a sound like wood splintering pierced his ears. He, and many others, hit the deck and cries of shock and pain arose around him.

Something had hit and stopped the ship.

Aimirgin jerked forward and grabbed onto Tase. "It came from below," she shrieked.

"Trouble, Tase-thing," Ciaran nodded to him. Tase swallowed hard and looked up.

Irrah was standing not far from him. His lips were thin, his eyes deep and focused. He took a deep breath and yelled, "Everyone to the battle stations. We are getting ready to be attacked."

Tase's breath caught. Attacked? His head began to spin.

The deck became utter chaos, Elves ran back and forth, stopping at certain points on deck. All of them had weapons and some were pulling more weapons from hidden areas on the railing.

The children were herded together and pushed toward the cabin.

"Wait," Caoimhe ordered. "Aednat will go below deck with the baby." She unsheathed her sword and held it out before her, examining the blade. "The others will fight."

Tase's heart leapt into his throat. "Pickled pixies," Ciaran cursed.

Ma turned suddenly, her black curls pinned into a ponytail so her disbelieving eyes could be clearly seen. "What?"

"Get them ready," Irrah commanded. He turned to his crew and began barking orders.

Ma's cerulean blue eyes were filled with horror. "You can't be serious!"

Aldabella ran up next to her, her green eyes just as large. "For Dia's sayke, tay are only children."

"And if we get defeated because we didn't have enough hands to fight, they will get massacred same as the rest of us," Caoimhe said. She turned to a sack on the floor that was filled with their weapons.

Tase began to feel lightheaded.

"This is horrendous," Ma yelped, advancing on her.

Caoimhe snapped herself around and made sure her head was higher than Ma's. "This is war!" she spat. "I have seen enough of them to know what is waiting for us in those waters. Besides, what do you think I have been training them for two years for? Hurling?" Her grey-blue eyes locked onto Ma's. "You've seen war too, Teagan, and you know as well as I they won't be spared if we are overcome."

Ma seemed beyond the ability to speak.

Caoimhe turned from her and moved over to the twins. "Here," she said, handing Tase his bundle.

Tase took it and tried to stop himself from trembling. Caoimhe handed Fadin his own bundle, which he took and began to untie the string. His hands hardly shook, and Tase tried to mimick him.

Clearie was given his golden bow and arrows and Aimirgin her flail and hand wrap.

"Prepare yourselves," Caoimhe said firmly, and busied herself with the other weapons in the bag.

"You will's be all right, things," Ciaran said, looking at Tase.

Tase gaped back at him. "Of course we will." His voice faulterd.

"We's will watch your backs," he nodded to Xemplose.

Fadin let out a sarcastic snort. "No offense, but what can you two do to help us? I don't even see weapons on you."

Xemplose actually grinned. "I suppose it's time to find out if our training worked, huh Ciar?"

Ciaran smiled back. "We's don't need weapons, things."

Tase didn't understand what they meant, but he was too overwhelmed to think about it.

Tase attached his half of Saint Patrick's shield to his arm, and held his part of Brian Boru's sword tight. Remembering who these weapons had belonged to gave him a slight sense of comfort. Besides, Caoimhe was right, what had they been training for?

Caoimhe passed Ma her two long silver knives. Aunt Kyna was handed her wrist blades – that came out from your palm when you squeezed – and her silver arches. She attached the arches to her boots, and as she pressed down with her right foot, a knife burst from it. "In good working order," she said. She put a hand on Teagan's back. "We won't let anything happen to them," she said.

Ma picked her head up, and nodded. She turned to her children and hugged each of them up tight. "Caoimhe trained you well. We'll be fine."

Tase made himself stay calm.

Aedant was ushered below deck with Glendan. Ruepricked was wrapped tightly on her small arm, and Lineth the elf followed, charged to watch over them. Aednat was not pleased.

"It's better this way, Aednat," Tase said to her.

"No, it's not!" she cried. "I want to be with all of you, not useless down in the cabin!"

"You aren't useless," Aimirgin assured her, touching her arm. "You're keeping Glendan safe. That's just as important as fighting."

Aednat snorted and gave Aimirgin an irritated look.

"You'll be all right, Freckles," Fadin said to her as the doors of the cabin began to shut.

She gave him a glowering look, furious to be locked away during the fight. The doors closed, and the last thing Tase saw was Glendan's large, frightened brown eyes.

Tase tried to steady his heart as panic rose inside his chest.

Uncle Lorcan had a knife that served as a sword, Enda had his talons out and exposed, and Mr Hogan held his whip tightly in his fist.

Irrah, standing at the helm, whispered to the bird on his shoulder and the little silver and green sparrow burst into the air and flew out towards the open sea.

Tase could hear his heart drumming in his ears, and his breathing sounded like it was a hundred times louder than normal. He stared at the water, waiting. He had never really fought before, how could he protect himself and those he loved?

*Whap!*

Tase jerked his head to the mahogany railing, and saw a black arrow – which almost looked like the tail of a stingray – and green rope – which appeared to be made of seaweed – embedded in the wood.

The sound of things being hurled in the air resounded all about the ship, and then there were several more *whaps*, as many ropes and hooks dug into the vessels railing.

"They are heres!" Ciaran shouted.

"They're trying to board us!" Irrah yelled. "Cut the ropes! Get them off *my ship.*"

Ciaran dove at one and his sharp black nails sliced through it easily.

Tase lifted his sword high and brought it down with all his force upon the rope. It swung up for a moment, and then vanished over the side.

More arrows hurtled through the air and onto the ship.

One came directly at Tase, and he lifted his shield just in time to block the sharpened sea shell used as an arrow. It bounced of his protection and landed on deck.

There was a blast from a horn that came up from the water.

Tase stuck his head over the side, and watched as the ocean became alive with creatures of sea. The name that came to Tase's mind as he stared at them was sea nymphs. They had flesh coloured skin, for the most part, but along their necks and half of their fingers were stripes of every colour Tase could imagine. All of them had pointed ears and hair that was styled into mohawks. However, as Tase looked closer at their hair – which ranged from every colour on the colour wheel – he thought that perhaps their hair wasn't hair at all, but fins, like those you saw on the tops of many fish.

A particularly large nymph, with brilliant green and purple stripes along his hands and arms, lifted his serrated spear high. He let out a war cry and hundreds of creatures flung arrows tied to seaweed ropes right for the railing.

Tase backed up and cut many of the ropes away. There were just too many. The remaining seaweed ropes became taut and Tase sucked in a terrified breath.

"They're climbing!" he shouted.

"Comes on!" Ciaran screeched. He jumped and in midair, as Tase watched, he burst into yellow. His whole body grew to three times his normal size and when he landed, with a loud thud, Tase saw the tips of his black hair were tinted orange. He turned his head slightly to Tase and he looked furious. His eyes were a blaze of gold, his pupils small and focused.

Tase couldn't deny, he was impressed. "Fire!" Irrah shouted.

Elves shot cannons, slingshots, and spears into the sea.

Tase ripped free one of the hooks embedded into the wood and, with a quick glance over the edge, hurdled it toward a nymph who was climbing with impressive speed up one of the seaweed cords.

He missed!

"Watch out," Enda billowed. He grabbed Tase and jerked him out of the way.

A knife made of sharpened seashell sped through where Tase's head had been, and buried itself into the wood of the mast.

Tase gaped at it, his eyes enormous. "You all right?" Enda barked.

Dazed, Tase nodded.

"Good lad," he said, patting him on the shoulder. "Now fight!" Enda vanished to another side of the ship and a frightening sound caused Tase to jump and look to the right.

"We're being boarded," someone yelped.

With a shock, Tase saw a purple toned nymph dash over the edge. "Don't let them climb over that railing!" Irrah shouted.

*It's a bit late for that!* Tase thought. He turned his sword in his hand and backed up a few steps, trying to prepare himself.

The attack came almost without warning. A serrated boomerang was flung at him and Tase, shocked by his own speed, blocked it. The boomerang ricocheted off his sword and began to swing back to its owner when Ciaran dove through the air and caught it!

In a flash the larger, yellow Ciaran flung the boomerang back at the nymph, who dodged it, allowing enough distraction for Xemplose to attack. The orange goblin had attached his left arm to one of the cannons on deck, and his whole body appeared to be made of the metal. He brought his cannon arm up, and slammed it into the purple nymph who, instead of being squashed or hurt, burst into nothing more than sea foam.

Some of the foam splattered on Tase, who could smell the saltiness of the sea from whence it had come. He tried to recover his shock and made himself move as weapons rained down upon the deck and saw the larger battle raging around him. They were being overrun, far too many seaweed ropes had clung to the wood, and swarms of nymphs poured from them.

WHAP!

Tase cried out as his shoulder was cut. A massive sword came crashing at his face and out of pure instinct from all of his training with Caoimhe, he deflected the blade before it sliced his nose. Another rapier came at his stomach and this time he lifted his shield and thrust forward. His sword missed but he felt the burning tingle of his magic. Without thinking, he cried, "Dhera éist!" He and the nymph were hurtled backwards. He slammed into the cabin doors and his stomach churned as if he would vomit. He had overdone the magic, Caoimhe was always warning them about that.

A nymph with zebra stripes made eye contact and began running at him. The creature was already far too close for comfort and Tase ripped himself upright but there was no time to do anything but raise his shield. Blow after blow hit his defense, and Tase's body in turn was repeatedly beat into the wooden doors. He had to escape; he would be killed if he didn't. The familiar burn of magic burst through him and suddenly, in a cloud of black, Tase saw where he wanted to be, right behind the nymph. And then he *was* there! How he had done it he didn't know, but without overthinking it Tase sunk his blade into the back of the nymph, who crashed to the floor as a splash of foam.

Tase bumped into something. He swung himself around and found himself staring at the edge of a sword. He turned his eyes upon his attacker and let out a relieved breath. It was Fadin.

"For the love of the fairies, Tase," Fadin huffed. He brought his sword down.

"Watch it!" someone called.

Tase and Fadin looked up and saw a sail and wood tumbling down right above them. They moved as quickly as they could and just missed the sail as it hit the floor, sending a massive tremor through the ship.

Tase peered at the remaining sails, and saw many nymphs climbing the wooden masts. They were trying to make the ship unseaworthy.

"Duck," Fadin demanded.

Tase did and he felt the rush of something heavy just miss him. As he stood he saw two enemies coming at them with tridents and, without a word, he knew what to do. He brought his shield up, blocking the first attack, and Fadin slid under his shield and turned the first attacker into froth.

Without pause, Tase spun, his sword making contact with the second trident. Fadin brought his shield in front of Tase as the trident nearly impaled him, and in a quick movement the second nymph splashed onto the wood at Tase's feet.

"We're good together!" Fadin yelped excitedly.

Tase agreed but his mind was on the tide of the battle, and from what he saw before him, they were losing.

There was a low resonating sound, like the blast of a deep horn, which came from the sea. Tase's heart sunk as he saw in the not too distant waves a swarm of new troops swimming at them.

"Reinforcements?" he cried.

"We can't beat the attack we have on us now!" Fadin hissed.

Tase realised this was very possibly the end. He would die here and now, at the age of fourteen, in a battle so ridiculously outnumbered that if it wasn't so terrible it would be comical, because of the sheer amount of over force.

Irrah's little green and silver bird suddenly dove over the railing and landed on one of the masts, chirping frantically.

Understanding flooded Tase's mind. "They're here to help us," he said, relief filling his voice.

The wave of reinforcements were mermaids and mermen, and Tase saw them beginning to shoot at the nymphs before they were close enough for hand to hand combat.

The tide of battle changed quickly. The battle in the water became fierce, and many nymphs hurtled themselves down into the waves, vanishing from sight.

There was a horn blast and the rest of the nymphs fell back. The attacking army retreated.

One lone nymph, with brilliant orange and red colouring, pulled something from his pocket and smiled. He ran right at Tase, who moved just in time to see him pull something off the object in his hand. As soon as he reached the cabin doors an explosion erupted.

Tase was on the floor, his ears ringing. Smoke and ashes were everywhere and the ship had a definite tilt. Voices sounding far away cried out. They were sinking.

As Tase stared at the smoking doors of the cabin something nagged at him. Aednat and Glendan! Tase ran towards the smoke and then quite literally was unable to move. His joints felt thick and numb, his heartbeat quickened, and his body trembled with cold. He was learning to recognise it, the Xoor was close and it debilitated him. He couldn't help them.

"Stay here!" Fadin called, flinging his weapons down, pulling off his jacket and hurtling himself into the smoking cabin.

Tase collapsed to his knees, fighting the shivering. He felt his stomach leap into his chest as his brother vanished into the cloud of smoke.

~~~

Everything was hot and smoke poured into Fadin's lungs. Fire burned on any piece of wood it could find and water spilled in from holes created by the blast the nymph had set off.

Fadin didn't see any movement besides the collapsing of wooden beams. "Aednat!" he called. He coughed and stumbled into the water. The shock of the icy sea after the heat of the air took his breath away and it was a moment before he recovered and made himself trudge forward.

"Aednat!" he called again.

He looked to the right and saw something caught under the water, where stairs had once led downward into other rooms. He acted without considering the pain of the water and dove in. His mind screamed at him to go back to the surface as the freezing water bit at him, but Fadin forced himself to swim. He grabbed the thing caught on a splintered piece of wood and knew it was Ruepricked. Without a logical reason, he *knew* Aednat and Glendan were trapped in the lower decks.

He shoved the unmoving Ruepricked into his trouser pocket and swam through the flooded stairway. He saw a light from somewhere as he left the stairs and, becoming desperate for air, he frantically moved towards it. His body compelled him upward and his face broke free from the water. He gulped in air as he heard the cries of a baby.

"Fadin!" Aednat screeched.

He turned to her and saw she was perched on a desk, Glendan bawling in one arm and the Xoor wrapped tight in the other.

"Where's Lineth?" Fadin asked.

"I lost her when the decks began to flood," Aednat explained. "A nymph made his way in and she told me to run. The water was comin' from everywhere and I knew I had to keep Glendan dry and warm. And I *had* to keep the Xoor away from the nymphs."

Fadin, shivering, gave her a questioning look.

"The mermaid must have given the Xoor to the elves, because Lineth handed it to me."

Fadin nodded, his mind starting to lose concentration from the cold. "S… she can't… t… take care of herself, w… w… we have to go." He reached out for her and the ship gave a horrifying jolt.

Fadin was jerked into the wall and Aednat and Glendan were thrust into the water.

For a terrifying moment the water rose around Fadin and he couldn't tell which way was up. The ship evened out and Fadin kicked his way to the surface. He drug in a breath of air, his head pounding in pain.

Aednat burst up out of the cold, gasping. If Glendan had been crying before, he was wailing like a banshee after the dunk in the icy water.

Fadin turned to the opening he had swam through and felt his heart sink as he saw it was now blocked by debris. "No!" he yelled.

Aednat tried to calm Glendan. "What are we going to do?"

"Fadin-thing!" Ciaran's voice called.

"Ciaran!" Fadin shouted. "W… where are yuh… you?"

"On the others side of this walls. You is stuck! We can'ts gets to you!"

Fadin closed his eyes in frustration. "C… can you muh… move the wreckage

182

that's b… b… blocking us?"

"I will gets Xemplose! He cans helps!"

"Wait!" But Fadin heard a splash. Ciaran was gone. Fadin smacked his fist against the wood. They wouldn't last long in the cold water.

Fadin saw, in the corner of his eye, a fishing pole with the symbol of a dove on it hanging on the wall. He turned his attention to it and recalled, for some strange reason, the fishing pole of the fisherman from his dreams. It was the same one! For whatever reason he remembered the pole distinctly. But, that wasn't possible. Those had only been dreams.

"Fuh… Fadin?" Aednat asked.

*What's the worst that can happen?* Fadin wondered, his teeth chattering together as his body tried to warm up. He went to the fishing pole and yanked it off the wall. The wood caved in where the fishing pole had been, and slunk to one side with a soft *clump*. The hidden door revealed a room that was only now being flooded as the water from their room ran into it.

"C… come on," Fadin said, holding his arms out for Glendan.

Aednat, looking dumfounded, gave him the baby and the two of them entered the room. There was a door to the right and just as Fadin went to it the door erupted open. Ice water crushed them and Fadin frantically tried to protect baby Glendan but there was nothing he could do besides plug his little brother's nose as the water began to drown them.

Fadin tried to open his eyes, but the force of the water twirled him around and he couldn't tell which way to swim. He became frantic as he knew baby Glendan was too little to hold his breath.

A mouth found his and air was breathed in his lungs. Fadin was beyond understanding it but he was grateful.

A hand was placed in his, which he clasped tight.

Another hand grabbed his wrist and before he could wonder what was happening, he was pulled forward. He clung tightly to Glendan, and onto the hand clasping his firmly back.

His head broke the surface and there was air. He clawed at the air, sucking it deep into his chest. He heard baby Glendan coughing and he tapped the baby's back and breathed some air into his mouth to make sure he could take in air on his own.

Aednat let go of Fadin's hand and gasped. He turned to see who had rescued them and saw Aldabella directly before him, only it didn't look so much like Aldabella anymore. She had changed somehow.

As Fadin looked at her blue hair he saw she had glimmering scales like the mermaids' around the sides of her face, on her neck, and shoulders. Her hand had become webbed, and Fadin saw small gills on the sides of her neck, just below her ears.

His mouth dropped open. All of Alassandra's warnings to her daughters about the sea came flooding out of his memory. The sea could claim them if they ever went in it, and here Aldabella was, as much a mermaid as Fadin had ever seen.

"Ah… Aldabella," he said. Sorrow and regret filled his chest as he realised she could never come home, that she would be separated from her family.

She shook her beautiful blue haired head, a single tear falling from her eyes. She pulled a piece of wood that was floating near them closer and Fadin grabbed on, Aednat almost sinking as she swam for it.

Aldabella gave them a small smile and touched her sister's cheek. "It's all right," she said, "help is coming. And I'll be ok, *he* promised me I would be."

"Who?" Fadin asked, bewildered.

She nodded to him, as if he should know. With a pained expression she dove down into the depths, a brilliantly blue tail the last thing he saw of her.

"M… Muh… Ma was right," Aednat whispered next to him. Fadin, wincing at the pain of the water, looked at her.

"Th… the ocean c… called to her," Aednat shivered, her auburn-hazel eyes filled with sorrow. "Sh… she'll never be able t… t.. to return to luh… land."

Fadin could feel a sting in his heart at the thought.

It began to rain and he turned round to see how far from the ship they were. When he did, his stomach rolled. The ship was all but gone. He could see the bottom of it sinking, a few figures bobbed frantically in the frigid water. All hope of rescue faded. What would they do now? Where were the others?

"Oh, nuh, no!" Aednat cried, when she saw the sinking underbelly of the ship.

Baby Glendan was howling in his arms, his body ached all over, and his strength was giving out, even just holding onto the wood. He wondered if he could put baby Glendan on the floating wood, but then he wouldn't have any of Fadin's body heat.

Hopelessness mixed with anger, and Fadin felt as though he may explode of both.

"Things!"

Fadin turned and saw Ciaran and Xemplos paddling to them in a little boat. His heart leapt in relief.

"We are's coming, things! Holds on!" Ciaran called, his body all green again.

"It's g… good to suh… see you, Ciaran!" Fadin called back.

"Popular demands, Fadin-thing."

Fadin chuckled despite himself, and then stared out at the wide sea, now beginning to rumble with waves. Aldabella was gone. Annoying as she had been at times, she had tried to save their lives. She had sacrificed her life for theirs, and now she would never be able to set foot on land again. His heart ached as he watched the ripples she had left disappear into nothingness.

The rain came down harder and Fadin turned to Aednat, who looked as though she could float away at any moment.

"Hold on, Fruh… Freckles," he said, shivering and clutching Glendan close to him. "Just hold on." He watched as Ciaran and Xemplose came closer, not knowing how long he could hold on himself.

# CHAPTER 12
## IMPRISONMENT AND SUPERSTITION

Tase definitely was dreaming. He knew that, because the last thing he had remembered was the deck giving a fantastically terrible jolt and the whole ship turning over. The freezing water was everywhere. That amount of cold, coupled with his body already becoming hypothermic from his proximity to the Xoor, meant that the added chill of the waves had done him in. He had lost consciousness.

Now, standing in a magnificent grape vineyard surrounded by trees with leaves of brilliant orange, ruby, and gold, the sun shining warm upon his skin, Tase wondered if this was a dream... Or had he died in that water?

"No, you're not dead, Tase."

Tase turned, startled.

Sitting on a fallen tree was a familiar looking man. He had tan skin and incredible jewel-like eyes.

The fisherman! Only, he didn't look so much like a fisherman now, this time he looked like... well like a farmer.

Tase glanced down as he noticed the man was stroking something, and with a start he realised the fisherman was petting Pathos!

"Pathos!" he cried.

The Bernese looked up to the fisherman, who nodded. Pathos ran to Tase and knocked him over, smothering him with kisses from his wet tongue.

Tase laughed and gave his faithful old dog a large hug, never wanting to let go of him again.

"He has missed you," the fisherman's warm voice said.

Tase sat up, Pathos staying at his side. "How is he with you? I thought we lost him."

"He was lost, but I found him. Pathos has been with me ever since."

Tase thought about what Fadin had told him, how Pathos and the dove had saved them all from Vladimir. Tase peered down at Pathos, who gave him his best dog smile, his long tongue hanging low. Fadin had also said their dog had spoken.

The fisherman gave a small rumble of laughter. "I must tell you, I was responsible for the talking bit."

Tase looked up at him.

"Your brother needed to know where to go, and he is not good at listening to still small voices. He needed something plain and clear, so I asked Pathos to speak for me. He didn't mind – in fact, he expressed to me that he quite enjoyed it."

Tase raised both eyebrows. "You can talk to him." The fisherman nodded, but didn't elaborate.

Deciding he would get no more information on the subject, Tase decided to move on. "I haven't seen you in a while," he said.

The fisherman smiled. "No, but that doesn't mean I haven't been with you."

That answer confused Tase, but he didn't argue. "Why didn't you warn us about the attack?"

The fisherman smiled and, at that moment, his ever-changing eyes looked distinctly blue. "What makes you think I didn't?"

"Ciaran warned us," Tase stated firmly.

"And who told Ciaran?"

Tase didn't have an answer.

"I won't always speak in the same way, Tase. But I always help those I protect, as long as they want my help." He turned his head slightly and the blue in his eyes was replaced with a cocoa brown. "I came to you, because the storm I warned you about is getting nearer."

"This isn't it?" Tase asked, thinking of the terrible battle at sea.

The fisherman shook his head. "No. This is rather like the hail leading into a tornado."

Tase shivered at the comparison, the thought of the Xoor sending the chill to his bones.

"I had you all hidden, and let you have rest on Bäle Rappõs," the fisherman said. "You needed the calm before the storm, and you," he nodded to Tase, "needed the time to be trained, for the battles ahead."

The word battles made Tase feel nauseated. "I don't know if I can fight again like I did today."

"You can," the fisherman assured him.

Pathos licked Tase's hand and he remembered his blackened fingers when he had first touched the Xoor. Now it felt like he would freeze from the inside out whenever he was around it. How could he fight if his body seemed to shut down whenever the book was close by?

"You will get stronger around the Xoor," the Fisherman said, as if Tase had voiced his concerns out loud. "Give it time, and fight against its voice when you are near it."

"Its voice?" Tase asked.

"You aren't listening for it, so you don't realise it's speaking to you. It whispers to you as it tries to freeze your heart."

Tase stilled as he considered that.

"Tase," the fisherman said, "the enemy is at your door. He wants something you have, only he doesn't know you have it yet, and you don't realise what it is you possess."

"What does that mean?" Tase asked. "What is it?"

The Fisherman stood up as if to leave and Tase moved closer to him, but Tase was no longer in the vineyard. He was lying on the shore, his body frightfully cold, his sword and shield next to him on the sand.

"He's awake," Coimhe's voice said.

"Tase!" Aimirgin cried.

Tase felt her hug before he could see her clearly. "I'm all right," Tase assured her, and sat up.

Caoimhe was there, her face pale, hair disheveled. Aimirgin, Clearie, and Desmond stood near him, all looking worn and wounded.

Tase looked around and saw a village not far from them, but nothing and no one else. "Where are the others?" he asked, trying not to sound panicked.

Caoimhe's face became angry. "After the bomb went off, everything became chaotic. The ship sank and we all were separated. Avalon, the mermaid, helped *us* reach the mainland, but the others…" She pushed her grey streak back from her face. "Some were taken prisoner by the naiads, others were wounded and cared for by the elves, who I believe found a way to get to the Elven Kingdom. I know for a fact that Alassandra was wounded; her and Arden went with Irrah, who promised to take them to his home. As far as I know, Fadin, Aednat, Glendan, and Aldabella went missing before the ship sank."

Tase tried to take all the information in. "I saw Fadin run below deck after the explosion to help Aednat and Glendan. I don't know if he found them."

She put her hand on Tase's shoulder. "We can only hope so." She gave him her hand, and he took it, wincing as she helped lift him to his feet. "The Xoor is missing too, but with any luck, Aednat still has it, and her, the baby, and Fadin are safe."

"What were they after?" Tase asked, knowing worrying about Fadin and the others would do him no good at the moment.

"To be rid of your family, and this." Caoimhe held up a wooden carving of an O with swirls of silver metal and six rubies inlaid in the wood. It looked strangely familiar to him.

"What is it?" Clearie asked.

"One of the six keys," Desmond answered, staring at it. "I spoke with Avalon. She told me the naiads had been entrusted with one of the families' keys many years ago, long before the night when the Six Key Families were wiped out. The naiads became untrustworthy, however, and the merfolk took it upon themselves to remove the key from their possession. When Cashlin Murrin was attacked the naiads tried to take the key back, but Avalon hid it, and the Xoor."

"These keys are what Vladimir has been after," Caoimhe said. "I don't know if he has any yet, but if he doesn't, the way he is going about it, he will soon enough."

Tase's head ached. "So what are we doing here?"

Caoimhe nodded toward the village. "One of the mermaids tracked Saoirse's progress in the sea. She said your sister came on land here, and that the sea creatures who helped her are in the service of Senssirra and Silass."

Tase sucked in an angry breath.

"I know, but there's nothing we can do about it, except go and get her." "We shouldn't waste any time in doing it," Desmond said. "If those snakes knew Saoirse was going to be here, they are bound to be waiting for her." His face was full of worry and he ran a hand through his thick dark hair.

"We can't let them take her," Clearie gasped.

"I have no intention of letting them get her, and I doubt they can capture her that easily." Caoimhe nodded, unsheathing her sword, Mella, and cleaning the blade. The sword almost sounded as if it were singing as Caoimhe stroked it with the burgundy dishtowel. It made Tase think of Ruepricked, and he had to control himself before he imagined the worst.

"Saoirse is unpredictable at best," Tase said. "They'll have a hard time

taking her against her will."

Aimirgin gave a little shiver. "Yeah, let them try and pull her off a wall, if she really gets angry."

Tase recalled when Saoirse had perched herself on Aimirgin's bedroom wall. She had been truly frightening that night.

Caoimhe stiffened.

There was an explosion of tingling all throughout Tase's body. His spine quivered, and his hair stood on end.

Aimirgin gave a little yelp of shock and Tase knew the others had felt it too. "What was that?" Clearie asked.

"Saoirse," Caoimhe said.

"What?" Desmond asked.

Tase rubbed his arms as the feeling subsided. "How did she do that?"

"I imagine she can't control it," Caoimhe sighed, looking toward the village. "She's there, in that town."

"You're sure?" Desmond asked.

She began to nod and then gasped, dropping her sword as she tried to sheathe it.

"What is it?" Tase panicked.

"The Bojins," Caoimhe breathed. "They're coming."

"HERE?" Desmond shouted.

Caoimhe looked at him, her grey-blue eyes wide. "They know she's here. I'm sure of it."

"How do you know it's them?" Tase asked.

"I have a lot more training than you sensing magic, Tase," she said. "It's them."

Aimirgin hugged herself. "We have to get to her."

Caoimhe picked up her sword and secured it in place. "We have no time to lose. Come on. Let's get to that village."

Tase swallowed hard and followed Caoimhe's lead. He watched as the sun rose over the ocean water. What a horrible night it had been, and so far the day wasn't shaping up to be any better.

~~~

Fadin awoke with a start and smacked his head. "Oh!" he hissed, clasping both hands to what was surely to be a nasty bump.

Aednat made a small squeaking sound next to him, but kept on sleeping.

It took him a moment to get his bearings but Fadin remembered Ciaran and Xemplose pulling them from the frigid water, making it to land, and somehow finding the barn they now slept in. He looked around him and saw baby Glendan nestled between Aednat and Ciaran, Xemplose snoring, his large arm wrapped around Ciaran's floppy ear. They were all wrapped in hay and horse blankets, and as Fadin watched his breath escape like a cloud in the air, he was grateful for the warmth. He turned to see what he had hit his head on, and glared at the handle of a wheelbarrow.

He wriggled away from the sleepers, and as he got out realised he was only in his pants. He spotted his trousers, shirt, and boots hanging up along with Aedant and Glendan's clothes. They had been soaking wet when they had stumbled into the barn the night before. He grabbed a stray blanket, wrapped himself up, and quietly walked outside.

The sun was blindingly brilliant and it shone little warmth down upon the rolling emerald hills. Nestled in the hills, near the shoreline, was a quaint village, where it looked as though many people were gathered near one particular building. The building was beautifully designed, Fadin could even tell that from his far away vantage point. It was made of stone, and had a high pointed tower. It made him think of Kavanagh Castle.

He stared out to sea, wondering where the others could be. He felt the anger burning just beneath the surface. How could this happen? They were all alone, with little Glendan, and the Xoor. What were they going to do?

He glanced back at the town. One thing was for sure, he wasn't going to risk going to an orphanage as they almost had the last time they had sought help from non-magic adults. He recalled Travis and Kathryn, the kind shopkeeper and his wife from Sligo. They had helped them the best they could, but their first thought had been calling the Guarda. Fadin looked down at himself, at the bruises on his knuckles from the battle the night before. He was sure there were bruises and cuts on his face as well, and he didn't know how to explain his wounds in a way that would satisfy adults with good intentions but closed minds.

No, he wasn't going to take the risk. He was going to stay as far away from that village as was possible.

He pulled the blanket tighter around himself and went inside to wake the others.

~~~

Tase was hungry and cold as they made their way into the village from the beach.

"We look homeless," Caoimhe commented as they neared the town. She looked them all up and down.

"We were in a battle," Desmond growled. "Of course we do."

"People will ask questions because of the way we look, Des," Aimirgin chided him.

"Indeed, they will." Caoimhe nodded, running a hand over her mouth. She turned her eyes to the village. "Desmond."

"Yes?" he asked.

"Do you still have that leprechaun gold Lorcan gave you?"

"Sure." He pulled out a small blue pouch from his pocket. "It won't do us any good though. You know leprechaun gold disappears as soon as it's in the hands of humans."

"True," she said, "but it may be good enough to get us some proper clothes."

Tase looked down at himself. He was a mess, they all were. "Isn't that cheating?" Aimirgin asked.

Caoimhe made a thoughtful face. "In a way, yes, but we'll find some way to properly repay them. And we'll need some backpacks to put our weapons in. We can't very well walk around with swords."

"Or bows and arrows," Clearie said, pulling his own bow off his back.

"Something to eat wouldn't be terrible either," Tase said, his stomach growling.

"All right, you all will wait for me, and I'll get what we need," Caoimhe said. "Come along, we'll find somewhere for you to hide."

They found an abandoned shack – which was just short of freezing – but Caoimhe took the gold and promised she would be quick.

As they waited Tase pulled the wooden K out of his pocket and twirled it in his hands. As his body shivered he wished desperately to be back at Kavanagh Castle. How nice it would be to take the K and use it to spend a day visiting with Ciaran in the attic. Things had been much simpler then.

He heard far away voices and looked toward the village. "Sounds like a bit of a ruckus," Desmond said.

Tase nodded. He could see from where he stood that many people were gathering in front of a tall building made of stone, with a tall pointed tower.

For some reason, he lifted his eyes past the town and saw a farm situated far off, high upon one of the surrounding green hills. He had a queer feeling that something important was at that farm.

"What do you suppose is going on?" Aimrgin asked, as the sounds from the village became louder.

"Got them!"

Tase jumped back and Aimrigin shrieked.

"For the love of fairies!" Desmond snapped.

Caoimhe smiled. "Sorry to startle you. I've got plenty here for everyone." She had a bag full of clothes, and another full of food. Tase could smell the food as its heat wafted out of the bag.

"Food second, let's get you all dressed. And Desmond," she pulled out a razor, "we need to do something about your hair. You'll frighten people."

He gave a snort. "Not likely."

It was clear from her expression there was no negotiating, so Desmond growled angrily but didn't argue.

"We have to hurry. I don't know what's going on in town but the shopkeeper I purchased from was eager to join the others. He seemed to think a monster had been prowling the beach last night."

"Saoirse?" Tase asked.

"It could be," Caoimhe nodded. "Get dressed quickly, and you can eat on the way." She left the shack and stood guard on the beach.

~~~

"Well, if we don't go into town, how will we get food?" Aednat asked, scratching at her rash through the covering of Ruepricked.

"Don't scratch it," Fadin hissed at her. He worried about it, and about Ruepricked. He hadn't so much as flinched since the battle at sea. After arriving on land Fadin had taken Ruepricked out of his pocket and re-wrapped him around Aednat's arm. He wasn't sure if the dishtowel would wake up, but he couldn't think about that.

"Oh!" Ciaran said, raising his green hand, "I can catches us some nice rats!"

Xemplose nodded. "They are quite tasty. Especially with some sugar sprinkled on top!"

Ciaran giggled delightedly and licked his lips. Aednat grimaced in disgust and gaped at Fadin.

"We'll make due somehow," Fadin said, looking down at his little brother. "But we aren't going into that town. Trust me, no good can come from it."

There was a ringing noise and Ciaran jerked upright. Smoke was billowing from his trousers. "AH!" he yelped.

"What is that, Ciaran?" Fadin asked, propping Glendan higher with both arms as the small boy slept on.

"Notes," Ciaran said. "Froms a friend." He pulled out a small piece of parchment.

"Hey," Fadin said, "that looks a lot like the paper Aimirgin gave us when she wanted to talk to us back at Kavanagh Castle." He recalled when he and Tase had been making the traveling potion to go to the Winter Fair. She had written to them on a piece of parchment just like that one. As he watched, writing appeared beneath Ciaran's fingers in silvery blue ink.

"Yes, the sames parchment," Ciaran agreed. His face contorted into a look of concern.

Aednat's auburn brown eyes widened. "What's wrong?"

Ciaran scribbled something back with one of his long fingernails and stuffed the parchment into a pocket. "The snakes is coming."

"Snakes?" Fadin wondered aloud, and then it hit him. "Senssirra and Silass?"

Ciaran nodded. "They aren'ts far, we musts goes!"

Fadin wondered who Ciaran's informant was, but it didn't matter as much as getting away safely. He didn't want Senssirra and Silass anywhere near them. He wrapped Glenden tightly in one of the blankets and secured his sword and shield to his back. "We'll get as far away from here as we can."

Aednat stood and plopped the Xoor into an old satchel she had found buried in the hay. "What are we goin' to eat?"

"We'll find something on the way," Fadin assured her. He moved swiftly to the exit. As he reached out to open the door it slid open ferociously on its own. Fadin gasped and the light of the day blinded him. Before he could react, Glendan was ripped from his arms and something dark was thrown over his face. He hit the floor hard just as baby Glendan started to cry. He began to struggle, kicking and trying to rip the dark bag from his face, but something hit him over the head. His mind swirled with fury and panic for a brief moment, but the hit to his head served its purpose and he blacked out.

~~~

The crowd in front of what Tase now could see was a church was extremely anxious and frightened. Many people shouted their concerns as one.

"Is she what we have feared, Creedy?" a woman cried.

"She must be!" a large man yelled. "How else do you explain the missing sheep?"

"There isn't sufficient proof she did anything to the sheep," the man who must be Creedy replied. He was standing at the doors of the church, holding the crowd at bay.

"Is that why she's being locked up?" an old woman screeched. "Lack of proof?"

Many other frightened voices shouted out questions as one, sounding like the buzzing of bees.

Caoimhe leaned in to Tase. "Saoirse must have lost control last night. She probably doesn't even remember what she's done. This crowd is too frightened." She shook her head, hair positioned so it covered her pointed ears. "Things could go badly."

Tase felt his heart pound and Aimirgin touched his shoulder. Desmond and Clearie were staying further back, in case things didn't go well. They wouldn't all be seen together, so if an attempt failed Desmond and Clearie wouldn't be recognised.

Tase looked about him, but none of the villagers seemed to notice the strangers in their midst.

The doors to the church opened and another man exited, this one older and balding, with a small half circle of brown hair about his head. He was perhaps fifty, and his eyes were kind, but weary. He held up his hands and the crowd became silent. "I have spoken with the council," the man said. "We agree there is not enough evidence to suspect this girl of taking our missing sheep."

There was a rumble of uproar.

"Except that she's the only stranger to come in last night," a man shouted, "and she was out of her mind this morning!"

"What do you suppose those stains on her clothes were from, Durick?" another voice bellowed.

"She had mud, sand, and seaweed on her clothes," the balding man said. "And she was bleeding from a cut on her head. The red stains on her clothes appear as if they came from that wound."

More shouts.

Tase felt his palms beginning to sweat. Caoimhe took a step forward.

"Enough!" the balding man shouted. Silence fell once more. "We are not just a bunch of superstitious country folk. We are proud rational Irishmen, and we shall behave as such. What we know is that we have a very sick girl on our hands. I am keeping her locked up for her own safety, and the council and I have agreed to discuss this matter in further detail. Until that time, I am *still* chairman of our town council, am I not? I promise the girl will be kept safe until we know more, and no one is to go near her, unless they have my express permission. Is that understood?"

Many heads nodded, and other voices shouted understanding.

"Now, we have all had enough excitement for one day. We should *all* go about our own business." He made a sweeping motion and everyone began to scatter, many talking amongst themselves.

"Come on," Caoimhe said to them.

Aimirgin stayed close to Tase's side as they made their way through the dispersing crowd.

Caoimhe was headed for the balding man but someone beat her to it. A tall man walked up the church steps and began speaking to him.

"Son of a motherless troll," Caoimhe hissed.

Aimirgin tripped and tumbled into Tase who lost his footing. The two of them began to stumble and Tase smacked into a lady standing near them.

"Sorry!" Tase managed as he tried to regain his balance.

The woman turned and Tase nearly fell again as he stared into the face of… Ma.

"Tase!" she yelped. She gathered him in her arms and Tase clutched her back.

"Ma," he sighed, breathing in her familiar scent.

"Oh, Aimirgin!" she cried, and gathered her into the hug as well.

Tase felt the relief wash over him, and for a moment he felt like a child again, safe in his mother's arms.

Ma let go and Tase saw the man speaking to the balding chairmen glance back. It was Mr Hogan!

Tase smiled at him, but Mr Hogan didn't smile back. He was in serious conversation with the chairmen.

"I'm glad to see you're all right," Caoimhe said, putting a hand on Ma's shoulder.

Ma smiled at her and, dropping any formality, flung her arms around the older woman.

Caoimhe let out a surprised chuckle, but hugged her back all the same. "Where's Fadin? Clearie? Glendan?" Ma asked, pulling away.

"Clearie and Desmond are with us," Tase said.

Ma's cerulean eyes filled with concern.

"They're only missing," Caoimhe said softly.

Ma became quite pale but she nodded. "We'll find them," she said firmly. Caoimhe touched her cheek. "We will."

Ma shook her head and looked back to Mr Hogan. "I'm sure you heard. Saoirse's here, and they have her locked inside."

Caoimhe nodded. "I was going to speak to the chairmen, before Lee beat me to it."

Mr Hogan shook the man's hand and came down from the steps.

The chairmen began speaking to the man named Creedy in hushed tones. Mr Hogan walked toward them and Aimirgin, unable to control herself, grabbed her father around the middle, and buried her face in his chest.

Mr Hogan smiled and patted her softly. "Aimirgin, I'm so glad you're safe." He kissed her on the head and opened his arm to give Tase a hug. "I'm afraid we have a bit of a problem." Mr Hogan told Ma and Caoimhe.

"What sort of problem?" Ma asked.

"I spoke with Chairmen Durick, and he is a reasonable man, but these people are extremely superstitious. He told me he doesn't think Saoirse is guilty of taking the sheep, but he insists he can't let her go."

"Why not?" Ma almost cried.

"He said he can't speak about it out in the open, but he offered us a meeting."

"I say we take it," Caoimhe said. "If the man is willing to talk, perhaps he can be reasoned with."

Tase ran a hand through his red hair. What sort of trouble had Saoirse gotten herself into now?

"I agree," Mr Hogan said.

"When does he want to meet us?" Ma asked.

Mr Hogan looked at her, his dark eyes soft. "Teagan, I know you're not going to like this, but I think having you come would be a bad idea."

Ma's eyes turned livid. "I'm her MOTHER!"

Caoimhe put her hand on Ma's arm. "That's exactly the reason it wouldn't be a good idea."

Ma pulled away.

"You can't stay objective," Caoimhe insisted. "You're too emotionally involved."

"Of course I am!" Ma growled.

"Because you're a good mother," Mr Hogan said. "But having you there could put Saoirse in jeopardy."

Ma couldn't have looked more furious.

"Not intentionally," Mr Hogan clarified. "But your emotions could get in the way of us convincing Chairmen Durick to release Saoirse to us."

Ma settled a bit. "I can't let them keep her locked up."

"I know," Caoimhe said. "Trust us, we will do everything in our power to have Durick let her go."

Ma seemed extremely doubtful, but she nodded. "If it's best for Saoirse, then I won't come."

Mr Hogan nodded. "You should stay with the children. We'll try not to take too long."

Aimirgin let go of her da, and Tase stood next to Ma as Mr Hogan and Caoimhe began to head toward the church.

"I sure hope they know what they're doing," Ma said, staring after them and biting her nails.

Tase felt a knot forming in his stomach. He hoped so too. He felt a tug in his heart and turned his eyes once again to the farm on the hill. He could see it a little clearer now, and this time the barn door stood wide open. He had a sinking feeling, but had no idea why.

~~~

Lee Hogan followed Mayor Durick, as he preferred to be called, through the main sanctuary of the church, with its beautiful architecture and stained glass windows, into a little office.

"Durick," he said, offering a hand to Caoimhe.

She took it firmly and gave him a small smile. "Ms O'Keefe," she said, giving her fake surname.

The mayor nodded and sat behind a shabby desk, with wood pieces chipped out here and there. The office was quaint, not done up like the sanctuary. Whatever money the church made, it wasn't going into making the other church rooms more comfortable.

"Please, have a seat," Durick offered.

Lee and Caoimhe sat down. His legs were longer than the average human man, and he had to allow them to sort of drape across the floor instead of being able to sit completely upright, one of the drawbacks of being so tall.

"Please excuse the office," Durick said, "I usually operate out of a building dedicated to village affairs, but we had a fire three days ago, and lost almost everything."

"A fire?" Caoimhe asked, giving Lee a suspicious look.

"Wasn't it raining three days ago?" Lee asked, remembering the storm that had hit the island that had distinctly travelled toward the mainland. Based on the location of this village, he couldn't see the storm missing it.

"Indeed, it was," Durick said, his face looking perplexed. "It happened under rather strange circumstances." He looked up at the two of them, his face appearing older than it had when Lee had meet him outside. "It was the first of quite a number of strange instances," he sighed. "I know you want me to release the girl to you."

"Saoirse," Caoimhe said. "Her name is Saoirse."

The mayor nodded. "I know you want me to release Saoirse to you, but I'm afraid I can't."

"Why ever not?" Lee asked, sitting up a bit in his seat. "You have no proof, as you so clearly pointed out to your townspeople. We have told you she is in our care and we will remove her from this village just as soon as you give her to us."

Mayor Durick looked saddened. "Mr Hogan," he said, "I know this seems unfair, but please trust I am not an unreasonable man. I have no intention of harming or keeping your ward longer than necessary." He paused and seemed to consider his words before continuing. "However, it is necessary for me to keep her until I am certain she is not a threat to my town or my people."

"In what way could she be a threat?" Caoimhe asked him.

"Ms O'Keefe," he said, folding his hands upon his desk, "I think we can all agree that the girl," he cleared his throat, "Saoirse, is troubled, can we not?"

Lee and Caoimhe didn't answer.

"I'm not saying she did anything to the sheep, but the timing is rather remarkable." He ran his hand over his balding head. "There is another reason I cannot simply release her, and this one you may find hard to believe."

Lee exchanged a meaningful glance with Caoimhe. "Try us," he said.

"All right," Durick agreed. He turned around to a burgundy coloured chest that was perched upon an old counter. The chest was the nicest thing in the whole office. He unlocked the clasp and pulled out an aged book. He placed it on the desk and opened it. "This is a history of our village," he said, "passed down many generations. Most of it is perfectly normal, intellectually believable, and intriguing." He turned to a page that had ink drawings of something lingering in the dark. "However, there is an entry or two that are more fantastical."

"Such as?" Caoimhe inquired, leaning forward.

"There is a legend about a creature that attacked this village. There are old accounts, some dating as far back as the 1500's but this one, which took place in the year 1917, is quite clear." He looked down at the book and took a deep breath. "18 October. We had a strange fire that took place during one of the worst rainstorms of the year. We lost five cottages, and in the chaos almost half of the O'Connell's sheep went missing. We don't know if they ran off because of fear or if they were stolen." He moved to another entry. "20 October. Food has been stolen from one of the local shops. We haven't seen any strangers in town for a few days, but there must be some foreigners sneaking about because no one here would dare steal from Tom Dingle. 26 October. Children have been stolen from their beds, we have searched for them everywhere, but we can't find them. There have been three now, we pray there won't be anymore."

Caoimhe looked at Lee. He felt the unease as well.

"28 October," Durick read on, "Twelve children have been taken now. Almost all the sheep in the entire village are gone, and two whole families have vanished without a trace. What is doing this to us? 30 October. It's a monster, I've seen it. It gets power from the moon, that's why it was so strong when it was full. The creature can shift forms, she can appear as a woman and then as a massive animal. She has taken three more families, I don't know how we will survive her. If she isn't stopped, she will consume the whole village." Durick sucked in a breath before reading the last entry. "31 October. The creature is vanquished, several of the remaining men and I hunted it down and slayed it. With the moon no longer at its peak she didn't have the same strength. It was a fierce battle, and five good men didn't come back, but their sacrifice will not be forgotten. The town is safe for now. We buried the monster, deep enough that no one will find her. I can only pray a creature like this will never return." Mayor Durick closed the book and looked up at them both.

Lee shifted uncomfortably in his chair. The fire, the missing sheep, they were events that had taken place in the village over the last few days and definite similarities could be drawn between them and the legend from the town's history. If Mayor Durick felt they were tied together, he would certainly worry things could escalate, and Saoirse, a stranger who appeared when a number of sheep went missing, was a prime target.

"It was an interesting story," Caoimhe said. "But I hardly see how this pertains to Saoirse. You're telling me that a fire and a few sheep gone astray is enough reason to hold a sick girl?"

Durick didn't answer. Instead he pulled something from a pouch attached to the book. He held it up before him and Lee widened his dark eyes. "This is the claw of the monster from 1917. It was found embedded in wood attached to stained torn cloth. The man who found it discovered it in one of the missing families' homes." It was about the size of a bear claw, except it was gnarled, twisted as if there were two claws not one. At the base it sparkled dully as if lined with old precious stones, and its tip almost looked dipped in silver. "And this," Durick continued, "was found in the field where the sheep went missing." He pulled from his pocket a bone coloured spike with a silver tip. It *could* have been a stone or a piece of jewelry, but it did appear very similar to the old claw.

"You found this?" Lee asked.

Durick nodded. "Not far from where your Saoirse was found." Lee stiffened.

"I know it sounds like a load of irrational nonsense, but I'm afraid you've come across a mayor who has seen a thing or two he couldn't explain in his day." He folded his hands on the desk. "I err on the side of caution, and though I do believe you have only good intentions with Saoirse I cannot not allow her to leave until the next full moon has passed."

"The next full moon?" Lee asked, exasperated.

"The full moon just passed," Caoimhe said, "surely —"

Mayor Durick held his hand up. "There's no good talking about it, my mind is made up. I will keep an eye on the girl, and if after the next full moon she remains unchanged, then you are all free to go." He stood to indicate the meeting was over. Lee and Caomhie followed suit. "She will be well cared for. Upon request I can let you see her, but it will be a supervised visit of course."

Caoimhe gave him a mock smile. "Of course."

He sensed her sarcasm. "You are welcome to go to the Guarda, if you think my decision unfair, but I'm afraid you'll find the Guarda around this town have heard of the legend too."

Lee forced himself to hold out his hand. "Thank you for your time," he said, as the mayor took his hand and shook it.

"If you need anything during your stay, come see me. I'll be here."

"Just one more thing," Caoimhe said.

"Yes?"

"Where is Saoirse being held?"

"Here, in the church, to ensure her safety." Durick informed them.

Caoimhe nodded, "Thank you, Mayor." She turned to leave and Lee followed her lead.

As they walked out Caoimhe leaned in to him. "We are in more trouble than we thought," she whispered.

Lee thought about the meeting and all the bad news. "In which particular way are you referring?" He arched a black eyebrow at her.

"That was no half werewolf claw," she said.

Lee grabbed her arm. "What are you saying?"

"I know what Saoirse is," she said, "and it's far more dangerous than we thought." She ran a hand through her copper hair. "Come on."

They continued though the sanctuary and out the door and Lee's heart raced. He had no idea what Caoimhe meant.

Teagan was waiting not far from the church. She saw them exit and all but ran to them. "Well?" Her cerulean eyes were wide.

"We need a way to get Saoirse out of there," Caoimhe said, "because she isn't going to make it until the next full moon."

~~~

Tase and Aimirgin waited silently. He held tight to the rope before him and took a deep breath.

Caoimhe walked into view below them. The town was having a meeting in one of the local stores. It was loud enough that they could hear muffled voices in the street. Caoimhe looked up and made eye contact with Tase.

He nodded to her and Caoimhe ran toward the town meeting and burst through the doors.

Gasps arose.

"Help! Please you have to help!" Caoimhe called. "There's something strange prowling the streets and it attacked my companion."

"What was it?" a man cried.

"Where is it?" another asked.

"It's right outside, please," Tase could see her plead with someone who was at the front of the meeting. "Mayor, you said if we needed anything to come see you." There was no answer. "We believe your stories, just please, help me!"

"All right," the mayor said, his voice sounding shaky. "Any volunteers to help me catch whatever is skulking about our town?"

Many male voices rose in volunteer.

Caoimhe lead the way and Tase readied himself. He looked back at Aimirgin. She looked terrified but she gave him a nod and a smile.

Caoimhe was pointing down the alley where Tase and Aimirgin were perched on the roof.

A group of men began to walk toward it.

"Help!" Mr Hogan called from below, and Tase saw him lying in his position near the back of the dark alley.

"I see him!" one of the men called, and the whole group, excluding Mayor Durick, Caoimhe, and two others went into the alley.

Aimirgin lifted the seashell to her lips, leaned over the edge, and blew into it. The sound that erupted was like a wail. If Tase hadn't known what it was, he would have been petrified.

The men staggered, unsure what to do. "What was that?" one cried.

Aimirgin blew into her horn again and Caoimhe caught Tase's eye.

Tase nodded and yanked on his rope. Blue powder tumbled down between Mr Hogan and the men. Tase watched from his vantage point as Mr Hogan outstretched his arm. The blue powder lit and the flames that erupted were five times higher than a normal fire.

The men jumped back and yelled in shock. That's when Ma jumped just in front of the flames, snarling.

She looked enough like Saoirse to be confused with her and no one but the mayor and Mr Creedy had paid any attention to her. The men cried out in terror.

"What?" Mayor Durick yelped, clearly only thinking of Saoirse. "How did she get out? She's under lock and key!"

Caoimhe, not being watched, pulled out her own pouch of blue dust. She flung it in a semicircle on the ground and lit it.

Screams of terror erupted all around, and other townspeople flooded from the town meeting. Others ran out of their homes, fright and curiosity driving them to see what was going on.

Tase smiled. It was working.

~~~

Clearie swallowed hard. "You sure this will work?" he asked Desmond.

"It has to," Desmond smiled. He looked much younger with his cropped hair and shaved face, hardly older than Quinlan. He patted Clearie on the back. "You have the potion my da gave you?"

Clearie nodded. "Yea, but Des, he is sure this actually does what it's supposed to do? Last time I heard Arden talking about it, it sounded as if he were still testing its reliability." His mind kept bringing up the memory of being stuck inside the Aislinn's walls in Cavan-Corr. That potion Arden had made was supposed to let you walk through walls, but they had fallen through the floor. He suppressed a shudder, trying not to think about what would happen if this potion didn't work.

"It's our one shot, Clearie." He looked him square in the eyes. "You ready?"

Clearie took a deep breath. "Yeah, I think so."

Desmond shook his tense body loose for a moment. "Wish me luck," he said, then burled through the doors of the church.

Clearie heard the howl and the cries of fright from the three men guarding Saoirse. He made sure he was well away from the door.

Desmond the wolf crashed out of the church and a gun blast tore through the wood of one of the doors.

Clearie jumped and watched as Desmond ran on all fours down a dark street. Two men ran after him, shouting angrily, the one with the gun letting off another shot.

"One left," Clearie whispered to himself. He grabbed the dishtowel tight.

There was an explosion from somewhere else. Clearie was startled but saw the blue light of the flames bouncing off the buildings not far from him. *Tase*, he thought.

The last man peeked his head around the corner, looking off in the direction of the huge fire.

Clearie jumped on him and tried to get the dishtowel over his mouth and nose.

The man was stronger than Clearie had guessed, but he managed to clamp the towel over his face. The man slammed Clearie into one wall, and another.

Clearie cried out, but did not let go.

The man staggered and after one more attempt at crushing Clearie against a wood door, he swayed and collapsed to his knees, then fell face first onto the floor.

Clearie got up and clutched at his ribs. He wasn't sure how much damage was done, but he couldn't wait to find out. He ran through the sanctuary and opened every door he saw. Each one lead to nothing, until he found a hall of six doors. He tried them one by one and felt the mounting stress as he realised this was taking too long.

He opened the third to last door and saw Saoirse locked behind a crudely made cage.

"Saoirse!" he cried.

"Clearie!" she yelled, her face contorted in fear. "Watch out!"

Someone grabbed Clearie from behind. "I don't think so!"

Clearie yelped as he was lifted off his feet. A tall man had him by the collar of his shirt. He was large and much too strong for Clearie, but he tried to fight anyway.

It did little good. The man jerked him across the room and with a set of keys unlocked the door holding Saoirse and threw him in.

"Good luck getting out of here," the man snarled. Before Clearie could rush him and try and get out the door the man locked them in.

Clearie cursed and slammed his hand against the bars.

"You came for me!" Saoirse cried. "Oh, Clearie, I'm so sorry for what I did to you! I didn't mean it. I —"

Clearie turned to her, put a finger to his lips and whispered, "I know, Saoirse, I know it wasn't really you." He smiled at her.

The big man lifted a gun which was leaning against a wall, glared back at them for a moment and then went into the hallway.

"Saoirse, we don't have much time," Clearie said, surveying the room and spotting what Mr Hogan and Desmond had confirmed would be there. A crack in the floor and wall, which led outside.

"What are we going to do?" Saoirse asked, watching cautiously for the guard.

He let out a breath and pulled the green and gold liquid from his pocket. "We're going to escape."

"What is that?"

"A potion Mr Aislinn had been working on while we were on the island." Clearie uncorked it and felt his stomach do summersaults.

Saoirse's green eyes became wide. "The liquid one?" Clearie looked at her and nodded.

She stared at the bottle warily. "If this doesn't work…"

"What other choice do we have?" Clearie asked. Saoirse didn't have an answer.

Clearie took out another bottle. "What's that one?"

Clearie gave her a doubtful smile. "The antidote." He spilled it through the crack. "I hope," he said, under his breath. "No one can give it to us, so we are going to have to land in it."

Saoirse turned pale.

He held the bottle out to her. "You first." She took it shakily.

"One swallow each," he informed her. "Make sure you're standing close to the crack in the floor."

She moved closer to the small opening, took a deep breath, and brought the potion to her lips. She took a gulp.

Clearie did the same and shivered at the bitter taste.

"Oh!" Saoirse cried.

Clearie turned to her and tried not to gasp as he watched her hand begin to drip to the floor in a pale puddle. "Oh," he gasped.

Saoirse let out a small scream and in a wink erupted into liquid that splattered to the floor.

Clearie covered his mouth.

The puddle of Saoirse began to leak out the crack in the floor and Clearie had a moment to be thankful for the slant of the tile before he felt his fingers prickle. He looked down at his hand and yelped. His whole hand began to ache and he watched it drip to the floor. The sight of his hand melting away was more shocking than he had anticipated, and as he watched his body drip to the tile he had a horrifying realisation. He was going to mix with Saoirse's puddle, why hadn't he thought of that before? Why hadn't he asked the question? What if they couldn't be separated?

The guard slammed into the bars and Clearie yelped. "Where is the girl?" he demanded. He began to fumble with the keys when he spotted Cleaire's dripping hand. He jerked away from the door, eyes wide, a strangled sound escaping his lips.

Clearie tried to turn around but his whole body suddenly felt like jelly and, with a spike of pain, he burst into liquid. It was the queerest feeling, being the liquid goop. He felt his body slide along the floor, and he felt himself touch Saoirse, almost like touching her hand. He had some thought but not as much as normal, and the only thing that consumed his mind as he tumbled out the crack was that he hoped all of him made it.

He splattered on the other potion and on top of Saoirse. He felt them mix together and had a feeling of panic as he wondered if they would ever find a way to separate.

The other potion sent a shock through him, and if he had a mouth he would have screamed. There was another shock, and then another. He felt his feet form, then his hands, his eyes, he could see properly again. After a moment he felt his whole body slide into place and he pulled himself up. He touched his hands, face, and torso. It looked like he was all in one piece. "Saoirse?" he asked, turning.

She was there, looking just as Saoirse should. She looked at him and gave a frightened laugh. "For a moment I thought we would be stuck together."

Clearie chuckled and put a hand to his face too. "So did I."

"Move it!"

Clearie turned and saw Mr Hogan and Tase running toward them. Mr Hogan's long legs propelled him forward and Tase strained to keep up.

Clearie watched as Desmond rounded another corner and heard angry voices close behind. "Oh!" he managed, and grabbed Saoirse's wrist. She didn't need explaining, she ran with him.

Ma, Caoimhe, and Aimirgin came through a different alley and almost collided with Clearie and Saoirse.

"Ah," Caoimhe said, running next to them, "the potion worked." Clearie tried not to think about if it hadn't.

Ma grabbed Saoirse's hand and they all tore out of the town. They ran to a tree Caoimhe had picked out, and Clearie spotted the string she had tied to a low branch.

They reached it and Clearie looked back to see a mob of the townspeople not far behind. "Caoimhe!" he cried.

"Everyone hold onto each other," she ordered. Clearie grasped Tase's arm and Aimirgin hand.

Caoimhe pulled the string and the world flipped. It felt as though he had been turned into jam and then sucked through a straw, traveling at an incredible velocity. *WACK!* They all tumbled to the ground, hitting it harder than Clearie thought necessary. He looked about and saw they were in the forest that lay not far from the village, intact and safe.

He grinned for a moment, but the familiar sensation of his stomach turning to jelly whenever he traveled by magic overtook him, and he hardly crawled a few centimeters away before he wretched. He spat the last bit of foul taste from his mouth and his stomach settled. He sat upright and, with a feeling of utter relief at seeing them all sitting there, let out a laugh.

The laughter was catching, as the relief tumbled through them all. Ma grabbed Saoirse in a hug, which she returned wholeheartedly. Though she didn't laugh, even Caoimhe couldn't keep from smiling.

Tase flopped back on the grass, his hand on his forehead. "We did it!" he laughed in a hiccup like way. "We actually did it."

Aimirgin rested her head on her da's arm.

Clearie thought about the terrible liquefying potion and shuddered in amazement of their success. "I honestly can't believe that worked."

Mr Hogan let out an incredulous sigh and ruffled Clearie's blond hair. "Nor can I."

Clearie jerked his head in the direction of the strange voice and felt his stomach drop.

Vladimir smiled down at them, his pale teeth gleaming. To his right stood the terribly breathtaking Dominique, her appearance this night more wild and frightening than lovely. On the Bojins left, Senssirra and Silass slithered, the look of pure pleasure unmistakable on their faces.

Clearie's breath caught, and terror bit into all his senses. He didn't know if this time they would make it out alive.

# CHAPTER 13
## STICKY WICKET

Fadin awoke with a start but he knew it was a hallucination the moment his blue-green eyes opened. He was standing on a rocky path in a valley, with massive mountains before him. As he turned around many landmarks of his life marked the road behind, such as a few trees from the fairy forest, the van he had escaped in when being chased by the Cavan-Corr guards, and even his old home which rested far down the road. There were places in the path he had travelled where dark clouds loomed overhead, where bogs oozed over the trail, and where large holes waited. There was a particularly massive hole that was in the path right before Kavanagh Castle. As he again turned forward, he took in the mountain's vibrant emerald colour, which at first was all he could see, but as he looked harder he saw the sheer drops and incredibly sharp rocks protruding from the only path up them.

Even though he knew it wasn't real, that somewhere he was unconscious with a sack over his head, he felt the hopelessness of the climb seep through him. He looked back at the long way he had come and sucked in a sharp breath as his feet suddenly stung with pain. He glanced down at his feet and saw they were bare and bloody. At some point on the path he must have lost his shoes.

His eyes were drawn to a pond, not far from the trail, with beautiful clear water glittering in it to the brim. Somewhere in his mind he knew he should try and wake up, but the pain of his feet was vivid and sharp, so he limped over to the pool.

He intended to put his feet in the cool water, hoping that would bring some relief to the pain. As he got up to the pond and looked down, he winced at his appearance. Dark bruises lined his right cheek and temple and he had a cut on his forehead.

An unnatural shadow moved swiftly along the ponds edge, directly toward him. Fadin felt himself shiver in response to it, and as the shadow shot behind him he ripped himself around, sure he would be confronted with a monster. Nothing was there, only the valley with the soft sounds of birds chattering to one another.

He turned back to the water and saw himself and someone else. He yelped in shock and stumbled backwards. Turning, he again found that no one was there. He got closer and peered into the glassy surface and saw the other reflection was still there. It was his father.

Seeing him made Fadin feel an ache he had forgotten he had. His heart yearned with loss, and he wished, more than anything, that Da could truly be standing beside him. A flood of memories of the past few years replayed in his head. He imagined what those memories would be if Da had been there. He and Ma could have explained everything to them, it wouldn't have been because he and Tase had found out on their own. They would have just gone to Kavanagh Castle for a visit, Mr Hogan would have come to see Da and they could have talked about old memories. Da would have been there for Glendan, Da would have taught them to fight, could have told them about his childhood, he would know what was the right thing to do. Things would have been *very* different.

The pain so overpowered him that Fadin fell to his knees. He had never felt so lost in all his life, and the gigantic hole Da had left had never before been so sharp. A tear fell down his cheek. Fadin touched it and felt the anger burn against himself. He was crying? He couldn't allow himself to be that weak.

He stood up and stared defiantly at his father's reflection. He picked up a stone and rolled it in his hands. "Where are you when I need you?" he cried. He suddenly felt mad at Da for leaving him, as irrational as that was. Da had left when Fadin had needed him most, and he was angry with him for it.

He hurtled the rock at the image of his father. The splash was magnificent, and as the water cleared Fadin saw that Da was gone. Somehow that made the hole in his stomach even larger and the tears came despite his abhorrence for them. He hadn't really wanted Da gone, he was just angry, he was *so* angry. He glanced back through his tears to see how his reflection looked, and sucked in a breath.

It was no longer his father, but this time it was the face of the fisherman. "Fadin," the kind rumbling voice came from behind him.

Fadin whirled round and saw the fisherman standing behind him, his clothing different this time, more designed for working in a field than for catching fish.

"You!" Fadin cried.

The fisherman didn't smile. "You are full of rage."

Fadin felt the fury bubbling again and tried to wipe away his tears. "Why am I here?"

The fisherman held his hands out to the road and to the mountains. "You see the road?"

Fadin nodded. "Yes, what about it?"

"It's the one you've travelled," the fisherman said, and as he said it Fadin knew it was true. When he knew the truth, the pain of his father's loss became even sharper, though Fadin didn't know why. In order to try and avoid the aching, he pointed at the mountain. "Will I be doing some hiking in the near future?"

The fisherman smiled at him. "Not all the mountains you will have to climb in your life are made of grass and stone."

Fadin let out a frustrated sigh as the thought of that made him wish Da were there all the more. He plopped himself on the grass and examined his bleeding feet.

The fisherman sat down in front of him. He put a hand on one of Fadin's feet, but there was no pain as he touched it.

Fadin looked up at him, into the eyes that shifted colour so effortlessly. They shimmered green and with a change of the light became grey. "What do you want from me?"

"Only to help you." His eyes were so kind, and though Fadin wanted to deny the goodness in them, he couldn't. "You are *so* angry, and that anger is eating at you, taking more and more of you each day."

Fadin closed his eyes. His head ached.

The fisherman put his hand under Fadin's chin and made him look up. It was hard to feel cross looking into those eyes. "It's all right that you are upset with your father for leaving you, but at some point, Fadin, you are going to have to start forgiving him."

Fadin took a shuddering breath. "How can I? When things keep getting worse and worse? We are here trying to pick up the pieces of what broke when he left us." Pain began to trickle through the cracks, even though he had tried to stop it, and tears formed again.

The fisherman was still for a moment. When he spoke, his voice was soft and kind. "He didn't want to leave you."

The pain became more powerful than he could control and Fadin felt his feet heal under the fisherman's touch. "Why are you showing me all this?" he asked.

"So you can begin to heal, Fadin."

"I just want him back," Fadin said as the tears fell freely. "I hate this path." He stared back down the way he had come. "I don't want to face that!" He pointed to the mountain. "I know I can climb it if I have to," he gritted his teeth, "but I'm sick of climbing."

The fisherman took both of Fadin's hands in his. "I know."

Fadin let out a groan. "Don't I get a choice?"

The fisherman gave him a sad smile. "You always have a choice. But if you don't climb the mountain, how will you ever know what's waiting for you at the top?"

Fadin thought that often things didn't feel like his choice.

The fisherman stood and turned to the open valley. He whistled and Fadin heard a bark.

He gazed at the long grass and saw a dog running right for him. The dog was large and had black, brown, and white markings. "Pathos?" he cried.

The Burmese knocked him to the ground and licked him generously. Fadin laughed and he heard the fisherman's rumbling chuckle.

Pathos got off him and when Fadin looked up the fisherman held out his hand. "Your father is in you, Fadin. You need to begin the process of forgiving him, and forgiving yourself. You couldn't have saved him, it was out of your hands, and it is okay to be mad at him. The time has come, though, to begin letting go."

Fadin felt the pang of the truth in his words, but he wasn't sure if he *could* let the anger go. He took the fisherman's hand and was pulled to his feet.

Fadin opened his eyes and found he was not in a valley, but was instead staring up at a ceiling that had been painted like the night sky, complete with sparkling stars that actually glowed.

Where was he?

"You okay, thing?"

Fadin sat up and found he had been sleeping in a fluffy bed stacked with fur and feather stuffed blankets. He focused his eyes and saw Ciaran leaning in close to his face.

"Ciaran," he breathed, "what happened?"

Ciaran smiled his stained teeth smile. "He's okay!"

Fadin looked about and saw he was in a queer sort of house. The walls were made partly of stone and party of wood, as was the floor, and in some places the stone of the walls curved out and in, almost like the curl of a huge wave. There was a rock fireplace that had a bookcase in the shape of a spiral over it, and hung here and there on the walls were beautiful wings that could have belonged to gigantic butterflies. The lighting in the house was made from several white sheets covered in small fairy lights, which hung from floor to ceiling, and other small hanging lanterns that were shaped like stars and moons.

Though the ceiling wasn't too high, there was a ladder which led to a short bridge of rope and wood that encircled the entire space, and along that bridge were shelves filled with books, food, drinks, bottles, and dishes. There was another ladder that lead up from the bridge, and it lead to a hole in the fake sky ceiling which was covered by leaves from a narrow tree that grew right inside the house.

"Glad you're all right, human!" Fadin turned and saw Xemplose next to Ciaran. He was smiling just as wide, but his teeth shone pearly white against his shocking orange skin.

Another goblin peered at him from near the fireplace, which was spitting out crackles as it consumed the burning log. This one was a girl, with brilliant blue skin and twinkling amethyst eyes. Her hair, which hung in a twisted braid over her shoulder, was stark white and was so long it almost touched her knees. Fadin had no idea how to judge beauty by goblins standards, but she did have a sort of prettiness about her.

"Who are you?" Fadin asked.

"Fadin-thing," Ciaran's voice said, "this is our friends, Rinnerwood."

"Rin," she corrected, in a pleasant voice. She gave him a small closed mouth smile.

"Hello," Fadin managed. He touched his aching head.

Ciaran added. "She has takesen us ins while we waits for help."

"Help?" Fadin asked, while the memories of being kidnapped replayed in his head. "Where are Aednat and Glendan?" He made to get up and found his bed was surprisingly close to the ground, so close it appeared as though the bed were no more than a mattress lain upon the floor.

"They are fine, thing," Ciaran assured him.

He spotted Glendan before his panic could rise. His small brother was playing with a small stuffed pegasus that was actually flying around his curly red head, and a toy troll that waddled around on its own. He looked up at Fadin and giggled, his single dimple standing out on his cheek. Fadin smiled back.

He spotted Aednat curled up on another bed, this one actually carved into the wall, only large enough for the mattress to fit in, and a person if they weren't too tall. Aednat was sleeping soundly but she had a large bandage on her arm, which was directly over where the rash had appeared on her skin.

"Is she all right?" Fadin asked.

The blue goblin nodded, not seeming concerned at all. She walked over to three jars, which hung on the wall. All of them were steaming, and each one was a primary colour. She flicked the bottom of the blue one and a bubble bounced out. She took a little cup from the shelf next to them and the bubble popped in the glass. "Drink this," she said, holding the cup out to him.

Fadin took the cup and saw steaming blue liquid inside. It smelt like some sort of tea, and he took a sip. His head began to ache less.

He looked at Aednat again and noticed she was quite pale. "That rash on her arm, does it make her sick?"

Ciaran nodded. "Yes, geartús gets very sicks when their mark gets close tos formsing."

Rin stood closer so she could see Aednat. "It takes a lot of energy. Her magic is choosing the shape, and she will be weak until the process is done."

"How long does it take?" Fadin wondered.

"It depends," Rin said.

"I hope it doesn't take too long," he sighed. He took another sip of the blue tea and eyed Rin. "Who put a bag over my head?"

She gave him a wry smile. "I didn't expect anyone to be so close to the door, you surprised me." Her voice was full of humor. "I'm afraid I overreacted."

Fadin touched his head where it had been hit. "I would say so." He blinked, remembering further. "What happened with Senssirra and Silass? Did they come?" He turned around in a circle. "Where's the Xoor?"

The goblin's all exchanged glances. Fadin eyed them suspiciously.

"The book is safe," a deep voice said from above.

Fadin looked and saw a man climbing down from the hole in the ceiling.

"The snakes are another matter." The man's feet found the bridge but he didn't turn enough for Fadin to clearly see him. He continued down the second ladder. "They made their way just north of the village." He stepped off the ladder and turned. "And I'm afraid your family has found not only them, but Vladimir as well."

Fadin's mouth hung open. "Robert?" he cried.

The older man nodded to him, looking cleaner and more youthful than last Fadin had seen him.

Fadin wanted to ask him many questions but the most important one found its way to his lips. "Vladimir has found my family?" His heart pounded at the thought.

Robert grabbed a small staff from a shelf on the wall and examined it. "Indeed, and I'm afraid they are in desperate need of help."

~~~

Tase felt the dagger of fear tear from his chest into his gut. The man standing before him didn't physically look like much, he wasn't tall, perhaps 1.7 metres, and he was old, his face lined with wrinkles, cheekbones prominent and underlined with shadow. But the presence he carried about him was one of absolute power, as if he could squash you as easily as he could an ant, and, looking into his hooded owl-like green eyes, Tase believed he could.

Vladimir laughed heartily, his mirth sounding smoky and bubbling deeply in his chest. "What a group of shysters you are, huh?" His gleaming teeth shone against his salt and peppered beard. He pointed his finger at the town. "Tricked those saps good, didn't ya?" He whipped his hand in a circular motion and a prickling sensation filled the air.

Tase jumped as barbed wire suddenly appeared and wrapped itself round and round several trees as if it were a turbo-charged snake. It stopped winding itself around the trees and Tase saw they were surrounded by the sharp spiked metal. It had made a circle of sorts, trapping them all inside, from the ground to a metre over Mr Hogan's head. Tase shivered in fear.

There was a rumble in the earth and Tase felt as though the very ground beneath his feet had come alive. He stumbled and fell, directly onto Aimirgin, who had already stumbled into the grass. There was a great sound, like an avalanche, and as Tase gaped he watched part of the earth behind Vladimir rise like a small mountain. From the crumbling dirt mound, a massive, weasel-like animal crawled. It was coloured brown with bits of grass and roots stuck in its hide. Its cruel silver eyes cut terror into Tase's heart like a nail driven into wood. He knew the creature, the same kind he had seen at Kavangh Castle all that time ago in the woods, when Dominique and the wolf had nearly captured him and Clearie.

"They have a lithian!" Aimirgin cried.

Tase swallowed as the animal growled and paced slowly behind Vladimir.

Vladimir smiled wide and looked directly at Saoirse. He waved to her. "Hi darlin', miss me?"

Ma growled furiously. "You MONSTER!" She lunged at him.

"Teagan, no!" Mr Hogan yelled. He caught her merely centimetres before she reached Vladimir.

The lithian snapped its jaws.

Tase's heart pounded. He couldn't have imagined what would have happened had she actually touched him.

Vladimir laughed in delight and clapped his hands together. "Oh, did I make the mama bear angry?" he asked.

Ma, her cerulean eyes wide with fury, spat at him, but missed. "You will stay away from *my daughter*!" she seethed. Mr Hogan, though much larger than Ma, was having a hard time keeping her held back. "You will not touch *any* of my children! Do you hear me?"

If Tase had been eating a bucket full of candy, curled up in the most comfortable blanket, on a fluffy couch, watching his favorite movie, laughing and joking with Fadin, Aimirgin, Aednat, and Clearie, he doubted that he would be enjoying himself half as much as Vladimir was at the current moment.

Vladimir's lined face was lit up, and his eyes shone with delight. "The stories of your ferocity pale in comparison with the real thing, Teagan, my dear," he chuckled, gesturing to her. "And as much as I admire your spirit, I'm afraid there's really nothing you can do to stop me from doing whatever I wish to your lovely children."

Mr Hogan crossed both arms around her to stop her from lunging at Vladimir's throat.

As he looked at him chuckling, Tase began to feel cold, his heartbeat pounding in his ears. He didn't understand, to his knowledge the Xoor wasn't close, but he was beginning to feel the effects of it all the same.

Vladimir saw Tase and beamed in his direction. "Tase my boy, how very good to see you." He winked at him. "Up and about this time, huh?" He tilted his head ever so slightly. "Feeling all right?"

Tase tried to suppress the shivers that were beginning.

"Why don't you just get to the point and stop playing games?" Caoimhe said.

"Ah," Vladimir said, holding both arms out to her. "The elf princess." Caoimhe's eyes were icy cold.

"Don't look like much of a princess now though, do you?" He raised both eyebrows. "You want me to cut to the chase? Not much fun that way."

Caoimhe said nothing.

"All right then." He smiled at her, looking as charming as a summer's day. He walked closer to her and held out his palm. "Hand it over, Milady."

Caoimhe looked as stiff as stone.

Ma and Mr Hogan looked at her questioningly. "Hand what over?" Ma asked.

"Come on," Vladimir said in an almost playful manner, wiggling his fingers. He inclined his silvering head to Tase and Clearie. "I can get you some incentive, if you want it."

Tase cried out as someone grabbed his hair. He heard the hissing in his ear, and looked up into the ruby eyes of Senssirra, who flicked a small blue tongue out at him. She yanked him closer to her and he winced. The end of her tail wrapped around his ankle and she used her other hand to place something cold at his throat.

Aimirgin let out a squeal and Tase heard Ma screech, "No!"

Vladimir inclined his head to her. "I know what you have. I *could* remove any obstacles in my way to get it," he said matter-of-factly, and Senssirra moved the cold thing higher up toward Tase's jaw, "but I would rather not see untapped potential go to waste." He held his hand out further. "I'm afraid you find yourself in what the humans call, a sticky wicket."

Caoimhe made her lips into a thin line and her frigid eyes burrowed into Vladimir's, but she did not test him. She pulled a small pouch from her belt and allowed the wooden O to fall into Vladimir's open hand. As soon as it touched him Tase felt the surge of power that gathered to Vladimir, who beamed delightedly.

The cold thing was moved away from Tase's throat and Senssirra's grip on him slackened.

Vladimir held the O up toward Caoimhe. "So good of you to collect the O'Neil key for me, it would have been so much harder to retrieve it from the mermaids myself."

Caoimhe gave him a glare that would have made Tase crumble into dust. "I'll admit," Vladimir said with a flourish, "I was hoping you would have the Xoor, but it appears as though, for now, your people have kept it out of my hands again. No matter." He slipped the wooden O into his own small pouch. "I'm patient, and it's only a matter of time."

"You will *never* get it!" Desmond growled, his tone almost sounding animal like.

The lithian flicked his root tail and snapped his dagger-like teeth in Desmond's direction.

"Desmond, hush," Saoirse whispered to him.

Vladimir chuckled openly. "Oh, such a tough lad. Are you going to keep me from it?"

"Desmond," Mr Hogan warned.

Desmond ignored his father and stood protectively next to Saoirse. "I'll do whatever I have to do."

Vladimir smiled. "You know, I am really going to enjoy playing with you." With a flick of his hand, Desmond was hurtled up into a tree by the lithian's root-like tail. He smacked several branches and began to fall back down.

"Desmond!" Saoirse cried.

Mr Hogan sucked in a terrified breath.

A cage was fashioned in seconds out of the tree's branches as the lithian's tail made fast work of them, tying knots, bending the pliable wood. The lithian caught Desmond with his tail before he could get too close to the ground and finished the cage, trapping him inside.

Desmond's black eyes were filled with fear and fury. He pulled at the wooden bars, but they were firmly in place.

Senssirra let Tase's hair go as she rumbled with mirth, and Tase, staring up in shock at the caged Desmond, began to slip away from her. He trod on something that gave a yelp. He jerked toward the sound and saw a small blue creature near Senssirra's tail. The blue creature put a finger to his mouth, warning Tase to be quiet. Tase obeyed and thought the creature looked familiar somehow.

"Brave boy you have, Lee," Vladimir said in delight.

Mr Hogan just stared at him, holding Ma the best he could.

The lithian swirled his root-like tail threateningly behind Vladimir.

Dominique smiled and stared up at Desmond. She gave a little swirl of her finger and one of the branches broke from the bottom of the cage. Desmond jerked away from the broken branch, his eyes wide with dread. Dominique laughed gleefully.

Tase began to feel light headed and he stumbled, his numb hands and knees hitting the floor.

Ma gasped. "Tase!"

Tase recoiled as Vladimir's face was suddenly before him. "Feeling weak, my boy?"

Tase didn't answer.

"Wanna know why?"

Tase said nothing, but the cold was taking him over, he could feel his heart slowing. He held his head high and refused to act afraid.

Vladimir stared at Tase for a long moment, and then let out a soft snicker. "You are something else, lad. It's no surprise the book cursed you." He turned his eyes on Ma and Caoimhe. "Have you two at least told him why he is feeling hypothermic? Or why he has that beautiful scar on his chest?"

Ma and Caoimhe remained silent.

"Thought not," Vladimir nodded. He took a step forward; so quick that Tase hardly had time to blink. He ripped Tase's shirt open and exposed the blackened bit of skin that streaked across his chest and branched off to his right shoulder. He then, in one swift movement, tore away the high neckline of Caoimhe's outfit, and made a gaping hole in the front of Ma's shirt, though Mr Hogan had tried to move her away from him. He stepped back and held his hand out to them. "There, what a threesome they are."

Tase, still trying to regain himself from the unexpected act, inclined his head to Caoimhe.

Her neck was splashed with blackened skin, it twisted and curled not far from her jaw line, and disappeared beneath the rest of her shirt. This was why she always wore turtlenecks, to hide the scar, a scar matching Tase's in appearance, though not in size or placement.

Tase then turned to Ma, whose eyes met his as he looked at her.

Her shirt had been ripped away, just above her chest, but it exposed her left shoulder. Tips of black flesh could be seen, curled near her arm. The black clearly travelled below her torn clothing, and Tase expected that the full scar was a much larger size.

"Beast!" Ma seethed at Vladimir.

Mr Hogan did not look at Ma's scar, but he kept his hands on her shoulders to make sure she didn't do anything foolish.

Tase took a deep breath and closed his eyes. Ma and Caoimhe had both, at some point, touched the Xoor, and been cursed by it, just as he had.

Vladimir rumbled with his laughter. "Well, although I'm having just too much fun, I think we ought to head back, don't you?"

"Back where?" Caoimhe barked at him.

Vladimir put his hands behind his back. "Our home, of course. I have such..." He strode along the line of prisoners and stopped in front of Saoirse. "...plans for you all." He held his hand out as if to touch her, he moved his fingers in the air and a strand of her hair moved by itself and tucked behind her ear.

Saoirse looked terrified, but she stared transfixed at Vladimir.

"Get away from her!" Ma spat.

Vladimir turned his head slowly to her. "You seem like such a good mother, Teagan," he mused. "I'm sure, by this point, you would have told your children everything." He moved and stopped in front of Clearie. "Did you always know you were different? Or did the news of what you are surprise you, Clearie?"

Tase, though feeling weaker from the cold spreading through his body, eyed Ma.

Ma looked frightened.

Clearie's face was so clearly confused it made Tase's stomach churn. He peered at Ma, questioningly.

"You don't know?" Vladimir said, looking surprised. "Oh, dear," he sighed, turning to Ma and putting a hand to his chest, "have I just been the cause of family turmoil?" He shook his head, acting sincere. "I'm *so* sorry."

Clearie's face portrayed his pain and Ma, staring at him in sorrow, seemed unable to hold the tears back that tumbled down her cheeks.

Vladimir let out a sigh and took a few steps backward. "Oh, the tangled webs we weave," he recited. "Bind them." He snapped his finger and the lithian drove his tail into the earth. It ripped up, attached to many pliable roots, making its tail twice as long.

"Dominique," he said, holding his hand out to her.

Her full lips curved upward and her eyes filled with inky blackness.

Tase felt himself become paralysed. He couldn't move, he couldn't do anything except breathe. Tase knew everyone else had been frozen too, there would be no fight this way.

Tase couldn't prove it, but he felt strongly that if Vladimir had not gotten that key Dominique would not have been able to use the power she had over them now. The key made them stronger, and Tase felt the fear flood him from the inside out as he thought about going to the Bojins home.

The lithian's tail began to bind them all, and Tase's stomach dropped in panic.

~~~

Maldorf shivered in terror, but he knew what he had to do. He dug into his skin pouch and slyly pulled out the Dragon's Tooth. He could feel the power seeping off of it. He clutched it in his paw and whispered, "Break the bond, allow me to disobey my mistress, remove the orders, so I may pursue my own interests. Loosen these shackles, give me the freedom to choose, away the slavery, give me the power to refuse."

Maldorf felt the break in the bond, like something had been sitting on his chest and it had gotten off, allowing him to breathe. His eyes darted to his mistress but she didn't seem to notice.

He took a few steps backward and again rummaged through his pouch. He pulled out the small scroll, replaced the tooth, and unfurled the parchment. His eyes gleamed silver and he put his sharp black nail to the scroll. He scribbled, *Help! Help! Help!*

He looked up, hoping no one had seen him writing on the scroll. It appeared they hadn't; everyone was paying attention to Vladimir, who was still speaking.

The little piece of parchment vibrated, and Maldorf looked down.

*Helps is coming.*

Maldorf took a deep breath and rolled the parchment back up. He stuffed it inside his pouch and eyed the forest tensely. He hoped the goblin would make it in time.

~~~

Tase wished he could thrash against his root chains, scream, try and get away, anything! But he was held motionless. His frustration and fear built and he wondered how long he could contain his emotions inside his head.

The lithian paced their small arena, growling and digging its brown claws into the soft dirt.

Vladimir spoke to Dominique in Romanian, she nodded and he strode over to Tase and the others, holding his arms out. "Thank you all for being so cooperative." He clapped his hands together. "We will be departing in just a moment. You will be traveling by lithian express, held motionless by Dominique security." He extended a hand to Dominique, whose eyes were beginning again to fill with black.

The lithian's tail began to twist toward Tase's bindings. "Just a warning," Vladimir said, "this *may* hurt."

Tase began to feel pressure build up all around him and wished he could wince.

A ball of light struck Vladimir square in the jaw. The blow hurled him backward, nearly knocking him to the floor, but he caught himself, and skidded to a stop, his hands and knees buried in earth.

Tase couldn't turn to see where it had come from.

Dominique screeched and jerked toward Vladimir, but her yell was cut off by a ball of light hitting her in the forehead. Her body snapped back, and she slammed into the earth.

For a moment Tase could move, he began to struggle against his restraints but Vladimir called something out and Tase became motionless once more. In his mind he cursed.

He saw Vladimir bolt upright and hold his hands before him. He was alert and eager to fight, but somehow he did not look angry. He howled and sent a burst of black into the forest.

Dominique was on her feet too, and she hissed in fury, though she kept her inky eyes focused on Tase and her other prisoners.

Another burst of light hurtled towards Vladimir, but he knocked it away with his fist, as if it were no more than a fly.

Tase was consumed with alarm. What was happening?

A woman, who was extremely tall and slender, erupted into the clearing. Her face was beautiful, with a flattened nose, large eyes that reflected every colour, and lips that were small and dainty. Her forehead held a lovely opal horn, and her face was framed in white and silver curls.

The horned woman! It wasn't possible that she could be the same unicorn lady who had rescued Tase and Clearie back in the woods near Kavanagh Castle, but she certainly looked like her.

She held her hands out before her, and the tips of her fingers looked like they were rough like hoofs. She flicked her long and exquisite tail, whipping it behind her, and glared at the Bojins.

Vladimir snickered. "Well, another guest to our party." He pointed towards Tase. "I'm afraid we are all filled up."

The woman brought her hand forward and a wide wave of the same light exploded from her.

Vladimir gritted his teeth and raised his hands. As the light came within centimetres of him, it suddenly vanished into nothing.

Three other unicorn people rushed into the clearing. One appeared to be male, but he was as beautiful as the women. They all stared at Vladimir and Dominique, their positions showing they were ready to fight.

The lithian snapped at them all and clawed the damp ground.

Senssirra and Silass looked as though they wanted to slink away, but they held their ground.

Dominique bit the air, but Vladimir hissed something to her in Romanian, making her become still. He did not give the order to engage, and it seemed Dominique was not allowed to strike without his consent.

Tase's heart drummed in his chest.

Vladimir seemed to be waiting for someone else. "Come out, come out, wherever you are," he sang. He took a step forward, his light eyes surveying the surrounding trees. "I know you're out there."

Another figure stepped into the glade, somehow slipping through the fence

Vladimir had created. He pulled down the hood that had been over his head and Tase saw it was the Lighthouse Keeper, Robert. However, he looked different somehow. He was cleaner, and his long white hair was pulled back. His pale blue eyes, heavily lidded and set beneath thick eyebrows, seemed brighter than the last time Tase had seen him, and he certainly appeared stronger.

Robert stood to his full height and glowered at Vladimir. "Here I am," he said, hands extended.

Dominique yipped and bared her teeth.

Vladimir held his hand up to her, cautioning her to stay put. "Indeed," he said wryly. He shook his finger at the old man. "However, the question is why, since what is going on here is none of your business." He took a few steps towards Robert. "You no longer interfere with human matters," he stopped and leered at him, "isn't that right?"

Robert took a step forward. "A few years ago and you would have been correct. However," he turned his eyes to Tase, "things change."

"Hum," Vladimir rubbed his hand over his beard. "The other question is, how did you know where we were?" He eyed Senssirra and Silass, who seemed to shrink under his stare.

Robert arched a silvery eyebrow. "Luck?"

Vladimir chuckled and flicked his hand back.

The lithian plunged his tail into the earth and roots, like snakes, broke through the soil and began coiling themselves around Robert and the unicorn people.

Robert and three of the unicorns sprang out of the way.

The other horned woman began to be consumed by the roots.

Without looking, Robert flung his hand behind him and the roots loosened, allowing the unicorn lady to go free. He ran at Vladimir, and in his hand appeared a large twisted staff.

Vladimir dodged him easily.

Robert swung around and parried the blow by Vladimir's long nailed hand with his staff, as his claws aimed for his face. He shoved forward with his twisted cane and hurtled Vladimir backward, who landed with cat-like grace, and roared with laughter.

Vladimir rushed forward, teeth bared. He jumped and turned one of his palms up. A glow of green appeared in his hand, and as he approached Robert he brought his arm up over his head and flung it at him.

As it soared toward the old Lighthouse Keeper, it turned into a long wide spear. Robert raised his hand and the spear spun and changed directions.

It flew at Vladimir with surprising speed, but he seemed unfazed and with a simple flick of his wrist it turned into dust as it hit him.

The two men continued to fight, but Tase's attention was taken elsewhere.

The lithian was battling the horned people, and they were getting dangerously close to Tase and the others. The lithian dove underground and when he tore up from the ground a tree behind him was pulled under the dirt. In a shower of dirt and grass the tree flung upward once more and Tase saw it was attached to the lithian's root tail. The massive creature began to use the tree like a club and tried to hammer the unicorn people with it.

Dominique was becoming restless, she wanted to fight and Tase felt her power over him flickering. He could move one moment, but was frozen still the next. It seemed her whole focus had to be on keeping him and the others motionless for the magic to work, and her attention was divided.

Eyes filled with black, Dominique took a step forward.

"No, Dominique!" Vladimir screamed at her as he dodged a blow from Robert. She stopped but hissed at him.

A horned woman got on top of the lithian and began to detach his tail from the tree.

Dominique took another step forward and Tase felt the top half of his body become free.

"No!" Vladimir ordered.

The lithian howled as another unicorn jumped on his back.

Dominique yelled and swung her left hand to her side. Black tentacles erupted from her palm and coiled around two of the unicorn women who tumbled to the floor.

Tase was free to move. He struggled against his root bindings. They were firm but he was sure he could struggle free.

There was a loud *crack* and Tase saw Silass trying to get up from the rock he had been hurtled into.

The unicorn man swung his head up, and from his horn a sword made entirely out of light thrust at Silass, but Senssirra deflected it.

"Dominique!" Vladimir called to her. She wasn't listening, she was immersed in her fight with the unicorn woman, and the lithian fought in sync with her.

Tase feared the unicorns wouldn't survive the both of them. "I'm going to help you!"

Tase jerked and spotted a little blue creature who had suddenly appeared at his side.

"I'm Maldorf, a friend of Ciaran's," he whispered.

"A friend of Ciaran's?" Tase gasped delightedly. He watched as Ma and Mr Hogan struggled against their root chains as well.

Dominique's battle was getting far too close to Clearie, he could be hurt if they fought much closer to him.

Tase watched as Maldorf touched the rope that bound him. He whispered something and the rope fell away. Tase took a shocked breath. "Thank you!" he said.

Maldorf nodded and moved to the others. Tase saw Ciaran and Xemplose were already helping set the others free.

Dominique flung herself onto the trunk of a tree near them, and began to climb. It were as if she had become a cat, she scurried up the trunk without reaching for any branches, and so quickly, if you had blinked you would have missed it.

Tase stared up at her in terror.

She began to jump, from one tree to the next. She hurtled herself from trunk to trunk, on all fours, sending a rain of black daggers at her attackers. Her hair became alive with motion, as if a wind had suddenly blown through it, and her eyes locked onto two unicorn people.

"Dominique!" Vladimir roared. "Don't!"

It was too late. She screamed, a sound so piercing Tase felt it cut through him, and magic so sharp it cut like a diamond knife. There was a word in the scream, but what he didn't understand what it was. He felt the power the word carried, however, and he knew at once what it had done as he saw the power hit the unicorn people. He stared in horror as the two unicorns fell down, their life ripped from them. Their eyes, once shimmering like opals, colourful like a rainbow, went grey and dark.

Tase thought it may have been an accident, considering it had been standing right behind the unicorn people, but the lithian, too, fell down dead. Its massive body caused a small quake as it hit the ground.

Vladimir cried out in frustration and Tase turned to see Dominique's face turn ashen. The black receded from the whites of her eyes and she staggered, her feet failing her, until they completely gave out and she collapsed onto the forest floor.

Her ebony eyes flickered and fell on Tase. He wasn't sure what to do. He grabbed his sword from his belt where Vladimir had left it and held it out towards her threateningly.

Though clearly affected by the magic she used, she was not afraid of him. "They are free!" she called, in a weakened and trembling voice.

Tase wished he had thrown some sort of magic her way, instead of just threatening to do so.

Vladimir shot his hand toward them. "Watch out!" Desmond called from above.

There was no time to move, a dome made of red glass trapped them all inside. Ma struck the glass, but it did no good.

"Ogre spit!" a blue goblin, who appeared to be female, growled near Tase.

Robert came at Vladimir and grasped his staff with both hands. He swung it over his shoulder and brought it forward towards Vladimir's face.

Vladimir caught it, holding the end a few centimetres from his nose. "Is this the best you've got, old man?" he howled in laughter.

Robert twisted his wrist slightly, and a long gold blade sliced through the end of the staff.

Vladimir released it and jerked away just in time. "Oh, ho, very good," he grinned. He ran at Robert, nails brandished, and sliced at him.

Robert blocked him and swept his gold blade at Vladimir's chest, missing him by a hair.

A flash of bright green caught Tase's eye.

He followed it and saw Ciaran was standing behind a tree. He had turned brilliantly yellow and held a sharp stone in his hand. He flung it right at Vladimir's head.

Vladimir whirled round and knocked the stone away with his palm, but his eyes were wide clearly searching for his attacker.

This distraction, which had taken no more than a few seconds, was all that was needed.

Vladimir was struck with a blow from Robert's staff, so hard that it must have been magically magnified. It sent him flying through the air.

Robert rushed to the dome. "Cover your eyes!" he commanded, and struck it with his staff. It shattered into a million pieces and Robert held his staff out. With a snap of his finger Desmond's cage fell apart and he landed near them. "Everyone grab on!"

Tase immediately obeyed, but as he was reaching for the staff Aimirgin tripped and clutched at his trouser pocket for support. She tore it and the wooden K fell to the floor.

"Tase!" Robert ordered as he bent down to grab it.

Tase clutched it in his hands and glanced up. Vladimir was staring at him. His smile was wide and sparkling, and his cold green eyes were fixed on the K.

Tase clutched onto the staff and they began to disappear as light surrounded them.

Vladimir shot something toward them, and Tase clamped his eyes shut. There was a great flash, and the woods and the clearing were gone.

# CHAPTER 14
## SHADOW OF THE PAST

They appeared in a flash of light in the midst of trees. Fadin shook his head, trying to orientate himself.

"What just happened?" Aednat asked from beside him.

"I guess the travelling potion worked," he said. "I'm just not sure where we travelled to." Robert had given them a potion, and a small bottle filled with the liquid for Glendan. They were all to drink it when the hourglass sand, which sat proudly on a twisted shelf, turned blue. They had obeyed, but Robert hadn't told them where they would be going.

Glendan gave a small cry and puked directly onto Fadin's arm. "UCK! Glendan!" Fadin complained.

Aednat snorted with laughter.

Fadin made a face at her and wiped the sick off with the blanket Glendan had been wrapped in. "Stop laughing and help me," he chided, trying his best to wrap the soiled blanket up one handed.

"I'm not touchin' that," she cackled.

Fadin gave up and flung the blanket on the dirt and leaf covered ground. He turned and sucked a breath. Before them stood Kavanagh Castle. He hadn't seen the castle in a long time, but there was no doubt about the changes to it. Many of its stained glass windows were broken, the vines that climbed its stone front were burnt and shredded, and one of the two towers that had stood on either side was now a crumpled heap. He recognised that it had been the tower that had led him and Tase into the attic, Ciaran's home.

"Whoa," Aednat said, turning as well and clutching her bandaged arm. "This is your castle?"

Fadin looked down at her. He had almost forgotten that she had never seen it. Aimirgin had, of course, been to the castle many times, but Aednat, who lived underground in Cavan-Corr, had not. "What's left of it, apparently."

Glendan made a hiccup-like sound and clapped his small hands together. Fadin hugged him tighter to his chest, already forgiving him for the vomit. He looked to see if anyone else was on the castle grounds. After all, they had appeared here so suddenly. Robert had hardly given them any warning before he and the goblins vanished.

He crinkled his nose as he noticed the forest was almost right to the castle door. That wasn't right; the castle had many grounds of flat fields, the forest lay beyond those. He wondered if perhaps more trees had been planted? That didn't seem right either.

"Fadin, Aednat, Glendan? Is that you?"

Fadin turned and saw Enda stepping out of the castle. "Enda!" he and Aednat cried as one. Fadin looked at him closely as he rushed toward them. He had never seen Enda look so disheveled, well, except for when he and the others had all been in Cavan-Corr Penitentiary. His hair was an absolute mess, his boots torn, his clothes stained, and he had a nasty bruise lining the right side of his chin.

Enda came and gathered them into a warm hug in one swoop. "Thank goodness you're safe," he sighed.

Fadin chuckled with the large arms around him. "I'm glad you're safe too, Enda."

Enda let them go. "Where are the others?"

"No one else is here?" Aednat asked.

Enda shook his head. "No, and I've only been here a few hours. I figured the others would come here eventually." He peered at them. "How did you figure out how to get to the castle?"

"We didn't, really. Robert left us with a travelling potion. He said to drink it when the liquid glowed. So we did."

There was another flash and Fadin jerked back as he saw Tase, Ma, and many of the others all huddled around Robert.

Enda rushed toward them. "Are you all right?" Fadin propped Glendan higher. "What happened?"

Ma turned her wide eyes, finding him and Glendan. "You're safe!" she cried. She ran to him and grasped him tight.

Fadin smiled, breathing her scent in. "Hi Ma," he said, hugging her back. Ma chuckled. She pulled away and touched his cheek before taking baby Glendan and kissing his chubby cheeks. He giggled and pulled at Ma's black curls.

Fadin saw Tase, who appeared pale and quite shaken. Aimirgin stood next to him, saying something to Clearie, who looked the worst of all of them. Fadin felt the wave of relief wash over him as he saw they were all all right.

"My parents and Annata aren't with you?" Aednat asked.

Mr Hogan looked down at her. "No, I haven't seen them since the attack, but I heard they went with some of the elves."

Aednat nodded, but looked concerned. "What happened?" Enda asked.

"Vladimir appeared," Robert said. "We almost didn't make it." Enda ran a hand over his chin.

"He's stronger than we thought," Caoimhe said, and let out a small groan. She pulled her hand away from her side and Fadin saw her hand was stained red.

"You're hurt!" Fadin cried, but before he could do anything Caoimhe swayed and collapsed.

"Caoimhe!" Mr Hogan shouted.

Robert bent over her. "Vladimir hit her with something," he said, shaking his head. "Let's get her inside."

Fadin watched as they picked her up and a thought occurred to him. "Where are the goblins?"

"Yes," Ma said, "I hope they're all right, we owe them our lives."

"They have their own troubles to attend to," Robert said, helping place Caoimhe in Enda's strong arms. "But they're safe."

Fadin nodded, grateful they weren't in danger. As they walked up to the castle he felt his stomach tighten. He was speechless as they entered. They stepped into the entrance way and saw that the damage was far worse on the inside than on the outside.

There were cracks in the floor, half the stairway had collapsed, and bits of wall were missing all over the place. The door under the stairs was broken and hanging on by a hinge, and it by no means looked like it led the way into the growing room they had escaped from over a year ago. There were stairs leading down into some blackness that Fadin had no desire exploring.

He turned to the Sun Room, to its burnt floors, couches that had been torn up, broken windows, and a hole in the wall about the size of a pumpkin leading into the Tea Room.

The Cavan-Corr Guards had ripped the castle apart.

"What were they looking for?" he asked no one in particular.

Mr Hogan put a hand on his shoulder.

"The Xoor, what else?"

"They've destroyed it," Tase whispered.

Fadin felt a wrench in his chest. Why was it that every home he had lived in ended up broken and left in ruins? His mind wandered to his old house on Little Hallow Road, now a heap of burnt wood and ash, haunted by the dark magic left by the Bojins. "Are we safe here?" Fadin asked.

"Yes," Robert answered, overseeing Enda as he lay Caoimhe on one of the old couches. "The castle has been moved. We are no longer in Glas Cavan."

Fadin blinked. "What?"

"It was a fail safe," Mr Hogan said. "If anyone ever broke in, the castle could be magically relocated. This isn't the first time it's happened."

Fadin peered out the front door and realised Mr Hogan and Robert were right. They were no longer on the castle grounds, that's why it had looked wrong to him when they appeared here. He could scarcely get his mind around the fact that the whole castle had actually been moved.

"They opened it up," Ma breathed.

Fadin turned to her and his eyes fell down the corridor and saw what she meant. Down the West Hallway, where the dead-end used to be, there was a huge gaping archway. Stairs, leading only to what he could think was the West Tower, began and swirled around a corner, and beyond them there was a huge room. It was more than a room, it was like another castle, and from that room stemmed more halls and doors, and from where he stood Fadin couldn't even see half of it.

Fadin gaped at Ma. "There's more to the castle?"

"A lot more," Mr Hogan said.

"Well, why was it closed up?" Aednat asked.

"Bad memories," Ma said, pushing Glendan higher on her chest and moving down the hallway towards the new opening.

Saoirse stood between Fadin and Clearie. "Something terrible happened," she said, her green eyes transfixed on the gaping hole leading to the new room. "Can't you feel it?"

Desmond put his hands on her shoulders.

Once he focused on it, Fadin found he could. There was a heaviness, a pained presence that seeped from the room. In his training with Caoimhe he had never felt anything quite like it. It felt older, and quite sad.

"It's the remains of old magic," Mr Hogan said. "Even I can feel something." He took a step forward and turned to the twins. "Listen," he said, bending so he was lower than they were. His dark eyes found theirs. "There were dark things that happened here." He eyed Clearie specifically. "I cannot express to you how difficult seeing that room is going to be for your ma." His face was sad. "We will explain things to you, but can you look at your mother, and tell me what you see?"

Fadin shifted his gaze to Aednat, who looked just as perplexed. "Explain what exactly?" He watched as Ma almost stumbled into the room.

"I see Ma as a woman who is lost," Tase said.

Fadin stared at Tase, and looked back at Ma. She looked incredibly small in the abandoned room.

Mr Hogan gripped their shoulders tight. "What she did, by not telling you all the truth, was wrong. There is no question there, but... as much as I loved your father, boys, he too made the decision to keep secrets from you. Together they made their life, and omitted to you all what they felt you should not know. However, your father is not here to reap the consequences of those choices. Your mother is left to have to fix the mess they both made, alone, and I think that she is overwhelmed by the vastness of it, and doesn't know where to begin."

Fadin looked at Clearie and noticed for the first time that he was extremely pale. What had he missed?

Mr Hogan looked deep into their eyes. "Even though you are angry with her, and have every right to be, remember that loving someone is not only loving them in the good times, but being by their side even when they disappoint you. It's accepting the good with the bad. That is what real love is, not a feeling but a choice."

Fadin had a sinking feeling. What hadn't Ma told them now?

He stared at her, at how broken she appeared in the destroyed mess of what once must have been a grand place, and didn't know what he wanted. So again he nodded, agreeing with himself that for now he would say nothing, and try to just take in what was in front of him.

Mr Hogan stood up and followed Ma down the hall.

Aimirgin and Aednat came to stand with Fadin and the others. "What could have happened here?" Tase asked.

Aimirgin shook her ebony head. "I don't know."

Fadin looked to the walls and started as he saw that the pictures that had once been black and blank were now filled with images. Some were broken on the floor; others were hardly held to the wall and looked as though they would fall any moment.

One of them was of a waterfall, and he could hear the water. It was a black and white photo of a mossy hill, and not far in front of it stood two people, a man and a woman. They held hands, staring at each other, and the waterfall fell down behind them, causing the mist to swirl around their ankles.

He prodded Tase in the shoulder. Tase stared at the image wide eyed.

Another photo showed the Irish Sea. As Fadin got closer he could actually smell and hear the ocean. He pulled away and knew now why the pictures had been blank.

Fadin turned and saw he was right at the opening to the new room. He sucked in breath and hesitated to go in, as did the others. The heavy feeling was stronger here. He swallowed and made his foot cross the threshold. The sadness that swept over him when he entered was like the wave from the moving picture, spilling over him. The magic left behind in this room was almost visible it was so thick, and it had sucked in sorrow from whatever tragedy had occurred.

Fadin picked his eyes up from the marble floor – where they had fallen when the heaviness had crashed on him – and stared at the gigantic oil portrait which hung over a massive marble fireplace, now covered in dust and cobwebs.

It was of six people. There was a man who was the furthest back; his eyes were cerulean blue, his hair was curly and brown, and his nose was long and elegant. A small smile was on his face, and his blue eyes crinkled up at the corners, the way Ma's did when she smiled. Next to him, resting a pale hand on the man's shoulder, was a small woman, with curly ebony hair, and Ma's face, only with brilliant hazel eyes and an upturned nose. He saw the inscription of their names underneath the painting, but he could have guessed who they were without it – Grandfather Declan, and Grandmother Igraine.

Fadin let out a heavy breath.

Sitting in front of them were four children. The first was a smiling boy who looked to be about eleven, with hair as black and curly as his mother's and eyes as blue as his father's. This must be Uncle Glendan, whom his youngest brother was named after. He even had a dimple, high on his face, like baby Glendan had on his cheek. The next child was no more than eight, and there was no mistaking her. It was Ma, her hair a mess of black curls, and her face round and rosy cheeked. Beside her was a boy, who couldn't be more than a year younger. He also had curly black hair, but his eyes were bright hazel like his mother's, and one of them looked permanently stuck to the side, a lazy eye. Dubhlainn, his betraying Uncle Dubhlainn.

Fadin swallowed hard and moved his eyes to the last child, who was no more than three. She had a full little face, an upturned nose, ringlets of brown curls, and big sparkling blue eyes. He read the name, because of all his mother's family, this is the person he had heard the least about: Etain Kavanagh.

There was another painting, this one of Enda as a young man, hung next to the family portrait, and a third showed a second family painting that had Enda in it.

Fadin turned from the pictures of his family and peered at the several old ropes that hung on both sides of the large family portrait. Some of them were uncoiling, and hung far above the marble floor, while others still held their form and dangled all the way to the ground. The longer ones had stains on them, dark stains, as did the fireplace. The hearth looked like it had been splattered with something long ago, and whatever it was it had pooled on the marble floor before it, leaving its dark handprint on the ground for years.

Ma walked over to it and Fadin could see her hand that clutched baby Glendan was shaking. "I need to explain some things to you all," Ma said. She turned and her cerulean eyes were filled with pain.

Enda grabbed Desmond and Aimirgin's arms gently and began leading them out.

"No," Ma said, her eyes falling kindly on Enda, "we are all a family now. They should know as much as my children." She put her head down for a moment and gestured to the ropes. "This is your past too, Enda, not just mine."

Fadin peered at Enda and noticed the grief which covered his features. He tightened his jaw and nodded.

There were old couches and chairs around the room, all of which were beautifully designed, almost appearing like thrones, and each one had a swirling K carved into the wooden arms. Mr Hogan helped turn a few right side up, and they all sat. Ma sat across from her three sons and Saoirse. Mr Hogan placed himself in a chair between them all.

"Clearie," Ma said, "you are my flesh and blood." She touched her heart and Fadin noticed the dark swirling scar that matched Tase's. "I couldn't love you more." Fadin had a sinking feeling and he watched as Clearie's blue and purple eyes widened. "You are *my* son, I just didn't give birth to you."

Fadin's mouth opened and he heard Tase suck in a breath. Hundreds of questions flooded into Fadin's mind, but he kept silent; he felt that Clearie deserved to be the first one to ask questions.

Clearie's eyes twitched, and he seemed to be trying to decide how to react. He nodded, and twisted his fingers around each other.

"I want you to know, before I explain," Ma said, her eyes shining with the tears that hadn't reached the surface yet, "we were going to tell you. It was always our plan to tell you together…" Her words fell away for a moment and she looked full of regret. "When Da died…" she folded her hands, "everything changed."

Clearie didn't say a word, he just listened, his face full of emotion. Mr Hogan watched Clearie closely.

Ma took a deep breath. "You are the son of my sister, Etain, and the elven lord Fintan."

Fadin knew the name, but from where?

"He is the elf who destroyed Afanasii," Mr Hogan said. Clearie nodded.

"They were young when they married," Ma said. "He loved my sister, and he married her without his father or people's consent." She looked down for a moment. "It caused some trouble because she was not an elf, but they didn't care, they were happy with each other, and that's all they needed. In the midst of all the terrible war, they became pregenant with you."

Ma swallowed and peered at the ropes. "Then the unthinkable happened." She rubbed her hands together. "Dubhlainn and Puceula betrayed us. In their lust for power they turned to Afanasii and his forces. Afanasii wanted inside information, and my family was at the centre of the rebellion, so they were a prime target." Ma's voice seemed to fail her for a moment as she looked at the stains on the floor.

Enda ran a hand over his face.

"It happened before Dia was killed," Mr Hogan said. "Many of us were out on missions, gathering information, freeing prisoners… Kavanagh Castle had protections on it, and no one could enter unless they were trusted people. It was our headquarters where we made all our plans, our hospital for the wounded, and a safe place." He shook his head. "Only your ma's family and a handful of others were there that night. Your ma, your da, Enda, and myself were far away."

Ma began to speak again. "We didn't know who betrayed us at first, but when we came to the castle and saw it burning," she bit her lip, "we knew someone had let them in." She closed her eyes for a moment. "You could feel it, the darkness on the castle, as you can now, but then, when it was fresh… it was even seeping through the front doors. You didn't have to have some special gift to feel what had been left here." She took a shuddering breath. "I could see the stains from the entrance hall. When I got to them, there was nothing to be done."

Fadin's heart felt empty, hollow.

Ma turned to the fireplace and walked over to the dangling ropes. "I couldn't take seeing them that way, couldn't be in this room… so I ran." She turned her face to her children. "Alroy and Lee tried to stop me, but I dodged them, and made my way to the garden." Her hands danced on her neck as she took in a gasping breath.

"There was something under a bench outside," Ma said, her eyes finding Clearie. "I was crying so hard, I almost didn't hear the noise it was making." She stood still as a statue. "I knew you were her's the moment I saw you. You looked just like her, and you had one of her eyes, and one of Fintan's." She took a breath. "I believe she gave birth and hid you before the enemy came in. You were under my favorite garden bench, where she knew I'd find you."

Clearie was gaping at her, tears falling down his own cheeks. Ma seemed unable to continue.

Mr Hogan helped her. "Fintan came not five minutes after we did. When he found your mother… he lost his mind, Clearie. He wouldn't leave her." Mr Hogan looked at Ma. "We all thought you had died with her. I even thought that until very recently."

Ma took in a sharp breath. "I *was* pregnant, but I had lost the baby a few days before I found you, Clearie. I thought it was too dangerous to tell who you really were because I knew Fintan was a target. So I kept it, and you, a secret. I was afraid because of the war, and after the war when Afanassi's body wasn't found…" She paused. "When the war was over, we left, but your father and I knew we had to tell you one day." Ma stood up and walked toward the fireplace. "We didn't tell the truth because we knew what that meant. Clearie, Fintan was the next in line to the elven throne after Caoimhe, because he is her cousin. Caoimhe is the king's daughter, but when she refused it, her father stepped down as king, and now Fintan is king of all the elves, which makes you the heir to the elven throne."

"Many elves won't want a half human on their throne," Enda said.

Ma nodded and pulled something from a small pouch on her belt. It was a beautiful silver bracelet, whith swirls and a diamond, surrounded by trees. "This is your fathers crest," Ma said. "It was an heirloom made for you, when you were in your mother's belly." Ma stared at him. "We were going to tell you on your sixteenth birthday and give this to you."

Clearie stood, walked over to Ma and took it.

"When you turned eighteen we were going to take you to meet him."

Clearie turned his eyes to her. "Does he know about me?"

Ma shook her head. "No, he thinks you died with your mother. We decided that was best, because he went mad after Etain died." Ma looked down. "I see that was wrong now, and I am so sorry, Clearie." Her face became streaked with tears. "I am so very sorry."

Clearie stood still for a moment, holding the bracelet in his hands. Fadin was overwhelmed, and didn't know what to feel.

Clearie threw his arms around Ma. "It's all right, I'm not angry with you."

Ma broke into sobs. "I should have told you everything about your real mother, how wonderful she was, how much I loved her. I should have told you about your father, and I should have let him have the chance to know you."

Clearie hugged her tighter.

Tase seemed speechless, and Saoirse was beside herself.

"No more secrets," Ma said, she looked up to her other children. "No more."

Tase got up and rushed to her. She hugged them both and Saoirse, with some reluctance, joined them. As she found Ma's arms Fadin felt the magic pulse from her, almost in a wave. It was a little unsettling how strongly he could feel it.

Fadin, wondering how *he* felt, realised that though angry at the dishonesty for so many years, knew Ma was trying to make up for it now. He went to her arms and hugged her tight. She had made some mistakes but she would always be their mother.

"I hate to interrupt," Robert said, "but we have a bit of a problem." Fadin turned and Caoimhe was *standing*, but only with his help.

"I'll be fine," Caoimhe insisted, but her voice faltered.

"If you would listen and sit down, you would be better," Robert chided.

Fadin's eyes widened as he realised he could see the veins under her pale skin become visible. They were blue for a moment and then began to darken into a sickly blue-black.

Caoimhe's face was agonised and she began to cough violently.

"She was hit by something Vladimir threw at us. His magic has become stronger, I cannot heal her."

Fadin felt a knot growing in his belly. "Can't you heal yourself?" Fadin asked her. "Like you do other people?"

Caoimhe smiled slightly. "I'm afraid not."

"She needs the help of her people," Robert said. "She must go to Irrial Ath Dara."

"No," she said, vehemently shaking her head.

"If you won't go, you'll die," Robert said matter-of-factly.

Fadin froze, his blue-green eyes transfixed on Robert. There was no doubt in that statement and it sent a shock through him.

Caoimhe coughed again and Robert led her to a chair where he sat her down.

Everyone went to her.

"Please, old friend," Ma said, "go to your father's people if they can help you."

Caoimhe began to shake her head again but Tase put his hand on her shoulder. "Please, Caoimhe, we need you."

Fadin nodded. "We can't make it without you."

Caoimhe gave them all a defeated look. "All right, I'll go."

"Thank you, for heaven's sake," Robert huffed. "It will need to be soon." He looked at her pale skin. "We can't wait more than a day or two."

Ma nodded. "Then we'll rest for a while, and move out." She took a deep breath. "I'm no Daireann, but I know there is a cupboard in the kitchen that never runs out of food. Who's hungry?"

She led the way into the kitchen, leaving Robert and Enda to attend Caoimhe.

As Fadin was leaving he heard Robert whisper to Enda. He strained his ears to hear.

"The girl is in trouble," Robert said. "Her power is unstable, she can't control it."

Enda let out a sigh. "I know, I noticed her emotions triggering it when she hugged Teagan."

"We need to get her help before she destroys herself, or all of you."

Enda nodded. "What do you suggest?"

"We take her to her father," Robert whispered.

"Teagan won't agree," Enda said.

Robert leaned in. "Which is why we won't tell her."

Caoimhe let out a weak incredulous snicker. "Good luck, old friend."

Robert arched a thick eyebrow at her. "What else would you suggest? You know I will take nothing but good care of that girl. And you must get to your father's lands. Teagan and the others can take you."

"I don't doubt their navigation skills," she said, peering up at him and wincing, "I would just hate to be you when Teagan finds out what you've done."

"We will be long gone by then," Robert said, bending down so he could look at Caoimhe's pale skin better.

"You better never see her face to face again," Caoimhe chuckled and then coughed.

He touched her forehead. "You need to rest, and not worry about it." He turned his attention to Enda. "We leave tonight, after everyone is asleep."

Fadin hurried out of the room before they noticed him lingering in the shadow of the twisting staircase. He made his decision in a split second. They may leave without Ma, but they weren't going to leave without him. Saoirse was his sister, and he was going to protect her, no matter what lay in store.

# CHAPTER 15
## SAOIRSE'S BURDEN

"We don't even know where they're going," Aimirgin cautioned. Her olive tan skin and dark spots stood out against the green walled room, and Tase noted the fear in her ebony eyes.

They had snuck upstairs to Tase and Fadin's old room. It was trashed, like the rest of the castle. It was sad seeing it that way, the room he and his brother had learned many truths about their past and who they really were in. They were quite different from the boys who had slept in the now broken bunk beds.

"Does it really matter?" Fadin asked. "Saoirse is in trouble and they are taking her. I'm going, whether the four of you come or not."

Tase blew out an exasperated breath, which flung back a strand of red hair that had fallen too close to his eye. "You know I'm coming," he declared, feeling the sense of dread more clearly.

"Count me in," Aednat volunteered.

Aimirgin rubbed her hands together nervously. "What about you, Clearie?" Fadin asked.

Tase looked at him. Clearie's face was worn out, but his eyes were bright. He pushed back his longer blond hair and turned his gaze on Fadin. "As much as I would like to go with you, this time my place is here."

Fadin looked equally as shocked as Tase felt. "You can't be serious," Fadin exclaimed.

"It's not because of what Ma told us, is it?" Tase suggested. "Because, Clearie, you are as much our brother now as you ever have been.

Clearie smiled. "No, that's not the reason at all. I know I'm your brother, no matter who I was born from. The reason I'm staying is because everyone here will need to go to the elven kingdom, and that's where I need to go, I know it deep in my gut. Besides, Saoirse will have enough protection, and I'll need to be here to take care of Ma and Glendan."

Fadin shook his head but patted him on the shoulder. "They couldn't be in better hands." He shifted his gaze. "What's it gonna be, Aimrgin?"

She let out a little moan. "Oh, all right, I'll come. But if we are all going we need to leave a note for your ma and my da."

Tase bumped her with his arm playfully. He was truly glad she would be coming along.

"A note we can do," Fadin said, moving away from Clearie. He grabbed a piece of crumpled parchment from the ground and found an old pen. "What shall it say?"

In the end the note was an apology, a vow to be safe, and a promise to return. Clearie was given the letter, but assured them he would act dumb, as if he was just as surprised to learn of their leaving as Ma and Mr Hogan would be.

There was a small satchel that still had some of Mr Aislinn's potions inside it. Aednat was able to pick out the potion that made them invisible and soundless, which were not always two things that went together in a magical mixture, she explained to Tase.

They packed themselves food, clothes, and blankets. They found satchels in an armoire, which was located in the large new room. They put more items than they should have in them, but they didn't have as much space as Aimirgin's bag she used to use. They also found fur bedrolls in the closet, and small square parcels that exclaimed:

O'Connell's Instant Fire!

Once packed, they hid their satchels in a hole in the wall which was conveniently close to the castle door. Then they waited.

Instead of everyone having their own room, Mr Hogan and Enda had pulled mattresses from the many rooms of the castle and put them all in the Tea Room. Robert had made some sort of tea that Ma, Mr Hogan, and Caoimhe drank generously. Tase suspected it had an ingredient that was used to help them sleep deeply. Desmond had lit a fire, and everyone fell quickly to sleep.

Tase had been having a hard time staying awake, but when he heard the slight footsteps in the foyer, his eyes shot open. They all got up as quietly as possible and watched as Robert, Enda, Desmond, and Saoirse left.

Fadin lead them into the hall and they quickly gathered their packs. "You'll leave the letter for them?" Aimirgin double checked.

"Of course," Clearie said, hugging her.

"Take good care of them," Tase urged, glancing in the direction of the Tea Room.

"You know I will."

"Come on, we don't have time to dawdle," Fadin said impatiently, holding a rope and the potion.

They all took part of the rope in their hands so they wouldn't get separated from each other, since they would not be able to see nor hear one another.

They took the potion, and Tase quivered at the sensation. It took but a few moments for them all to flicker out of visibility.

Tase watched the door open and he gripped the rope tight as it pulled him forward into the night.

"Be safe," Clearie wished, as he closed the door. Tase sincerely hoped they would be.

"They're gone!" Ma screamed.

Cleaire's eyes shot open and he felt the guilt attack him instantly. He sat up and saw Mr Hogan shoot from his mattress toward the entrance hall. "Who's gone?"

Ma came into the Tea Room with the letter. "The boys, Aimirgin, and Aednat!"

"Gone? Gone where?" Mr Hogan demanded.

Clearie did his best to act surprised; it really wasn't that hard, since the guilt of knowing the truth made him feel panicked.

Caoimhe, her pale skin and blackened veins looking even worse in the light streaming in from the open window, leaned up weakly against her pillows. "They're with Robert." She held her own letter, which lay unsealed in her lap.

Ma's frantic eyes found it and Coaimhe handed it to her. Ma covered her mouth as she read it, and Mr Hogan paced. "Robert has gone to take Saoirse to her father."

Mr Hogan's ebony eyes widened in fear, "He would take children into that kind of danger?"

Ma shook her head. "The children snuck off even without his knowing."

Mr Hogan growled under his breath, "Why didn't he tell us he was taking Saoirse?" He suddenly turned to where Desmond had been sleeping and closed his eyes. "Desmond too." He sighed and covered his face in his hands. "All my children are out there somewhere, and I can do nothing to help them." He slumped into one of the torn couches, looking defeated.

"Anything could happen to them," Ma began to sob. "They are just children, out there in the wild. What if something is out there waiting for them?" She sunk onto the mattress next to Caoimhe's.

Coaimhe touched her hand.

Clearie swallowed, the responsibility of his brothers' and the girls' lives feeling like a massive weight he should have to carry until they returned home safely.

"Robert will take care of them," Caoimhe reassured her. "If they are safe with anyone, they are safe with him. He will protect them with his life."

Ma squeezed her hand back and a worried tear fell down her cheek.

Clearie honestly hoped he had made the right decision. The more his heart swarmed with fault, the less sure he became.

The potion lasted for several hours, but nothing can last forever. It felt strange to make noise again, and Tase had to get used to making a conscience effort to remain silent.

They travelled a good way off for about another hour when Robert abruptly stopped. Tase could just make out their shapes ahead and suddenly Robert vanished.

"Where did he go?" Aimirgin gasped.

There was a small *thwump* and Robert appeared before Fadin, his staff pointed right at his chest. "For the love of —" Robert roared.

Fadin smiled at him. "We thought we'd come along too." Robert lowered his staff and glared angrily at all of them.

"What is it?" Enda called through the trees.

"A band of fools," Robert barked back. He pointed at all of them. "If time were not of the essence I would march you all back to that castle and give you a good smack in the head for your stupidity!"

Tase felt a twinge of remorse.

"Whoops?" Aednat said, holding her hands out, palms up.

Robert rolled his eyes. "Come on."

~~~

They covered a lot of distance even though they walked by foot. When Aednat asked why they didn't just use magic to travel, Robert told them that spies were watching for magic use and that certain creatures and Dalbhach could track where a travelling potion and other such means of magical transportation ended up. So walking it would be.

Tase was exhausted when they stopped to make camp, and frustrated. Robert refused to tell them where exactly they were going. He was certain it was for their own protection, but it didn't make Tase feel safe.

They ate a simple dinner; dried meat and fruit. Robert would not allow them to have a fire.

Tase curled up in his fur bedroll and listened as Robert informed Enda and Desmond that the three of them would have the night watch. Tase fell asleep almost instantly, Enda being placed as their first guard.

He awoke with a start and saw that Desmond and Robert were missing. Desmond was standing guard. Tase wrapped his blanket around himself and snuck out of his bed. He tiptoed to Desmond, who turned as he approached.

"Hey, Tase," he whispered. "I'm surprised you're awake."

"Where's Robert?" Tase asked.

"Left, said he'd be back by morning."

"Left?" Tase gasped. "Left where?"

"I don't know. He got some sort of a message from someone." He patted Tase's shoulder. "He's fine, don't worry about it."

Tase was rooted to the spot, fear consuming him. He wasn't worried for Robert's safety, but for theirs. How could Robert have left them? They had Enda, sure. But he wasn't the same. What if he didn't come back?

"He'll come back," Desmond assured him. "Now go on and get some rest."

Tase still felt unsettled, but he got up and made his way toward his bedroll.

Something moved.

He jerked backward and fixed his eyes on the place where he saw something dash behind a tree.

The sound of scurrying footsteps flashed to his left.

Tase whirled round, and a moment later was on his feet. He saw the bag with their weapons out of the corner of his eye and wished desperately he had been wise enough to at least grab his sword.

Something dashed across his peripheral vision causing him to spin to his right. He grabbed a large branch leaning against the tree trunk and held it out like a weapon.

"Don'ts hit me's please," a small voice said.

Tase let out a gasping sigh and let the branch fall from his hands. "Ciaran!" he whispered.

"Comes to see ifs yours all right." The little goblin came out from behind a tree. His green face was gaunt and he had large circles under his eyes.

"Ciaran," Tase said, taking a step forward, "are you all right?"

"Nevers mind me. I comes to see you. You barely escapes Vladimir."

"I know," Tase nodded. "Thanks to you we made it to the castle safe. What happened to you? How did you find us?"

"Had business to attends to, but I is fine, so is blue goblin and Xemplose."

"I'm glad to see you, Ciaran." Tase smiled.

"Same, Tase-thing," he grinned, showing yellow teeth. He walked up to Tase and clutched his leg.

Tase smiled and sat down, pulling the blanket close to him. "Why are you here, Ciaran?"

"I has something for you, Tase-thing." He held out a wad of papers.

"What are these?"

"Newspaper clipsings," Ciaran said. "You's had all been aways from the magical ministry fors too long. Bads things are happenings. Shows theses to the lighthouse keepers in the morning."

Tase flipped through them, but couldn't see anything in the dark. "Where did you get these, Ciaran?" he asked, but when there was no answer he looked up and found Ciaran was gone.

He stuffed the newspaper clippings in his shirt and crawled over to his warm bed. He curled himself up and within a matter of moments drifted to sleep, his mind spinning him into dreams of what could possibly be on those pieces of paper.

When he woke up it was to the sound of rain and shouting. He sat up and saw a canopy had been pitched over them during the night, so the rain didn't touch them. He also saw that Robert was back, and that he had a young girl and a man with him. The man looked terrified, but the girl seemed ecstatic about the rain. She had her arms open wide and was trying to catch droplets of them in her mouth.

"Who are they?" Fadin asked.

Tase shook his head. "I don't know." Aednat popped her head next to theirs.

"Well," Aimirgin said, "what are we waiting for?" She got up. Tase, Fadin, and Aednat followed.

Enda was quite upset. He pointed to the man, who looked as though he may faint. "Was there really no other option than to bring an Ainondhall?"

Desmond paced back and forth, while Saoirse was still deeply asleep under the canopy.

Robert saw the children join them. "Fadin, Tase, Aimirgin, Aednat," he nodded to them, "this is Dr Jason Guilfoyle."

Dr Guilfoyle eyed them; he looked surprise by their presence. "Children?" he asked Robert. "Isn't what we're doing dangerous?"

"They can take care of themselves, Doctor." Robert said.

Dr Guilfoyle, though still appearing confused and frightened as ever, smiled at them. "Hello," he said. He kept his blue eyes on the girl and she swirled in a circle.

"This," Robert said, "is Marie Whelan."

"Hey," Fadin said, "she's the girl who was locked in with Saoirse at the Cavan-Corr Penitentiary."

Tase shook his head. "Oh yes! She is." He recognised her green eyes. "Isn't she the one who escaped from the asylum?" he asked, recalling the newspapers reporting a missing girl over a year ago.

"This is the girl," Robert nodded. "She was brought back to the hospital, but I have been watching it to make sure Vladimir didn't try and get her back. I entrusted Marie to Dr Guilfoyle here, and another friend who works at the asylum. I put protections around the castle, the Bojins should not have been able to enter it."

Desmond paused. "Did they get in, somehow? Is that where you went last night?"

Robert took a deep breath. "Yes, I warned Dr Guilfoyle to look out for a black dog, and for anyone asking about Marie. He contacted me last night, and good thing too."

Dr Guilfoyle ran a hand through his thick dark hair. "There was an old lady asking about her, a Mrs Cunningham."

Tase and Fadin looked at one another. *It can't be,* Tase thought. Fadin's wide blue-green eyes seemed convinced.

Enda seemed to have recognised the name too. He gave the boys a surprised glance.

"She came in asking about the Whelan girl, claimed she was a relative. I have never known any visitors, besides Robert here, to come asking about her." He took a steadying breath and watched Marie as she picked up a multicoloured leaf from the ground. "I contacted him, and good thing too. The old lady had some sort of weapon in her pocket; it made fire appear from a bottle, it wasn't long before the whole hospital had to be evacuated. Nurse O'Malley and I got Marie and were headed to my car when the black dog attacked." Jason held up his arm and Tase saw several nasty gashes. "We managed to get inside the car, but there were two of them. The other was a young woman, and somehow," Jason seemed to be trying to decide what was real and what he had imagined, "somehow she lifted the car." He shook his head. "Robert saved us, but Ms O'Malley didn't make it." He covered his face in his hands.

Roberts's features were grave. "She was a wonderful woman. A good friend of mine." He cleared his throat. "She sacrificed herself for Marie, and now we must do whatever we can to keep her safe."

"Why does Vladimir want her?" Enda asked.

"She knows the location of the missing Whelan key," Robert said. "Only she doesn't realise she knows it." He smiled at Marie, who picked a mushroom and showed him.

"See Bobby?" she asked him.

"Don't eat it," he beamed at her.

Tase had never seen Robert's face look so soft. She nodded and simply plopped it in her pocket.

"Is she a little, off?" Aednat asked Tase.

Tase nodded. "She does seem to be."

"We have to keep her away from him at any cost," Enda said. He looked at Saoirse. "The mission we are on now may not be the best one to take this girl and Jason on. Perhaps we should change our plan."

Desmond became defensive. "We have to help Saoirse, you can see yourself she isn't doing well!"

"Calm yourself, Desmond," Robert said. "I agree Enda, but we really don't have a choice. If we don't get help for Saoirse, she is going to light us up like a beacon."

"What do you mean?" Enda inquired.

"You know how she is becoming unable to control her magic?" Jason's eyes became wide at the word, magic.

Enda nodded.

"She is extremely powerful," Robert inclined his head to her. "Vladimir has spies looking for large bursts of magic, and if she loses control she will send out a blast of magic that will bring down the enemy upon our heads. We need to find her father so he can teach her to control the power she has."

Enda got close to Robert so Jason couldn't hear his words. "If we continue down this path we could very well condemn an innocent man to death."

"I will do my best to make sure that doesn't happen," Robert stated. "But we have very little choice in the matter."

Tase felt his stomach twinge.

"I hope nothing happens to us," Aimrgin whispered. "Robert and Enda don't sound too confident."

"Wherever we are going," Fadin said, "it sounds dangerous."

"Quick breakfast," Robert told them, "And then we'll set out." He moved to Jason. "Until things are safe, you will be with us."

Jason nodded.

Robert went to Saoirse and woke her.

Tase made a face. She was incredibly pale and her eyes were glossy. "How are you feeling?" he asked.

"Sick," she admitted, "and weak."

"We'll be there soon enough," Robert assured her. "Get yourself some breakfast."

Tase suddenly remembered about the newspaper clippings Ciaran had left for him. "Robert," he said, grabbing them from his blankets. "Ciaran visited me last night. He said to give these to you."

Robert came to him and took a handful.

Enda did the same. "They're newspaper pages."

"Yes, Ciaran said you needed to see them."

"The King Fallen Ill," Enda read.

Robert let out a snort. "The King has been ill for quite some time. It's just taken this long for his people to notice."

"The article on the king's health is dated for two weeks ago," Enda told him.

"Council Plots Against the King," Desmond said aloud. "Treason, Council Members Arrested?" His face was concerned.

"Arrested?" Enda asked. "I know many of the members on the council. They are good, honest people. What could they have possibly done to be arrested?"

"I haven't been involved in political matters for a long time," Robert said, scanning the newspaper page in his hands. "And you all have been missing for quite some time. It looks as though big changes have occurred lately."

Fadin grabbed a page from the bottom of Tase's pile. "Listen to this." He read: "'Several members of the Council of Princes have been arrested today, on the charge that they have committed treason by plotting against King Raegan. These individuals have been loyal, trusted members of our city and ministry for many years. How is it that suddenly, they have become the enemy? What plot have they created against our king? What is defined as treason? Do we even have a king to plot against? These previous council members have been taken to Cavan-Corr Penitentiary for no other reason than not agreeing with Advisor Lynch. Whom, I'd like to point out, has been put in a great position of power, now that our king has fallen ill. Fallen ill? Where is our king? Has anyone actually *seen* him in the past few years? Are we to just believe he had suddenly become so sick he cannot make decisions? Or has he been sick for quite some time, the seal being in another's hands, and now it is just official? Perhaps there is indeed a plot going on, but it is not against our king. No, it seems to me the plot is against us. Do we sit by and allow our Ministry to be taken over? Or do we do something to stop it?' Argonne Nugent." Fadin put the paper down.

Saoirse pulled two pages from Enda's pile. "'Argonne Nugent to be Arrested for Treason. Writer Nugent, Voice of the People, In Serious Trouble.'"

Enda read another headline, which had been cut out. "Argonne Nugent, Marvel or Mental?" He made a sound of disgust.

Robert straightened out a piece of newspaper in his hands. "Argonne Nugent Escapes Ministry Arrest." He let the paper fall to his side. "That name sounds familiar to me."

"You keep up on Cavan-Corr Post?" Desmond asked. "If so, you should know the name. Argonne Nugent is the main reporter. His column has been called The Voice of the People, and he doesn't mind speaking his mind. The citizens of Cavan-Corr love him." He looked back down at the parchment in his hands. "I'd be lying if I said I wasn't a fan of his work."

Robert shook his head. "I don't read newspapers. The world is in shambles whether or not I bother myself reading about it."

"Uplifting thought, that," Desmond said, handing a page back to Enda. "King? What king are we talking about?" Jason asked him.

Tase put a hand on his arm. "It's all quite confusing at first," he consoled.

"We wondered if we were completely mental ourselves, when we first found out we were magical," Fadin added.

Jason let out a deep breath. "You didn't always know about... uh..." He seemed unable to say the word. "... all this?"

"No, we found out when we were twelve," Tase told him. Jason nodded, he seemed to take some comfort in that fact.

"Well, it looks like old Nugent got away," Enda said.

"Good for him."

"At least Ciaran has warned us about what's going on," Robert said.

"It's gotten much worse since we've been gone," Desmond sighed.

Robert nodded. "Nothing we can do about it now." He handed the remaining pages in his hand to Enda. "Gather them up, we don't want any evidence of our being here left behind."

Enda grunted his agreement and collected the newspapers.

Tase felt concerned about many things, but worrying about them all wouldn't solve the problem they were in. Only action would. He followed Roberts's orders and began packing his sleeping things away.

~~~

Tase fitted his hood more securely over his head as the pounding rain picked up momentum. His feet ached from all the travelling they had done over the past few days, but Robert was showing no signs of stopping.

Saoirse had worsened over their travel. Her eyes had become sunken, her face gaunt and pale. She had also had at least three convulsing spells. Enda helped by trying to bundle her at night, holding her still while she had her fits and watching her every move, but that was all he could do. Robert was as much at a loss as Enda was, he tried many herb mixtures in the evenings, but nothing improved her condition. Whatever was wrong with her, they needed to find the help she needed, and fast.

Jason became more comfortable with them all, and Marie was like a small child trapped inside a thirteen year old's body. She liked to walk and to talk, though most of what she said was complete nonsense. The more the days passed, the healthier she looked and the worse Saoirse got.

Tase suspected where Robert was headed sometime before they got there, and when he saw the North Atlantic Sea before them, and column upon geometric column of stones at his feet, he knew he had been right. He had been here with Da before, and it had been loads of fun then.

"The Giant's Causeway?" Fadin said. "This is where Saoirse's father is?"

"No, my lad," Robert declared, "this is the bridge to where he is."

"Where exactly is he?" Aednat questioned.

Tase thought she had better luck teaching a duck to tap-dance than getting a straight answer out of Robert.

"The lost city of Nóinín," Robert surprised Tase by answering.

"Nóinín?" Aimirgin blurted.

"Should I be concerned about where that is?" Jason wondered.

Enda muttered something under his breath and Robert smiled. "We will be all right." He looked at the children. "Haven't you ever heard of the legend of this place?"

Aednat turned to him. "What? The story about Finn McCool, the giant who built this as a bridge to Scotland, to fight the giant Bernandonner? Of course I have! Finn McCool thought he would come to Ireland and battle Bernandonner because he was smaller than he was. But when Finn finally got the bridge built, Bernandonner was sleepin', and his wife dressed him like a baby to trick McCool. When Finn arrived and saw how large the baby was, he was terrified of how huge Finn must be since his baby was so gigantic, and he ran back to Scotland, tearin' up the bridge he made as he went."

Robert smiled. "Well told. What is important about that story is this incredible formation of rock, which also exists on the Isle of Staffa."

Saoirse gave a small shiver. "Scotland."

Desmond moved next to her and rubbed her shoulders with his hands in an attempt to keep her warm.

Tase stared out to the sea, where he could indeed see Scotland. "Are you telling us that story is true?"

Jason listened intently.

"Really?" Aednat questioned, her face incredulous. "After what I told you about Brian Boru?"

Robert grinned. "I'm telling you that most legends are based loosely on fact." He walked towards the water and blew into his hands, which burned silver. "I'm telling you that this formation also exists in Scotland." He began to touch several columns with his silver fingers. "I'm saying, Finn McCool wasn't a legend."

Robert stood up and slammed his staff into the ground. Magic sped off in a dome around them.

"What did that do?" Aimirgin questioned.

"It keeps unwanted visitors away," Robert informed her. "If anyone wanders nearby they will change directions, deciding to go walk somewhere else."

"Coast seems clear," Enda nodded.

"Clear for what?" Jason asked.

Robert pressed a few of the columns hard.

There was a deep rumble and Tase nearly stumbled off his feet. Jason jumped up, slack-jawed.

Fadin moved next to Tase and they stared, in shocked awe, as the sea seemed to be growing, but then more columns appeared, rising from the water.

They kept rising up and up, until finally, they were all the same height, and made a wide and long bridge all the way to the distant landmass that was Scotland.

"WOW!" Aednat exclaimed, jumping up and down. Aimirgin covered her mouth in surprised delight.

"Oh," Jason gasped. He leaned against one of the stones. Tase's mouth hung open, amazed.

"This may be one of the most incredible things I've seen magic do yet," Fadin said.

Robert ruffled his hair and began crossing the bridge, Marie right at his heels. "Come along, Jason," he called.

Jason obeyed shakily. "I am getting myself a full examination if I ever wake up," he told himself. He stepped carefully on the wet stones and kept muttering.

"Last one there is rotten dragon dung." Aednat winked at them and began crossing the bridge.

Tase smiled, his red hair being tousled by the wind. "Aimirgin, it would be better if you didn't race. We don't want to have to dive in and save you."

"Ha, ha," Aimirgin mocked, but she tread her way carefully.

It didn't take too long to cross, but it was no quick matter. The stones indeed were slippery, thick with sea moss and covered in water, some fish had even gotten beached by the sudden rise of the stones. Tase, Fadin, and Robert had to help Aimirgin along several times. Her hoofed feet were not graceful like Desmond's on the slick stone.

Tase was grateful when they made it to the Isle of Staffa, and felt safer once the bridge was lowered. He kept fretting the whole time that someone or something may see the bridge and realise where they were headed, even with Roberts protection.

Jason leaned against the rock wall that stood along the beach and put his head in his hands.

"You did good," Enda smiled at him. "Didn't lose your head once." Jason looked at him.

"I'm impressed," Enda winked. He whistled and flexed his talons as he walked by.

Jason's eyes became huge as he watched the talons retract. "Enda," Robert scolded.

Enda just chuckled and Saoirse even smiled at him. Her body looked so frail.

Tase looked around. This area of Scotland was uninhabited, and it was eerily silent, except for the waves crashing upon the rock. "Now what?" he asked.

"I thought Nóinín was an Irish story."

"Nóinín has been around for a long time," Robert said. "It is a Celtic story, not simply an Irish one. The city has been lost for many years, and only a handful of people know where to find it."

Tase was confused but didn't press the issue.

They walked along the shoreline until Robert had them come to a halt.

"Is it close?" Fadin questioned.

Robert walked up to part of the stone that burrowed in like a cave and climbed up the cliff edge. "Closer than you think." He breathed into his hands again, touched his silver fingers onto the stone and took a step back. A hole suddenly appeared, marked by blue light and part of the stone pulling inward.

Tase took a step forward and watched with wide eyes.

Robert pulled out an old amethyst stone that had flecks of gold here and there. He placed it into the hole and turned it three times clockwise, twice counterclockwise, and once more to the right.

Everything was silent for a moment, and then the stones moved. They folded in upon themselves, and up into the cliff, and down into the floor. After a moment an opening could be seen. The rocks continued to clear away until a large arch stood before them. In golden letters, on a smooth piece of stone that was a part of the stone entrance, was the word *Nóinín*.

"This is *so* not normal," Jason whimpered.

"It will be all right," Aimirgin consoled him.

Tase took a deep breath, feeling the mounting apprehension.

"Don't expect a warm welcome," Robert said, moving under the arch. "Those who live here now, are not keen on guests."

"Wonderful," Aednat sighed.

Marie was like a shadow behind him.

"Wait," Jason said, his voice quivering, "we're going in there? Are you serious?" He followed closely behind.

Tase bit his lip and followed into the dark.

It was like a narrow cave, which bent steadily downward. It was dark, nearly pitch black. Robert created a purple flame in his hand, and led them on.

Tase pulled his cloak around himself as the temperature quickly dropped. The passageway spiraled, and became narrower. Tase began to feel panic creep up his spine, but he tried to fight it, and remind himself they were here to help Saoirse.

All at once the walls fell away and Tase gasped at what stood before him. A massive city, looking like one large castle carved out of the stone itself, towered in the large open cave. It was old, and showed signs that there had been battles fought there long ago. If Cavan-Corr was big, this was enormous. Tase could almost hear the battle that must have raged when poor King Nuadu was betrayed.

Aimirgin gasped. "Oh."

"Bless me," Enda breathed.

"Welcome to Nóinín," Robert said, his voice echoing against the stones.

They entered through a massive broken stone gate, and Tase's heart leapt into his throat as they crossed the threshold, but nothing stirred.

Much time passed as they climbed the city, undisturbed. How much time, Tase wasn't sure, but the fact that they had gotten so high up made Tase think it had been hours.

"Not to complain," Jason said, clutching to his jacket. "But what is it we are supposed to find here?"

"He's right," Saoirse said, leaning against Enda for support. "There's no one here."

"I'm sorry to say I disagree with you both," Robert said. "But there is most certainly someone here. And they're watching us."

He pointed up to a sheer cliff, where a balcony once protruded from a house built into the rock.

Tase looked up and clutched Fadin's sleeve.

Fadin let out a shocked breath. "I see it," he whispered. Hiding in the shadows were a pair of bright green eyes.

# CHAPTER 16
## NÓINÍN

Fadin gulped as he stared at the pair of eyes watching them. The irises were so pale they could easily be mistaken for white, just like Vladimir's when he became a wolf.

Jason clamped his eyes shut, and Enda stood protectively in front of him. Marie nervously clutched onto Robert's trousers.

"What do we do?" Fadin whispered, keeping his eyes fixed upon the creature in the shadows.

Without warning a great cry rose up. There was the sound of climbing against rock; growling and scornful sniggers flooded the great cave.

Aimirgin squeaked and clutched onto Fadin and Tase's sleeves.

In an instant at least fifty people clothed in fur and leather were surrounding them, knives brandished, claws extended, and bright green eyes filled with murderous intent.

Everyone huddled against each other.

Fadin felt his stomach drop in terror. They were in a close-knit circle with nowhere to go. He kept his sword drawn but wished for nothing more than a place to run. They were ridiculously outnumbered.

"This is a plan?" Enda spat at Robert.

"I didn't know there were so many," Robert acknowledged.

"No kidding," Enda hissed.

A man stepped forward, shabby and vicious looking. "Lost, are we?" he asked, his voice sending shivers up Fadin's spine.

"Not unless this isn't the kingdom of Nóinín," Robert answered, not sounding the least bit frightened.

Fadin stared at the man's face. He appeared to be thinking.

"Well, in that case," he grinned, "better take you to our queen." He bowed mockingly and yelled, "Wrangle them to the throne room, boys!"

The wild looking people cried out with frightening excitement.

Fadin was shoved against Tase as their entire group was pushed forward, securely surrounded, with no place open for escape.

They were herded along several curving streets, wide arching corridors, and large tunnels. Fadin was poked by the tip of a knife more than once, which sent a shudder of laughter through the wild looking man who prodded him.

They rounded a wide corner and came to what looked like the equivalent of a town square. It was a large oval area, open and peering over part of the city below it. It appeared there had been foliage here once, because large bits of ground were marked out that looked like gardens. Now the earth was grey and hard.

Near the back of this open courtyard, there were corridors clearly leading to the rest of the city. Before them a wide swirling throne sat; even in its decrepit state it was a sight to behold. It was a seat made from green marble, and it had a dazzling piece of mirror that glowed of its own inner light, where the head of the king would have rested. The arms looked to be large petals, made of gold, now dull but still brilliant. Other golden flowers lined the throne, and made their way to where the footrest ended. On the sides of the throne were three stone statues carved in the shape of three girls, with small tiaras. Each of them had hair made from gold that swirled below their feet and wove into the throne itself.

Directly in front of the throne there was a great tomb, made from marble and encased in gold and diamonds. The top looked like a man, laying face up, holding golden flowers in his folded hands. Etched into the sides of the tombs were the faces of the four women with golden hair.

"King Nuadu's Tomb," Enda whispered as they were pushed towards it.

Fadin was overcome by the reality of the place. He had only known this kingdom in a story, and now the tomb statues of the golden princesses stood before him. He turned as a glimmer caught his eye, and saw a pile of mirror pieces on a large flat rock, some pieced together, beginning the forming of a mirror statue. Queen Duana's mirror statue.

Their captors stopped pushing them, and backed up, giving them a wider space to move in.

Fadin took a deep breath and looked up. He suppressed a gasp and snapped his mouth shut.

A multitude of light green eyes were staring out at them from the shadows. "Oh, m... my," Jason breathed, clutching Marie to him.

Marie did not look happy. Her eyes were wide and frightened, and she clung onto Jason as if he were the only thing keeping her tethered to the floor.

"Robert," Enda said, his deep voice disturbed.

"I know," he answered, not taking his eyes off the things watching them.

"There are too many," Desmond hissed, watching the ones they had been captured by, and looking at the many eyes staring at them.

Saoirse began to tremble and clutched Desmond's whole arm against her. Enda brandished his talons. "If this goes sour," he murmured.

Fadin moved so he was shoulder to shoulder with Tase, and he grabbed Aednat's sleeve and pulled her closer while Tase already had Aimirgin's arm. "Keep close," he said, steeling a glace at them. "We are more of a threat together," he said to Tase.

Tase nodded and put his hand on the hilt of his sword, which was securely attached to his belt.

"If there's a fight," Tase said, directing his words to Aednat and Aimirgin, "you both stay right next to us."

Aednat nodded and gulped, taking a step behind him. Aimirgin put her hand on her flail.

"Still glad you came, Freckles?" Fadin whispered at her.

She glared at him and gave him a small punch in the shoulder.

An odd clicking noise resounded in the courtyard. It bounced off the old walls and rang in Fadin's ears. Someone was clicking their tongue to the roof of their mouth.

"Who dares to disturb this place?" a woman's voice slid out of the darkness.

It made the hair on Fadin's arms stand on end. He could feel the power behind that voice. It was unlike the rumble of magic being called upon. It was deeper, and more potent somehow. It was like a smell wafting off a hot meal. Whoever this woman was, her magic ran deep within her, not even needing to be called forward to be present.

"Someone in need of your help, Lady," Robert said, stepping forward just in front of the tomb.

There was a cold laugh. "*My* help? Surely you must be joking." The voice moved, though Fadin heard no footsteps. "You cannot possibly be so stupid as to have come willingly into our lair, Old One, and think we will help *you*."

"Stupid, no," Robert answered, his eyes moving in the shadow, "but desperate." He turned to Enda and nodded.

Enda looked at Desmond, who reluctantly let Saoirse go.

Saoirse, clutching to Enda as tightly as she could, followed him out to where Robert waited. Her curly black hair swirled around her, making her look even paler than she actually was.

As soon as Saoirse actually crossed the threshold into the oval courtyard, hisses rose up all around them. More eyes joined the others already looking on, and the voice in the blackness growled.

Fadin's heart pounded louder, and he held his breath.

Robert put his hand on Saoirse's shoulder. "This child is ill, and it is my belief the one who can help her is in your ranks."

"This child *should not exist!*" the voice rumbled. "She is an abomination, an unnatural creature, a half breed! It is because of her very nature that she is ill." The voice moved again. "You will find no help from us here."

"You would deny your own kind? The child of your own kin?" Robert asked.

There was a heavy silence. In the blink of an eye a woman appeared from the dark. She was wild looking, even more so than Dominique. Her hair was a long wavy mess of several colours, auburn, silver, chestnut, ash-blond, and golden-brown. It was pinned back away from her face, and pushed up, so it looked like a small ball was perched beneath her hair, while the rest of it fell around and over her shoulders in tangled waves. Her eyes were such a light green they nearly looked white, the same as all the other eyes staring out at them. Her skin was dirty, looking to have a thin layer of grey and brown dust caked on it. She was clothed in leather bottoms and high brown boots. Her arms were covered in bracelets of leather, her hands in thick rings, and she wore a heavy fur cloak, with the head of a wolf adorning one shoulder.

Fadin tried not to stare at her, but he couldn't help it.

Jason was staring too, though his was a look of sheer terror.

She came so close to Robert, they were nearly touching. Her green eyes were very large, almost unnaturally so, and they had the faintest hint of pink in the whites, making the green stand out all the more. She scanned him with those eyes, seeming to bury into him. She cocked her head from side to side and grabbed a small handful of his cloak. She breathed it in, and let it fall away. "You are not what you seem," she spat.

He leaned in closer to her. "Neither are you, Yessult, Queen of this Cavern."

A smile broke out on her face, and showed perfectly white teeth. "You know of me?"

"I would be a fool to come here if I did not."

"You are a fool already," she hissed back. She stepped away from him, the smile still colouring her pale lips. She turned her vivid green gaze upon Saoirse, who cowered in its wake.

The woman moved around her, shifting her position almost like a lion examining its prey. Yessult grabbed a handful of her thick, curly black hair and breathed deeply. She flung it away from her and grasped Saoirse's chin.

Saoirse let out a little shriek but did not pull away.

Yessult let out a cold laugh and pushed her face back. "She is a half-breed all right." She took a step backward. "This thing is forbidden," she said to Robert. "It is against our laws."

Fadin stiffened. He wasn't sure, but he had a feeling this woman was not a werewolf. So what was she? And what did that make Saoirse?

"Against your laws or not, she is here, and she needs help."

"I'll bet she does," Yessult sniggered. "Her other half has been choked and stuffed, and is just aching to come out." Her eyes were like green ice. "She is half changeling half human; whoever created her doomed her to death. I will not help her."

"She is the daughter of one of your kin. One who I know to be here." Robert said. "Faolan Hennessey."

Yessult stopped smiling. "That is a great accusation to make." Her face was contemptuous.

"She is his." Robert stood firm and looked her in the eye. "Therefore he must take responsibility for her."

Yessult looked like she could break Robert's neck, but she nodded her head. "If what you say is true, then this cannot be pushed aside, and the one who has disobeyed must indeed be held for his actions." She turned her gaze to the shadows and screamed. "Faolan!"

Fadin's heart leapt into his throat. He *was* here. Whatever Saoirse was, whatever was wrong with her, their hope was that Faolan, her real father, could help. Saoirse was part human, but she was part whatever Faolan was too. It had seemed she was half-werewolf, but Robert seemed to think that was not the case.

Throat dry, Fadin turned his eyes to the spot where Yessult was glaring.

From the shadows stepped a man who had only the vaguest resemblance to the singing picture of him that hung in Fadin's old closet. That picture had shown a twenty something boy with a wide smile, silvery-blond hair, and sparkling green eyes. The man who stood in the courtyard before them was small and too thin. He had to be in his fifties, at least, and his face was gaunt and sallow, covered in a silver beard and mustache. His hair, which nearly hung to his shoulders, had gone completely silver, and his eyes had lost their sparkle. His skin, like Yessult's, seemed to have a layer of dust covering it, and his clothes were made from leather and fur.

257

He stared in pained disbelief at Saoirse, his hands quivering. Saoirse was just as still as he was.

Yessult turned to Faolan. "You claim her, Ciotógach?" Faolan didn't move.

Fadin held his breath.

Yessult smiled. "Do you claim this child?" Faolan slowly shook his head.

Saoirse let out a gasping cry.

Fadin hissed under his breath, fury burning his cheeks. Aednat clutched his sleeve.

Desmond cursed and took a step forward, but Tase put a hand on his chest to hold him back.

Yessult chuckled. "Well, Old One, unless you have proof, that this girl is indeed his, then —"

But Faolan, head continuing to shake, walked up to Saoirse and cupped her face in his hands. His bottom lip quivered, and his silver brows were pulled together, making a firm dent in his forehead. "My daughter," he choked between the tears that ran from his eyes. "Bless me," he gasped, "*you look just like her!*"

Saoirse was etched in place, her mouth hanging open.

Yessult's features had contorted malevolently. "This child is *yours*?" she spat.

Faolan released Saoirse's face, and turned to her. "Yes, my queen," he looked back at Saoirse, "she is."

Yessult gave a low growl.

Robert pushed Saoirse and Enda back behind him.

Enda held onto Saoirse protectively, and she gaped at her father and Yessult in dread.

"You have broken one of our highest laws!" Yessult roared.

Faolan fell to his knees and bowed his head at her feet. "I know, my queen. I cannot make penance for what I have done. I was foolish then, I did not want to accept what I was. I made a terrible mistake."

"Mistake?" Yessult howled.

There were roars and growls from the shadows and around them. The watching green eyes narrowed into glaring slits, and those in the courtyard bent low as if ready to pounce.

Fadin's stomach churned. He didn't see how they were going to get out of this cave alive.

Yessult began to circle Faolan. "If memory serves, making a child is no *mistake!*"

Faolan kept his head bowed. "No, my queen, you are right. I broke our laws, but I have lived many years following them and serving you."

"Is that supposed to make up for what you have done?" she screeched, her voice echoing to great heights.

Tase caught Fadin's eye.

Fadin shook his head. This was not going well.

"Of course not," Faolan answered. "Nothing can, but my queen, I have been loyal to you. You have taught me all I know about my true nature, and I understand why such things are forbidden."

Yessult snarled at him. "Do you?"

"Yes," Faolan answered. "But I cannot take back what has been done."

Yessult's eyes flickered up to Saoirse. "No," she agreed, "But you can set things straight."

At this Faolan lifted his head. "My queen?" Fadin had a bad feeling.

In the blink of an eye Yessult dashed behind Robert and snatched Saoirse away from Enda.

Robert could have attacked her, stopped her, but he remained still, and Fadin could only guess this was to keep the masses of eyes and crouched bodies from pouncing on them all. One wrong move and they would be in an incredibly outnumbered battle.

Yessult flung Saoirse's cloak off and made her get down on her hands and knees before Faolan.

Enda's face was furious, but Robert kept his arm in front of him, keeping him from moving.

Desmond was almost beside himself. It was only because Robert stood in the way that he did not attack.

Faolan was as surprised by Yessult's actions as anyone else. He stared up at her.

"Kill her," Yessult barked. Saoirse let out a terrified cry.

"What?" Faolan gaped.

Fadin's stomach gave a great lurch. "You heard me, Ilchruthach. Kill her!"

Desmond roared at the top of his lungs, his teeth bared, his fingers beginning to take on the shape of claws.

Suddenly, Saoirse began to change. Her demeanor was no longer cowering, she became stiff, and her eyes narrowed coolly. Her hands went slack and her breathing evened out.

Yessult noticed the change because she turned her attention away from Faolan.

"Kill her?" Saoirse's voice rumbled, much deeper than it should have been. "I think not!"

Yessult clenched her teeth and hissed.

Saoirse ripped her arms away, her nails turned to gnarled claws with silver tips. She slapped Yessult, leaving a bloody gash, and jerked a few steps away from her. She whirled around, her black curls falling in her face, and she growled at Yessult.

Snarls, howls, and screams rose all around the courtyard.

Yessult touched her dripping cheek and turned her wild eyes on Faolan. "Do

259

you see why they are forbidden?" she scowled, looking at the blood on her fingertips. "They have no sense of the order of things. They are untamable, disloyal, not knowing of our ways." She spat at Saoirse's feet.

Saoirse let out a terrifying roar that could not belong to human lungs.

Fadin nearly stumbled backward and Jason clutched onto the shoulder of his shirt.

"Prove to me I am your queen," Yessult hissed at Faolan. "Kill her!" Faolan slowly got to his feet and Saoirse brandished her claws at him.

"No," he said firmly.

Yessult's face lost all expression. Her large green eyes pierced Faolan, but he neither backed down nor made a sound. She glowered, brandishing her white teeth. "So be it," she snapped. She roared, a terrible deep rumble that reverberated through the ground. Yessult began to change, she became taller, her legs and arms widened, her face elongated, and her fur coat clutched to her skin and began to cover every inch of her. In her place, standing nearly four metres tall, was an enormous bear, with the head of a lion and a long lion's tail that had a sharp spine protruding from it. Her fur was of silver, chestnut, auburn, ash-blond, and golden-brown, and her eyes burned with fury.

What happened next took only a matter of seconds but Fadin saw it all in slow motion. Faolan grabbed Saoirse's arm, Robert whirled round and shoved Enda towards Fadin and the others.

Enda yelled for them to run, his claws displayed, and Desmond exploded into the grey wolf. Fadin pulled his sword from its sheathe, his eyes staying on Robert.

Robert pulled a large hammer from beneath his cloak, and held it high. In a brilliant flash, which caused Yessult and her people to turn their heads to shield their eyes, he, Enda, Saoirse, and Faolan vanished from where they had been standing and were teleported into the midst of Fadin and the others.

"Run!" Robert commanded.

Fadin didn't need telling twice. He, Tase, Aimirgin, and Aednat dashed side by side.

There was a bloodcurdling shriek from behind them, and Fadin couldn't help but look back.

Swarming from the shadows, climbing on the walls above the courtyard like great spiders, scurrying over the cliff edge, and dashing around and past Yessult, there were hundreds upon hundreds of green-eyed men, women, and every kind of predatory animal Fadin had ever seen. Lions, Panthers, Bears, Wolves, Tigers, and a battalion of others.

Fadin screamed. There were too many, and they were too fast. They could never outrun them.

Fadin turned his eyes ahead at the stone walkway before him. His eyes widened as far as they could go. Hundreds of the creatures were already clambering over the walls ahead of them, and the ones behind were gaining.

"Weapons out!" Robert ordered.

Jason let out a horrible yelp as he too saw what was before them. "Behind me!" Robert boomed at him, ripping Jason and Marie directly behind him.

Fadin held his sword at the ready.

"Charge!" Robert screamed, picking up his speed, hammer above his head.

Enda let out a battle cry. Saoirse ran full speed, claws out.

"Keep close!" Fadin demanded of Aednat. He positioned his sword like a spear before him and ran in unison with Tase. He let out a scream as they approached the throng coming right at them. He was so afraid that his teeth chattered as he ran, but he did not stop, there was no turning back.

They collided with a terrible thundering crash.

Fadin's blade sunk deep into the chest of a leopard and the animal seemed to explode into glittering dust. He tore the blade away before he could think, his heart pounding. There was a snarl to his left and with a jerk of his arm he sliced at a large brown wolf. He missed, and the wolf lunged to bite his leg. He dodged the bite and kept moving.

"Fadin!" Tase cried.

Fadin turned and saw the massive horde of predators from behind ram into their small group. A lion pinned him down and Fadin sliced at it.

There was a bright blast and before he knew what happened Enda had him by the arm and was dragging him forward.

"Keep moving!" Robert ordered. "Do not stop no matter what."

"Easier said than done," Fadin hissed as a large bear got in his way.

The wolf Desmond jumped on it and bit at its face. Fadin sliced at the bear and it tumbled off the stone walkway.

"Look, look!" Jason wailed.

Fadin peered where he was pointing and saw a great mass of beasts that would force them to stop just ahead.

"Bloody hell!" Enda billowed.

"You're right," Faolan yelped. Fadin had almost forgot about him. "We can't stop, they'll overcome us, and she won't make it," he said, nodding to Saoirse.

Saoirse looked confused and terrified, but back to her old self. Her skin was whiter than snow though, and her hair was sticking to her face because of sweat.

"Follow me," Robert cried, suddenly jumping from the street off the sheer drop to the left.

"What!" Tase yelped. Fadin's jaw dropped.

"Don't think," Enda told them, rushing at the edge, "just do it!" He vanished over the side.

Fadin could see nothing but black over the edge but one look at the oncoming stampede, and the sound of the one behind, and he turned towards the edge.

His lungs burned as he cried out, nothing beneath him except air. His feet hit something solid and he stared in awe as he realised they were on a great, round cog. What it had been used for he had no idea, but it was large enough for them all to stand on.

"What are you doing?" Fadin cried as he saw Robert smash one of the cables holding it to the stone wall.

"Improvising," he called back. He smashed the last supporting cable and the gear moaned and shuttered.

"Are you crazy?" Jason screeched.

"Get ready to run," Robert barked, grabbing onto Marie's hand. Her chin was trembling, and her eyes were squinting with fear.

Something jumped onto the cog behind Fadin. He turned and jerked back as he came face to face with a huge hyena.

That was all it took.

The great wheel began to roll.

Fadin nearly fell on his face, he had to run forward, finding he was at the front of the spinning wheel, but in his terror of being eaten by the hyena he kept his balance.

Screams from the others rang in his ears, but all he could think about was moving his feet.

The hyena tried to run at him, but it lost its footing and fell off, exploding into the same glittering dust. Fadin risked a glance over his shoulder and saw the others running with the wheel too, and that the cog was rolling of its own accord down the broken streets.

The cog hit a wall and it caused it to shutter and slow, nearly stopping. Fadin kept his balance, but only just.

The cog regained its momentum and the creatures chasing them swarmed on the walls and buildings next to them.

"In a moment," Robert suddenly yelled, "follow my lead and jump off!"

Fadin turned to him and saw a wall and a large bridge coming at them. If they stayed where they were they would become decapitated by the bridge, or squashed by the wall. "We can't possibly make that!" he cried.

There was no choice, however, the bridge and the wall were coming.

Just as Fadin was wondering how they were all going to jump when the wheel was turned the wrong way, the giant cog snagged on something beneath them and it swung like a door on hinges, positioning them the right way.

"Face it," Robert barked.

Everyone turned, the wheel wobbling dangerously under their feet. "Take my hand," Robert instructed Jason.

Jason didn't argue.

"Use the momentum for your jump when we hit the wall," Robert instructed.

Tase gripped Fadin's hand.

Fadin closed his fingers firmly around his brother's. "Now!"

They hit the wall and Fadin sprang forward. There wasn't much need to jump, other than positioning, because the force of the impact caused them to fly forward with great speed.

They all landed on the bridge, Enda nearly overshooting it. "Go, go!" Robert ordered, pointing to the right.

Fadin, Tase, Aimirgin, and Aednat fallowed closely behind.

There was a crash just before them and several beasts dropped down, crashing right in their path.

Robert swung with his hammer and a large portion of the street fell away, taking the predators with it.

Fadin kept running and immediately saw a problem.

Where there once used to be a whole stone bridge, there were now parts, with great gaps between the firm stone, and some of the standing pillars looked shaky and unstable.

"No time to stare at it," Robert boomed. He grabbed Aednat and flung her across the first gap.

She screamed, flew through the air and landed, rolling along the floor, nearly falling off the other side. Her face was filled with horror when she ripped around.

Robert turned to Fadin, but he leapt out towards the first landing before he could touch him.

"Go, Freckles, go!" he yelped. He grabbed her hand, and together they jumped across the next gap.

He could hear the others following behind and with Aednat he ran and took another leap across the great opening that led far down into blackness.

"The next one is too far," Aednat wailed, trying hard not to cry.

"No," Fadin said, staring at the hole that looked like a wide-open mouth. "We'll make it." He doubted it. The gap was too long.

"Fadin?" Tase yelled, landing on the stone and helping Aimirgin with her footing.

All four of them stared at the space before them. "Nothing for it," Fadin cried, taking Aednat's hand firmly in his.

Tase did the same with Aimirgin. "What are we waiting for then?"

Fadin nodded, his heart plummeting in terror. They ran towards the hole, pushing their feet as hard as they could into the stone. They came to the edge and jumped off. Before they were midway Fadin knew they weren't going to make it – they were much too far from the other landing – and his stomach did panicky somersaults. There was nothing any of them could do; it was too late, they were all going to fall to their deaths.

Black smoke suddenly consumed them, and in a blink Fadin's feet hit solid earth, so hard in fact that he groaned in pain. He jerked back, feeling Aednat's hand still clasped to his own, and stared down at the stone beneath his feet. They all had made it.

"How?" Tase gasped.

Fadin turned to him, mouth open.

Before Fadin could say anything, his eye caught something to their right. Hordes of angry beasts were gathered at what used to be the end of the bridge. Desmond and Jason landed on the pillar with them.

"That's gonna be a problem," Desmond said, eyeing the wall of howling animals.

Robert and the others landed on the stone as well. "We're trapped," Enda panted.

"Not if I can help it," Robert said. He raised his hammer high and let it collide with the stone.

The pillar gave a groan.

"Are you mad?" Desmond asked. "You'll bring the whole thing down."

"That's the point, boy," Robert grunted. He brought his hammer down again, and the pillar wobbled. "One more ought to do it," Robert said. He raised to strike once more.

Suddenly the great bear with the lion's face hurled itself through the air, just as Robert brought his hammer down towards the ground.

Fadin saw it as if in slow motion. The bear, which he knew was Yessult, aimed at Marie, but Jason flung himself in the way. The bear grabbed Jason with her massive clawed paws and wrestled him to the ground as he screamed and fought her. She roared at him and then sank her teeth deep into his shoulder.

Roberts's hammer found its target and the stone pillar broke free and began to fall forward.

Fadin and the others leaned back to keep from tumbling off, but Yessult and Jason rolled off the edge and vanished into the black.

"Doctor!" Marie called, but Robert held her firmly. The pillar began to slide on its own.

"Get down low so you don't fall off," Robert commanded.

Fadin crouched down, and it was a good thing he did. The pillar began to slide down, at incredible speed, what was once streets, but now was almost an avalanche of rubble.

The sounds of animals behind them became loud and hateful, but there was no way the beasts could gain on them at the speed they were going.

"We're nearly at the bottom!" Enda cried as their piece of bridge soared towards the flat ground near where they had come in.

Everyone was hurled forward unexpectedly as the pillar collided with something protruding out of the slide of rubble.

Fadin rammed into the floor, his shoulder hitting first then his face and side. He yelped in pain but stood up as soon as his body stopped its sliding.

"Go," Robert yelled, pointing with his staff towards the way they had come in.

Fadin glanced up the streets now filled with broken bits of city and saw an alarming stampede headed right for them. He saw Aednat standing up, a terrible burn from the ground across her right cheek, and grabbed her arm. He snatched up Aimirgin's hand and jerked them both along. He felt Tase just behind him dash into the dark corridor.

He ran up the winding path, the sounds of the others at his heels. Sunlight crept around the snakelike tunnel and he pushed himself harder, nearly dragging the girls beside him.

They burst through the opening in the rock into blinding light, but Fadin didn't stop, he kept running, tripping and stumbling over the beach rocks beneath him. He could see the causeway not far ahead. Perhaps if they could make it there they would be safe.

"Fadin," Tase cried, "we'll never make it that far!"

Already Fadin could hear the beasts erupting from the cave.

"Dry up and run!" Fadin barked through clenched teeth. They had to make it, *they had to*! He flew across the stone, his eyes adjusting to the light, and saw that the giant bridge was disappearing back into the water. "No!" he screamed. "No, no!"

Aednat wailed at his side. "Oh, what are we goin' to do?"

Aimirgin screamed and Fadin turned to see Saoirse pinned beneath a panther, her eyes wide green balls of fury, but though she fought vigorously the panther was far stronger.

Aimirgin cried, "We have to help them!" Fadin slid to a halt and drew his sword.

Desmond the wolf flung himself towards the panther that had Saoirse, but a blonde and grey jackal met him in mid-air and the two tumbled along the rocks, barking and sinking their teeth into one another.

Enda was wrestling a giant gorilla, his talons slicing open whatever they could come in contact with.

Robert was sending several beasts hurtling through the air, with one swipe after another with his hammer, but more kept coming. Marie was clutching his cloak and screaming, her terrified and lost eyes seeming to swallow up her whole pale face. The creatures appeared to be trying to reach Marie, to snatch her up.

Fadin felt his heart collide against his chest, and shivered at the sweat pouring off his face and down his already damp shirt. There were too many, there was no way they could beat this number of creatures.

Aednat let out a gasp and Fadin turned his eyes to where hers fell.

Two hyenas, a panther, and a wolf had their heads turned in Fadin, Tase,

Aimirgin, and Aednat's direction. There was a brief moment of pause, and suddenly, like a rocket, the four beasts turned and came galloping at them.

Tase drew his sword too, and stood at Fadin's side. "We can't beat them," Tase gulped.

Aimirgin drew her flail. "We have to try," she said. She pushed Aednat behind her. "I want you to run, Aednat."

She let out a whimper. "I won't."

Fadin wanted to argue Aimirgin was right, but there was no time. He ripped his sword forward just as a hyena smashed into him.

He could hear the other one slam into Tase.

Fadin cut the beast's right leg, but it didn't stop the vicious attacks of its teeth. It clamped his sword's blade over and over, and it was all he could do to keep its fangs from sinking into him. He held its neck back as far as he could with his open hand, digging his fingers into its fur.

"Fadin!" Aednat screeched.

He turned his eyes and saw the blue-black panther flying through the air towards him. He tried to push the hyena away, but it was no use, it was too strong. He turned his body so the hyena was facing the leaping cat. It landed on top of the hyena, which yelped, and Fadin groaned under the weight, but its reach was long and its claws slashed into Fadin's skin. He gasped and cried out, unable to help himself. The pain was blinding, the cuts from the panther had gone deep.

Aimirgin attacked the panther, setting its fur on fire, but the panther did not seem to mind. It tumbled on top of her.

Aednat shrieked. She was suddenly in his line of vision, throwing a large rock in the direction of the panther.

He kept his sword between the hyena's teeth, which kept attacking him, but his strength was faltering quickly, and in a wave of panic he saw the panther pull away and give chase to little Aednat, who was now running toward the water.

Next to him, Tase fell to the floor and cried out.

Fadin cried out, not with pain, but in desperation. He couldn't hold on much longer, and any magic he possessed was squashed by pain and fear and he could find no way to let it out.

There was a great crash of power that burst from behind them. It caused Fadin to crumble to his knees, and the golden wave sent the hyena colliding with the stones.

His ears began to ring and all sound was blocked out except a beeping that seemed deeper, as if it were imbedded in his skull. He watched as the wave of something that appeared hot crashed its way through beast and human alike, sending everything it touched to the ground. The things the golden wave did not touch took off running in the opposite direction.

Fadin began to feel dizzy and lightheaded. Before he understood what was happening, his head hit the ground. His eyes rolled up and he stared at the sky, his ears still hearing nothing but the ringing.

A shape appeared before him, and as his eyes adjusted he had just a momentary picture of something gigantic, with huge silver eyes, and great wide wings.

# CHAPTER 17
# THE D.E.R.T.H.S.

Cormick, Colmcille and Quinlan Hogan had made it to the castle safely. Clearie noticed the relief in Mr Hogan at having three of his children under one roof.

Colmcille had broken his leg during the sea battle, and had a hard time getting around, but he had seen where most of the others had gone. Alassandra Aislinn had been seriously injured, and Irrah had taken her, Ardan, and Ananta personally to his home. Aldabella had been spotted in the ocean; after that no one seemed to know what happened to her.

Aunt Kyna had deliberately gone off on her own; where, it wasn't clear, but she had denied help from Irrah, insisting she had an important task to attend to.

There was absolutely no sign of Arden, and that news made Clearie's mind imagine the worst possibilities.

It was decided they would leave for the elven kingdom the next day, and Clearie, already packed, feeling anxious, decided to explore the newly opened up castle. Ma asked if he wanted company, but he insisted that he was fine and wanted to be alone. He knew this part of the castle brought up bad memories for her.

As he ventured into the new rooms he wished Fadin and Tase, ever adventurous, were with him. He missed Aednat's sassy comments and Aimirgin's gentle spirit. He prayed they were safe, wherever they were.

He discovered an even larger kitchen than the first, a room that had nothing but books – which he spent a significant amount of time in – and another that was an inside garden complete with waterfall.

As he made his way back downstairs he spotted a door that lead to a steep narrow stairway that spun downward. He considered not going inside, but something pulled at him and he opened the door. The stairs led deep underground and when he came to the end he saw an underground cavern that was undoubtedly the dungeon.

There was a large pool in the middle of it and Clearie walked cautiously to its edge. Something moved beneath the surface. Before Clearie had time to panic, a face appeared and broke the water's surface.

It was a mermaid, and, by the looks of her, quite an old one at that. She had green hair, pale blue eyes, and milky white skin. "Do not be afraid," she said. "I am Noelani, the mermaiden of this castle. I have been here many years, given sanctuary by your grandfather, Declan Kavanagh."

Clearie swallowed, his purple and blue eyes wide.

"I only want to help you," she assured him. "I helped your brother once, when he fell from the goblin's slide into my pool. I promise, I won't harm you." She kicked her lovely ashen green tail, which billowed out behind her like the tail of a betta fish.

Clearie recalled Tase telling the story of being trapped in the well and something breathing air into his mouth to save him. This mermaid must be the creature. "What do you want from me?"

"To warn you, as I have been asked, and to give you this." She held a bright green dagger in her glittering scaled hands. "It was given to your brothers by Aimirgin Hogan, but I am afraid it was not hers to give. It was in her father's study, and it was a gift to him from the true owner." She nodded to him. "It originally belonged to your elven father, Fintan." She held it out for Clearie to take. "It can unlock any door, and in the future you will be in need of such a skill."

He took it from her and held it carefully. "Thank you," he said, examining it. "How did *you* get it?"

"Your brothers dropped it, and when they did I had the castle bring it to me." She must have noticed his confused look because she gave him a small half smile. "When you have been in one place as long as I have, you learn a trick or two." She touched Cleaire's arm. "I also am to give you this." It was a brilliant emerald stone. "You must not use it here," she warned. "Use it in a safe place."

"What is it? How do I use it?"

"When the time comes, you'll know," she nodded. "I must leave you," she said. "Keep that dagger safe. Good luck to you, young one." With that, the mermaid vanished under the dungeon water, swimming away into one of what Clearie could see were many tunnels.

Clearie took a steadying breath. The knot in his stomach grew and the worry felt like it would swallow him up.

~~~

Tase moaned and rolled. The bile choked out of him before he really understood what was happening. Another wave of nausea took him, and he shuddered as the last of the sick left his sour mouth. He turned back to the position he had first awoken in and slowly opened his eyes.

He was staring up into hexagonal cubes of stone, which made up a vast high ceiling nearly twenty-one metres above him. As he slowly arched his head he realised he was in a cave, a cave made completely of these strangely shaped stones, and that in certain areas the stones became hexagonal pillars, and they looked familiar. As he stared at a particular pillar a switch in his head set in place. It looked just like the Giant's Causeway. This thought flooded his mind with other images and memories, Saoirse trapped under a panther, a great stampede of

269

carnivorous predatory animals, a wolf pinning him down, searing pain in his leg as teeth sunk into his skin. He jerked up at this sudden remembrance and the pain in his leg was no longer a memory, but extremely real. He squinted his eyes and yelped involuntarily. The sound carried across the cave and bounced off the hexagonal pillars.

"Ah, careful, laddie," a deep voice rumbled beside him.

Tase again jerked, this time to the right, and the pain spiked. He kept his cry of pain to himself and blinked confusedly at the face beside him.

A white haired man, with chiseled features, bright icy blue eyes, and a long nose that had been broken at least twice, peered down solemnly at Tase's leg. "I hope it'll heal properly, but ye have got to rest it." His brilliantly light eyes found Tase's, and Tase saw a clawed scar, which went up into the man's hairline.

There were so many things that didn't make sense to him, but the most immediate concern rushed out of his mouth before he could stop it. "Where are the others?"

"Safe," the man answered.

"Hey, Duff," a woman's voice echoed across the stone, "that one awake?"

"A'yep," the white haired man, clearly named Duff, said.

Tase turned his eyes to the woman. She was somewhere in her thirties, with blond hair cropped extremely short, a scar on her lip, and some sort of bandage over her left eyebrow. She wore warm clothing, and rough looking trousers that seemed to made of a durable material. She carried a large blanket, made of some sort of fur, and a bottle of steaming liquid.

Tase took quick inspection of his surroundings and realised he was in a small cove of a much larger cave. His view of whatever else was nearby was blocked by the curved wall of stone pillars arched around his makeshift bed.

The woman strode over to Tase and nodded to him. "Can ye walk?"

Tase didn't know if he could or not, but he was going to give it a try if it meant he could find out where Fadin and the others were. "Yes," he said firmly.

Duff looked up at the woman, disapproving.

"He can heal after we have some things settled," she answered his stare. "Follow me."

Tase began to get out of bed, but as he placed his leg upon the floor from the low mattress and saw the bloodied wrapping around it, he began to feel light headed and feared he may vomit again.

"Here," Duff said, slipping his arm under Tase's.

Tase leaned on the older man, and with his help followed the woman around the curved wall.

The first thought that struck him was that he surely should have heard some sort of noise from the colossal creature in front of him when he was in that small cove, for the wind was wailing like the cry of a banshee through the cave tunnels.

Tase's jaw dropped, and he had the most powerful desire to turn the other way and run, but, besides that not really being an option with his injured leg, he was most certain it would also be an incredibly stupid idea with those enormous eyes watching.

Tase took in the massive creature in the huge stone cave. He saw auburn and gold scales, a long snake-like neck, gigantic black spikes from the tip of its snout to the end of its enormous tail, and reptilian silver eyes, with pupils which contracted into a diamond shaped slit. The colossal unchained dragon, which had to lie down to fit properly in the cavern, stared at him, its eyes unblinking.

Tase's mind crashed to the memory of the dragon he had seen in Cavan-Corr, the one that had to be tethered down by twelve men and muzzled, just so they could remove some barbed wire it appeared the creature had gotten tangled in. As he noted again that this dragon wasn't held down by anything or anyone the fear rose in his belly and his heart thudded frantically against his ribs. Then he felt it. All the training Caoimhe had done with him to feel magic began to take effect. The power he felt emanating from the huge dragon made him shudder. It was a different feeling than one he had ever sensed, it was a deep, low rumble, a suppressed roar like an underground waterfall, and the magic was firmly controlled, but there was so much of it within the creature, such a vast quantity flowing through it, that if it were to lose control, even for an instant, it could easily wipe them out.

The dragon inclined its head slightly to him, and Tase had the most intense feeling that it was smirking. He stumbled backwards.

"Don't get yer knickers in a twist, laddie," Duff chuckled. "She ain't gonna do nothin' to ye."

The dragon snorted.

Tase gaped at Duff, and for the first time he noticed something that looked familiar to him. The older man was wearing a silver breastplate, and upon it was inscribed D.E.R.T.H.S. He puzzled over this, for he remembered it from somewhere. It suddenly clicked. Aednat's room in Cavan-Corr, the poster on her wall. "You're the Dragon Entrapper, Rider, Tamer, Huntsman Squad?"

Duff smiled. "One of them, yes."

"They're the Scottish division!" a familiar voice shouted.

Tase turned to where the voice had come from and saw Aednat, her face beaming, her bandaged arm in a sling, sitting on a fur puff of sorts.

Another man was with her, this one middle aged with auburn-brown hair.

The man stood and looked approvingly down at her. "She is quite a fan of us, it seems."

"Oh, yes!" Aednat grinned broadly.

Tase couldn't keep himself from smiling a little. It was good to see Aednat, but where were the others?

"And why shouldn't she be?" the woman asked. "We did save their skin, did we not?"

"No need to be rude, Ness," the second man scorned.

The questions in Tase's head began to bubble over, and he could no longer contain himself. "Where are the others?"

"Fadin is in the next cove," Aednat answered, and her face fell. "He was badly hurt."

Tase's stomach did a back flip. "How bad? Can I see him? Where's the cove?"

"Calm yerself," Duff soothed.

"He's fine," Ness said. "Yer old man did somethin' to him, and gave him some sort of potion. He'll live."

"The others are in another passage of the cave," the man with the auburn-brown hair told Tase. "I was informed the dark haired girl is your sister?"

Tase nodded, his stomach in knots.

"Well, they are tryin' to work with her. It seems she is having a hard time keeping control of herself."

"Oh, let's not candy coat it, Ronan," Ness barked, walking up to the dragon and stroking its large neck. "We have gotten ourselves into quite a mess here, takin' them on."

Ronan didn't answer her, instead he turned to Tase. "Why don't I take you both to them? We'll get your brother first." He left Ness with the dragon and led the way to another wall of the hexagonal pillars.

Duff supported Tase as they walked and Aednat hurried alongside him. "Where are we?" Tase asked, peering up at the high ceiling.

"Fingal's Cave," Duff answered. "On the Isle of Staffa."

"The cave that was said to be the end of Finn McCool's bridge from Ireland to Scotland?"

"The same."

It made sense now why the stones looked like the Giant's Causeway. "We're still in Scotland then?"

"Oh, yes. Thought it would be best. Took ye to the nearest safe place. Ye were all pretty badly injured."

"My leg seems all right," Tase said, testing his weight on it.

"It's better than it was, laddie. Ye wouldn't have wanted to see it when Tara started on it."

Tase decided this was true. A thought occurred to him, knowing now where they were. "How is this Fingal's Cave? I thought it was a sea cave, the bottom only water?"

"The part the humans see is only a sea cave with the ocean for the bottom. But they don't always see whats really there, do they?"

Tase looked over at Aednat, who seemed to be having the absolute time of her life.

"There is a secret entrance through one of the cave walls!" she blurted. "We are in the middle of Staffa, right in her heart. I was awake when they took us here."

Ronan smirked. "Here we are," he informed them as they turned the corner of a wall.

Tase's eyes fell on a small mattress with fur covers. Fadin was lying motionless, his eyes closed.

"Fadin?" he blurted, and nearly pulled away from Duff, but the older man held him fast, and together they made their way to the bed.

Tase put his hand on his brother's arm and his blue-green eyes opened. "Tase?" he asked groggily.

"Yeah," he answered, a wave of relief washing over him. He was going to be okay.

"Ahh," Fadin winced as he tried to sit up. "My chest." He placed his hand lightly over it and pulled off the covers.

Tase stifled a gasp so as not to alarm Fadin. He was bandaged from shoulder to shoulder and all the way down to the brim of his trousers. Blood, and lots of it, had seeped through the gauze.

Fadin's eyes widened. "What happened?"

"You were injured, rather badly," Ronan said. "You'll be all right though. It looks worse than it is."

Aednat whispered in Tase's ear, "You should have seen it at first. It was absolutely awful."

Ronan placed his hand on Fadin's foot. "You can get up if you'd like. I was going to take these two to the others."

Fadin nodded and Ronan began to help him up. Tase winced, as Fadin did, as he adjusted himself to Ronan and started forward. Ronan and Fadin lead the way through more intricate tunnels.

"Well," Fadin said, inclining his head backward as he hobbled along, "aren't we just a couple of crippled old men?"

Tase chuckled as he held onto Duff. It was true, the more he thought about it, the harder it made him laugh and he had to work to contain himself.

They made several turns and crossed through many cove-like rooms, until they came to the end of a long twisting tunnel and rounded the corner. As soon as they did the noise of shouting voices bombarded Tase's ears. They should have heard this kind of noise echoing from several caverns back, which made him conclude that some sort of magic stifled sound from traveling in the cave.

They were in a large open cavern, with beds protruding from the cavern wall, stalactites that gave off the light source in the room, and an open area of water that moved like the ocean.

The shouts were coming from Robert and Enda, who were in what seemed like a heated conversation.

The troubled girl, Marie, was plopped on the floor, talking with a woman Tase had never seen before, but she looked unharmed.

Aimirgin, who was standing at the cavern entrance, spotted them. As she turned Tase saw her arm was in a sling, and in her natural form he noticed the tip of one of her pointed ears looked like it had been bitten.

Robert could help patch them up, but he couldn't heal them the way Caoimhe could. He missed Caoimhe. Tase felt his mind grab at the thought, and he felt his stomach fill with worry for Caoimhe, Ma, Clearie, Glendan, and Mr Hogan.

Aimirgin came to stand beside them, limping slightly on one of her hoofed feet. She gave them a disapproving look with her ebony eyes concerning the yelling emanating from Enda and Robert.

There were four other men, not all of them appearing human, in the cavern as well, all wearing the clothing of the D.E.R.T.H.S. They were talking quietly amongst themselves.

Faolan Hennessy, Saoirse's birth father, stood still, his face in his hands, his lank silver hair covering any other part of his face that would have been visible. He looked small and broken as he waited there, and Tase was unsure how he felt about him.

"It was an ambush!" Enda continued roaring. Tase swallowed.

"There were far too many," Desmond added.

Robert took a deep breath. "She knew we were coming."

"How was that something you didn't consider? If you knew those creatures waited there, why did we go?" Enda was livid, his grey eyes giving off the slightest hint of a silver burn. He came up close to Robert, in a surprisingly hostile manner.

Robert eyed him dangerously and stood to his full height. "I did not know she had that many under her control. If I had we would have approached a different way."

Enda backed away slightly. "Be that as it may, we were comically outnumbered! What did you hope to gain from taking us there?"

Robert's blue eyes pierced Enda's. "Your niece has a serious problem, and she was held by the Bojins for no short period of time. The power she possesses she has no control over, seeing how she nearly killed her brother and the Hogan boy on the fairy island. I would say she was in some pretty desperate need of help. Don't you think it is even remotely possible that the Bojins had something to do with that? I, for one, do not understand how to help her control it, and if she doesn't learn she could be a danger to herself and others."

Saoirse, who was standing on the opposite of the cave from Tase, rubbed her forehead as if it pained her.

Enda let out a snort. "So the solution was to bring back this," he motioned to Faolan, "pathetic broken shadow of a man I once knew?" His voice rose and quavered at the end.

"You have a better idea of who could have helped?" Desmond asked coolly, standing at Saoirse's side, who began biting her nails.

Tase wondered at the anger Enda was clearly feeling. It seemed misplaced considering what they had just been through was clearly not Faolan's fault. Tase ran a hand through his red hair, remembering that Faolan had left Ma when she was pregnant with Saoirse. Perhaps that was where the anger came from in Enda.

Enda ran his large hands over his face and shook his greying head. He strode over to Faolan so swiftly that Tase was shocked. He growled in the smaller man's face, "How could you have abandoned them all those years ago?"

He was mad about the past all right. Robert moved forward. "Enda!"

"How could you have done that to her? How could you have deserted your wife and unborn child?" Enda's voice was at such a high volume that it hurt Tase's ears.

Tase clutched harder to Duff's arm as there was a drastic change in the cavern. There was the smell of something burning for the briefest moment, and the air lost its stillness. There was a slight cool wind that crept over Tase's body, and a tingling like static that crackled all around him.

Robert made to grab Enda's arm but there was no need.

Faolan began to change before their eyes. His skin changed to silver hair, and his body grew. Enda pulled his arm away as Faolan shook his new massive body. Standing before them was a creature that looked a lot like a silver gorilla, but he had twisted claws tipped in silver and had a unique look about him unlike that of a normal animal.

Tase nearly fell backward and Duff became rigid next to him.

A deep voice resounded from the gorilla that had been Faolan. "This is why." He addressed Enda. "I could not control my shifting then, and I didn't want to hurt them." His eyes, the brilliantly light shade of green, fell on Saoirse. The gorilla shrank, his fur pulled away like water receding on the sand, and skin could be seen beneath it. The face shifted back to that of a human with a turn of Faolan's head, almost as if it had been an illusion, a trick of the light. No longer was a beast standing enormous in the cavern, but a small and broken looking man with grey hair. "I'm so sorry."

Saoirse stopped biting her fingernail and gently removed Desmond's hand from her shoulder. She walked over to her father and stared at him. "Is that really why you left?"

He nodded and his lip quivered. "I have thought about you every day," he choked.

"You can help me?" she asked. "Because I have no control at all when I start to shift, or whatever you call it."

"Yes, I can teach you how to control it."

Saoirse turned. "I need his help, no matter what choices he made in the past, Enda."

Enda examined Saoirse's eyes. "You're right, I'm sorry." He directed the apology to Faolan as well. "My nerves are a bit on edge."

"All of ours are," Robert said matter-of-factly. He spotted Tase. "You're awake," he half smiled at them. He acknowledged Ronan. "Thank you for your hospitality."

Ronan ran a hand over his face. "Of course. We are glad to help." He lowered his voice. "Robert, the two of us go way back. But I have my people to think of as well. I have a dragon in this cavern, and if she feels we are in danger, you know I cannot control what she does." He eyed Faolan. "I have never seen creatures like them before. They are quite powerful, and if they don't have control, extremely dangerous."

Saoirse looked down. "You're not wrong." Tase felt a pang in his chest. It wasn't her fault.

Ronan made a face. "I don't wish to be cruel," he sighed. "May I ask, Faolan, what exactly you are?"

Robert changed his attention to Saoirse's father as well. "That is something that is a mystery even to me."

Faolan took a step toward him. "I am an ilchruthach. At least that's what we call ourselves. We are human in almost every way when we are born, and it isn't until or unless our lives are threatened that our magic is woken up. We can shift into a predatory creature when provoked, but it takes time to shift at will. Once that part of us awakens we hear the call of our Queen. As if we have a tracking device embedded in us, we find our way to her." He eyed Saoirse. "I don't exactly know what this power will mean to you, since you are half human, but I can teach you what I know."

"How do we know you are truly on *our* side?" Robert asked. "Yessult called you her *left hand*, so you were clearly close to her."

"She trusted me," Faolan agreed, "which gave me the ability to learn more about her than any of her other subjects know." His face turned bitter. "She is the Ard-ilcruthóir, the high changer of many shapes, our Queen. While the rest of us are limited by one shape we can shift to, she can change into whatever predatory creature she desires, whenever she chooses. I thought it was because she was our queen, perhaps she was the first of us to ever exist." He let out an angry chuckle. "But I found her using her magic upon our water supply in Nonín. I investigated what she is doing, and found that she is stifling our abilities. She claims she is queen because her shape holds no boundaries, but I know that if we were left to develop naturally, the rest of us could shift into whatever creature we choose. My ability has been stifled for so long by Yessult, that I hold no hope of reclaiming the power to shift into whatever I desire." He addressed Saoirse. "However, I think *you* do have that power, which means one day you could challenge Yessult."

Saoirse's features were frightened and unsecure. She met Tase's eyes, seeming to plead for some sort of help.

"You're scaring her," Tase said, watching the fear grow in Saoirse's eyes.

Faolan noticed the look on Saoirse's face. "I'm sorry, I don't mean to. I only want to help you."

"I know," Saoirse answered.

There was a fierce rumble in the cave and it felt like an earthquake beneath their feet.

Ness came sprinting around the corner, Aimirgin next to her, who had a bandage on her shoulder.

"She's angry about something, Ronan," Ness reported.

Aimirgin turned. "Who's angry?"

Aednat was watching everything with the greatest interest. "The dragon. Their dragon is angry," she said, her face breaking into a smile. "This is amazin'!"

"Robert," Ronan said, "I can't control her. If Unundine doesn't want the girl here, it is best you leave. I don't have any power over a dragon. Our relationship is built on mutual trust."

Aednat made an ecstatic face. "Did you hear that?" she whispered. "Their relationship! He is friends with a dragon!" She made a face that looked as if she were screaming with excitement.

Tase shook his head at her. She was enjoying this far too much.

"I'm afraid we have overstayed our welcome," Robert decided. He turned to gather Marie, but froze.

Tase felt the shift in the air. He snapped his attention to Saoirse. It was as if a magical explosion went off. Tase gasped from the power of it and saw that standing where Saoirse had been was a colossal, midnight coloured jaguar with faint silver spots.

He pulled away from Duff, staring. "Whoa!" Fadin cried.

"She can do that?" Tase panted.

Robert stepped back. "Apparently so."

The jaguar Saoirse was quite beautiful; her silver markings made it look as though her fur almost shone, her tail was striped with silver, and her paws adorned the distinct gnarled and silver tipped claws that marked the ilchruthach.

Aimirgin made a small gasping sound. "I didn't know she could change!" Tase let out the breath he was holding.

Enda and Robert exchanged glances. "Saoirse," Robert tried to calm her, hand out, "It's all right."

Her green eyes were frightened, and in her fear she bared her teeth and yowled at them.

The cave shook again, and Tase heard the cry of the dragon, Unundine. The jaguar Saoirse growled deeply and backed against the wall of the cave.

She swiped with one of her dagger-like clawed paws, and gave a frightening yowl.

Ronan cried out. "Please, Unundine, we are all right, the girl will not harm us."

The dragon roared again, and the cavern gave a massive quake, causing two stalactites to crash into the floor. Saoirse dove away and arched her back.

"I don't think Unundine believes you," Ness implied.

Faolan walked toward Saoirse. "Calm yourself," he told her. "It's all right."

She hissed at him.

Faolan stood his ground. "You're too upset," he told her. "You have to get control of your fear."

She swung her claws towards him, but he was quite swift; he dodged her attack easily.

"I can't get through to her like this," he said.

"Well we are open to any suggestions." Enda stated, a note of sarcasm to his voice.

In a wave of magic Faolan shifted into the silver gorilla. It shocked Tase almost as much as it had the first time.

"If they shift out in the open," Ronan whispered to Robert. "There will be nowhere you can hide. Their magic is so potent it will be easily located."

Robert sighed. "I know. What I wouldn't give if this country were larger." Tase eyed Fadin, Aimirgin, and Aedant.

Faolan held his large clawed fingers out to Saoirse. "Will that work?" Fadin asked incredulously.

Saoirse's body relaxed and she touched Faolan's fingers with her dainty black nose.

"You are not an animal, Saoirse," Robert said as he moved closer to her. Her eyes turned to him, her pupils wide, still fearful.

Faolan shifted, as if it were a trick of the light, into a man once more. His eyes, which Tase had only seen look sad or terrified, were filled now with something else. He moved his hand up Saoirse's nose and stroked her head. "You can control this," he told her. "Take a deep breath and control your fear."

Saoirse the jaguar seemed to listen. Her chest heaved as if she had indeed taken a large breath.

Faolan stroked her chin and stared at her in the eyes.

The jaguar once again became human Saoirse in a shift of the light. The magic in the room subsided.

"Good job, Saoirse," Faolan smiled at her.

Saoirse was panting, and slumped on the floor, but she managed a grin. The roar of the dragon resounded through the cavern.

Saoirse jerked upright, but there was no sign of the jaguar.

"I'm sorry," Ronan insisted. "But I don't want anyone to get hurt. Unundine feels as though you are a threat to us. If we don't have you leave, she'll take matters into her own claws."

"We understand," Robert said. He smacked Ronan on the shoulder. "Let's move out," he called.

Duff helped Tase turn around as he changed directions, and Fadin made a face as Ronan aided him.

As they walked swiftly through the cavern Tase couldn't help but wonder: what now? Saoirse let off huge waves of power when she shifted. Vladimir had spies watching for magic use. They would be found for sure, the amount of time simply depended upon how many spies he had who possessed the talent for sensing magic. Tase ran a hand through his red hair as he realised how bad of a situation they were in.

"Here," Ronan said as they reached a new cavern. He pointed to a pile of clothes on the floor. "Put these on."

Tase saw the pile was made up of clean regular human clothes. He let go of Duff to dress but had difficulty getting his jeans on. It was rather more painful than he would have thought.

Marie was a bit difficult, but Robert and the woman D.E.R.T.H.S. finally managed to get the flowery dress on her, and she clutched onto Robert's side.

Tase suddenly remembered Jason, and wondered what had happened to him, but knew this was not the time to ask.

"There is a ferry," Ronan said, "with tourists that has landed on the isle. You all look convincingly human enough." He handed Robert a stack of bank notes and Tase caught a glimpse of a £50.

"Thank you again," Robert said.

Ronan nodded. "I wish we could do more. If you ever need help," he handed Robert a small bit of parchment, "don't hesitate to ask." He and Robert gave each other a one armed hug, and Enda shook Ronan's hand.

"By the way," Ronan said, turning to Aednat, who gaped, astounded, up at him. "As I have heard, you are quite the fan of us?"

Aednat nodded. "Oh yes, I want to join the D.E.R.T.H.S. when I'm old enough."

He got down low so he was closer to her height. "Well, I think you certainly have the passion, and after what you all went through in Nonín you are definitely brave enough." He pulled a bracelet from his arm and held it up to her. "Can you take care of this for me?"

Her aburn hazel eyes were wide with honour. "Yes, sir," she answered.

He squeezed the bracelet and for a moment his eyes glowed silver. The bracelet shrunk and he handed it to her. "Keep it on you at all times, and if you ever come upon any other D.E.R.T.H.S. you show them that, and tell them you are a friend of Ronan's. You'll never be turned away."

She took the bracelet with supreme care and snapped it on her wrist. "Thank you, so much." She smiled at him, her dimples standing out on her freckled cheeks.

There was a thundering quake from the cave. Ronan stood and looked toward the sound.

"Time to go," Robert smiled. He followed Duff as he pointed to a narrow passageway that spun upward.

Robert entered first.

"Good luck," Ronan said to Tase and Fadin as they walked by him. "This won't be the last time we meet."

Tase and Fadin nodded to him and moved into the stairway-like passage. "I hope he's right," Fadin whisperd.

Tase managed to walk on his own, but he was slow moving, especially since the passageway was at an incline.

Adenat bounded next to them. "I am SO joinin' the Scottish Division of the D.E.R.T.H.S. when I grow up!"

"I thought you wanted to be part of the African Division, Freckles?" Fadin said.

She waved him away. "I didn't even know there *was* a Scottish Division, and you didn't see how incredible their rescue of us was! I want the Scotts, and I'll tell you what, it's a heck of a lot closer than Africa."

Tase chuckled despite his worry.

"I have no doubt you will be a part of the D.E.R.T.H.S. when you are an adult, Aedant," Aimirgin smiled.

Aednat tried to peek under the bandage on her arm. "Do you think my mark could be a dragon? Oh my fairies, what if it is a dragon? That would be so COOL!"

"Will you children hush up?" Robert called to them.

For whatever reason this sent them all into a fit of giggles, which caused Robert to roll his eyes.

For a moment even Saoirse laughed with them, and when she did she reminded Tase of Ma. It wasn't the same without Ma there. He hoped she was safe.

# CHAPTER 18

# NO REST

Fadin breathed in the cool air as it whipped on his face from the sea. They had made it safely onto the ferry from the Isle of Staffa to the Isle of Mull, still in Scotland. From there they had to board another ferry to get to the Scottish mainland. It took several busses to make it to Troon, and it was from Troon that they boarded the ferry that would take them home.

Fadin longed for home, though he wasn't quite sure what that really meant anymore. The place that was home had become much larger. It was no longer a building that meant home, it was Ireland that was home. As he saw the beautiful green in the distance, he understood how much he had missed it. He also knew that it was more than a place, home was where those who loved you waited, and he had a longing to see Ma, Clearie, baby Glendan, Mr Hogan, and everyone else. He wished he knew where they all were.

He suddenly felt like someone was watching him, so he turned and saw a pair of sparkling blue eyes staring up at him. He smiled down at the girl, who could be no older than ten. She was a pretty child, with long brown hair, and skin that had been sun-kissed.

"Hello," Fadin said to her.

She smiled up at him, her grin the kind that made you want to smile too no matter what mood you were in. "Hello," she said back to him.

There was a moment of strange silence, in which Fadin was not sure what to say. He didn't know if he should walk away or try and find her parents.

"I think," the girl said, still studying his face, "that I know you from somewhere."

She was an American, he could tell by her accent. He had never met anyone from America before, so he knew she couldn't know him. Fadin smiled at her again. "I don't think so," he said.

She arched a brown eyebrow. "You're looking for someone." It wasn't a question.

"Am I?" he asked.

"Yes," she said, matter-of-factly. "He told me you were."

"He?" Fadin asked.

"He also said you won't find them."

"I won't?" Fadin tried to hide the chuckle rising in his chest. This child was quite sure of herself. Who did she think she was talking to?

"They aren't where you think they are," the girl said. "They didn't make it that far. Someone stopped them."

This sent a chill down Fadin's spine and made his stomach churn as he thought of Ma, Clearie, Glenden, Caoimhe, and Mr Hogan. They were supposed to travel to the elven kingdom, what if they hadn't made it? He was no longer amused with the girl. "Okay, well I'm going to go and find my family," he said, turning away.

She grabbed his arm with a light touch that made him stop. "Here," she said. She put a white feather in his hand. He stared at it; it glimmered strangely in the light. Fadin jerked his head up from the feather to her eyes in shock. He thought of the dove in the forest that helped him and Clearie find their way out, and the dove who was with Pathos right before he spoke to them and sent them away from Vladimir, the dove that landed on the fisherman's shoulder. He blinked and focused on the child in front of him. That was silly, it was just a feather, it could be from any bird. Still, though, he wondered.

"Where did you get this?" he asked her.

The girl smiled her dazzlingly bright smile and pointed. "He gave it to me."

Fadin looked to where she was pointing and felt the shock crash over him. Standing on the shore of Scotland, no more than coloured lines at this distance, was a dog. It was a Bernese, there was no doubt; black, white, and tannish-red fur. "Pathos?" he whispered, his quiet voice full of wonder. Fadin could feel the disbelief creeping into his mind, it couldn't be Pathos, it just couldn't.

"The man who was with him told me to give it to someone. When I asked who, he said I would know when I saw you."

Fadin, still staring after Pathos, shook his head. "What did the man look like?" There was no answer.

"Was he a fisherman?" Fadin asked, turning. But the girl was walking away from him towards an older man who had the same dazzling smile.

"Come on, Alexa," the older man grinned at her, extending an arm to receive her.

"Okay, Poppy," she answered him. The girl leaned against her grandfather and took one last look at Fadin. She waved to him and together she and Poppy both vanished around the corner to stare out the other side of the ferry.

Fadin scrunched up his face and shook his head. He looked back to the shore where he had seen Pathos, but there was nothing at all there. "Perhaps I'm just going mad," he wondered aloud.

"Nah, if you were goin' mad, I'd be one of the first to tell you."

He smiled despite himself and glanced down at Aednat. "Hey, Freckles," he said warmly.

She nodded to the feather clutched in his pale hand. "Where'd you get that?"

Fadin turned to see if he could spot the girl, but she was nowhere within sight.

"I don't know really," he said.

"Pretty," Aedant whispered, running her finger along the side of it. She looked out toward Ireland, the wind tousling her dark red hair. "Do you suppose they all made it safely? To the elves, I mean." She turned her wide auburn-hazel eyes to him.

Fadin felt a tug of panic in his stomach but he smiled at her reassuringly. "I'm sure they did." He looked out to the ocean, filled with tumultuous waves, and realised that he wasn't sure of that at all.

"I hope my family is okay," Aednat wondered. "I don't know for sure where Ma, Da, and Annatta are. She stared at the waves. "And I hope Aldabella is all right, wherever she is."

Aimirgin suddenly appeared at Fadin's side, looking human and in a long green coat. "I'm so sorry about Aldabella," she said. "I miss her. Even when she acted like a know it all."

Aednat laughed and wiped her eyes before any tears could form. "She did think she knew everythin'." She shook her head. "And she sure loved that blue hair of hers."

Tase appeared on Fadin's left, his cerulean eyes sad as they stared at Aednat. Fadin swallowed the sadness that bubbled up inside him.

Aimirgin hugged her. "We'll find them all, Aednat," she assured her. "We'll find them."

"Of course we will," Tase added, putting a hand on Aednat's shoulder. "Besides, with your dad's inventive mind, I just know they're safe."

Fadin nodded. "Nothing could keep him from protecting your ma and Annatta."

Aednat let go of Aimirgin and forced a brave smile.

"Nearly there," Robert said, coming to stand near them. He wore a long grey coat that fit him nicely and a grey, black, and white scarf with a perfectly respectable cap atop his head. It was strange how normal he could look, when Fadin knew how normal he was not. His staff was supporting him, like a walking stick, and it looked to simply be a fancy and expensive cane made by an old man who obviously must have money.

Marie was clutching onto Robert's side like always, though she appeared to become worse as the trip wore on. It seemed as though all the travel was distressing her; she would get panicky but Robert always seemed to be able to calm her down.

At the moment her little fingers were interwoven with Roberts's jacket, her large green eyes staring out at the sea.

"Is she all right?" Fadin asked.

Robert shook his head. "We need to get her somewhere safe for the night. And we must be very careful not to use magic. Vladimir will be looking for us."

Fadin nodded but felt his heart spasm as he thought of waiting to go find Ma and the others until the morning. He wanted nothing more than to go to the Elven Kingdom now, to make sure they were all safe.

~~~

When they got off the ferry in Larne, Northern Ireland, Fadin felt a wave of relief at being home, even though his feeling of worry for Ma and the others still clung to him.

Robert produced a map from his pocket and Enda got them two cabs. In what felt like a blur of time they wound up in four rooms of a bed and breakfast not far from the ferry terminal.

Fadin shared a room with Tase and Desmond.

Fadin sat on his bed, full from the wonderfully warm dinner Enda had brought them from a restaurant close by, and fingered the feather in his pocket. The boxes and crumbs from the meal were strewn along the small table in the room, and bits of food and trash had also found their way to the floor, displaying how ravenously the three of them had eaten.

Desmond seemed restless; he paced the length of the narrow room, seeming to be in deep thought. "I understand why we had to settle in for the night," he said to neither of them in particular, "but I don't like waiting to find the others." He turned round, his left hand on his face, the other wrapped round his waist. He was biting the thumbnail of his tan left hand absently.

Fadin nodded and pulled the feather from his pocket. "I don't like it either." Clearly he wasn't the only one feeling ill at ease. He turned his eyes on Tase, who had been incredibly quiet since they had begun their journey home.

He was staring blankly at the flower pattern of his bed, twisting a strand of his red hair between two fingers.

"Tase?" Fadin asked.

"Hum?" Tase looked up.

"You okay?"

Tase said nothing, but looked back down at the blanket. "I don't know. I sort of have this…" He seemed to be searching for the right words. "… this uneasy feeling in the pit of my stomach." He looked Fadin in the eye. "I'm worried about them."

Fadin bit his lip, remembering the little girl's words.

"Well, we can't help them by worrying," Desmond said. "Better get to sleep, that way we are rested. When the morning comes, we can get an early start."

They all got in bed without another word. The room was dark and quiet, but Fadin knew none of them were asleep. It felt like a long time until sleep took him, and even when it did it wasn't deep. His mind was filled with the faces of everyone they had left, and the little girl's voice hummed in the dark somewhere, "You won't find them."

A hand slapping down over his mouth made Fadin jump awake. His sword, which had been hidden in a long backpack by his bed, was almost in his grasp when a voice hissed at him.

"Hush, things! No, leaves sword alones!"

His eyes widened in the dark at the familiar voice. His body relaxed and he pulled his hand out of the backpack.

"I lets you mouths go, but keeps quiet, okays?" Fadin nodded vigorously.

The small body on top of him moved and slid next to him. "Ciaran," he whispered. "What are you doing here?"

"Maldorf's," Ciaran said. "Little blue creature, you knows him?"

Fadin racked his brain and then remembered the blue creature who had helped them when Vladimir attacked. He had shown Fadin Da's old tooth necklace, he had protected Fadin and the others, risking his own life. "Yes, I remember him. He's all right then?"

Ciaran's face was nothing but blackness in the dark room, but Fadin felt the pained look in the silence Ciaran let fall between them. "He is alives." Ciaran finally whispered. "He and I, we beens talksing to each others, keeping tracks of whats been happening. Things is becomesing mores and mores dangerous."

"Well, that's just great," Fadin said, a little too loudly. Tase stirred.

"Shhhh!" Ciaran hissed.

"Aren't we going to tell Tase?"

"He isn't whats I'm worried abouts hearings you."

Fadin's breath caught. "What *are* you worried about?"

Ciaran came a little closer to Fadin's face. "Maldorfs, he tolds me they is comings for you things."

The knot in Fadin's stomach became tighter. "Who? The Bojins? The snake people?"

Fadin could see the slight outline of Cairan shake his head. "No, Cavan- Corr guardses. Maldorfs say there is ten ofs them. They is coming heres, now."

Fadin jumped out of bed. "How did they find us? We have to get everyone up! Get out of here!"

"Shhhhh!" Ciaran whispered again. "We musts not have thems panic, otherwise coulds cause magic, magic makes them knows right wheres you are. They only knows you in Larne, not knows you in this little houses."

Fadin nodded, more to himself than to Ciaran. "Okay, let's wake them up quietly. We have got to get out of here."

He moved towards Tase when he suddenly felt something. It was sort of a shiver, one that ran along his bones, but it was a warm shiver, like nothing he had ever felt before. "Ciaran," he whispered.

"I feels it too, Fadin-thing," he said.

Fadin didn't know why, but he moved toward the window. He could hear by the quiet clacking that Ciaran followed him. He pressed himself against the wall, slightly moved the curtain back, and peered out into the dark street.

There was a man walking slowly toward the bed and breakfast. He had a thick long coat on, and walked with a cane. Fadin couldn't see his face, but he felt the shiver become stronger.

"Who is its?" Ciaran whispered.

Fadin lowered his arm so Ciaran could climb up.

Ciaran scurried up and perched himself on Fadin's shoulder.

The man came closer, and the light of the closest street lamp fell upon his face.

The sharp intake of breath felt like a knife in Fadin's throat. The face was pale and hollow, lime-green eyes sat beneath black brows, and the hair, though it was under a cap, was clearly white. As he turned to look at the bed and breakfast Fadin saw that half his face was scarred, as if it had been burned a long time ago. The thick lips curled into a horrible grin and he pulled the twisted staff close to his chest. Fadin saw the red ruby glint as it caught a ray of light from the streetlamp.

"Oh," Fadin breathed, his heart pounded against his ribs. "Puceula Lynch."

"Haves to go, haves to go," Ciaran hissed in his ear.

Fadin moved away from the window and rushed to Tase's bed.

Tase sat up before he could even touch him. "What is it?" he whispered at him.

Desmond was suddenly standing behind Fadin. "Why are you up? What's that on your back?" He spoke quietly too, but there was panic in his tone.

"It's Ciaran, but we have to go, right now. Puceula is outside."

"What?" Desmond almost cried.

"Ciaran?" Tase asked.

"Yes, Tase-thing," Ciaran's voice sounded like he smiled.

"Oy!" a strange voice whispered in the darkness. "We 'ave got to go, go! The Advisor to the King himself is outside! What on Ireland's green land you waiting for?"

"We comings," Ciaran said. "Gots to get the others, you make distractions, okay's?"

The strange voice mumbled something then said more clearly. "Others are waiting, no wasting time. You come soon soon, or we leaving without you." There was a quiet poof, like a small cloud of dust being shoved out of a vacuum bag.

"Who was that?" Fadin asked.

"Another goblin friend of mines. I can introduces you laters, it's times to go." Ciaran hopped off of Fadin's shoulder. "Grabs stuffs, times to wake others!"

All three of them gathered their things at lightning speed. They opened their door as silently as they could manage and went to the room next door.

"It's locked!" Desmond growled.

"Here," Ciaran said. He took his small, long-nailed finger and placed it in the lock. He twisted and the door unlocked.

"Useful trick," Desmond commented as he opened the door. Ciaran shrugged.

Enda was already on his feet. "What is it?"

"Puceula's here," Desmond said. "Let's go." Enda woke both Aednat and Aimirgin.

Fadin, Tase, and Ciaran went to the next room but the door opened, Robert had his staff brandished and Marie on his hip. Her legs hung limply at his side, and her head was lolled on his shoulder. He nodded without a word and jerked his head in the direction of their last room. With a twist of his finger, Ciaran had the next door open.

Nothing stirred in this room. As Robert and Tase woke Faolan, Fadin peered out the window once more. Puceula now had several men surrounding him but they looked confused. One of them was pointing soundlessly at an inn not far down the street, but Puceula seemed intent on the bed and breakfast, though his expression was unsure.

There was a small brilliant flash from the inn down the street, and Fadin felt the small surge that was magic. Puceula saw the flash, but didn't seem to feel the magical surge. He bit his lip, but the man next to Puceula seemed to have felt it, he gestured toward the inn, in absolute certainty.

"Got to go, now," Fadin whispered. It was only a matter of time before they came back.

Everyone was up except Saoirse. Faolan's thin face was filled with worry.

Enda moved to Saoirse and shook her awake.

It was only in the brief second before it happened that Fadin felt that may be a bad idea.

Her eyes shot open, the shockingly white-green of the ilchruthach, and she transformed into the black jaguar with silver markings. The magic she sent out was like a crashing and devastating wave. Fadin had to catch his breath after it struck him and he dashed to the window to see Puceula staring right at him. "Bleedin' troll! They know, they know!"

In a wink Saoirse transformed back into a human. "What happened?" she cried.

Robert yanked her up by the collar of her shirt and shoved her towards the door. "We have to go!" he ordered.

Faolan was at her side in a flash, and her green eyes turned toward the window in fright. "Keep your fear under control," he ordered.

Fadin ran forward and grabbed Ciaran, who was hobbling next to Tase.

There was flash and the sound of a horrible high-pitched scream. All the glass in the room broke.

Fadin jerked his head backward for an instant and saw Puceula and three guards coming into the window. Just behind them he saw the hooded woman, her cherry red curls spilling out from under her hood. He hadn't seen her in such a long time, it made his spine tingle in recognition of her.

"Fadin, let's go!" Tase cried. Fadin turned and ran.

"What the!" The owner of the bed and breakfast had emerged in a thick nightgown and robe. Her hair was tousled and her eyes were wide. "What in the Good Lord's Name are you…"

Whatever she was going to call them Fadin never heard, for there was another scream and more glass shattered around them.

"Here!" Enda's voice cried.

Fadin saw him outside another broken window and he rushed towards him, Aimirgin, and Aednat.

Robert jumped through the window with surprising agility, and Fadin and Tase were right behind him. They had emerged onto the street and the other guards who had not followed inside turned to them.

With his one free hand Robert pulled a bottle from his jacket and threw it at them. There was a purple explosion and the guards fell back. "Won't hold them off for long, come on!"

They ran down the street to the left, passing house after house. Fadin felt a pang of guilt at the damage that had been caused to the bed and breakfast, but what could be done?

"Goes to the park!" Ciaran called.

"What's at the park?" Robert asked.

"Help," Ciaran told him. "Ways to get you outs of here."

Robert said nothing, but with a flick of his staff a map made entirely out of light appeared before him. "All right then, to Larne Town Park it is." He closed the map with another swish of his staff and turned his head.

Fadin turned as well and saw that Puceula was not far behind them. He clutched his own staff in his hands and thrust it forward. With a silvery gust he was suddenly at their heels.

Fadin cried out and pulled his sword from his pack. He didn't know what he was going to do but his eyes burned silver and a jet of clear wind spat from his sword. It hit Puceula dead in the face and seemed to freeze him. No, that was the wrong word, it seemed like it just stopped him, kept him in that moment, and he was unable to move. Though it had worked, it was not a good idea to act without thinking. The magic cost him and he felt suddenly as if he would fall, his legs felt like lead, and his stomach heaved.

"Whoa there, boy," Enda said, appearing at his side. He steadied him and put his hand on his back. "Keep moving, and don't think."

Fadin tried to listen. They couldn't afford for him to fall.

"The others aren't far behind," Desmond called. "They are using something, I'm not sure what it is, but it looks like they are passing it between them."

Fadin couldn't imagine what it could be.

"If they are passing it between them," Robert said, "then it's either a travelling potion, or..."

Something kicked Fadin in the spine. He yelped and tumbled, Ciaran jumped from him and he felt his face scrape along the asphalt.

"Ah ha!" a deep voice cried, and Fadin heard someone else hit the road.

He looked up, and felt the hot and sticky liquid stream down where his face had collided with the pavement. He tried not to think about it and instead focused on standing. He turned and gathered that the ten guards, now fighting violently with the others, had somehow flown to them. How, he wasn't sure, but it didn't matter. He was thrown to the ground again and he felt his wrists suddenly bound by something hard and metal.

"By the authority of the King of Ireland, you are under arrest." It was a woman's voice and Fadin felt all the angrier for it.

He kicked hard and tried to buck her off him but a knife was suddenly at his throat. "You better shut your gob and get up," the voice hissed.

Fadin froze. "Get up!"

She stood him up and he gaped. They had been overcome so quickly.

One of the guards had Marie, who was kicking and screaming. She was trying to bite the man who was struggling to hold her. He watched as another man came up and injected something in her neck. In the briefest of moments her eyes became dark and slid closed. They were going to take her back to Vladimir.

Enda was pinned to the floor by three of the men, all of them displaying wounds caused by his talons, which were fully brandished. They injected the same substance into his neck and he too closed his eyes and his body slackened.

Aimirgin flung her flail at several of the guards, wounding a few, and sending some magic their way, but her kind nature kept her from harming any of them too severely. They pounced on her and she smacked her head hard against the pavement. She instantly became her Faróg self, and tried to kick at them with her hooves, but it did her no good.

Aednat, Saoirse, and Desmond were nowhere to be seen, but one guard appeared either dead or unconscious, next to the now bound Faolan, whose eyes were the most brilliantly light green. The bindings on him looked like they were made from a thorn bush, and his eyes glowed ever brighter as the bindings tightened around him.

Robert sent a guard flying across the road into a tree with one swipe of his staff. Another guard used a dart gun and shot it at Robert, hitting him in neck. Fadin saw, wide eyed, that there were four others already in Roberts's arms, and legs.

A female Cavan-Corr guard sent a wall of red magic hurtling into Robert. He deflected the attack but it seemed to cost him. He stumbled but turned and opened his mouth wide. He brought his free hand to his mouth and blew. Ash and smoke collided with the woman and she coughed and spluttered, falling to the floor. As he watched, the grey stuff was sucked into her mouth and she seemed unable to catch a real breath.

Another dart found its way into Robert's chest and he stumbled again. He pulled the dart out and yanked from his coat another bottle. It was filled with green stuff that Fadin saw was labelled *Ogre Snot*. Robert threw the entire bottle and the guard who had shot him yelped as the green goo spread all over him and then sucked onto the floor. The guard was trapped to the ground and, no matter how hard he struggled, he seemed unable to break free.

Fadin felt the magic burn in his chest. He knew he should be careful, if he wasn't he could hurt himself as much as anyone else.

Desmond was suddenly dragged forward by a different guard and one of the ones who had pinned Enda. He was bound in the same metal Fadin was. He growled furiously, and his eyes burned silver. It looked like the metal electrocuted him, and he had a spasm and cried out, little silver lightning strikes emitting from his bindings and striking him in his back, neck, and arms.

Fadin controlled his anger. His magic would do no good.

"Too bad," the voice of Puceula Lynch chortled behind him. He walked up, his cap gone, white hair a disheveled mess. His scars didn't look as bad now that Fadin could see them more closely. He wished he could make them worse.

Robert turned his staff toward Puceula.

Puceula, the Advisor to the King, shrugged his coat off and exposed his own twisted cane and something else clutched in his other hand. "Ah ah ah," he grinned, shaking the glass bottle.

Robert's eyes became a bit wider, but he did not lower his weapon.

Fadin looked at the glass bottle hard. There were three braids of golden hair locked inside it. They shimmered and seemed to possess their own light source, though they were not that bright. The glass had the symbol of a flower with four petals and three stars between each petal. It was the symbol of Nóinín, and Fadin had seen the glass jar before, in Robert's house on Inish Tearaght. He suddenly found himself wondering if those braids belonged to the three golden princesses, but how could they? If they did, how was it Robert had come to have them?

Puceula smiled wider, brandishing his brilliant teeth. "If you so much as let a spark loose, this bottle will shatter and all that will become of these precious relics will be the ash and dust of those they came from."

Robert reluctantly let his staff fall. "So," Puceula said bitterly, "still in the company of those who dwell in the dark?"

"Where else would I be?" Robert snorted.

"It looked as though the snakes would have their way first," Puceula mused. "I guess it will be me who brings you to our master after all."

"The better to save your hide!" Desmond spat.

Puceula turned his own red jeweled staff on him. His eyes became cruel and silver and he sent a red wave of smoke colliding into his face.

He screamed as the smoke made his bindings shock him all over.

Puceula snapped his fingers and one of the guards stuck him with a syringe. Desmond passed out immediately.

Fadin looked around and realised that Tase and Ciaran were nowhere in sight either.

"So where are the rest of you?" Puceula questioned.

Robert turned his gaze from the limp Marie in one of the guard's arms, to Lynch. "You think we are foolish enough to all stay together?"

"I think you were foolish enough to bring two ilchruthach into a small town and not expect us to catch you." He eyed Faolan, who snarled at him, and seemed to search for Saoirse.

Robert said nothing but glanced back at Marie.

Puceula followed his gaze. "I heard about what happened to the poor doctor." Robert stiffened.

"Too bad, that's what happens when you involve normal human beings."

Fadin saw Tase peer around a bush from the corner of his eye. He swiveled his vision and Tase pointed to something below Fadin.

Fadin thought to him, *What?* It suddenly felt like something slapped and bit

Fadin in his neck, then his arms, wrists, and chest. The worst pain, however, came when whatever it was hit his spine, he felt like a hot knife had penetrated his skin and had sunk down to the bone where it twisted and shocked him. "Ahhh!" he cried and jerked. His chains had shocked him, just like Desmond's.

"Didn't you see what happened to the wolf boy?" the woman holding him hissed, pulling on his restraints. "Don't be stupid, boy, stop trying to use magic."

The pain stopped and Fadin's eyes grew wide. He hadn't known his ability to speak to Tase through their thoughts had been magic, at least not in the way he thought about magic. That ability seemed natural, but clearly it wasn't because he could not talk to Tase with his mind now, bound as he was.

Fadin slid his eyes back to where Tase had been, but he was gone. "... of playing games," Puceula was saying. Fadin hadn't been paying attention.

He got right in Robert's face. "It's only a matter of time before we find all the keys. We found your little hiding space easily enough." He brandished the braids in the glass. "Where are the Seven Seals?"

Fadin felt the surge, but didn't understand it at first.

Robert cocked his head as if he heard a high-pitched sound, and Fadin noticed a few of the guards do the same.

"Sir, watch out!" one of them cried.

It was a fraction of a second too late. Saoirse flung herself from a tree and in a blink was the black jaguar with the silver markings. She collided with Lynch, who flung her from him, transforming his staff into a shield made from red light. It was a narrow miss.

Robert kicked the jar out of Puceula's hands and grabbed it. He sent a wave of magic at the guards now fighting Saoirse the jaguar, knocking them down briefly.

Ciaran was suddenly there, on Fadin's shoulder, causing him to jump. "Hello thing!" he smiled, and threw a bottle of blue and silver powder in the female guard's face.

She screeched and dropped the knife, trying in vain to wipe the stuff away. Fadin ducked out of the way of her flailing arms and fell to the floor.

Ciaran jumped on top of her, pulled her hair and began to unbuckle her belt. "Almosts has its!" he grunted.

In a puff of black smoke, Tase was at Fadin's side. "You all right?" Fadin stared wide-eyed at his brother.

"Here's!" Ciaran shouted, and flung a set of silver keys to Tase.

Tase caught them and thrust them into the lock on Fadin's wrist. With a screech the lock unfastened and Fadin's hands were free. He jumped up and searched for his sword. It wasn't far from him on the floor.

Ciaran jumped back and brandished his claws, creating a ball of red a yellow magic between his hands. He flung the magic at the female guard, but she blocked his magic. He threw himself on top of her but after a furious and brief struggle he was flung from her with a cry and he rolled sickly on the asphalt.

"Ciaran!" Tase cried, as Fadin moved for his weapon.

It was as if Fadin's ears unexpectedly exploded. The sound that pierced them felt like a hundred needles were burrowing their way to his eardrum. He clutched his ears and fell to the floor, any other thought flung from his mind because of the pain.

He opened his eyes and saw that standing in the middle of them was the hooded woman, the banshee, her cape vibrating with the horrendous sound of her scream.

Everyone, even Robert, was on the floor, clutching at their heads, except for Puceula. It looked as though Robert had pinned him to a car but he pulled himself away from it and picked up his staff and the glass bottle from the street.

Fadin watched, wincing and pushing his palms to his ears as hard as he could, but trying to focus on what Puceula was doing.

He picked up the crossbow that had sent the other darts into Robert's body. He held the weapon firmly against him and aimed. In a stream that was almost not visible, Puceula unloaded the roll of ammunition into the older man.

Robert blocked a few of them, but it seemed as though the Banshee's scream disrupted his normal abilities. Robert's eyes fluttered and he sunk further to the asphalt, though he kept his hands firmly clenched on his ears.

Puceula dropped the crossbow, satisfied that fifteen darts should do the trick, and aimed his staff at Roberts face.

Fire, unlike any Fadin had ever seen, erupted onto the street. It was blue, brilliantly blue, and so hot that it melted the roof of a car it briefly touched. It changed directions slightly and a burst of it shot in Puceula's direction. He dodged it but it hit the Banshee.

Her cape caught on fire and she stopped screaming. She whirled around towards the direction the fire had come from, not bothering to even try and put the flame out, and froze.

Fadin found he could move so he shifted his gaze and saw Aednat standing in the middle of the street with what looked like an ancient flamethrower, but beautifully designed.

Aednat set her face furiously at the Banshee and pulled the trigger. Her gun sent a huge blast of blue flame directly in contact with the hooded woman, but it also sent Aednat flying backward. She collided with a car but stood her ground and shook her dark red head in shock.

If they hadn't been in so much danger, Fadin would have laughed himself sick.

The hooded woman vanished with the flames, not around a corner, or into the foliage, not in a puff of smoke; she just simply wasn't there anymore, no good explanation why.

"She's gone!" Aednat yelled.

As soon as she was, a wave of goblins emerged from the trees and bushes around them and threw what looked like glass balls at the guards beginning to stand. One was Xemplose, large and orange, and another blue goblin Fadin recognized as Rin, though there were others he had never seen before. When the glass bottles hit they caused a small explosion of the same blue flame Aednat had shot from her weapon. These bombs, of sorts, worked at first, but then several guards caught on and began to block them.

"Get up!" Tase hissed in Fadin's ear, breaking his concentration.

Fadin obeyed. He grabbed his sword and the pack that held his shield. He changed his gaze and saw that Robert held Puceula by the collar of his shirt and that he had placed his hand on his chest.

Puceula writhed beneath Robert's touch and Robert flung him to the ground. "You coward!" he yelled. "No wonder you feel nothing. You would rather have a heart of stone than feel all the guilt for what you have done."

Puceula reached for his staff but Robert stepped on it. "Don't pretend you never did the same!" Puceula spat.

Robert held up the glass vial with the glowing braids. "For a time, but I learned that's no way to live." He uncorked the vial and stared Lynch in the eye. "You really think my hiding places will be that easy to find?"

Puceula Lynch's eyes grew wide.

Robert dropped the vial on Puceula's chest and it shattered, turning into little glass snakes that began to burrow their way into his clothes. Puceula yelped and his eyes burned silver as he tried to remove them in vain.

Robert smiled and lifted his staff. "You won't be a problem for us any longer, Lynch." He placed it on Lynches forehead.

Puceula's silver eyes widened. "No! Don't!" he screamed.

Fadin understood what he was going to do, and he felt sick as the realisation hit him. "Robert, wait…"

Something massive hit Robert with such force that it flung him across the street and into a tree, which cracked with the impact.

Fadin whirled and saw two familiar faces among a small army of guards. Colin and Holtunson, the two guards who had chased them when they had found the Xoor in the museum in Dublin. His jaw fell open.

"Times to goes, times to goes!" Ciaran yanked on Fadin's arm.

Fadin peered down at his little friend and winced as he saw the scrapes and gashes on his small green face and body.

"We cannot's stay, thing! Musts goes, NOW!"

Fadin nodded and with one last, horrified glance saw Holtunson pick up the massive sword he was dragging behind him.

The next blast missed, but it came horrifyingly close to Tase. Tase jerked out of the way just before it collided with his right side, and hit a car instead, sending it smashing into a fence.

Lights were turning on and voices could be heard shouting and screaming inside.

"Bombs! They are bombing us!" a man yelled.

"Is it terrorists?" one woman cried out. "I thought we were past all this. You have to call Lauren! I want to make sure they haven't been hit!"

"Follow!" Ciaran hissed, and Fadin did. He and Tase realised the others were already out of the street.

"Where have they gone?" Tase wondered.

"Justs follows me!" Ciaran ordered.

They ran toward the green ground of the park and Fadin heard the dragging sword be lifted off the asphalt.

"Watch it!"

Fadin shot out of the way as Aednat appeared, the massive gun in her arms and Aimirgin stumbling next to her. Aednat fired and the blue flame aimed true. It hit Holtunson, but he blocked it with his weapon, though the remnant flame broke off into two smaller streams as it hit the blade, which collided with some of the other guards. They screamed in pain and fell to the floor, trying to roll the fire out.

Fadin turned back to Aednat and saw that she was on the floor, a good two meters from him. He let out a small laugh despite the situation. "Good shot, Freckles."

She stood shakily and grinned. Aimirgin pushed her forward. "Come on," she ordered, holding her wounded arm close to her. Fadin hoped no people came outside, with Aimirgin in her true spotted, hoofed, and long necked form. Not to mention the magic flame-thrower and the goblins.

"Go, go!" Ciaran growled.

Fadin grabbed Aednat's hand and Tase helped Aimirgin. They ran until they rounded a few trees and saw everyone piled in a sort of circle on the grass. Desmond, Marie, and Enda were unconscious. Saoirse was human again, Faolan was no longer bound, and Robert leaned on his staff, seeming to truly need its support.

Fadin turned his gaze to the outside of the circle and made himself do a double take. There were five of them, and though they looked different than Ciaran, they were all goblins. They each stood around the circle in the grass, and one of them stared directly at Ciaran. "Get friends in circle. We must go."

Ciaran nodded and pushed them inside.

Fadin, Tase, Aednat and Aimirgin squashed themselves against Desmond, Faolan, and Robert.

Ciaran took his place on the outside of the circle and Fadin saw that with six of them they made a perfectly even pattern.

"Now," the goblin who had spoken first nodded.

Each of them put a clawed fist out. Their fists grew larger and everything outside the circle began to lose colour, turning black and white. At the same moment the goblin's all opened their hands and the world outside began to go all black.

Before the dark consumed them, Fadin saw Puceula, Colin, and Holtunson appear around the trees. Puceula yelled something, but the dark also blocked out sound, so all he knew was that Lynch's face contorted into a shout of fury, and they were gone.

# CHAPTER 19
## THE GOBLIN GUILD

Tase opened his eyes and the darkness was gone. He wasn't sure where they were and then arms were around his neck. He was about to fight and yelp, but a voice in his ear said, "You're okay! You're all okay!"

"Uncle Lorcan?" he asked, bringing his hand up and feeling his uncle's small, round body.

Uncle Lorcan pulled back from the hug and Tase saw his bright round face, which looked so much like his fathers. Tase beamed at him. "What happened to you? We didn't know where you had gone."

"I went with Kyna," he said, nodding, and Tase saw Aunt Kyna letting go of Fadin and Enda.

Uncle Lorcan hopped to Fadin's shoulders and Aunt Kyna gave Tase a brief but caring hug. She wasn't a very warm woman, nowhere near as gentle as Uncle Lorcan or Mr Hogan, but Tase knew she loved them all just the same.

"We went off on our own," she said. "I knew someone who could help us, but it was dangerous, and since we were all separated anyway," she turned her attention to Robert as she continued, "I thought it best to take the opportunity and keep everyone else safe. I told Lorcan to go, but he insisted."

Uncle Lorcan let Fadin go and bounded onto Aimirgin's left shoulder. "I wasn't about to let her go alone."

"Have you seen my family?" Aednat asked, her hazel eyes hopeful. "I know that Aldabella was lost…" She had to stop for a moment to even out her voice, but couldn't seem to find it again.

"Aldabella saved us," Fadin said, and Tase looked at him in surprise, "but she had to sacrifice her freedom. She went into the sea, and she…" he seemed to try and find the right word, "she can't return to land."

Tase and Aimirgin exchanged a shocked glance.

"Oh no," Uncle Lorcan choked. He put a hand to his mouth and looked to Kyna.

"I'm so sorry, Aednat," she said, bending down so she was the same height as the eleven-year-old. "I haven't seen your family, but I know for a fact that your ma and da were escorted by Irrah himself, I can't imagine your sister wasn't with them."

Aednat nodded and wiped at her eye before anything could form there. Tase felt a great hollowness at the thought of Aldabella at sea, her blue hair swaying with the movement of the ocean, unable to come home.

"We will find them," Robert insisted, putting a hand on her shoulder.

Aunt Kyna spotted Faolan and she recoiled in disbelief. "Faolan?" she all but shouted.

"I'm here for Saoirse," he said.

There was tension between them, and Tase could tell there were words being passed to one another that didn't need to be spoken aloud. What they were, he could not guess.

"Well," Uncle Lorcan said, landing on Saoirse, who smiled at him. "I'm glad we have help for my Saoirse, wherever it may come from." He eyed Kyna, who broke her stare with Faolan.

Aunt Kyna took a breath and refocused herself on Robert. "Our decision to go on our own paid off. We found who we were looking for, but it was because of Carian and his Goblin Guild." She held her hands out to Ciaran and the other goblins.

Tase liked the name Goblin Guild. He had almost forgotten about them, and at Aunt Kyna's remembrance he examined the lot of them.

One of them was yellow, with hair so red it seemed unnatural. He had a small red mustache and beard, and his right eye was pure white with four large, pale scars over and under it. The marks stretched down to his chin. His ears were large, nearly Ciaran's size, though they both stuck out straight. His good eye was pale grey and it swivelled to Tase, staring at him, and he grimaced. "What is it you be lookin' at, human?"

Tase blinked.

"That's Leafold," Ciaran nodded to him. "He nots always the warmest goblins, but he is braves." He smiled his crooked, stained toothy grin.

Tase suppressed a chuckle.

Ciaran said, "We goblins comes together because we knows the truths." He looked at the boys. "We knows who is trying to hurts you, we knows about the Bojins, and we don't wants to sits by and do's nothing."

"That's right." Xemplose nodded. He patted a band on his arm that held a symbol of an obscure goblin head wearing a crown that made two G's around a crystal, clearly standing for the Goblin Guild name.

Ciaran patted the heavy orange goblin and came to a much smaller and thinner goblin. He was a chocolate brown, and both of his ears flopped down, giving him the look of a puppy. He had small fangs that protruded from the top of his mouth over his thin lips, and his face was adorned with golden freckles that almost sparkled against his dark skin. His eyes were deep green, and his hair was messy and white. He smiled shyly at Tase and Fadin as Ciaran put his arm around him. "Thrilt," he said. "He is youngs, almost as youngs as you things."

Thrilt nodded. "Xemplos, my brother." As his face turned, Tase saw that the small goblin had what looked like old burn marks on his face. They were not the random pattern of some accident. Instead, the old wounds were set in designs, swirls and knots. "Ciaran find us both, brought us here."

Ciaran nodded, confirming this. He hobbled over to a light blue goblin that Tase had seen before when Vladimir had attacked them. Her white hair was cast in twists and braids. Two small black horns appeared from her hair, and from her smaller pointed ears dangled many silver earrings, some lined with jewels. "Rinnerwood," she said, her voice high pitched but deeper than Tase expected. "You can speak my name as Rin if you would like. Ciaran found me, too."

"To be fair," a voice, which sounded like a cross between a machine and a man who had smoked himself to the state that normal speech was no longer possible, said, "Ciaran found us all."

Tase looked and saw that the owner of the voice was quite an old goblin. His skin was the same shade as Tase and Fadin's, though it was covered in scars and was worn, like old leather. His head was bald, and one horn was pronounced in the middle of his forehead. His eyes were a light purple, and the left side of his face looked as though it had been melded to what once may have been a metal helmet, and he had a white scraggly beard. He was missing an ear on his left side as well, and the other ear looked like it had been shredded. His throat was covered in a sort of metal choker, and it was from this that the sound of his voice emanated, robotic sounding as it was.

"I am Pilous," the old goblin said. "Ciaran is the one who brought us together. He is the one who knew help was needed." His worn face turned up into what may have been a smile, a smile made around two fangs that protruded out from his lower jaw. "The time for sitting in the shadows is over." He looked around the room at the wounded others. "As I can see you know," his purple eyes locked onto Tase and Fadin's, "we are not ordinary goblins, as I am sure you can all see."

Tase wasn't really sure what ordinary goblins were, but he did know, from things Ciaran had told him, that most goblins were lowly creatures, mistreated, and had little importance in the magical Irish world. He nodded all the same.

Pilous pointed with his missing hand to the yellow goblin with the missing eye. "Leafold worked for the enemy during the Great War, he has much information on enemy tactics. Xemplos and Thrilt," The heavy orange goblin and the small brown one inclined their heads, "were taken to the enemy's side when they were very young. Experiments were done on them that have left them hurt, but they are more powerful than many. Rin was raised in the ministry; she is the last in the royal line of goblins. She knows many things and knows secrets none of us could find on our own." He paused and touched his own chest. "I was part of the resistance in the Great War. I lead a secret team of goblins, trained for the purpose of assassination by stealth. I was captured, and as you can see I did not escape unscathed. I know how the enemy worked last time, and you can learn much about the future from the past."

Robert seemed to enjoy the goblins. He gave them all a nod of approval. "You will all be quite useful, I see. And please, who is it you all helped Kyna find?" Robert asked.

A man stepped forward. He had apparently been there the whole time, but among the brilliantly coloured goblins, Tase had missed him. "Me," the man said. He was in his mid to late forties, Tase decided, with blue eyes, curly brown hair, and scruffy bristles on his face. His most distinctive feature was his nose, it wasn't large but it was a unique shape, a feature you wouldn't forget. His eyes were weary and it looked as though he hadn't slept in a long while. "Argonne Nugent," he introduced himself.

Enda smiled wide and stepped forward, taking Argonne Nugent's hand in his massive one. "It is a pleasure, Mr Nugent," Enda praised. "Your articles are the only ones that speak the truth."

The reporter grinned back at Enda, seeming to like him right off the bat. "I thank you for that, but I'm afraid my rather large mouth and articles in the papers have gotten me into quite a lot of trouble."

"I'll bet," Robert noted.

Desmond stayed next to Saoirse, but he seemed in awe of Mr Nugent as well. "I'm glad you're all right, from the last things I read I wasn't sure you were still a free man."

"For a time I wasn't," Mr Nugent said. "My cover name is Fergus Daly, and I committed a small but punishable crime while under that name and was thrown in jail. Kyna here was actually thrown into Cavan-Corr Penitentiary on purpose so she could speak with me."

"Wait," Tase said, remembering a few years ago when Aunt Kyna had been thrown in jail for slander against the king, "Are you talking about when she was taken off the Cavan-Corr Council?"

Mr Nugent inclined his head, affirming that was the instance he was talking about.

"But," Tase protested, "I remember you writing an article about Aunt Kyna being thrown in prison. If you were both in jail, how is that possible?"

Mr Nugent pointed to Rin, the blue goblin. "She and Kyna got me out. I won't go into the details, but it was a daring rescue. I won't forget what she sacrificed to get me out of there."

"For a good reason," Kyna said. "He has contacts who keep him well informed, and he has information that can help us."

"For example?" Robert asked.

"You have been away a long time," Mr Nugent addressed Robert and then widened his range to Enda, Desmond, and the rest of them. "Many changes have occurred in the ministry. Puceula Lynch has been given far too much power. Though they have not made themselves publicly known, we are aware that the Bojins control Lynch, and many others. Currently the best thing they have going in their favour is the ignorance of the magical community's people. The majority of the population doesn't have any idea of the plotting the ministry and Puceula are doing. Beyond that, the Bojins have left the country on a number of occasions lately, I followed them myself and from what I was able to gather at least some leaders from magical Russia, Egypt, and Germany have met with them. About what, I don't know, and I do not know their plan fully, but one sure fact is that at this point Vladimir possesses three keys." He spotted Marie and his eyes widened. "Is that Maire Whelan?"

"Yes," Robert confirmed. "I rescued her and her doctor, Jason Guilfoyle, from her asylum when the Bojins attacked it. Unfortunately, Dr Guilfoyle was lost to us."

"I'm sorry to hear that," Mr Nugent said. "Not to sound insensitive, but we must keep the girl away from the Bojins and their followers at all costs."

"That is my intention," Robert huffed. "You seem to put a special emphasis on her, above the others. Is there a reason?"

"Yes," Mr Nugent said. "Right now, Vladimir only believes that Marie knows where the lost Whelan Key is."

"Doesn't she?" Enda asked.

"Yes and no," Mr Nugent said.

Tase was beginning to get confused.

"She *is* the missing key."

"What?" Robert incredulously asked.

"She is one of the most important pieces, without her nothing can be opened. If Vladimir possessed Marie and knew how to use her, he could unlock more power each time another key was taken. As it is, his power only increases ever so slightly with the taking of the keys. Without Marie, he cannot get the Xoor open even a crack, whether he possess the book or not."

"How is it possible that she is a key?" Robert inquired.

"I don't know how it happened," Mr Nugent told him. "I only know it's true. She is the only one who can actually use the keys to begin to unlock the book, and once Vladimir figures that out his whole desire will be for her."

"We must hide her," Enda said.

"Agreed," Robert nodded. "However, we have a safe place to go. We should join the others in the elven kingdom."

Tase felt a wave of relief at the thought.

"There's somethings we should tells you," Ciaran grimaced.

"What is it?" Tase asked, panic filling his chest.

"Your family was ambushed, before they arrived in the elven lands," Rin replied.

"What?" Tase and many others voices demanded.

"We's were checksing in on thems," Ciaran said, "ands we saw them be tasken prisoner."

"By who?" Robert asked, frustration in his tone.

"Fairies," Ciaran trembled.

Fadin made a snicker. "Fairies? Are you kidding?"

"Do not," Faolan said, coming to stand behind him, "underestimate what fairies can do." His pale green eyes shimmered.

"Where are they, Ciaran?" Enda questioned.

"We cans takes you to wheres we last see's them," Ciaran answered. "Froms there we wills have to do ours best."

Enda rubbed his head as if it ached.

"We will leave soon," Robert announced, "but first we need a chance to rest, or we will be no good to them."

Tase wanted to argue, but he knew Robert was right. He was beginning to feel a bit hopeless at the odds against them.

"You're in the right place for that," Uncle Lorcan stated. And for the first time Tase realised they were underground somewhere, but that the ceiling looked like the inside of the mushroom. "We have a bit of a ways to go on foot," Uncle Lorcan informed them. "So take a moment of rest, and then we will get everything we need to continue the journey. My family's Leprechaun Lair is just down this passage."

"A Leprechaun Lair?" Fadin asked.

Uncle Lorcan smiled. "I wish I could show it to you under better circumstances."

Tase slumped to the floor and leaned against the stone wall. Aimirgin was asking Uncle Lorcan a question, and Robert was checking Saoirse. Aednat was trying to peek under her arm bandage while Desmond chided her. "It won't develop right if you keep trying to peek at it!"

Ciaran giggled and pointed at her, and Aednat stuck her tongue out at him.

Tase was vaguely aware of Fadin collapsing down next to him, and he turned to his brother.

"Alive?" Fadin asked, the side of his face horribly scraped from the last attack.

"I suppose," he acknowledged, looking down. He saw his shirt had been torn and he could see his blackened scar on his chest. He quivered as he thought about the Xoor.

"You two okay?" Enda questioned, coming to sit with them. He folded his long legs beneath him, and checked them over. He made a face at Fadin's cheek. "That's a nasty cut, Fadin."

Fadin winced as he lightly touched it. "I know."

"I can't believe how much has happened," Tase said. "We were safe on that island. It was home, and then the naiads came, the island sunk, Saoirse was held hostage, Vladimir took the key the mermaids gave us, and we ended up at the castle learning that Clearie isn't even our real brother!"

"Ah ah, don't forget," Fadin chimed in, "Saoirse is an ilchruthach and can change into a huge cat, plus Aldabella is now a mermaid, Aednat's family is nowhere to be found, Puceula just tried to kill us, and Vladimir has three of the six keys needed to open the Xoor."

Enda sighed. "Plus Caoimhe, Lee, Cleaire, your ma, and Glendan have been captured by faires." He ran his large hand over his face and stared at the boys. "I'm sorry this world has been nothing but trouble for you two."

Tase rested his head on one knee. "It hasn't all been bad. Just particularly dangerous lately."

Enda rumbled with laughter. "I'm glad you boys are here with us."

"So are we, Uncle Enda," Tase grinned.

"I don't know," Fadin considered, "being captured by faires may just be pretty cool."

Enda grabbed him playfully and ruffled his red hair.

Tase smiled for a moment but it faltered as he looked at Saoirse. She made a face that reminded him so much of Ma he almost thought she was Ma for a moment.

He suddenly felt the pain of her absence incredibly strongly. He missed her! He wanted to see Ma's sparking cerulean eyes, he wanted to feel her comforting arms around him. He wanted to hear her voice assure him everything was going to be okay, and to see her smile.

"Tase?" Enda asked.

"I miss Ma," he admitted. "It's not the same without her."

Fadin seemed reluctant, but he nodded in agreement. Tase assumed his brother didn't want to admit he needed their mother as much as Tase did. But Tase knew the truth, Fadin missed her every bit as much as he did. Fadin just didn't like to be vulnerable, where Tase really couldn't care if he appeared too soft to some people. He needed his mother and he wasn't ashamed of it.

"No," Enda agreed, "it isn't." His grey eyes were sad. "I miss her too."

"Without her, Da feels so far away," Tase acknowledged. "I also miss him, Clearie, Glendan, Caoimhe, and Mr Hogan." His thoughts lingered on Mr Hogan.

He thought about his kind, tanned face, his warm black eyes, and his calming smile that felt like home. He had become like a second father to him, and Tase wished he had some sort of father now. He stared up at Enda. "We have to make sure they're all all right."

Enda put his large hands on both the boys' shoulders. "I swear to you, I will not rest until our family is safe and all together. I love your mother every bit as much as you do. I didn't ever want to give up when she and your father disappeared all that time ago, after the Great War. I probably never would have, but Kyna and the others were convinced that they had been killed or captured. I just lost hope."

Tase thought back to when they had first arrived at Kavanagh Castle. He and Fadin had overheard a conversation between Ma and Enda once, a fight. Enda had told her that when Ma and Da had run away after the Great War he had gone looking for them. He had searched for seven years, and after all that time he had asked for her forgiveness for not finding her, and had become a professor in the underground city of Cavan-Corr. Years went by and he had learned Ma was alive. He, Aunt Kyna, and Daireann found their family, but did not interfere for ten whole months. Enda had even disguised himself and had been Tase and Fadin's substitute teacher, Mr Donovan. In fact, it had been Enda who was their teacher the day the Banshee shattered all the glass in their classroom, the day of Da's accident. After Da died, Enda pretended to be the butler in Aunt Kyna's castle so that Ma had time to recover before telling Tase and Fadin the truth. Enda was all right pretending to be a servant if it helped his sister, he was okay with her leaving him for all those years. He forgave her, and Tase thought he would probably forgive her anything. If anyone loved Ma as much as Tase and his siblings, it was Enda.

"I promise you, we'll find them. We'll do whatever we have to do to get those faires to let them go."

Tase smiled at him. "I believe you, Uncle Enda."

Enda's face lit up at Tase calling him uncle. He often forgot to give Enda that title, just because he had firstly come to know him only as Enda. It made him so happy, however, that Tase promised he would call him *uncle* from then on.

Fadin gave Tase a look that told him he had heard Tase's thoughts about Enda too. He nodded. "You would do anything for Ma," he said. "We are lucky to have an uncle like you."

Enda, who usually was strong and didn't show much emotion, seemed as if he was struggling to keep tears back. He grabbed them up in a massive hug, and Tase felt quite fortunate that despite all their troubles he was part of this world that had given him an uncle who would do anything for them.

Enda pulled back and ruffled both their hair. "Try and rest for a bit," he instructed them. "After we rescue your ma and the others from the fairies we will be going to the elven lands. And I don't know what to expect when Clearie meets his father, Fintan."

Tase widened his eyes. "That's right. Clearie's birth father is the king of the elves, right?"

Enda ran a hand through his greying hair. "Yes, he is. Which means Clearie is the next in line for the elven throne. I guarantee you many elves will not be happy about a half human being the heir."

Fadin's mouth had fallen open. "You mean Clearie could be a king?"

Enda pinched the place on his nose between his eyes. "In theory, yes."

"That's terrible news," Fadin said. "I'm not sticking around the elven kingdom if that's what's gonna happen."

Enda chuckled despite the stress he was clearly feeling. "Oh, Fadin. I wouldn't worry too much about that. What I am concerned about is certain elves seeing Clearie as a threat."

Tase had not considered any of this, and the new information gave him a stomachache.

"The problems just keep coming," Fadin sighed.

Enda stood up to his full and immense height. "Try and sleep if you can, our troubles will keep. I will wake you up when we move to Lorcan's Leprechaun Lair." He took a deep breath and stared down the passage. "We still have a long way to go."

Tase felt though Enda was only referring to what was immediately before them, the words had stronger meaning. So much had happened, but there was much ahead. Their journey was far from over.

~~~

Tase was leaning against the stone wall one moment and the next he was staring into the face of a large dog. He jerked back in alarm and then covered his mouth. "Pathos?" he breathed.

Pathos licked him and the fisherman's chuckle was unmistakable.

He looked around and realised he was still in the passageway with the mushroom ceiling, but everything and everyone besides the fisherman and Pathos seemed layered in fog.

"Am I asleep?" Tase asked.

"Your body is resting, but your mind is not," the fisherman said.

Tase pet Pathos, enjoying the feeling of his fur on his skin, when a thought struck him. "Why is Pathos always with you? And why did he run away that night in the woods when all the guards attacked?"

The fisherman nodded at Pathos, who in turn stared at Tase with his large brown eyes.

Tase felt something tugging at him. Pathos didn't run away that night... but something happened. There was a drop in Tase's stomach as in his dog's deep brown eyes he understood. "Pathos," he breathed, "did you... were you..." He couldn't make himself finish the sentence.

Pathos put his head on Tase's knee.

"It is any dog's honour to lay his life down for his family," the fisherman said gently. "That was his job, to protect you, and he was proud to do it."

Tase stifled a gasp. It wasn't until after that night that Pathos had been able to do such strange things. Even though Pathos had been gone for so long already, the fact that Tase understood now what had happened brought fresh pain. "Who did it?" he made himself ask.

"Vladimir," the lighthouse keeper said.

Tase remembered seeing Vladimir there as a wolf that night. He looked at Pathos with sorrow. "You were such a good dog," Tase choked. He couldn't keep his emotions in.

Pathos moved closer and laid his head on Tase's shoulder. Tase grabbed him around his neck and let himself cry. It wasn't just Pathos he was crying for, it was for everything he had lost, it just felt like too much with this added to it.

"Don't be sad for him, Tase," the fisherman said. Tase pulled back and looked at him.

"He is quite happy, and I promise you I am taking superb care of him."

Tase smiled and wiped away the stray tears. He took a shuddering breath and eyed the fisherman. "Why did you come to me?"

"To warn you. You know of the storm," the fisherman said. "Yet you don't know how close it is, and that the closer you get the more you will feel the thunder before you see the lightning. Ciaran is unintentionally leading you into a trap."

Tase felt his insides twist. "A trap? I have to tell the others, I have to stop them! If it's a trap then are Ma and the others all right? How do we find them?" There were more questions but they all became jumbled and he couldn't decide which one to ask next.

"Tase," the fisherman said, "you have to follow him anyway."

"WHAT?" Tase spluttered.

Pathos watched him. "This is training, Tase."

"Training? For what?"

"There is no avoiding or stopping the storm that is coming," he said softly. "There is only preparing yourself to face it."

Tase could hear his heart pounding in his ears. "What do you want from me then? If I'm not supposed to stop everyone from following Cairan?"

"I want you to be on your guard," the fisherman said. "There's more just around the corner, Tase. Things you couldn't see if you tried to imagine every possibility. But, such is life. You just have to know that when these things come, you are not alone."

Tase thought of everything he had already been through and it weighed on him. "I'm tired," he said.

The fisherman touched his cheek. "I know. I'll help provide you with the strength to keep going."

Tase wanted to ask something but he could feel himself slipping away. "Sir?" he asked.

"Yes, Tase?"

"Have you seen Da?"

His jewel-like eyes transformed into a warm brown. "Yes, Tase, I have." He scooped Tase into a strong hug that was so powerful with love and understanding that it quite literally took Tase's breath away. Tears of loss tumbled down his chin, but in the fisherman's arms he felt such an overwhelming sense of home that it helped dampen the pain of his father's death. The fisherman let him go after a few long moments and put his hand under Tase's chin. "Prepare yourself, your journey is a long way from over." He moved back and began to walk away, Pathos trotting after him.

Tase wanted to call to him, but he had no strength left to do so. As he watched he saw someone in the distance bend down and call to Pathos. Tase wasn't sure, but he could have sworn whoever it was had bright red curly hair.

Tase smiled as he thought of Da and drifted off. As his mind fell into deeper sleep he thought he felt the rocking of a boat, and heard the quiet lapping of waves upon wood. He could have sworn he smelt the scent of fisherman's nets, and heard the fisherman's voice singing to him softly:

Away from the safety of the day, And into the wild of the night.
Though the earth shall crumble and the mountains fall,
Though the waters of the sea roar and the mountains quake in fright,
Though the sky may fall and the darkness eat the light,
Into the storm we shall go.

Away from the safety of all we have known,
Into the shadow of the mighty wing,
Though the darkness has swallowed up all hope,
Though all we have loved has fallen and to the edge we cling,
Into the wild we shall wander, our hearts though sad will sing,
Into the storm we shall go.

# CHAPTER 20
## THE GROWING DARK

Jason Guilfoyle woke with a start. It was dark and cold wherever he was. Where was he? He tried to remember. The last thing he could think of was being at the hospital. He was having particular trouble with Marie Whelan, and then something had happened. An old woman had been brought in. What had her name been? Cunningham? Was that it? Yes, Mrs. Cunningham, she had somehow been delivered to the Juvenile Ward. He remembered he had gone to sort it out, when something blew up. There had for certain been a bomb of some kind, and then the fire alarms had gone off. For some reason he was hesitant to evacuate the patients, why had that been?

There was something about the fire, it wasn't regular fire, but a sort of green fire. There was a black wolf in his memory too. That didn't make any sense, and neither did the memory of trying desperately to find a candle and light it for help. What good would lighting a candle do? Unless he had been at church and had wanted to pray for a patient, but he rarely went to church anymore.

As if it had crashed into his body at that precise moment, he felt an aching pain in his head, right arm, and all over the left side of his ribs. He let out a groan as he tried to move. Some of those ribs, he was sure, were broken. Had that been from the bomb?

There was a low and distinctly feminine chuckle from somewhere in the dark.

The hair on his arms and the back of his neck stood on end. He realised, as he tried more aggressively to move, that besides the pain, he literally was unable to go anywhere. His wrists and legs were strapped to whatever chair he was sitting in.

"Good to see you're awake, Doctor."

The voice was somehow familiar, and it filled him with dread. He thought he should say nothing, but his mouth did not catch up quickly enough with his mind. "Who are you? What do you want?" He tried to sound in control but he spit the words out too hastily, giving his voice a frightened pitch.

"You're afraid?" the voice asked. "*Good.*"

He could hear one set of footsteps moving around him. Whoever the voice belonged to they were slight, the footsteps did not fall loudly on what he assumed from the sound was a stone floor.

"I asked what you want," he said, succeeding in sounding calmer this time. The chuckle sounded again.

"What do I want?" The footfalls stopped. "Well, Doctor, what I want, I already have."

He swallowed too loudly and his heart thrummed against his sore ribs. He thought again that perhaps the right answer was to say nothing at all, but his mouth seemed unable to keep quiet. "And what is that?"

The slight footsteps moved closer. The first thing he saw was a leather boot coming into the dim light he hadn't really even realised was there. The rest followed swiftly. She was a wild-looking woman, with a long wavy mess of hair that reflected many colours. It fell thick around her face and over her shoulders, giving her the appearance of having a lion's mane. Her eyes were such a light green they were almost white, and she was clothed in leather bottoms and high brown boots. She wore the same heavy fur cloak that she had when he first had seen her, the head of a wolf adorning one shoulder.

He knew for certain now that he had seen this woman before, and he remembered being in the cavern city, in the ruins. He remembered all the light green eyes peering back at him. Even though he wished he didn't, he knew he had seen this woman change, become something else. He remembered the great multicoloured bear and how her teeth had sunk into his skin, pulling him down into the black.

She smiled, and her white teeth stood out against her dirty skin. "What I want, is you."

He felt a terrified shiver go up his spine as her pale green eyes gleamed. Somehow he knew, in that instant, that his being here was a planned thing. "For what?" he demanded.

"I have great plans for you," she chuckled as she began to circle him. "I happen to know, though you've lived in Ireland for quite some time, that you were raised in America, though your family originated in Ireland a *long* time ago." She circled behind his chair.

Jason froze. He did not know the extent of this woman's power, but power she did have, if she knew who he was, who his family was.

"You did a good job hiding your past. Changing your name, putting as much distance between you and your family as you could." She stood in front of him again. "Not good enough." She leaned forward and put her hands on either side of his chair. "I know who your daddy is."

Jason felt terror and regret surge through him.

"He is in quite the powerful spot in the American Government." She smiled wide. "You're going to help me blind that country so they won't lift a finger in the chaos that's coming. Then, you'll help me tear it apart, from the inside out."

Jason sat up as far as he could. "*Never!*" he growled.

She raised one eyebrow. "Oh, you're going to help me all right. Whether you want to or not."

"If you think I have any power over my father," Jason snorted, "you've got another thing coming, lady."

Her eyes gleamed. "Unfortunately for you, I know things you don't." She suddenly jumped and was perched on his chair, directly above him.

He startled and shook the chair, wishing with all his might he could pull himself free.

"In a war," she whispered to him, "sacrifices must be made." She touched her thumb to his forehead and gave him a small scratch with her nail.

He felt pain burst from that spot and course through his whole head. He let out an involuntary cry of shock.

She flung herself backward, landing gracefully. "You're in for a rough night, Doctor," she said, turning and beginning to walk away. "Don't plan on sleeping much."

Through the pain he saw her stride towards two large doors that became visible as she neared them. She raised her left hand and a massive guard stepped to one side, and the doors opened.

Jason cried out again as the pain became worse in his head. *Oh no*, he thought, his mind racing to his father. *Oh no!* His vision suddenly went black and he cried out in fear.

~~~

Yessult didn't smile when she heard the doctor scream. She knew the fear and pain of her poison all too well. She truly didn't wish it on anyone, but war was war, and the good doctor was leverage she needed.

She entered the lavish room with opulent couches, brilliant fur rugs, and luxurious curtains of the finest silk strewn from the rafters and across sharp corners.

Dominique Bojin, the wild and beautiful, leaned against a pillar, fiddling with her ruby necklace inscribed with a B. Her midnight eyes flicked up to Yessult, and her thick red lips turned into a pout. She was paler than usual, and had a sickly look to her. Yessult had heard talk that Vladimr and Dominique had gotten into a fight with the Kavanaghs and their allies. It looked like Dominique had overdone it during the battle. That was always the girl's problem; she was exceptionally powerful for a short time, but she had no restraint and would wear herself out too quickly. Yessult didn't much care for her.

Judging by the look of disgust Dominique was giving her, Yessult guessed the feeling was mutual.

Now, Trandafira on the other hand, Yessult feared and respected. She spotted her coming out of the shadows near one of the two fireplaces. She had her long black hair flowing freely around her, and her appearance was quite lovely, though her eyes were cold and ruthless. Trandafira was much like her brother in the way that she was always in control. She calculated, she planned, and she was patient. She allowed Vladimir to lead, but Yessult suspected Trandafira greatly influenced him, though she would make her suggestions in such a way that it seemed everything was Vladimir's idea.

From the shadows she stepped from, there was a chair and Yessult knew who sat in it. She bowed in that direction. A hand came up, informing her to rise.

Gabriel also emerged from the shadowed corner. He was young and strong in appearance, but Yessult knew better than to accept everything your eyes saw. He was powerful, she could feel that, but what power he possessed she was not sure of. She didn't remember a time when Gabriel's magic – whatever it was – had been used in the open. His murky eyes and blue-black hair glimmered in the firelight as he watched her turn to the thin man leaning over papers on a beautifully decorated wooden table.

"You weren't wrong," Vladimir said in his crackling rumble of a voice. "The doctor will be of great use to us." He looked up and straightened. "You are willing to use him to get what his family has?"

She bowed her head. "As long as you hold up your end of the bargain. Your people have been stopping me from creating more ilchruthachs. I need many subjects. You know my strength relies in how many beings follow me. I have control over them, they are only allowed as much power as I allot. In return for letting me collect as many subjects as I desire, I will help you with the doctor, and you can use my ilchruthachs for any purpose and in any way that you wish."

Vladimir eyed Trandafira, who gave him a snide smile. She strode across the room and set a tray down on another vividly carved mahogany table.

Vladimir chuckled, and clapped his hands. "It's a deal!" He strode over to her and held out his hand, his green eyes dancing malevolently.

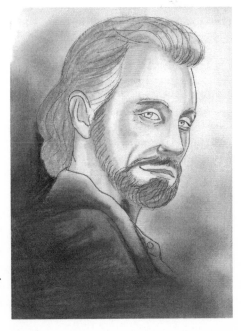

She hesitated for a fraction of a second, but, pushing aside any worry, she clamped hers around his.

Gabriel took a blue stone from the desk and they each placed their free hand on it. Trandafira and Dominique both placed a single hand on the stone as well. None of them flinched as ring shaped brands were burned around their middle fingers. The pain was fleeting, and as long as they each held up their end of the bargain, there was nothing to fear from the brand.

Yessult let go first.

"Now that you are in our inner circle," Vladimir sang, "I want you to travel to America as soon as you are able."

She had been expecting this. "I am able. I will need Jason to be well enough."

"Yes," Vladimir chuckled, putting his hands behind his back, his white teeth gleaming. "The two of you playing husband and wife shouldn't be too difficult with your poison coursing through his veins. You'll just have to convince and win over his daddy." He circled her as he spoke. "We need to clean you up a bit." He clicked his tongue to the roof of his mouth. "Living in that ruin of a city has made you forget about appearances, my dear."

She glanced down at her dirt and dust covered clothes and skin. "I suppose you're right."

He smiled. "I *am* right." He snapped his fingers. "Maldorf," he called. A pathetic looking blue creature appeared, with large chocolate brown eyes and silver shackles on his wrists and ankles.

"Yes, Grand Master?" the creature asked.

"Take this woman and draw her a bath. While she cleans up send one of my servants to bring a magical tailor here so clothing can be custom made for her. I also want a hair dresser, and someone who knows how to do make up." He looked Yessult up and down. "We'll have to have this lady looking her best to play her part."

"As you wish, Grand Master," Maldorf bowed.

"And, Maldorf," Vladimir said.

"Yes, Grand Master?"

"If you ever try to pull a stunt like the dragon tooth again, I will have no more use for you. Do you understand me?"

Yessult looked at the creature better and saw he clearly had taken a beating.

"Yes sir, Grand Master, sir," Maldorf shuddered.

Vladimir kept his eyes on Yessult but addressed the small creature. "Good, now lead our new ally to her quarters."

"This way, lady," Maldorf said to her.

Yessult turned to the dark chair once more and bowed. "Thank you, my king, for this opportunity."

The hand raised once more to tell her she could stand. She looked into the darkness and saw the weakened but clear face of Afanasii Egorov, the man who had killed Dia, the monster who had nearly taken Ireland over seventeen years ago. Vladimir was helping him regain his power. It would only be a matter of time now.

She headed for the door but stopped as she reached Vladimir. "You know, after this is all over, it is *his* name they will all remember. Afanasii Egorov is the name that will strike fear into people's hearts, not yours. No one will ever know that you were the one who gave him the throne. That it was you that made him king."

Vladimir's smile was dazzling. "I don't need my name remembered. What I want is to steal the Xoor and its keys, to kill anyone who stands in my way, and to destroy Ireland."

"Is that all?" Yessult grinned.

He smirked and opened the door courteously for her to leave. She followed the servant Maldorf out.

She laughed quietly as she crossed the threshold of the door. A war was imminent, the time had come to pick a side. Like a game of chess, survival depended on the moves you made, and with Vladimir holding the only kings on his end of the board, she had clearly picked the winning player. She had lived long enough to know that power never lasted forever, but it was better to have it for a while than not at all.

~~~

Vladimir smiled wide as Yessult left. He eyed the dark corner and inclined his head to Trandafira. She signalled the other two. He led all of them out a beautiful arched wood door and into another lavishly decorated room. This one had walls made of grey marble, with pillars and gold molding along the ceiling. The floor was magnificently polished cream, gold, and mahogany flecked marble with beautiful fur rugs set here and there. Several murals and portrait paintings adorned the walls, but Vladimir's favorite part of this room was the prisoner who was trapped within the walls themselves. He chuckled wickedly as he watched the marble covered Ardan Aislinn run from one end of the room to the other, stuck in the marble walls. He had caught Ardan shortly after the battle with the Kavanaghs. He had been alone, searching for his youngest daughter, and Senssirah had caught him. "Kind of ironic, that your own failed potion has ended up being one of my favorite weapons," Vladimir chatted, "don't you think, Ardan?"

Ardan smacked at the wall and tried to yell back, but the spell would never allow him to leave, or speak, unless Vladimir wished it. "The only way you're getting out of there is if you accept my offer and use that creative mind to serve my purposes."

Ardan clearly mouthed, "Never!"

Vladimir chortled, leaned against a wall and grinned broadly.

"Afanasii is quite veak," Trandafira informed him. "But, he vill regain his strength eef ve keep nurturing him."

319

"He will play his part well," Vladimir affirmed. "I am not concerned in the slightest." He sauntered to the glass case where three of the six ruby pillows were holding their treasure. He let his fingers dance over the glass as he peered down at the wooden O, M, and D. "Three of the six," he said, his voice rumbling. He turned. "Only three left, and last, the Xoor. Then all the power we could ever want will be ours. No one will be able to stand against us." He smiled broadly and grabbed his sister's shoulders. "We are closer now than we ever were seventeen years ago."

Trandafira beamed back at him and touched the glass. "Only za Kavanagh, Whelan, and Guilfoyle keys left."

"Ve are so close," Gabriel boasted. "Yessult vill take za Guilfoyle Key. Ve just need to knov za loation of za Kavanagh Key and feend za Whelan girl."

Vladimir snickered and held both arms out. "I know the location of the Kavanagh Key."

Trandafira, Gabriel, and Dominque's eyes were on him. "Vhere is eet?" Trandafira asked excitedly.

Vladimir raised both eyebrows. "The Kavanagh boy, Tase, has it on him."

"The child?" Trandafira laughed. Vladimir nodded his head in delight.

Gabriel's face grew dark. "Zat fool Puceula almost had za boy only a few hours ago! He lost them. Ve could have had za Kavanagh key in our grasp!"

Vladimir put his hands on the younger man's shoulders. "Don't fret, Gabriel. The boy doesn't even know what he's got. The Kavanagh key will come to us when the time is right." He felt the amusement growing in his chest and the laughter that erupted from him was unquenchable. He let his emotions roll with it, letting Gabriel's shoulders go, unable to contain his glee. "Oh, it's just too easy," his voice rumbled with his mirth, "like pushing a child off a rolling log." He took a steadying breath, his chest light with delight, and watched Ardan try in vain to find a way out of the walls.

"Should Puceula be punished for his failure?" Trandafira questioned. Vladimir considered the suggestion, staring at her,  and shook his head.

"No, he has successfully made himself invaluable at the moment. He is right where we want him to be. He will take over the ministry, and open the doors for us to overthrow the entire government."

"Everything ees een line," Trandafira purred.

Vladimir spun to face them all. "All according to plan." He eyed Dominique, who was still pouting. He arched an eyebrow at her. "How long are you planning to sulk for, Dominique?" he asked, placing his hands behind his back. Trandafira exchanged a look with him, but Vladimir raised his hand. He would take care of it. He strolled over to where she leaned against a marble pillar.

She looked up at him, her pouting lips in a deep frown.

"You did not obey me, did you?" he asked her, standing extremely close to her face. She turned her eyes down. "Did you?"

She shook her lovely head.

"No, you did not. When I tell you to stop, you *must* listen to me." He put a hand under her chin and tipped her head so she had to look at him. "You are *exceptionally* powerful, my pet. But you must understand, you are like a cheetah. You can sprint and outrun any animal in your sights, but once you use your power you wear yourself out, and you cannot run again until you regain your strength." He turned her head from side to side, examining her appearance. "You are still not fully restored from the power you expelled during our battle with the Kavanaghs. That is far too long to be useless." He inclined his head to her. "I need you to learn self-control. When this war comes your power will be needed but you must brace yourself."

She nodded.

"Good girl." He turned to Trandafira and Gabriel. "To you both, my right and left hand." He took Trandafira in his right hand and Gabriel in his left. "I have held you both back until this point. Now I am going to need you to take a more active role."

Gabriel grinned.

Trandafira bowed her head.

"We will get the last keys and find the Xoor. The Kavanaghs cannot evade us forever, and the time has come for us to actively seek them out. They are gaining their own allies, and that is something we do not want."

Trandafira's expression was irritated.

"Do not fret, sister," he soothed her. "Their group is separated, and everything is in our grasp." He walked to the window that overlooked a portion of their land. The night shone brightly with the light of the moon. "We will not have to be patient much longer. Soon Afanassii will rise, Puceula will take the throne from Raegan, and the Kavanaghs will die." He took in the sheer number of ilchruthachs behind their castle walls. There were hundreds of them, and Yessult was itching to gather more. All in human form, a few here and there began to shift into animals. They were like bubbles popping on the surface of near boiling water. "And now, thanks to Queen Yessult, we have a *graaaaand* army." He chuckled darkly, extending his hand to the increasingly changing multitude. Several of the ilchruthachs began to howl and roar. "Our time of waiting is nearly over."

Trandafira stood at his shoulder and beamed down at the great horde. The yips and growls began to rise in volume as more of their army shifted.

Gabriel and Dominique stood on his left, Dominique leaning against Gabriel's shoulder. She giggled, as nearly the whole mass of ilchruthachs became predators.

Vladimir looked to the sky and saw lightning strike in the distance, the noise of his new army had reached a peak, their howling cries like a symphony of war reaching its climax. He smiled wide, his perfect teeth gleaming. "A storm is a comin'." His deep smoky laugh rumbled with sheer pleasure. "And I am ready for it."